Missy Goes to West Point

P. G. Allison

Cover design 2015 by Cormar Covers
www.cormarcovers.com

Missy Goes to West Point

Missy.Werecat@verizon.net

Also by P.G. Allison

Missy the Werecat

Missy Goes to West Point

Table of Contents

Prologue

Dec 2017

"Hey, Patrick? Promise not to tell?" Missy laughed. It was fun to tease her brother and she was in a great mood. Christmas vacation and everyone was home.

Patrick looked at her with a very pained expression on his face. His sister was always baiting him like this. "Only if I like what you tell me. If I don't like it, then nothing doing. I'll rat you out."

Missy laughed and picked up on his choice of words. "Rat me out? But, that's not much of a threat, once you hear my secret. You see ... cats kill rats. You know that, right?"

"So?" Patrick looked around and the fact that his entire family was sitting there, already smiling at what Missy had just said, made him very suspicious. Obviously, they knew something and he was the only one in the dark about her secret.

"So, I'm a cat." Missy laughed. "That's my secret."

"Very funny, very funny!" Patrick looked at the others and wondered why they were now laughing at him so hard. Missy could be such a pain sometimes.

"Sorry, but I'm not joking. Mom and Dad said it's okay for me to tell you now. They think you're old enough. Not to tell anyone on me. You won't, right?"

"Riiiight, you can be quite sure I'm not going to go around telling anyone that my crazy sister is a cat." Patrick looked at her like she had two heads. "You don't think I want everyone thinking that I'm crazy, do you?"

Missy said, "I knew that I'd have to show you. But, everyone agrees I can do that right here. I don't need to bring you out to the State Forest like I did for them. You don't mind if I spend the next few hours lying around in here, watching TV and stuff with you guys, while I'm being a cat do you?"

Patrick was getting a little concerned, mainly because no one else was acting like she was crazy. Why not humor her, since that's what everyone else was doing. "Sure, sure. No problem. Be a cat if you want. I won't mind."

"Actually, I have to warn you. Prepare you. So, you won't get nervous. You know those pictures in my bedroom? The mountain lion pictures? That's me. Mom took those. I'm a werecat."

Patrick suddenly realized she was being serious and that everyone else was going right along with this. Seriously!

Missy stood up and so did his mother and his sister Heather, who suddenly were holding up a blanket. Missy said, "I have to get naked now, so I can Change.

7

You understand. Okay?" She walked over and stood behind the blanket.

Patrick could see she was taking off her clothes but only her head was showing above the blanket. He looked at his Dad and his brother John but they were just calmly sitting there like this was no big deal. "Isn't anyone else going to say anything?"

John said, "Missy's a werecat, Patrick. It's in our genes, so you really need to know this. That's why she disappeared for those two years. She stayed in the mountains until she figured out how to Change back. She's been Shifting back and forth ever since, but we haven't been letting her out of her room when she does that at home. Until now." Looking at Missy and laughing, he said, "Okay, Missy. You can stay out here tonight. No more hiding out in your room as long as you promise to be good."

His Dad got up and said, with a big sigh, "I better go get those raw steaks out for her. You know how hungry she gets whenever she does this." Chuckling, he walked into the kitchen.

Patrick looked over at Missy who seemed to have finished undressing. She smiled at him and said, "I'll be back in a *flash!*" Then, she ducked down and for a few seconds, nothing happened. Suddenly, there actually was a flash, a great shimmer of light behind the blanket and he could feel a mysterious burst of energy in the room. Heather pulled the blanket away and there stood his sister. Missy the werecat.

8

Chapter One
Jan 2018

"Michelle, have you seen Missy?" asked Mike.

"She's down at the front desk or maybe over talking to the Concierge ... making sure everyone is either already back here or else on their way back. We apparently are now getting a huge snow storm that's blowing in here tonight, in spite of the forecast for this weekend supposedly being clear. Missy tells me she can feel it coming and you know how she's never wrong about stuff like that, right?" Michelle had long since stopped questioning any of the amazing things Missy could do.

Mike's twin sister had become really close with his girlfriend. He and Michelle's boyfriend, Aaron, had little choice but to go along with whatever crazy plan the girls came up with -- the two of them had definitely been in charge of things for this entire weekend. Not that this ski trip up here in New Hampshire was a bad plan or even a crazy one. It was the chemistry between the girls that was crazy, but he and Aaron were actually quite happy about that. Their lives had been much richer these past few months.

Aaron looked up from his smart phone, watching as Michelle came over and joined him on the couch. He and Mike had been waiting patiently for the past half hour. "Wow, this must be pretty important if she's not waiting until after we eat. You know how she is about her meals." It was a common joke amongst the three of them. You just never wanted to get in Missy's way when it was time to eat. They'd returned from a great day on the slopes and had all stopped up at their rooms to change for dinner. He and Mike shared one room and the girls shared another.

"Oh, I know, I know, but she insisted. I can't say whether they'll take her dire warning seriously or not, since the forecast hasn't changed yet. But, she claims she heard some folks talking this morning about hiking up to the peak. She's worried about them." Michelle snuggled up to Aaron and then looked over at her brother. "Did you know there's been at least one fatality each year on Mount Washington for the past hundred and fifty years?"

"Yeah, she told me about that. She also told me how she was all over up there, that first winter she was gone ... that's all she'd say about it, though, except how beautiful it was and how cold it was." Mike had accepted that Missy just wasn't ready to share her secrets yet. She'd disappeared from soccer camp in July 2013 over in Keene, New Hampshire and had returned two years later. She had assured him there had not been any sexual predator involved but she wouldn't explain things beyond that. He did know her first year had been in the White Mountains and then she'd gone south, finally reappearing on the Blue Ridge Parkway down in Virginia. Two years in the mountains which she just wouldn't talk about.

"Really? She actually discussed that with you, huh?" Michelle had also accepted Missy keeping her secrets. Missy was Missy. "I'm surprised she opened up to say anything. Aaron and I haven't heard her say one thing about the time she was gone other than last year, when we first got to meet her. Remember? I'd been a bit pushy, asking her to explain all those scars on her back and shoulder. So, she admitted it was a black bear that gave her those. And then she went on to say something about a bullet causing a scar on her thigh and how she'd been forced to live in the mountains for two years but wasn't going to talk about it."

Aaron said, "Yeah, but she also blurted out how she was *not* damaged goods -- she got kind of emotional just from telling us that much. And, then the two of you had that Missy and Mike moment, off in your own special little world." After saying this to Mike he looked over and smiled at Michelle, remembering how he'd discussed it with her afterward. Michelle had not expected to like Missy at all because of all the negative things she'd heard. Those things had all turned out to be just rumors being spread by a few girls who'd been upset with Missy. Upset and jealous.

"Yes, your first *moment* with her was too cute; we couldn't stand it the way you both were suddenly so into each other." Michelle had already been going with Aaron for two years at that point but had never had moments with him like what her brother and Missy had suddenly been experiencing that day. Seeing such love at first sight happen before her eyes had been amazing, notwithstanding the fact that her brother had actually

12

chased after Missy for months before she'd finally agreed to his even buying her an ice cream. She'd then gone to his prom and he'd gone to hers, but that had all happened a bit later. "We did give you our approval after that, of course. How could we not? Your magic mojo still affects that girl like nothing we've ever seen before. You know that, right?"

Mike laughed and said, "Well, I hope so. But, these mountains also affect her. Last summer when we spent that weekend near here -- over on Ossipee Lake with Senator Maxwell and that family she'd rescued? The Stratton's from Washington D.C.? Well, it was very obvious how Missy was being drawn to all these mountains. That's why she wanted to go skiing with us. At least, that's one of the reasons." He grinned in acknowledgement that being with him was probably an even greater reason. "She'd never done any skiing until last month, remember?"

"Well, she sure learned fast," said Aaron. "From the bunny slopes to black diamond trails already. How is that even possible? We've all been skiing for a dozen years and she's already better than any of us." Missy was an unusually gifted athlete, having demonstrated some extreme abilities in various other sports. But, still. Although Michelle was not that athletic, both Aaron and Mike were expert skiers. What Missy was doing was beyond amazing. "If she never was skiing before, what about those two years she spent in the mountains?"

"Those were some difficult times for me, guys!" said Missy as she walked up. She'd been able to hear most of their conversation while approaching the

13

lounge. "Maybe someday I'll even tell you about them. But, not today. A girl has to keep some of her secrets, right Michelle?" She plopped herself down next to Mike and wrapped both arms around his big chest. Placing her head on his shoulder, she just squiggled a bit, pressing herself against him as he responded automatically with his arms going around her. This elicited groans from both Aaron and Michelle.

"I'll say right, Missy, provided you two don't go have another of your magic moments, right here in front of us." Michelle was laughing as she then added, "Can we go eat now?"

Sure enough, Missy jumped right up and poor Mike was completely forgotten. But, then she turned and grabbed his arm and yanked him up also. "Yum, yum! You guys just have no idea how hungry I am. I could truly eat a horse right now!"

Two hours later, they were still sitting in the lodge restaurant, watching the flames flicker in the big fireplace. Missy had enjoyed a huge steak, extra rare, which the others had all laughed about. She was always so physical and her metabolism did really seem to need all those calories. Her usual intake was about 4,000 calories per day, which she easily burned off while staying at her normal weight of 135 pounds. She and Michelle were the same five foot eight inch height and could wear each other's clothes. But Missy was solid muscle with very little body fat. Even so, with her wide hips, wide shoulders and narrow waist, her body was

14

very curvy. Whenever she dressed up in a low cut gown, with a push up bra for her 34C breasts, and went strutting around in her four inch heels, it would take the breath away from all who watched her.

"That was wonderful … just what I needed to fuel me back up after all that fun we had today, racing down those slopes!" Missy looked at the others, who were obviously quite satisfied with their meal. "And, those jumps I made on that last run? What a rush! You guys really ought to try those …" She sat back, looked at Mike, and began thinking how he was making her feel right now rather than about her feelings out skiing earlier.

They all assured her it had been scary enough just watching her make those jumps. Mike Ryan was big at six three and quite a handsome guy, very masculine with a strong jaw. He was also very physical and had played well on various sports teams. He and his sister had the same dark hair and amazing blue eyes. They both had nice smiles but, in contrast to her brother, Michelle was very pretty and feminine looking. Aaron Brooks was a couple inches shorter than Mike but was also athletic and good looking. His hair was a dirty blond and his eyes were a dark blue.

Missy had gorgeous dark red hair, which would now fall way down her back when she let it all out. She usually had it up in braids or a bun, but tonight it was in a high pony tail. Her deep green eyes were beautiful and she had a very nice proportional nose plus a beautiful smile with vertical crease lines in her cheeks like dimples. She had a fair complexion that would tan

15

rather than burn out in the sunlight. Her classic facial features and bone structure were very attractive and, when combined with her somewhat "feline" appearance, could look anywhere from just pretty to very attractive to absolutely stunning. When aroused or excited, her cat endowments would manifest in her eyes, with yellow or gold speckles appearing and making them almost glow.

When really content and happy, the way she was this night, Missy would relax her controls and allow herself to really enjoy both of her natures, cat and human. She had not shared her werecat secret with any of them, so Mike didn't yet fully understand many things about her. But he knew his Missy was getting amorous once again and the way she kept looking at him, his own arousal in response was making him fidget. Her eyes were definitely giving off that golden glow, filled with those speckles which Mike recognized right away. Since Missy was so fully aware of his arousal due to her enhanced senses, it was definitely turning her on that much more.

Not only were Missy and Mike physically attracted to each other, they somehow had bonded in emotional ways. So, whenever Missy allowed herself to indulge, as she was doing right now, Mike was able to experience her energy and emotion and it was intoxicating. They indeed could easily go off in their own world, leaving everyone else behind. With a deep sigh, Missy realized what she was doing and pulled back. She had tuned out for a few moments and had allowed those pleasurable feelings to wash through her. Tuning back in, she looked at her friends. She noticed the way Michelle was studying her and right away she spoke up. "Mmmm, sorry everyone! I just am enjoying tonight so very much. If I seem a little spacey or anything, please forgive me." Looking at Mike, she saw he was now coming back into the real world once again.

Michelle laughed and said, "Missy, you and Mike really do space out sometimes, but it's very special. And, you're doing that thing you do with your eyes. Aaron, can you see all the gold speckles? Now do you believe what I was telling you about?" She reached over and hooked her arm through one of Aaron's arms and pulled herself closer, sliding her chair around so it was next to his and she could snuggle up to him. They were both going to the same university in Boston and had been sleeping together for a few weeks. They just hadn't shared that information with anyone else yet. Maybe this would be a good opportunity. They already had agreed about telling Mike this weekend … the timing was perfect right now for doing that.

And, since Mike and Missy were clearly so into one another, why not also give them a little push? Michelle looked at them both and asked, "Hey, why don't you two get a room? Oh, that's right … we already have some rooms, don't we?"

Aaron of course picked right up on this and said, "Sure, I'll be more than happy to clear all my stuff out of Mike's room … then you guys can have that, no problem. And, I'll just go bunk with Michelle." Aaron paused and stared at his friend, Mike. Then he added,

"We've actually been doing that for awhile now anyway."

Missy laughed. She recognized right away what they both were doing and saying; since she'd known from their scents how they'd been having frequent sex for awhile now, she had actually anticipated this. They'd all driven up together yesterday and she'd wondered why Michelle hadn't said anything last night. Looking at Mike, who was processing this news about his twin sister bunking with Aaron, she decided to have some fun. "Gosh, really, you'd be okay with switching rooms with me, Aaron? That's so thoughtful. Helpful, friendly and considerate. Kind. Were you a Boy Scout, maybe?" Giggling, she paused for a moment and then added, "Or, maybe you just really want to have more sex with my best friend, here. Michelle? Talk to us, Michelle!" Her laughter after saying this was contagious.

Mike was now watching the two girls explode in hilarious laughter. As usual, they were on the same page together. He looked at Aaron and noticed his friend was a bit uncomfortable, but was waiting for him to react. "Okay, okay. I'm not all that surprised, Michelle. In spite of how well you might think you guys were keeping this a big secret, it's actually been very long in coming. Ha, ha. But, I am not going to sit here and listen to any further conversation about my sister's sex life. Nor am I going to discuss anything about … well … anything."

"Oh, relax, Mike! Just because we're letting them share a room together doesn't mean you and I are going to have any sex, so there's nothing to discuss. You

don't have to say anything about … well … anything."
Missy was still laughing and was only barely able to talk.
"Besides, remember how we have those *boundaries* that
we agreed to, right? On Thanksgiving?" She knew she
was playing with fire since she hadn't ended up actually
setting any boundaries at all. She had agreed that night
to going with Mike over to his dorm in Medford, which
would be practically empty and where they'd be alone in
his room. That had been their first time actually being
all alone with one another. She had agreed to that after
telling him they would have some boundaries. Where?
Oh, she would tell him where those boundaries were …
once he reached them. Ha, ha.

Missy had never really relaxed all her controls
until that night. She had never even allowed anyone to
get past first base with her. But, that night? Once
things got started and she began to enjoy all the things
Mike was doing … his fondling, kissing, sucking her
breasts and nipples … his touching her … her first time
for such intimacy … she just couldn't stop. Her
enhanced senses allowed her to experience pleasure
that was above and beyond anything she'd ever
dreamed possible. Her wild, passionate, werecat
instincts drove her to higher and higher levels of
excitement and anticipation. She became oblivious to
any thoughts of stopping or setting any boundaries.
Instead, she had demanded that Mike touch her more
and more.

She had been grinding her pelvis against him and
-- when he'd placed his hand on her abdomen, merely to
push her back and adjust their positions -- that had felt

so wonderful that it had triggered her to beg and plead - - she'd become that much more insistent. When his hand had slipped inside her jeans and down to touch her throbbing pubic mound, she'd gone crazy. Just his hand cupping her there, moving his fingers over the slick folds inside her wet panties, applying pressure ... she'd exploded. She had shattered and splintered, bucking uncontrollably while screaming at the tremendous release this was giving her. Her orgasm had just completely overwhelmed her, with convulsions going on for more than a minute plus those delicious aftershocks that had lasted far beyond that. As her quivering body had finally lay still, limp and spent on top of Mike, her emotions and sexual energies had all drained away and she'd begun making incoherent sounds, cooing and mewling; she'd been so exhausted she'd then fallen asleep.

Mentioning *boundaries* to Mike now was indeed taking things to a new level with him. Sure, they'd talked about that night. A lot. He'd been so wonderful, willing to lie there while she'd slept. His own raging passion had eventually subsided although he'd finally admitted to something the next day. It had been the worst case of blue balls that he'd ever experienced; the aching had lasted for hours and hours. She'd promised him that would never happen again. At least, it wouldn't happen if there was a next time. They'd not actually had that conversation yet. About a *next time*.

Or, had they actually just now had that *next time* conversation? Missy knew what her body was saying. It was definitely saying yes, yes, YES in answer to *that* question. A delicious thrill went zinging through her, making each nerve ending wake up. Wow! Was she getting aroused or what? She was suddenly very wet and her nipples were starting to ache. All her senses were so alive! She knew her mysterious bond with Mike was causing him to also get equally aroused and excited. Breathing in, drawing air through her nose and also scenting with her tongue and the roof of her mouth, she could clearly sense the high state of sexual arousal all four of them had now reached. And, such a turn on that was!

"Have we signed the check yet?" Mike's voice was almost a squeak, but a very low, husky, sexy sounding squeak that only amped things up for Missy that much greater.

Aaron and Michelle actually got up and left them. Michelle gave Missy a conspiratorial wink, waved good bye to her brother and off they went. Missy knew Michelle would move all her things for her while Aaron was collecting his gear from Mike's room. Her pulse began to pound that much harder. She watched as someone approached their table.

But, instead of presenting Mike with the check, the man actually addressed her instead. "Miss? Are you Missy McCrea? You asked them to let you know. Down at the desk? They said you wanted to know about that group that went out hiking? Umm ... they just received word. At the desk. Apparently there's a problem. One member in that party had a minor injury ... a sprained ankle ... so it now looks like they're not able to get back down ... and, ahh ... the reason that's a problem?

21

Communication with them has just now been lost and there's no GPS location for them. You see, the thing is … in that last communication … they also reported getting hit by a big storm up there. The guy at the desk said you were very positive about there being a storm coming in and I guess you were right."

Chapter Two
Jan 2018

James Murray was worried. This hike had started out as a glorious experience for the four of them and now, as the blizzard raged around them and the darkness and cold of a night on Mount Washington set in, they were in trouble. They'd started that morning with a clear forecast. They'd reached the peak just after noon, as planned. After enjoying a fabulous lunch and resting up there for an hour, looking out at the spectacular views, they'd started back down. Thirty minutes later, Bob Rollinsworth had slipped and badly sprained his ankle.

James was an EMT and they had prepared for this trip with plenty of provisions. First aid kit, flashlights, satellite phone, extra batteries, food and water, and a tent. Just in case. But, Bob's sprain definitely had slowed them down and had ruined their plan to be better than half way down before it got dark. Instead, they'd still been at an elevation over 5,000 feet at dusk, which is when the snow had started. And, the wind. They'd called down for a weather forecast update and had learned this huge storm had come roaring down from Canada, surprising everyone. While not that big a deal down below, up here it had soon become a raging blizzard and any further attempts at descent had not been feasible. They'd had to prepare for a night on the mountain and those provisions were being put to good use.

Bob's wife Joanne and their friend Luther Jenkins were experienced hikers and campers but none of them had done this before in a blizzard. It had taken a while to get the tent set up, but they'd managed that okay. The real problem was their satellite phone. In spite of their batteries being good, the damn phone itself had suddenly died. Modern technology. Great. They'd not really had a chance to call in their approximate location and, once the phone had died, they were now isolated. And, that situation would continue for however long the storm raged, and depending on how much snow might accumulate, perhaps for much longer even afterwards. So, he was worried.

They were inside the tent and they had brought along enough warm clothing. But, it was cold and getting a lot colder. They ate their dinner meal and tried to remain optimistic. There really wasn't anything else they could do.

Missy knew the hiking party was in trouble. She actually had recognized one of the group, an EMT named Murray whom she'd met last summer. She'd been driving home from Revere Beach, her first week as a lifeguard, and had stopped to help at a fire in Lynn. She'd saved a nine year old boy, jumping out a second floor window with the boy in her arms, but had broken her leg. Murray had been one of the EMT's on the scene and, after treating the cuts she'd received from broken glass, he had loaded her into the ambulance that took her to the hospital where they'd treated her leg.

She'd hoped they'd be back down before the storm came in, but now she knew the group was still somewhere high up there. Whether it was fate or bad karma, they'd been slowed down by someone's sprained ankle and now they were stuck on the mountain. Supposedly, they had adequate provisions and should survive the night. But, with communication being lost and no GPS signal, no one knew their precise location. That meant, since they'd only provided a general description of their planned route up and back, that depending on how much snow came in, they might be trapped up there and very hard to locate. Without help, they might easily become yet another statistic, adding to the death toll for Mount Washington.

"Mike, those people need help and I'm hoping you'll be okay about some stuff. Stuff I wasn't planning to explain just yet, but this is forcing the issue. I have to go help those people." Missy looked at Mike to see his reaction. He'd gone with her to the front desk where they'd learned all the details about this hiking party being still somewhere up on the mountain.

"But, Missy, you heard what they said. Those people are probably okay up there. They brought along supplies and everything, right?" Mike really wasn't seeing why she was so concerned. "And, what do you mean you have to go help them? You can't do anything. Let the search and rescue folks do their job. I'm sure they'll be out there tomorrow, with helicopters and everything. Right?"

Missy said, "You don't understand how lost those people can be up there. With two or three feet of

25

snow, the drifts can be ten to twenty feet. And, the helicopter search might never find them. I know. I've been up there. That's part of the stuff I have to tell you about."

Now Mike was confused. He knew she'd been in the mountains for those two years, but surely she hadn't been living up there during snow storms. Had she? "What are you saying, Missy? What sort of help are you talking about?"

"I'm going to bring them a satellite phone with GPS. That way, they can be located by those search and rescue folks."

"But, that's crazy! How …?" Mike left the question hanging and studied her.

"I can do that, Mike. I can find them and bring them a phone. And, I'll be leaving very soon, so they'll have that phone by morning. Let's go up to our room so I can explain some things. I've wanted to tell you my secrets for awhile now. Ever since Thanksgiving. Ever since … you know …" Missy grabbed his hand and led him over to the elevator.

Mike walked with her to the elevator and pushed the up button. She was going to share her secrets? This whole relationship with Missy was suddenly going to new levels and at a very fast pace. He'd been okay with taking it slow, since he'd thought that's what she wanted. But, he could sense she now really wanted to talk to him about some important things. Important things about herself and not just about this crazy idea to go bring those people a phone. While that was wonderful, finally having her share some of her mysterious secrets, he was pretty sure their spending a nice evening together and maybe even having sex was somehow not going to happen. Oh, well!

They went into Mike's room, which was now *their* room, since Aaron and Michelle had swapped things around. Missy went over to her suitcase and opened it up on top of one of the beds. Pulling out a small backpack she turned around and held it up to show Mike. "See this? I'll be bringing the satellite phone up there in this." She then rummaged in her suitcase further and pulled out a satellite phone. "I brought this along. Just in case."

Mike went over to the backpack and noticed it looked a little bit strange, the way the straps were set up on it. "I don't get any of this, Missy. You know that, of course. What are you trying to tell me?"

She sighed and studied him for a minute. "You know how I feel about you, Mike. But, you also know I'm going to West Point, hopefully, and after that I'll be serving at least five years in the Army. So, I can't really ask you for any commitments right now. But, I am asking that you agree to keep my secrets. Or, really, my one secret, which is a pretty big one. No matter what happens with our relationship, you have to promise me you'll keep my secret. Even if, once you know about me, you never want to see me again." She stared into his eyes and let her own eyes reveal to him how much emotion she was feeling. She knew her eyes were probably glowing with yellow in them.

27

Mike saw the way her eyes were suddenly flashing yellow and green in a way he'd never seen them do before. He knew this wasn't her being sexually aroused. This was her being vulnerable and open about something that really, *really* mattered. "Missy, I can promise you that I'll never tell anyone your secret. Never. Not ever. No matter what. Okay? And, if and when you're ever ready for any other commitments from me ..." He raised his eyebrows as he left the rest of that question for her to guess at. He could *feel* her energy now, throbbing and pulsing right there in the room.

"Okay, I trust you." Suddenly she smiled. "You actually have seen me, you know. I have a dual nature, Mike. I have two forms. I have photos of me in my other form, back in my room at home. You told me you thought I looked really beautiful. Last Thanksgiving." She watched the way he tried to solve this puzzle, unsuccessfully. "Mike, I'm a werecat. That mountain lion in those photos? That's me. In my other form. That's my secret."

She watched the way he tried to process this information. She figured it might help if she continued with a bit more. "When I disappeared for those two years? It was because I Changed to my other form and didn't know how to Change back. I was afraid I might hurt people so I went up into the mountains. I think it's some sort of genetic anomaly, but no one else in my family is like me. As for someday ... if I ever should have any kids of my own ... I just don't know, Mike. I'm still figuring this out as I go along."

"You can Change? Into a mountain lion?" Mike didn't know whether to believe this but he knew he definitely did *not* want to say anything that might show Missy he had any doubts. He'd listened to her babbling but was too shocked to really get what she was saying. Why was she bringing up kids of her own? He definitely wasn't ready for the conversation to go in that direction. "Um ... okay. I guess. I can live with that. You're still you, right? Or, when you're in this other form ... are you not really you anymore?"

Missy laughed with a huge sense of relief at this question. "Yeah, I'm still me. Mostly. But, I do live as a cat, not as a human. I experience things as a cat. I allow my cat instincts to guide me, so I attack and kill my prey just like a cat. I'm not out there thinking about Bambi or anything. I mean, deer are my favorite food source."

"But, what about ... I mean ... you won't attack humans, right?"

"Well, not really. Not unless my human mind says there's a reason to. My mind, in either form, is the same but it has many *places* it can go to, if that makes sense. It's why I can ignore pain. I feel it, but I can ignore it. I've learned to *control* myself. Mostly." Suddenly she blushed, as she recalled that one time when he'd seen her completely lose all control.

Instead of picking up on that, however, Mike asked about her earlier comment. "When you say *unless there's a reason to* ... about attacking humans? Are you saying you actually have had reasons? To attack humans?"

This conversation was now going places where Missy did not want it to go. "I never attacked anyone during those two years that I was gone, Mike. Not even when that hunter shot me in the leg." While this was all true, she was purposely omitting what she'd done *after* she'd come home. "I avoided humans and anything that might draw attention to myself. And, I still avoid having anyone find out about me. I've only told my family, my friend Alice, and now you."

"Alice knows? Okay. Never mind." He could keep asking her questions all night but he knew that wasn't going to happen. "I guess you really want to talk about this plan you have, right? For getting that phone to those people up there? You think you can do that ... in your other form?" Mike was trying to process a lot of things and realized he didn't want to push her. She would share all her secrets when she was ready. In her own way. But, he wasn't sure he really understood her intent right now. "Can you really do that, Missy?"

"Yes, I can and I will. I'll put some clothes into that backpack, along with the phone, and I'll wear it while I'm a cat. I can find them. It won't be easy but I can move well enough, even in this blizzard that's blowing up there. And, I'll be able to scent where they are. My senses are actually pretty amazing. I'm similar to a mountain lion when in my cat form but I'm not really just a cat. Sort of like I'm similar to a girl in my human form but I'm not really just human, you know? I'm enhanced. That's why I can do the things I do, eat the way I do, heal the way I do."

Mike was beginning to see how a lot of things, a lot of strange unexplainable things about Missy, might now actually have an explanation. "All that martial arts sparring? You really do heal up the way you told us? By bedtime?"

"Well, the bruises, yeah. When I fracture a rib, it might take a day or two longer. Unless I Shift. Then, I heal really fast. My body does this crazy thing with energy being used? I think that energy heals me. Amongst other things. I'm still figuring all this out as I go along, Mike."

Mike knew the best way he could assure her about the way he felt about her was to be supportive. If she believed all this, then he'd show her that he believed it too. "How can I help, Missy. What's your plan, here?

"Well, I'm going to fix up my backpack and we're going to drive over to the base of the mountain, then see how far up we can go. When we need to stop, I'm going to get out and take off all my clothes, strap that backpack on, and Change. If you'll pick up the clothes I leave behind and then come back down here to wait for me, that will be great."

"What happens when you find them, Missy? I get that you'll Change back, get dressed and bring them the phone. Then what? How do you protect your secret?" Mike was watching her as she began to actually pack things into her backpack.

31

"I'll give them that phone and make them promise not to tell anyone. They can say they had this phone all along but only got it working the next day. I'll be staying with them for at least two hours and then I'll leave. They're not going to ever understand how I got there anyway. So, they can't really tell anyone else my secret, since all they can do is tell some unbelievable story about me, which I'll just deny."

"And, the two hours? I suppose it'll take longer than that for any rescue party to reach them. But still ... why wait?" Mike was trying to show his support by acting as a sounding board for her, so she could fully explain her plan.

"That's because of this recuperation thing with my Shifting and the energy I use doing it. Once I Change, it takes over two hours before I can Change again and a total of six hours before I can Change a third time." She laughed. "Just be waiting with lots and lots of food for me when I get back down here, because I'll be so starved. I'll probably lose close to ten pounds and I've not bulked up for this adventure, so I'll be really, really skin and bones."

Chapter Three
Jan 2018

Mike drove them up the mountain but they were stopped before they could get very far. The snow was really coming down now and the roads were already blocked off; no one was allowed to go up any further due to the severe blizzard raging up there. Mike turned their car around and once they were out of sight, he pulled off to the side at a convenient turnaround. He'd been making only idle chit chat with her as they'd been driving up, not wanting to play twenty questions. If she really was a werecat and could Change the way she'd said she could, he'd know soon enough. Suddenly, he began chuckling to himself.

"What's so funny?" Missy was amped up now and her tension and anxiety were taking their toll. She could use a good laugh to relief some stress.

"Well, I'm just thinking how my silly sister ... I mean ... she obviously planned on getting the two of us together this weekend, right? So she and Aaron ... you know. What's funny is I'll be getting to see you naked in just a few minutes but, instead of this being a night of our making wild, passionate love in our room, you'll be off doing this St. Bernard rescue dog thing -- as a cat, no less -- and I'll be going back down to wait in that lonely room and worry about you. And then? When we finally see her tomorrow? I think I'll leave it for you to explain

33

things then, Missy!" Mike started laughing and Missy could only join in.

Suddenly, she began laughing even harder, with tears streaming out. "The best part? When she sees how *skinny* I'll be? Losing ten pounds during one night of wild sex with you? Yes, I'll be telling her all about *that*, Mike. Count on it!" More laughter for them both. And, she did feel a lot better.

They got out of the car and walked a little ways into the woods, which were now completely white everywhere. The snow was really coming down and it was windy. "Once I Shift, I'll only stay a minute, Mike. This really means everything to me, that you're being so supportive. I promise I'll make it up to you somehow. Later. Enjoy the show!" Missy began taking off her clothes and it was indeed a strange experience for them both. Mike was not able to see in the dark the way she could but even so, this was a bit weird.

Once she had all her clothes off, she strapped on her special backpack and she was ready. She'd already left all her jewelry back in their room. She was freezing and her nipples were aching like crazy but she had to show Mike she loved him, so she ran over and gave him a huge hug and kissed him. He was surprised but quickly responded, hugging her and kissing her back. She broke away and took a few steps to separate them. "Wait for it, Mike!" She crouched down on all fours, paused to let her mind go to that special place, began that strong exercise of her will that she was now so comfortable with making, and she Changed.

Mike was watching and waiting and when she crouched down, he was prepared. Even so, when he saw the great shimmer of light and felt the burst of energy right there in front of him, it was a shock. Even more shocking was the huge cat animal now standing where Missy had been, staring at him with those glowing yellow green eyes that were definitely still Missy's eyes. A mountain lion wearing a backpack. Unbelievable. She slowly approached him and he could suddenly hear her purring. That was even more unbelievable. He reached out his hand and she actually licked his glove with her tongue. She pushed her head against his leg, turned around and suddenly she was gone. He wasn't even able to hear her. He waited for several long moments and then bent down to pick up all her things.

Missy was actually thrilled to be doing this. She was back climbing on Mount Washington, in her cat form, finding her way through deep snow, and all her memories from four years earlier when she'd been doing the exact same thing were flooding back into her mind. It was exhilarating and she knew she'd been missing this. She was somehow meant to do this. Her powerful cat body was now just as familiar to her as her human body and she loved being able to once again move as a cat.

She had only been provided with a general area for where the group was supposedly planning to go on their way back down. And they'd reported being stopped somewhere above the 5000 foot line. So, she climbed. The storm was blowing snow with the fierce wind driving it horizontally, in huge gusts. There were deep pockets she needed to work her way around and slippery ice she navigated with care. Up she went, higher and higher, hour after hour. And, then she searched.

Dawn eventually broke and she was still searching. The storm had let up for brief intervals only to come howling back. It didn't seem in any rush to go away. She continued to cover ground, traversing various ravines and pathways and had actually gone up to the peak a few times. And then, finally, she found them. She scented them while still a long distance away but that was enough. It took her half an hour to work her way over to where they'd set up their tent, but she managed. They'd picked a decent spot, protected from the wind, but one that would never have been visible to anyone from the air. And, the snow drifts had filled the area with plenty of deep snow.

She was able to smell the four people inside the tent and they seemed okay. She looked around for someplace to Change, picked out her spot and went there. No one was outside the tent so her secret was safe. She Changed. Then she removed her backpack and pulled on her clothing. It was freezing cold but Missy was able to tolerate a lot of things which a normal human would find unbearable. Her outfit was not all that warm, made of that thin space age material, similar to those space blankets, but it was adequate for her. She pulled on her boots, hat and mittens and picked up her backpack which still contained the satellite phone. She was ready.

James was just thinking about going outside to relieve himself. They'd all managed doing that during the long night, once for each of them, and it was a brutal experience. Pissing outside with the freezing blizzard snow blowing with such ferocity was indeed just that: brutal. He'd also gone out with Bob, who couldn't put any weight on his ankle, and had needed his help. Joanne was still making jokes about how frozen her ass had gotten when she'd been out there, even though it had been during one of the lulls in the storm. They kept hoping for some further letup in the wind and snow and, with the dawn of this new day, he thought it perhaps was lessening.

Suddenly, as unbelievable as it may have seemed, they all heard a girl's voice calling. "Hello the tent! Anyone awake in there? Can I come inside?"

He zipped down the tent flap and looked outside. Standing ten feet away was this girl wearing a silver suit, black boots, black stocking cap and an unbelievable amount of gorgeous red hair blowing all around her head. And, he even recognized who she was! It was that girl Missy that had jumped out of a burning house with a boy in her arms. Last summer. In a bathing suit. She'd had her hair tied up then but he'd never forget her.

He also would never forget the way she'd miraculously healed up. She had definitely broken a bone in her leg, which had needed to be set. But, when he'd checked at the hospital a few days later, he'd learned how she had stopped in on her way to work, again in her lifeguard bathing suit, and had then paraded around in front of everyone. Her leg was fully healed and they even had x-ray's that proved it. Fully healed in four days? That definitely had gotten his attention and he'd then read up on her. There had been quite a bit out there on the internet, including video clips on YouTube. She'd won an amateur first place trophy in mixed martial arts at some big Expo in New York and the videos of her doing that had almost gone viral. She was indeed spectacular to watch.

"Hi Mr. Murray! I understand your phone went dead. I brought you one that works, with GPS and everything. Can I come inside?" Missy smiled one of her brilliant smiles at him, which made the creases in her cheeks almost look like dimples.

"Of course you can! Missy, right? I remember from last summer. But? How in the world? Come in, come in!" He waited as she squeezed through the opening and came inside. With five of them, they were very crowded but they all made adjustments so there was room for her. She sat down, opened the backpack she was holding and pulled out a satellite phone which she handed to him. He took the phone and said, "Are you an angel, Missy? This can't really be happening, can it? How did you get here and how did you find us?"

Missy laughed and said, "Can you introduce me to your friends? Then we can talk about stuff." She looked at each of the others and could see they were all staring at her in total amazement. But, those amazed expressions were also happy ones, so she smiled at them.

James introduced everyone to Missy and Missy to them, explaining how he'd treated her after firemen had carried her out on a stretcher from behind a burning house. He looked at her now and asked, "I'm not going to ask you about the leg since I already heard from everyone at the hospital." He looked at the others and added, "She somehow mended her broken leg in just a few days. She apparently isn't a normal girl. Maybe that's why she's able to appear up here out of thin air, like magic."

"Actually, guys, that's not far from the truth but, since it's magic, I can't really explain it to you. You know. If I told you? Then I'd have to shoot you? Yadda-yadda-yadda, right?" Missy laughed and they joined in, but still looked at her with puzzled expressions.

James turned on the phone and could see that, indeed, it was working. "How did you even know we needed this, Missy?"

"I'm actually staying at the same lodge as you folks and I was there yesterday morning when you went out. I overheard you all talking at breakfast about the hike and everything. Then, they told me last night at the desk about your situation and how your phone died. So, here I am!" Missy knew they would never understand, so she tried to keep it simple. She'd been way across the cafeteria when she'd heard them talking and they'd not even seen her there. They'd all left before she'd had a chance to say hi to James.

Joanne spoke up and said, "Here you are? That's it? Just like that? Please, Missy, we are thrilled about the phone, which might even be saving our lives. But? How is this possible? Surely you can explain this. I mean, is there any rescue party out there or anything? You can't just show up all alone like this …"

Missy now got serious and explained, "Actually, I can just show up like this and I am completely alone. You folks are going to have to just accept this because I'm not going to explain it. Sorry! Way too complicated and you still wouldn't understand. Or, believe my explanation. But, more important, you all have to promise me that you'll never tell anyone else. About me being here or anything. You're going to say you got your phone working this morning and that's all. Okay?"

This of course caused them to all talk at once and the discussion then went on for several minutes, with Missy insisting they just accept the mystery and agree not to say anything about it. She also insisted they make a call and activate the GPS signal so they could be located. After several minutes on the phone, James was advised there would be a helicopter coming for them once there was a break in the storm and it was safe to fly up there. James assured them they were all fine and could wait until then, no problem. Everyone in the tent was greatly relieved. Help was on the way, even if that might still be several hours away.

Missy turned to James and said, "I really do want this to be a secret. I'll stay for awhile but then I'll be leaving. You'll probably see me again down at the lodge, though, later on … when you guys all get back, safe. I just can't explain things for you folks any better than this. But, as you already said. I'm not a normal girl. I hope you can just leave it at that. Okay?"

James studied her and slowly nodded his head. "I get the feeling that if we tried to explain about you being up here, you'd just deny it. Right? So, we'd be left trying to tell everyone about something no one would ever believe. They'd think the altitude sickness got us or something."

"Exactly, James! I'm really glad you understand." Missy then looked at the others and, after some further discussion, they all had to agree. They were actually wondering if she was really there or maybe they were experiencing altitude sickness. That conversation brought on more laughter and they continued to talk about how bizarre and crazy this whole weekend was ending up for them.

What they thought was even crazier, however, was when Missy announced it was time for her to go. The storm outside their tent had only reduced its fury by about half and was still fierce. The cold and wind were unbearable, as the guy's had each discovered when they'd once again gone out to relieve themselves. All three had gone out there together. Joanne was still waiting, although her bladder was telling her she'd have to go out there sometime soon.

As Missy got ready and was pulling on her hat and gloves, Joanne asked, "How can you even survive out there, dressed like that? I didn't pay that much attention before, but that's not really warm enough. Not unless you're an alien and have a space ship out there, hidden away. Is that your secret?"

Missy laughed and said, "All I can say is that I'm definitely not an alien. Sorry to disillusion you but ... actually ... if that's what you'll all be comfortable with believing, then go ahead. Just think of me as an alien." With that, she hugged Joanne and then gave each of the guys a kiss on the cheek. "Gotta go! My boyfriend's been patiently waiting for me. See you all tonight!"

She emerged from their tent and walked out into the storm. After a few steps, she turned and waved at James who was watching her, and then she continued on until the tent was no longer visible. She picked an appropriate spot and removed all her clothes which she stuffed back inside her backpack. As she strapped the backpack on she took several deep breaths. It was exhilarating, standing out there in the midst of a raging snowstorm like that, freezing in her naked human form as she prepared to become a cat. Then, she crouched down and Changed. Moments later, now warm enough in her furry form, she headed back down the mountain.

Mike had been checking with the front desk and they'd called him that morning when word was received about the hiking party. There was good news from the group up there, who were all okay -- they'd somehow gotten their phone working and managed to send out their GPS location. There would be a rescue team bringing them in once the storm let up, probably sometime that afternoon.

He hadn't been able to sleep at all, with so many thoughts about Missy going through his head. His girlfriend was a werecat. The girl he'd already realized might be the one, the special one that maybe was meant for him, if those feelings they seemed to have for one another would continue -- she was a werecat. He'd actually seen her Change. And, knowing the phone call from that hiking party was because she'd actually managed to find them, just as she'd said she would, was just further proof.

He'd worried all night long and up until getting that phone call, the many possible scenarios had been tormenting him. Was any of this even real? Would she be okay? Would he ever see her again? What if she was to get hurt or worse, might die out there? As his thoughts continued to whirl around, processing everything and somehow making the unbelievable become believable, his heart was telling him something else. The only thing that was changed by his learning Missy was a werecat was that now he loved her more than ever.

Before? He had been pretty sure. He had allowed his imagination to play out a zillion possible scenarios, all with her in his life. And, he'd realized there really wasn't anyone else who could possibly compare. He'd hoped they could continue to grow closer and, if she did end up going off to West Point, he'd make whatever adjustments might be necessary to be her guy. If she'd have him.

Now? Now he realized he couldn't think of living without her in his life. The thoughts he'd been having about her maybe not coming back? Those convinced him. Life without Missy would just never be what his life could be with her in it. No matter what that required. If she was willing to accept him in her life, he was totally committed now. She owned him. His only concern was whether he could possibly own her in return. The fact that she'd now shared her secret was very encouraging. If she was willing to give him her love the way he was hoping he could give his love to her, that was all that mattered.

His phone rang with the special ringtone he'd selected for Missy. She was back! He answered right away and heard her voice, telling him where to come pick her up. She'd come down as far as she could, in her cat form, and then had Changed. Now she was hungry, so could he hurry?

"So, what excuse did you make up for Michelle?" asked Missy. They were still in the restaurant but she'd finally finished eating. She'd not actually lost ten pounds but she had indeed looked much thinner when Mike had picked her up. Their waiter hadn't quite believed her when she'd ordered that second complete steak dinner, before she'd even finished devouring the first one. Mike had laughed quite a bit at that.

44

"Oh, you know. I said you were sore in some special places and wanted to just stay in your room. Stuff like that." He laughed, knowing she knew that was a huge lie.

"Very funny. After I showed her my bruises that time, from sparring? And explained how I heal up so quickly? Even if she believed that I did manage to get sore, from having monkey sex with you, she'd never believe I'd stay in my room because of them. Special places! Ha!"

"Monkey sex? Is that a cat thing?" Mike laughed. He was so enjoying having her back and being able to tease her was great fun. "Actually, I told them both at breakfast that you'd gone over to that Rescue Center. That we'd both gone there last night since you knew that EMT who was in the group and you'd wanted to be close to whatever was happening. Then, after a night when we did *not* have any sex, you'd gone back there this morning to check up on any developments. So, be sure to stick with that story when you see them. They're out on the slopes again, waiting for the storm to blow over and hoping they can ski some more today. We are still planning to all drive back home late tonight, right?"

"Good story. And, I'll stick with that, don't worry." Missy looked at him closely. She knew he'd love to have her suggest staying over another night. Maybe not for any actual monkey sex but he probably had some very specific thoughts along those lines. She could scent that he was now aroused and it was actually making her feel very horny. Sighing, she said, "And,

45

yeah. We are driving back tonight. We all talked about this, remember? All those big commitments we each have for this week? We can't stay."

"What about the blizzard, though? Doesn't that give us a good excuse?" Mike was kidding with her, since he could sense she really wanted to stay and spend the night with him, just as much as he wanted them to do that. She really was able to make him know how she felt, when she wanted to. And, her eyes were showing yellow specs again, so he knew she was getting aroused.

She looked at him and suddenly it was just the two of them sitting there with this pulse of energy happening between them. She felt her cat flooding her senses and knew her eyes were glowing with gold inside the green. She told him, "Mike, what we have is really special and I want our *next time* together to be really special too. But, it just can't be tonight. Okay?" She knew he understood what she meant by *next time* and that she was actually telling him that she was ready for that. Sometime soon. She would make certain of that. Sometime very soon.

Missy actually was still there later that afternoon when James and the others made it back, after being picked up by helicopter. She and Mike were in the lobby, waiting for Aaron and Michelle. Since they'd heard about the successful rescue they were not surprised when the hikers showed up. She smiled at them, giving a little wave and Joanne stopped and just stared at her, shaking her head.

Joanne had almost convinced herself that Missy had only been a dream, but now she could see that Missy was really there, in the lobby of their lodge, like it was no big deal. James and the other guys waved and the four of them were then greeted by several other people all crowding around to welcome them back. There were a few reporters in the group but none of the stories that went out about the rescue included any mention of Missy McCrae.

Michelle showed up shortly after that with Aaron and the four of them then checked out and drove back home. Missy insisted that Aaron drive so she could sit in the back with Mike. She then put her head on his lap and fell asleep for the whole ride back.

Chapter Four
Jan 2018

Missy walked into the coffee shop and waved to Robert Ulrey, sitting in the far corner, furthest booth from the entrance. They'd been meeting there every once in awhile and it had now been over a month since the FBI had arrested Frank McCarthy and eight of his associates. The arrests were for money laundering and tax evasion charges; the FBI had put together a very strong case after receiving a wealth of information all about one of Frank's childhood buddies, Tony Gonzales, who'd successfully been laundering money for Frank during the past twenty five years. That had helped Frank rise to the top of the criminal organization in East Boston. And, the wealth of information had all been provided by Missy.

Robert had been the lead investigator for the FBI when Missy had disappeared and everyone had assumed she'd been kidnapped. When she'd reappeared two years later, she'd let Robert and everyone else just assume she'd been held by a sexual predator, under threat of something terrible happening to her family; a predator whom she'd eventually managed to kill. She didn't actually admit to that but it was the only logical conclusion they could get from her evasive answers and her unwillingness to explain what she'd been through, plus all her assurances it was now safe and there was no one out there who needed to be brought in.

Robert had indeed actually believed just that, back then. He'd written it up that way in his report, along with his conclusion that whatever had happened to her unknown kidnapper, it must have been justified. The FBI was not going to bring any charges against Missy, a fifteen year old girl who'd been forced to live through some terrible experiences for two years. He'd then helped Missy and her family get through presenting her story to the media. At a news conference to announce her return, it was his participation that had prevented the media from learning any actual details concerning just what had happened during those two years. Things had quieted down and Robert had been very pleased. Few of his cases had ended as well as Missy's case seemed to have ended.

Then, a year and a half later, she'd come to him with all that info she'd obtained from Tony Gonzales, asking for an audience with the FBI's Organized Crime Division. That had led to the FBI making their big case and making all their arrests months later. But, there was a lot Missy had never explained concerning what she'd given the FBI and about how she'd obtained it. She'd kept her secrets, some of which Robert had now gained at least a partial understanding of. He had a secret now, too. A month earlier he'd joined the US Government's Paranormal Branch, or "P" Branch, led by Drew Martinson. Drew had recruited him because of his special relationship with Missy. Drew knew she trusted Robert. Drew also knew Missy was a werecat and had explained all that to Robert.

"You're looking lovelier and lovelier each time I see you, Missy." Robert had often met with her right after she'd either been working out at the gym or else after one of her karate or martial arts sessions. For each of those meetings she'd still be wearing her karate gi with her hair all up on top of her head. Today, she was wearing a pair of dark green slacks and a matching green sweater, which he noted really made her figure look lush and curvy. He'd complemented her right after she'd removed the big jacket and scarf she'd worn when she came in. Her hair was in a loose pony tail and cascaded nicely over one of her shoulders. Since the dark green of her outfit was also a match to the color of her incredible eyes, his comment was in fact an understatement. She was looking like a model from some glamour magazine that didn't need any airbrushing whatsoever.

"Thanks, Robert, you look nice today too. A girl loves to get compliments like that and you're such a sweetheart for giving them to me." Missy slid across from Robert and smiled at him. He really did look nice, with his close cropped grey hair and that military bearing he still managed having, even after leaving the Army's Military Police and being in the FBI for over twenty years now. She knew he worked out at the gym and ran on weekends to keep in shape. Since she ran five miles almost every morning and worked out at her gym as much as she did, she could relate. She'd grown very fond of Robert. She not only liked him but also trusted him. He was a great friend.

"When the girl looks as fantastic as you do, Missy, the words are hardly a gift. Merely an acknowledgement." Robert had let that just slip out and he saw that Missy was actually blushing now. He hadn't really been quite so forthcoming before and realized he'd better watch his words with her. He didn't intend to ever cross any lines. Especially today, when he planned to admit what he knew about her and reveal how the US Government had brought him on to handle her. Sort of.

"You know I have a boyfriend already, right?" She laughed and so did Robert. "Now, what's the latest news about Frank and the boys? Are you keeping them all locked up for me, nice and safe? So, all of us peaceful citizens can relax in our beds at night and not be worried about *bad things happening*?" She'd actually used those same words with him years ago. From a fifteen year old, *bad things happening* had sounded a bit differently than how they did now from her at seventeen. Of course, a lot had happened over the past two years. She knew he'd finally figured out that she'd played him back then. And, he obviously knew she was playing him now.

"Yeah, they're all safely tucked away. Their lawyers tried for bail but due to everyone having prior criminal records and being such a huge flight risk, having access to millions of dollars the way they do, the judge has denied any bail." He looked at her and marveled at how she could be so playful about this. Sometimes, she was obviously a lot more mature than any teenager. "The court has tied up all the funds and assets the FBI knows about, but there are likely some offshore accounts we don't know about. Hell, we'd never have found those funds of Tony's you gave us, as you well know."

When Missy had given the FBI that wealth of information she'd also given them over ten million dollars, free and clear, which Tony had managed to accumulate. That had been over and above the five million dollar estate his wife had inherited, which had just gone through probate. So, yeah, Missy understood about hidden assets.

She'd had to learn a lot of things about Tony after two guys had grabbed her, using a syringe to inject her with a knockout drug. When she'd awakened two hours later, she'd found herself lying on Tony's bed in handcuffs. Naked. Tony had Missy kidnapped because she'd interfered and stopped him from raping his stepdaughter, Alice Morris. He'd been molesting Alice for three years, starting right after he'd married her mother, when Alice was just thirteen. That had ended once Missy had confronted him and he'd planned to get his revenge. She was going to be tortured -- raped and ravaged over several days -- and then murdered. She'd never be found.

But, Missy had escaped from Tony by Changing and then had completely terrorized him in her cat form. When she'd Changed back, he'd freely given her all the information she'd asked him for including all his passwords and codes. Although she hadn't actually killed him herself, she'd blackmailed the two guys Tony had used to kidnap her and had forced them into disposing of Tony.

A month later, she'd had Robert arrange her meeting with the FBI and had *traded* all the info from Tony for some information she'd wanted. And for some surveillance software which she was now using to monitor those same two guys, Billy Martin and Donny Delgato. Just in case, as an early warning system, she was monitoring them with spy cameras she'd hidden in their apartments. She'd get a text message from that FBI software if her name came up and she then could watch the video to see what had changed and what had happened. Yes, she had her secrets.

"Robert, I really appreciate the way you FBI guys are continuing to look out for me and trusting me. I know I never explained about all that stuff from Tony but he had his mob buddies and there were things ... things that I learned about those guys that I haven't shared. I just can't." Missy looked at Robert and she thought about what she'd learned. She and Robert had talked about this before. Or, to be accurate, they had talked about her *not* telling him these things.

Yes, she'd learned it wasn't just Tony and those two guys Billy and Donny. When Tony had wanted to arrange for things, like the murders of his first wife and then, later, his daughter, he'd asked his buddy Frank McCarthy and Frank had then called someone in New York who'd sent up these two hit men. The same arrangement had then led to these guys coming after her. But, she'd trapped them and shown them Tony's confession about those earlier murders as well as her own kidnapping, all on video tape. And, she'd learned these guys actually worked for the head of one of the mob families in New York. To avoid exposure, they'd told her everything and had agreed to all her terms. In addition to disposing of Tony, they'd named their boss Salvatore and had implicated him in arranging for everything. All on tape, added to the same tape she'd recorded Tony on.

And it was information about this mob boss Salvatore D'Amato that she'd wanted from the FBI. She didn't explain why but had insisted she needed this info to protect herself and her family. What had started out as her simply trying to help protect Alice had led to her being targeted by both the East Boston and New York criminal organizations. Hopefully, with the arrests of Frank and his gang, the East Boston organization would be leaving her alone. Her joking about *bad things happening* really wasn't anything to joke about.

"Missy, I wish you would share some of those things. So, maybe I can help. And, as bad as those things might be for you? I'm afraid I have to give you some new information. And, this information might be just as bad as those things you're not talking about." He sighed as he studied her. He and Drew had discussed this new situation at great length and they'd both agreed. Missy needed to know this. Even if it meant he had to admit to her that her werecat secret wasn't really a secret.

Missy could tell that Robert was serious. Crap! What now? "New information? Is it about Frank and his buddies?"

"Not exactly. But, it's related in a way, since our arrests have created this vacuum for organized crime in East Boston." Robert thought how best to present all this. "You see, I've been advised that an individual named Carlos has come up here and is taking over what's left. Carlos has several aliases but we think he's using the name Carlos Mancini up here. He's originally from South America but has been operating in Miami for the past ten years."

"Okay. But, why can't Armando just take care of this Carlos? Why is this of any concern to me?" Armando was the head of the FBI's Organized Crime Division in Boston and the one to whom she'd given all the information about Tony. And, the ten million. Robert had merely arranged for the meeting. And, Armando had provided the info she'd wanted about Sal.

"Oh, Armando will indeed have his team going after Carlos. Who knows? Maybe someday, he'll be able to make a case. But, that's going to probably take a few years, just as it did for the case against Frank. Without that info you provided, he'd still be trying to make a case."

Missy nodded and said, "Yes, I get that. But, you haven't explained why this affects me?"

"It's because we're pretty sure that Carlos is similar to you, Missy. We think he's a werecat."

Now Missy sat back, in shock. This was a lot to process. Robert knew about her? And, there were other werecats out there? She also picked up on his saying "we" and she decided to ask about that. "You know you're saying some very shocking things to me. And, you're saying *we're pretty sure* and *we think*. Why would the FBI ...?" She lifted one eyebrow to leave her question hanging at that.

"Ahh, it's not the FBI, Missy. But, I've been asked to join another team. There's a US Government agency ... their Paranormal Branch or "P" Branch ... I trust you will keep all this confidential, right? This is very secret. Just as secret as you being a werecat. If this guy Carlos hadn't come up here? But, he did and we think you have a need to know." Robert felt really bad about having to explain all this. But, it was necessary. Looking at her now, he could see she was very troubled. "Missy, did you think you were the only one? The only werecat?"

There were a lot of things racing through her mind as she continued processing this. Yes, she wondered about that. "I'm still trying to figure things out as I go along. Since you know my secret ... and maybe a lot more ... we really do need to talk." She looked around but there was no one else in the coffee shop anywhere nearby. "One of my biggest fears is ending up in some government lab. Now you tell me this "P" Branch knows ... do they have a lab? What's my risk, here, Robert? You're my friend. Please. Help me understand."

"No, they don't want to put you in any lab. Drew Martinson, the head of this "P" Branch, is very excited about you. He brought me on to help with you, because I'm your friend. He's thrilled you want to go to West

56

Point and everything. I can't tell you everything his organization knows, because they haven't told me. But, if I can answer a few of your questions, and I know you have some, let me try."

Missy thought for a minute. "How did he find out about me? Are there a lot of us werecats? Why hasn't any information about us ever been published? I've been looking, you know. Lots. Nothing but obvious fiction."

Robert said, "He heard about your saving that Stratton family and began investigating you because of that. You'd revealed your superhuman ability, right out there in plain sight. His "P" Branch has unlimited resources and was able to learn everything in our FBI files -- even what I'd only saved in my private file about you on my laptop. I hadn't even put that on our FBI database. I'm actually embarrassed to admit that, but ... at any rate, there's really an awful lot of information available about you. Once he started looking, it was obvious that you were really enhanced. Superhuman powers, able to heal ... plus all the articles, write-ups that I'm sure you know about. Being a great athlete in high school, second degree black belt in karate, amateur trophy in mixed martial arts at that Expo a year and a half ago? You know."

Missy sighed. Yes, she knew. "But, how did he know I was a cat? When I Change? Or, is that the only kind of wereanimal?"

"Now you're asking about some stuff that I don't really know much about. That is, about other kinds of wereanimals. But about you? You left those cat tracks last October. You pretty much admitted you were responsible for killing those two guys ... for kidnapping Alice? Remember? Drew read about that in my private file and it made it conclusive. He realized you'd more than just been responsible; you'd actually done that ... you'd gone in there yourself and broke their necks as a cat. You're a werecat." Robert smiled, as he remembered how difficult it had been for him to accept everything, at first. But, once he'd accepted it, many of the mysteries about her had suddenly been all cleared up.

Missy suddenly let her cat energy come flooding in and her eyes changed from the deep green they normally were and began filling up with gold speckles so they were flashing yellow to green to yellow. Then, she *pushed* some of her energy at him. And, with a playful smile she actually growled. The sound was definitely an animal sound and not something that would ever be coming from any girl.

Robert felt her energy and realized she was letting him see her, the real Missy, probably for the first time. "Wow. You do know about all this energy you're giving off, right? That's incredible, Missy. I was not briefed about any of that." He shook his head as he stared across the table at this incredible person. Her eyes were wild and mesmerizing. He was very glad she considered him to be her friend.

Laughing, Missy pulled back, tamping her feline nature back down, and her eyes now showed only a few specs of yellow. "I told you I'm still trying to figure things out as I go along. Is that anything your crazy "P" Branch can help me out with?"

Robert said, "Maybe. They have been monitoring a few of you werecats. And, there really are only a very, *very* few. That's why you can't find anything. Some have more abilities than others. You seem to have even more than anyone they've ever studied or learned about. That rapid healing you do? And, wait until I tell them about this energy push thing you just did. Then again, I don't really have to share that with anyone just yet. Maybe I'll keep that secret for now." He smiled at her.

"Interesting. I can only say that my various abilities all seem to be getting stronger, now that I'm older and now that I've managed to really meld my two natures into one. I actually have been going very slowly, since I do *not* want to lose control. I work the hardest on my controls, believe it or not." Missy felt as though she was sharing a burden, just being able to discuss this stuff.

"Well, I'm in your corner, Missy. Believe me when I say I'm only trying to help. That's why this warning about Carlos. He's a serious gangster and we don't trust him at all. It's really unfortunate that he's now up here in East Boston. If he ever learns about you? We don't have any way of knowing what he'd do." Robert looked around, once again making sure no one was listening in.

Missy said, "I was going to ask about that. Why is this Carlos a threat for me?"

59

"Isn't it obvious, Missy? You're a female. And, as far as we know, you're the only female werecat alive today. We're concerned this Carlos could not ignore you and since we've no way of predicting just what that might mean, we wanted to warn you. We don't think it would be anything good."

Chapter Five
Feb 2018

"He did it! He won!" Missy was jumping up and down and her excitement was contagious. Her best friend Alice Morris was with her and had brought her boyfriend, Mark Mathews. Mark was also a good friend of Missy's brother John and Missy had known him all her life. They were watching Mike compete at his college varsity swim meet and he'd just won the 200 meter butterfly event. Missy loved coming to these swim meets but it was difficult to schedule being there and even more difficult to have her friends join her. Alice and Mark were both at the same university in Boston and Mike's university was nearby in Medford where he was studying pre-med courses. She, of course, was still in high school. They were always going in different directions with all the many activities and commitments each of them had.

But, today was Saturday and they were all going out after the meet, as a foursome. Date night. Wow! Missy hadn't seen Alice since Christmas although they talked several times each week. She knew Alice's relationship with Mark had continued getting better and better and that really made her happy. Especially since she'd helped with that. Mark had been the one who originally had confided in Missy, asking her to help with his girlfriend Alice, who wasn't comfortable with his advances. She would say she wanted him to touch her but her physical reactions were clearly saying no. Could Missy maybe find out what might be the problem?

That had led to Missy confronting Alice's stepfather Tony Gonzales, of course, with all the events after that. Tony was now dead, Frank McCarthy was in prison, the New York mobsters were being monitored and now this guy Carlos had moved into the area. But, the progress Alice had made over the past two and a half years made everything worthwhile. Her sexual healing had been slow but steady, with assistance from her therapist Dr. Susan Thomas. Missy's constant support and unconditional love had also really helped. Alice had never told her mother and probably never would. But, she'd finally been able to tell Mark. They were now a real couple and really enjoyed a very healthy sex life, which Alice was very open about with Missy. She continued to tell Missy everything since being able to do that, back when she had no one else she could talk to, had made all the difference.

"Congratulations, Missy, your boyfriend is a super star!" Alice was thrilled with the way Missy now seemed so into Mike and this was actually the first time the four of them had gone out together. She turned to Mark and said, "Tell her, Mark. You're impressed with that performance too, right?" Mark was not a huge guy and had not been an athlete. But, he was handsome and smart and perfect for Alice, who was only five feet, five inches and had not been an athlete either although she had a very nice figure. They really were soulmates and looked great together. They both had blue eyes but Alice was a blond while Mark had dark brown hair.

"Of course I'm impressed. But, where are all the girl swimmers? You and Missy are getting to ogle all those guys out there, standing around in their little Speedo swimsuits with, you know, their *big packages* all bulging out. Where's the eye candy for me? That's the performance I'm interested in." Mark had provided elaborate gestures to go along with his comments, which made the girls really break up laughing.

"Now, Mark! Behave yourself and just sit there. This is a men's swim meet, remember? You're not getting any eye candy tonight ... until we get home. Now, let Missy enjoy herself and don't embarrass her." Alice looked at Missy and suddenly broke out in further laughter. "Damn, look what you've done now, Mark. Missy's eyes are getting all those yellow specs in them and I know what that means. You had to go and mention those *big packages* on display out there, right?"

Missy had actually been noticing how spectacular her Mike looked, with solid muscles rippling everywhere. A real swimmer's build, with fantastic muscle tone but not a lot of bulk. Broad shoulders, narrow waist, great abs, powerful legs. Long arms with those big hands ... just thinking about all the places she'd like to experience having him touch her with those hands... Mmmm. That always got her so wet, feeling slick and slippery between her thighs. Ever since that night with him last Thanksgiving, when his hands had indeed touched many of those places ... she shivered as a little sexual thrill went zinging through her. Yeah. She knew her eyes were doing that thing she did when she

63

was aroused. She inhaled deeply, to let the heavy chlorine scent help clear her mind.

"Guys, we're not going to discuss eyes or eye candy or big bulges, we're going to watch the wonderful performance my man is giving us *inside* the pool, not standing around *outside* the pool. Right?" Missy laughed and, suddenly feeling extra playful, she pushed out one of those energy pulses of hers, right at them, just as she'd done at Robert the other day. Mark had no idea what had just happened but Alice immediately broke out laughing like crazy. She'd actually seen Missy Change a few times and she knew what that energy pulse had felt like. She hadn't realized Missy could do that without the shimmer of light and the Shifting that went with it.

"Oh, you're being naughty tonight, Missy! We are still all going out to eat dinner together, right? My treat, okay?" Alice knew talking about food would probably distract Missy and she was right. Meanwhile, Mark was still looking around with that "What just happened?" expression on his face.

"Your rich girlfriend just agreed to buying me some lobster tonight," exclaimed Missy, looking at Mark with a huge laugh. Alice's Mom had insisted on giving Alice one million dollars and Missy delighted in teasing her "rich heiress" friend about that, every change she got. This was after the five million her Mom had inherited from Tony, which had caused her to give up her job at Walmart and make a lot of adjustments in her life. "Of course, you know I always have *two* lobsters for my poor starving body, to keep up my strength and everything. But, she can afford it. Thanks, Alice!"

Missy and Mike were walking into the parking garage after seeing Alice and Mark off at the subway station. Earlier, Missy had picked Mike up at his dorm and driven them into Boston for the swim meet and the meal afterwards. The meal had ended up being very special. What had made it special wasn't just that Alice had treated everyone or even that Mike's team had dominated at the swim meet. It was the news about Alice and Mark getting engaged. They'd taken turns explaining all about it right after placing their order and while everyone was waiting for their lobsters to be served.

Three days earlier, on Valentine's Day, Mark had surprised Alice. When she'd shown up at his off campus apartment, he'd insisted she go on a little scavenger hunt that he'd arranged. He'd obviously gone to a great deal of trouble and she was thrilled to comply. He'd left clues in a half dozen places, each leading to the next place, and at each of those places he'd hidden a gift box as well. It had taken her a good half hour to find each of his little gifts, which were all special and meaningful. Flowers, earrings, tickets to a play, a box of chocolates, a lovely bottle of wine and finally a candle light dinner for two all arranged right there in his apartment. He'd explained the wine was the reason for having the dinner right there at his place since they weren't twenty one yet. Then, when it was time for dessert? He'd gotten down on his knee, pulled out the little velvet box, opened it in front of her to reveal the engagement ring and popped the question.

Alice had been so overcome with her emotions that it had taken several minutes before she'd been able to say yes. Of course, the way she'd been hugging and squeezing him, with those tears of happiness making mascara tracks down her face, had made her feelings pretty clear. They'd been pretty much exclusive for years and had always loved each other. Once Alice had escaped from Tony's abuse, had realized being a victim had not diminished her and had started to highly value her own self worth, her love for Mark had allowed them to gradually get more and more physical. If anything, because of all the communication between them, their sex life was extra special. Alice was now very adventurous and really enjoyed all their lovemaking.

"Will being a Maid of Honor be something you can do? You know, if you're accepted to West Point?" Mike knew she'd submitted everything for this, done great on her interviews and was now just waiting to hear if she'd be accepted. She'd already explained how, if accepted, she'd be going there in late June and her trips home would be few and far between for that first year.

Missy said, "Yeah, Alice knows all about my plans. So, she and Mark are planning their wedding for Thanksgiving weekend, my first real opportunity to get back home. John's the best man and that'll work for him as well." Six months. Wow. She felt a little bad she'd not be there for all the typical Maid of Honor stuff leading up to the wedding. But, Alice wouldn't consider having her wedding without Missy and had pulled her aside right after their dinner to confirm this timing would work. When Missy had agreed it was definite and Alice could go ahead and send out the "Save the Date" notices, they'd both gotten really excited.

"I'm happy for you," Mike told her. He was thinking about how happy the two girls had been when Alice had put on her ring. She'd waited until they'd announced the engagement at dinner and then she couldn't wait to show Missy. They'd only heard the cute story that went along with that as part of the show and tell. Since the two girls had been so ecstatic during the show part, it had taken quite a while before getting around to the tell part. "I know Alice is really special for you. I mean … you even told her about being a cat before you told me, right?" He laughed a little at this, but when he looked at her his eyes were really asking her to explain that.

Missy could not only see by his eyes but she could actually *feel* his asking her about this. "Actually, I didn't *tell* her, exactly. I was forced to *show* her. She was kidnapped last year and I managed to find out where she was being held. To minimize any risk the guys might hurt Alice, I broke in there … as a cat. After … when it was safe … she saw me Change back." They'd just gotten off the elevator at the floor where her car was parked but Missy stopped walking and turned to study Mike's reaction. She didn't really want to explain all the sordid details that had led up to that night. She definitely wouldn't be telling him details about how Tony had abused Alice for three years. Mark was the only other person who knew about that, aside from Missy and Alice's therapist.

Mike stopped when she did and looked back at her. "That sounds pretty serious, Missy. I guess I hadn't thought that much about what secrets you might be keeping as far as after … you know … *after* you came down from those mountains." They'd had several long talks since coming home from the ski trip. She'd explained all about her life as a cat for two years in the mountains.

And, he'd already met the Stratton family that she'd rescued on her way out of those mountains. Their car had gone over a cliff and dropped down a hundred feet. She'd noticed the smell of leaking gasoline and had gone down and pulled the three of them out of the car. When it had exploded, she'd been holding the five year old girl, Emily, and had been badly injured when her head hit a rock. He'd read all about that. Now he was realizing she had some more secrets. Alice had been kidnapped?

Missy was about to ask him to be patient with her and that she'd tell him more stuff later. But, suddenly she recognized a familiar scent. Marco. She never forgot a scent; her scent memories were even stronger than her visual memories. Why would Marco be here in this parking garage? She instantly went on the alert and pulled Mike over so they were between two cars, close to the elevator.

When she'd rescued Alice from those kidnappers it was by confronting Frank McCarthy. Either he told her where Alice was being held or she'd send her video tape to Salvatore D'Amato. She'd shown him her video containing Tony's confession along with confessions by Sal's two guys, Billy and Donny. Since this evidence clearly was implicating Frank and Sal in the murders of Tony's wife and daughter, Frank would be in big trouble with Sal. After all, it was Frank and Tony who'd messed up, right?

To confront Frank, she'd walked into his favorite nightclub and had met two of Frank's guys at the door: Ramon and Marco. Ramon was one of the eight guys that had been arrested by the FBI, along with Frank, but not Marco. This couldn't be a coincidence; Marco had to have followed her here. And, he probably wasn't alone. She inhaled deeply and could scent three other guys who were also up ahead, somewhere. Somewhere near her car which was on this level but at the opposite end of the garage.

"Mike, we're going to get back on that elevator and go downstairs. Right now." She pulled him back with her while her mind raced with all the possible scenarios they might be facing. If they'd followed her here, they had to know Mike would be with her. Was this a hit? An abduction? Would Frank risk that? Whatever it was, she wasn't going to have Mike exposed.

Both the sounds and the smells she could sense from Marco and the three others were far enough away that she and Mike could get back on the elevator. When the doors opened, they went in and she pushed the down button. She took off her gloves, her hat and her coat and handed them to Mike along with her purse. "There are some guys waiting up there for me, Mike. For us, actually. Down by my car. Please just trust me about this, okay? I promise I'll explain things later."

When they got to the bottom level, she was wary. Surely there had been someone acting as lookout who'd have called up to the guys above, alerting them. Where was that guy now? When the doors opened, she and Mike remained inside, out of sight. She began parsing scents over her tongue and across the roof of her mouth. There. A man was out there, somewhere on the street, but nearby. Near enough to have watched them go in. Breathing deeply, she couldn't sense anyone else.

Mike was very concerned but she was holding a finger to her mouth for him to be quiet and signaling with her other hand that he stay there with the elevator locked open. She took off her boots and socks and was now standing there barefoot in her dark jeans and navy blue sweater. The New England Patriots lettering across her chest was white but otherwise, her outfit would look pretty dark. Especially since it was not that well lit outside. After a final check, she slipped out of the elevator and approached the entryway to the street. If this guy was only an innocent bystander, too bad. Missy wasn't about to take any chances.

She rushed out and went straight to the man standing out there next to a lamppost. He was definitely surprised and before he could react, she grabbed him by the neck with her right hand. She was fast and she was also very strong, especially when she allowed her cat

70

abilities to come surging into her body. She'd learned to control this and, at times of danger or great need or under extreme conditions like right now, she was indeed superhuman.

Inhaling his scent, so there would be one more person she'd never forget, she demanded, "Who are you? Let me see your cell phone."

He was unable to breathe and tried to break her hold but she easily prevented him from doing that. As she continued crushing his throat he sank down onto his knees. He reached a hand inside his coat and she told him, "That better be a phone because if you pull out anything else, I'll kill you." She was pretty sure he was part of the gang that had come out here after her and Mike.

The guy slowly pulled out a phone and handed it to her.

While still holding him by the throat, she dialed the last number he'd called. She recognized Marco's voice when he answered with a loud bark. "What the hell, Lorenzo? Where are they? It's been almost ten minutes now since you said they were on their way up."

"Lorenzo can't come to the phone right now, Marco," said Missy. "Do you want to tell me why you're up there with my car? Who sent you?" She put the phone on speakerphone and slipped it into her pocket. Then she suddenly grabbed Lorenzo's hair with her left hand and released his throat, freeing her right hand. She immediately used that to strike a blow behind the guy's ear, hitting his carotid artery. He was out cold and she lowered him to the sidewalk.

"Oh, shit! You bitch, what have you done to Lorenzo?"

"He's resting now. But you? I'm coming up there after you, Marco. Remember what I did to Ramon? Did Frank send you after me?" Ramon had given her a full body pat down, searching for weapons or a wire, before ushering her in to see Frank. That search had been very humiliating; after groping her between the legs he'd cupped her breasts and pinched her nipples. She'd really enjoyed kicking him in the jaw in Frank's office a bit later on. Right after she'd kicked him in the groin. His jaw had been wired up for several weeks after that.

"Frank's not around to call the shots anymore. I figured I'd do Ramon a favor. The four of us all doing you up here in front of your big boyfriend? That'll help Ramon do his time inside. Every visiting day? We'll show him the video, over and over." By the way Marco's voice was sounding along with the changing background noises, it was obvious he was moving around up there.

Missy knew it was time to get going. "Bye for now, Marco. I'll be right up." She hung up and went back in to see Mike. He had already called for the second elevator and had locked that one as well. Nobody up above would be using the elevators at this end of the garage. Missy grabbed his hand and they raced over to the stairway.

72

Chapter Six
Feb 2018

"Mike, these guys are all part of the same criminal organization that kidnapped Alice last year. I want you to call Robert Ulrey for me. His number is in my cell phone, which you have right there in my purse. He knows I'm a werecat and he's with the government. Tell him where we are and that we may need Plan WP tonight." She looked at him and could see all the thoughts racing behind his eyes and all the emotions he was struggling with. But, he nodded his head and she pulled him close and kissed him. "Please stay right here. If anyone gets past me, just let them go. We can deal with them later. Just be careful and don't get hurt."

Then she raced up the stairs to find her would be attackers. Her enhanced senses were all working at an even higher level. She'd also removed her earrings and put them in her pocket. Just in case. She knew she'd probably need to Change before this night was over. It really helped that she no longer needed to worry about anyone who might learn she was a werecat.

The Plan WP she and Robert had discussed was for disposition of anyone she needed taken care of. People she'd allow to live but only if they couldn't stay around and be a threat for her, her family or her friends. Robert had explained his "P" Branch didn't want her to be a vigilante and were willing to help. No more of her killing the bad guys. They'd force these people into witness protection and make it very clear that all their other options would be far worse. "P" Branch had the resources and could easily frame anyone as an informant and reveal evidence to their mob boss that proved it.

As she approached the fourth level, where her car was located, she could hear two of them. They were near the elevator, whispering. She paused and tried to sense if anyone was watching the stairway. She could scent three guys, none of them Marco. She needed to move fast and she did. The guy waiting at the top of the stairs was able to yell a warning but that was all. Her approach on bare feet had been silent and by the time he saw the blur of her movement towards him, it was too late for anything else. She dove right in front of him and then swept him off his feet with her legs. She was very experienced with maneuvers like this from all her karate and martial arts activities. He hit the ground hard and she was on him right away. Another sharp blow and he was out cold.

She turned to face the two guys at the elevator and noticed they were wearing ski masks, just like the guy she'd knocked out. Apparently, Marco's plan had been to rape her, just as he'd said, but leave her and Mike alive. Maybe they were thinking it was less of a risk that any evidence would trace back to them. Murder investigations of two people might somehow get more attention than any complaints of their attack by a bunch of guys that couldn't be identified.

Both guys were holding knives which sort of confirmed her suspicion. They still thought they could subdue her and weren't pulling out any guns. Yet. These were big guys and had probably been more concerned about Mike than about her. In spite of all that had been written up in the media about her winning trophies in karate and martial arts, she still was only a girl in high school. Right?

She tried to sense where Marco might be but he wasn't close enough, so she wasn't sure. Not wanting to take a chance he might actually be sighting down on her with a gun, she decided to run from these two guys rather than expose herself. She quickly managed to elude them and race away, dodging in and out of cars, keeping to the darker areas as much as possible. The two guys followed behind and probably figured they were forcing her towards a place they wanted her to go. To Marco.

She wanted to go to Marco also; or, really, to at least identify where he was. She eventually located him, down by the other bank of elevators and near her car. She was so glad she and Mike hadn't used that entrance into the garage and possibly been grabbed getting off those elevators. She'd have to be more careful and always check for scents before getting into any elevators in the future. Pausing to check again before stepping out of them would also be a good idea.

She let the two guys chasing her succeed in "herding" her towards Marco. One had a red ski mask and the other wore a black one. Then, seeing where some columns were blocking Marco from getting any clear shot at her, she suddenly jumped up onto the roof of one car and began leaping from roof to roof as she raced back towards one of the guys behind her, the guy with the red mask. When she got close enough, she dove, putting her hands on the roof of the car in front of him, and executed a perfect cartwheel, flipping right over his head and landing behind him.

The guy tried to slice her with his knife but her movements had completely surprised him and been much too fast. He tried to turn around to face her but she had already dropped down onto her hands and kicked back with both feet, hitting him hard and shoving him against one of the cars. Before he could recover, she kicked him again. Another guy who'd be using a straw to eat with for awhile until his broken jaw healed up. He was out cold.

The guy in the black mask had come charging over but was not even close. He stopped and yelled over to Marco, "That fucking bitch just took down Pedro! What the hell! I'm gonna kill her!" He reached into his jacket and pulled out a gun. But, this gave Missy enough time to escape. And, Missy had learned a thing or two about handling various weapons during all her karate training. She hadn't reached second degree black belt without knowing how to handle a knife. She grabbed the one Pedro had dropped and dove behind a car before this guy could get a clear shot.

Marco's voice called back, "Hector, just make sure she doesn't get away! She knows who I am and I want her dead."

Trying to distract the two of them, Missy called out, "Hey, Marco, what happened to your plan to just fuck me? Don't you guys want a piece of me? Come and get me!" She was slipping between cars and was about halfway between them both now. Marco had been approaching from his position and she could see he was now holding a gun also. It was "shock and awe" time. Putting down the knife she took off all her clothes. Then she picked the knife back up and moved silently around towards Hector.

He had been closing in on her location but when she suddenly jumped up a little bit on his left, completely naked, it definitely caught him off guard. He was not fast enough to get a shot fired. Suddenly, there was a knife sticking out of his arm and he couldn't even hold the gun; it dropped onto the ground as he yelled out in pain.

After throwing the knife, Missy had continued her charge straight at him. She was a blur and her kick was not blocked. Down he went, unconscious from the kick to the side of his head. She'd known exactly where to hit him with the heel of her foot. Since he was no longer feeling any pain from that knife, she figured she was doing him a favor. She hadn't even broken his jaw.

Marco had glimpsed all this, of course, and was now ready for her. "Nice move, you slut, showing those tits like that. But, those won't save you now. You wanna try to grab that knife, maybe? Go ahead ... you feel *lucky*, bitch?" He was close enough now to have a clear shot at her if she indeed were to reach for that knife. And, she really didn't have any clear escape routes where he couldn't get a shot off. She was making the logical assumption that he indeed was a very good shot with that gun, since he'd been one of Frank's bodyguards.

She had managed to get behind a car, where Marco wasn't able to shoot her. But, in spite of her speed, she didn't want to risk exposing herself any longer. Not as a human. She Shifted.

Marco saw the shimmer of light behind the car and could feel the strange energy pulse. What the hell? And then, some kind of animal was leaping over the car's roof and landed right in front of him, letting out the most awful scream he'd ever heard. He tried to aim his gun which he'd been holding out in front of him, but this was unbelievable and couldn't really be happening, could it? He fired off a round but then his wrist was being crushed by the animal's jaws and he dropped the gun. A cougar was eating his arm!

Missy didn't bite Marco's arm off, in spite of how tempting that was. She just continued to hold his wrist with her jaws and dragged him away from the cars and into the middle of the driving lane where he couldn't reach his gun or the one that Hector had dropped. She didn't let him get up but just pulled on his arm whenever he attempted anything. After several hard yanks he got the message. Don't move.

And then, they waited. Missy enjoyed being in her cat form, gnawing on Marco's wrist. Her eyes were blazing and at any sign of his resistance, she would bite down and chew some more. Finally, after about twenty five minutes, she heard Robert on the stairs. He had another man with him and they came up and then out slowly and carefully, guns drawn.

Missy let go of Marco's wrist and stepped on his chest, letting out a loud chuffing noise. Robert came around and saw her there. "Anyone else we need to watch out for, Missy?" When she shook her head side to side, he put away his gun. Bringing out a set of handcuffs he came up and stood there, staring at her. "Wow. If you're not a sight to see, Missy! Hey, is it okay if I have Lester take a couple of photos? For our files ... we don't really get to take photos very often, you know?" He then dropped down and put the handcuffs on Marco, who winced and cried out in pain. Yes, that had to hurt, since Missy had torn up his wrist pretty badly. Tough.

When Lester stepped out, he first went over to where Pedro and Hector were lying and put handcuffs on them. He then injected them with a drug using a different syringe for each of them, so they'd not be waking up any time soon. "Any others, besides these two and the one back there by the stairs? We already got that guy out on the sidewalk." He was studying her and it was obvious this was indeed his first time, face to face with a werecat. Missy shook her head side to side and he reached into a pocket and pulled out a camera. She preened, and proudly turned so her left side was facing the camera. Let them get some photos showing the scars on her shoulder and back. The photos her Mom had taken, which she had hanging in her room, didn't show any of her scars.

Robert said, "Lester Goodding ... Missy McCrea." Looking at Missy he explained, "Les is up here from our main office in D.C. He and his wife have actually been the ones keeping track of you for our boss, Drew. Believe it or not, they're both up here on vacation. Weekend after Valentine's Day. There's this play and ... well ... when I got Mike's call, I was able to reach Les and Marsha at their hotel here in Boston and they came along with me. Les doesn't actually carry a gun, normally, but I loaned him one of mine."

Les spoke up, looking at Robert, and said, "Marsha's down with Mike. Okay if I call them to come up now? Marsha's going to want to see this ... and, ah ... meet Missy, of course." Then he looked at Missy again, and couldn't hide the way he kept checking her out. He pulled out his cell phone and dialed without even waiting for Robert to respond.

Marco, meanwhile, was finally regaining enough composure to sit up and, after wriggling a bit further away from Missy, he said, "You guys obviously know that animal is some kind of a witch, right? I mean, Missy is a witch, or something ... right? And, you assholes have her running around ..."

"Shut up, you idiot," said Robert. "Missy is just your normal, everyday werecat, right Missy? If you and your buddies here had just left her alone, you never would have had any problems. From her, anyway. You're lucky she called us this time. Remember Luis and Jose? Those other guys that Frank would sometimes get to do his dirty work?" Frank had kept Alice's kidnapping a big secret but his association with Luis and Jose was well known.

Marco remembered those guys alright. And, how they'd supposedly been killed by some wild animal. He paled and tried to back even further away from Missy. Since he was still seated, it was difficult and Robert didn't let him move very far. He reached out and put his hand on Marco's shoulder to stop him. "You have no idea how lucky you are, Marco. You're going to do a lot of talking to us. All about how things are in East Boston. First, about Frank McCarthy, and now I understand a guy named Carlos Mancini has taken over and is running things there. You've already been identified as one of his guys, so we want to hear all about him as well."

Marco said, "I'm not giving you guys shit. I want a lawyer. You haven't read me my rights yet. I know my rights. I want …"

"Les, you tell him. I'm sick of looking at him and I want to make sure Missy is really okay." Robert went over to Missy and held out his hand, which she licked with her tongue. She sat down on her haunches and purred.

Lester looked at Missy and asked, "Did anyone else see you Change, Missy?" When she shook her head, side to side, he then told Marco, "You don't have rights but you are lucky. Your buddies? They'll all have to come forward and give testimony. But, they don't know about Missy like you do. You? You're never going to testify and you'll never tell anyone about Missy.

Understand? See, if you don't behave? Instead of our witness protection, we'll either lock you up in solitary or give you back to Carlos, with a lot of convincing evidence about what a great informant you've been." Smiling, he then looked over at Missy. Then he looked at Marco again and added, "Unless Missy wants to have you. Then, we'll just give you back to her."

Missy had been enjoying the whole discussion and decided she could help reinforce things. She stood up and bared her fangs at Marco and growled. Then, for even more fun, she let go with one of her piercing cougar screams again. This caught everyone by surprise, including Mike and Marsha Goodding who had just entered down at the other end. They both stopped dead in their tracks, but then Robert started laughing and it made them relax. Mike was quick to come running up to Missy and sat down next to her, putting his arms around her and pulling her close. He'd adjusted to what she was and he loved her. He wanted to show her just how much and he didn't know how else to do that. She seemed to really like this and began purring like crazy.

"Damn, will you just look at them? Marsha, come up here and meet Missy McCrea." Lester knew he and his wife would both be remembering this meeting for the rest of their lives. Did Robert really tell Marco she was just your normal, everyday werecat? Marsha was going to get a big kick out of hearing that.

Missy stood on all fours and wriggled free from Mike but looked into his eyes. Then, she walked over to where she'd left her clothes. He followed right after her, figuring she must want him to do that and when he saw her clothes, he smiled. Then, he stooped down and picked them up. She went back to the group so he followed after her. She went up to Marsha and sat down on her haunches and raised her right paw. Everyone laughed as Marsha shook her paw and said, "Missy McCrea? So pleased to meet you!" Then she looked at Mike and asked, "Does she need some privacy now? To Change back? When will she be ready to do that?"

Mike answered, "Not yet, but she will. He looked at his watch and said, "Probably in another hour, hour and a half. You guys know about this, right? She needs at least two hours to recharge or recuperate or whatever it is before she can Shift again. It's a huge drain of energy. At least, that's how she explained it to me."

Robert looked at his two colleagues and said, "Actually, no. We don't know anything about that, Mike. None of us has ever seen anyone Change and the various descriptions we've heard about it have been very vague. We really don't know all that much about werecats, in spite of how closely our Paranormal Branch has been trying to study them and follow their activities all around the world. Most don't seem to get themselves into as much trouble as your Missy does." With that, he laughed and the others all joined in. Missy made one of her loud chuffing noises and that set them off laughing even harder.

The next hour passed by easily enough. Robert had arranged for police to be outside, controlling the

83

situation as needed and preventing anyone from going up to their level. There actually had only been one couple plus another guy who were forced to wait for their cars down below until the level was cleared. Other levels were okay and cars had been allowed to come and go from those.

Missy hid while some guys came up with stretchers to collect the three guys who were still unconscious; they were loaded into two special vans, joining Lorenzo, and then they were whisked away. Lester took Marco down to another of these special vans that he had waiting. "P" Branch really did have unlimited resources and all five individuals would soon be getting processed. Hopefully, a wealth of great information would be learned about the East Boston criminal organization. Eventually, they'd disappear into the witness protection program where, hopefully, they wouldn't be causing any further trouble for Missy.

Mike and his new "P" Branch friends talked about Missy's car. Robert agreed to get it checked it out for any bombs or possible sabotage and then have it delivered to her home the next day. Although it was unlikely that Marco and his guys had actually tampered with it, no one wanted to risk anything. Let the experts do their thing. Mike had already called Missy's Mom and explained they'd be staying at a hotel in Boston that night. She knew Mike was aware his girlfriend was a werecat and if Missy wanted to stay in Boston that night, it was okay with her. She'd stopped having any rules for Missy once she'd learned her daughter was a werecat.

They all kept commenting about how special Missy was and it was obvious both Les and Marsha felt a bit strange, standing around and treating a huge cat as though she were a person. But, both Robert and Mike had little difficulty with that -- they both were still seeing Missy's eyes looking at them. The color was more golden than green but there was no doubt. It was Missy and those were her eyes.

She finally stood up, signaling she was ready to Change. Mike had placed her clothing over in a secluded area but she went over and picked them up and placed them in another spot, where she would be hidden behind a car but where she knew they'd be able to experience the shimmer of light and feel her energy burst. When they were all gathered out there, Missy came out and stared at them. Then she came up to Marsha and made it clear by the way she moved her head that she wanted Marsha to follow her. She led her back to where she'd have a full view of Missy when she Changed.

Marsha got really excited and exclaimed, "Oh, my God, Missy! Really? I'm so thrilled. This is such an honor for me. Wow!" She looked at her husband and they exchanged meaningful looks at one another. Yes, they had strange jobs but this would be a special moment for them and Missy had obviously tuned into that.

Missy stood behind the car for a moment and then, once again she came out and approached the group. She went up to Mike and looked into his eyes. Suddenly, they all felt the pulse of energy she gave off.

And, Mike understood. Missy wanted him to watch her Change also. Again. He walked over to stand next to Marsha and smiled.

Now Missy returned to her spot and got ready. She was facing Mike and Marsha and then, growing very still as she once again focused with her mind and exercised her will, she Shifted. And, of course, once again there was that great shimmer of light and mysterious burst of energy which went out this time in an especially powerful wave that everyone was able to feel. She knew she was showing off and she enjoyed letting everyone there experience some of this magic which she herself really didn't understand. She picked up her sweater which she modestly draped in front of herself as she stood up. "Hey, everyone! Great to finally be able to talk once again. Enjoy the show?" She laughed and she looked at Mike. She did not blush at all.

Mike and Marsha went back to join the others and let Missy get dressed. Marsha was still deeply moved and suddenly broke out and began babbling. "That was just so amazing. Missy, I thank you for letting me see that. Oh, that was incredible. One instant you're a cat and the next you're this beautiful woman. And your gorgeous hair! I had no idea; those photos don't do you justice. Does your hair always come out like that? All straight and perfect, with no tangles?"

Missy began laughing and said, "Yes, it does. Any time I'm having a bad hair day? All I need to do is Change, wait a couple hours and Change back. Presto! Perfect hair again!"

After several minutes of pleasant conversation, they agreed to all get together the next day for a late brunch. It was now well after midnight and Robert agreed to drop Mike and Missy off at a hotel. Then, Marsha spoke up and said, "Hey, why not check into the same hotel that we're staying at? Then, we can meet for our brunch right there at the restaurant in the hotel?"

Missy said that was perfect. She did have one request, however. "Is it okay if we stop on the way and get some takeout? Like, maybe a half a dozen burgers, perhaps? I'm guessing it's too late now for room service at the hotel and I'm really starved." Everyone laughed and Robert promised that would work. He and Mike knew all about Missy and her need for food after Shifting. Les and Marsha were learning fast. There was still so much they hadn't learned yet about what it meant to be a werecat.

Chapter Seven
Feb 2018

Missy and Mike walked into the hotel, bags of burgers in hand, after Robert dropped them off out front. They'd already said goodbye to the Goodding's back at the parking garage. When they went over to the desk and checked in they learned two adjacent rooms had already been paid for. Yes, "P" Branch was taking care of things. Evidently this was a further reward for Missy's *bringing 'em in alive*, rather than merely going up and slaughtering everyone in her cat form. She'd exposed herself to a much greater risk in order to do that and Robert had already told her how proud everyone was. Finding these rooms already paid for was just another little treat, and it made Missy feel very happy.

She hadn't told Mike yet, but she only intended for them to use one of these rooms. But, first she had to eat. That also would give her an opportunity to give Mike all the details about her little adventure up there tonight. She'd not really explained all that to anyone yet. They'd all just taken it for granted that she was able to knock out four guys, while still in her human form. Missy the superhuman. No big deal, right? Jeez, Robert and those "P" Branch folks were maybe giving her too much credit. Taking her special abilities for granted. That was something she herself was determined she never wanted to do.

She also wanted to provide Mike with the background about Tony and Frank and how she'd ended up helping the FBI. So, in between munching down on those burgers, she walked him through all the things that had led up to Marco and his guys going after them tonight. And, she logged into her website with her smart phone and played the full video tape she'd made. Tony and Billy and Donny, all confessing and naming Frank and Sal. She was still explaining things to him, long after all her food was gone. She didn't provide many details about what Alice had experienced but otherwise, it was pretty much a full disclosure.

"So, let me see if I understand all this, Missy," said Mike. "Tony molested his own daughter for years and when she grew up, he had his wife murdered. Then he married Alice's Mom and was molesting Alice. You confronted him, threatening exposure, forcing him to stop and move out. To cover his tracks, he then had his own daughter murdered. He arranged for both murders by having his buddy Frank McCarthy call Sal D'Amato in New York who sent up the hit men. Then, making similar arrangements, he had those same guys kidnap you. He wanted revenge."

"Yes, but I had no idea when I made him leave Alice alone that he was connected. He'd been washing money for Frank for twenty five years, so they were pretty tight." Missy sighed, thinking about poor Roseanne, Tony's daughter. "I wanted to protect Alice and she really has managed so well, even after being kidnapped by Frank's guys last year. They wanted her to tell them where Tony's money was. You have to promise you'll never tell anyone what you know about Alice."

Mike nodded. Then he asked, "Frank knew there had to be a lot more money than just what was going through probate as Tony's estate for Alice's Mom? That's why he had Alice kidnapped?"

"Sure, and he was right. He now thinks I have it all." Missy smiled. She'd already explained to Mike how she'd given the ten million to the FBI but when she'd confronted Frank, showing him Tony's confession, he naturally had assumed she'd kept it for herself. "Frank did figure out I was somehow responsible for Tony's death. And, of course, he's right about that as well. Mike, if all this bothers you ... about me ... not only having Tony killed but my killing those two guys that grabbed Alice?"

"Missy, please! Everything you've done was more than justified." Mike stood, came around the table and pulled her up and into his arms. "And, I don't want you to ever doubt me. I'll never judge you. I know what's in your heart and if you are forced to do these things, I only want to know how I can help." He lowered his mouth to hers and kissed her. It started out as just a nice, warm little kiss to reassure her. Somehow, as they continued kissing, it became something else. He could feel her energy and her passionate response and suddenly, the awareness that they were all alone, in a hotel room, caused his arousal to become very obvious.

90

Missy was through talking; after hearing Mike proclaim his complete acceptance, which she'd not wanted to take for granted, that was all she needed. Her response to his kissing her had started slowly, with a warm glow spreading throughout her body, and she'd kissed him with a gradually increasing amount of heat. When she sensed his arousal, with his erection suddenly so hard, poking against her, she wanted more. She didn't let herself over think this but instead just let her full dual nature freely seek all the satisfaction she had long been denying herself. She could easily have died, earlier that evening. Without ever experiencing the fulfillment she knew was possible with Mike.

She now wanted to give him all and everything, to whatever extent it was possible to do so. She felt herself getting very excited but this time, it was different. This time, her passion was focused on giving Mike pleasure rather than feeling all those delicious things that he made her feel. She slowly pushed him back a few steps and then broke away from their embrace and led him over to the bed. She reached up and slowly began unbuttoning his shirt. After several buttons were undone, she pulled the shirt out of his pants and her pace picked up as she raced to finish all the buttons; she then pulled the shirt back, off his shoulders and helped him remove his arms until his shirt was off and he was standing there with only his undershirt on his upper body.

Mike was watching her do this and not really sure if he could believe what she was doing. He wasn't sure yet just what her intent really might be but he was quite happy to go with it. She tugged at his undershirt pulling it out and she slipped her hands underneath and slid them up his chest, feeling his skin. All those fabulous muscles! His chest was huge and she'd always wanted to do this. Then, she moved her hands under his arms and around to grab his back, pulling him forward so her breasts were being crushed against that wonderful chest. She stopped to just hold him and breathe in his wonderful musky scent.

"Missy, are you trying to drive me completely crazy? There's a limit to how much a guy can take, you know ... are you going to start telling me about those *boundaries* pretty soon?" Mike was thoroughly aroused now and wanted to know if she'd really allow him to respond. She had to know what this meant, right?

"Oh, yes! Those *boundaries* of mine?" Missy chuckled. "I'm not going to talk about those, Mike. Not until I've finished ravishing *you* this time. Now, help me get the rest of your clothes off, okay? I want to see what you keep teasing me with ... that *thingy* of yours that keeps pressing up against me." She ground her pelvis against him, making her point in a way that could not be misunderstood. She was being very insistent and then she suddenly backed away, only so she could grab his belt and begin unbuckling it. "You've already seen me naked twice ... it's my turn now, Mike!"

He started laughing at her and reached down to grab the bottom of her sweatshirt, which he easily raised up and pulled over her head, forcing her arms up and out. "Those nanoseconds of nudity don't count, Missy! Definitely fun, watching you Change, but now I want to really see you ... I'm a hands on guy, so I need more than just those moments." He was kicking off his shoes and finished loosening his belt and un-zippering his pants. Then he reached out and grabbed her around the waist with both hands, lifting her up and depositing her on the bed in one smooth movement. He immediately grabbed her shoes and pulled them off.

Missy began giggling and said, "You first, you first! Take it all off! Show me, show me!"

Mike ignored her and grabbed her jeans which he quickly unbuttoned, unzipped and tugged off, all the while with Missy squirming and laughing, making feeble protests. Then he grabbed her feet and peeled off each of her socks, leaving her lying there in just her panties and her bra. Finally, he pulled his undershirt off and threw that away and dropped his pants, stepping out of them and kicking them across the room. "Socks?" he asked her, raising his eyebrows. She had been watching him with those incredible eyes of hers that definitely were now looking very feline with gold sparkles glowing.

"Everything, Mike! Take it all off!" Missy unhooked her bra straps and let them dangle loosely, holding the bra cups over her breasts while she slipped one arm out and then the other. She waited until he had his socks off and was holding the waistband of his underwear, which was now tented out by his prominent erection. As he slowly lowered his underwear she laughed in glee and threw her bra right at him. When he stood back up, with his prominent male member pointing right at her, throbbing, she immediately sat up and squealed. "That's so big! I mean ... I've read stuff and looked on the internet. But, Mike … your thingy there is my first one and … um … it is mine, though, right?' She laughed and her joy was so genuine that he had to laugh with her.

"It's yours if you'll just stop calling my penis a *thingy!*" More laughter, which was not really helping him maintain his thingy at its full size, in all its glory. But, when Missy reached out and began to fondle it, with such an awed expression, it sprang right back to full attention. She cupped his balls and his hard-on swelled to even greater size and a few drops of precum glistened on its tip. She found those right away and touched them with her finger, spreading them around and making the head of his member all slick.

Before she could get even more excited, he pushed her back onto the bed and fell on top of her, cupping one breast with his hand while he immediately sucked the pale pink nipple on her other breast into his mouth. No gradual teasing tonight; he knew her breasts were craving some much stronger attention. And, he was right. She moaned and her nipples hardened and he could feel the way her pleasure was washing through her entire body. He could also feel an energy about her, radiating from within but enveloping him as well. This was all happening so fast and he'd not been expecting this at all. He was completely naked, making love to Missy, and she was thoroughly enjoying this, encouraging him with a passion that was so strong and powerful he almost couldn't believe it.

They both began exploring each other's bodies, touching and feeling one another … finding special places ... caressing those areas that would make the other person moan or cry out in pleasure. Seeking satisfaction for their own curiosity, which they both had an abundance of. Mike had never done this with any girl and, like Missy, was still a virgin. He suddenly peeled her panties down and her beautiful pubic mound, covered in curly dark red hair, made him gasp. Against her milky white skin this made a very neat triangle and he immediately brought his right hand up to cover that area. His fingers began to explore the slick folds between her thighs and he was amazed at how wet she was. When he slid two fingers along her slit, her lubricating fluids came pouring out and she shivered, spreading her thighs apart.

Missy was beginning to feel her excitement build and build as wave after wave of delicious pleasure went coursing through her body, making every nerve tingle. Mike's touches were magical and she craved them, wriggling underneath the weight of his body which felt so wonderful pressing down on top of her and her hands were constantly caressing him. She buried her face in his neck and inhaled, allowing all her enhanced senses to experience Mike. Her Mike. She wanted him inside her, something all her instincts were crying for. And, she wanted to make this all about his pleasure. She had climbed to a high plateau and was now enjoying the way she could just stay right there, waiting for Mike.

Mike suddenly stopped and said, "Oh, Missy! I don't have any condoms ... what about ... you know ..."

Missy hugged him and put her lips to his ear. "It's okay, Mike. Don't worry ... I can't get pregnant tonight. Not right after I Shift back from my cat form ... it takes several days before I'm fertile again. I'll explain tomorrow, okay?" She slid her hand down his abdomen, tracing the hairs arrowing down from his belly across his groin to the thick patch above his manhood. She wanted that male member thingy inside her but it just seemed so huge! She pulled it down, adjusting her position so they were both lying side by side, and she began to rub the tip of his huge *thingy* along the slippery folds of her sex. Down, then up to where her sensitive clit was aching and throbbing and then down again, letting her juices flow out and make everything so wet, so slick, so ready. She flipped onto her back and said, "Mike, can you play like that for a bit? Just rubbing me with your ... you know ... up and down ... go really slow, okay?"

Mike knew she was concerned ... he was about to take her virginity ... and he was happy to oblige. He knelt with both knees between her legs which she now spread wide apart, letting him guide himself all along her entrance, using one of his hands while he bore his weight on his other hand. She put both her hands on his chest. As he moved himself all along her sensitive flesh, he began probing and pushing the tip inside, just a little bit each time. She was so incredibly slick and wet down there! She began to move her body under his, anticipating his movements. And, suddenly, she moved just as he moved and he found himself inside her. He'd slipped right in and he brought his hand away, shifting his body so his weight was now on both elbows.

Missy had felt him enter and she'd thrust her hips forward just enough to make that happen. Wow was that different! Yes, there had been a slight pinching sensation but now she felt him inside and she began to move her pelvis up and down, slowly sliding him into her, deeper and deeper, feeling herself stretch and become completely filled. Her body was now joined with his and they were one! She felt him shift his position, starting to draw back out just slightly and she wrapped her legs around him, clearly asking for him to push in further yet. As he did, she rose to meet him and she felt him penetrate her all the way, their pubic bones crushing together. What an experience!

They began to move, quickly establishing a rhythm that was wonderful, with her lubrication so slick that her warm sheath firmly held him while he glided in and out, in and out, moving so smoothly and easily. Their bodies were made to be doing this. She felt herself climbing to a higher plateau as her awareness of his movements began to make various things build inside her entire being, all while feeling the exquisite pleasure of having Mike inside of her. Too soon, Mike began to jerk and spasm as his orgasm made him move with uncontrollable thrusts, and she felt him ejaculate with his warm seed being spurted inside her.

"Oh, Missy! That was just so wonderful! Thank you, thank you, thank you!" Mike stopped moving and just laid there, still buried deep inside her. For several long moments, he didn't move and she felt so close to him, clinging with her arms around him, listening to his breathing slowly calm down and his heart rate subside.

Inside her warm and throbbing entrance she could feel him lose his hardness as he gradually became more and more flaccid. She squeezed just a little with her kegel muscles, wondering what that might do. She'd read various things about sex but this was her first experience and she was thoroughly enjoying it. No, she had not achieved any release yet, but the plateau she was now on was so satisfying!

Mike could feel the strong muscles of her female sheath grab and massage his limp member and he didn't want to pull out. His heart was pounding and he was overflowing with all the feelings he had for Missy. This had been the most fulfilling moment of his life and he couldn't believe how special Missy was, somehow knowing just what to do and how to do it so his pleasure had been beyond all expectations. Ahhh, that was nice. Mike was only nineteen, of course, and his recuperation period was very fast. As Missy kept doing those wonderful things, clenching and releasing, he began to feel himself growing firm inside her. Could that be happening? Yes, it could and yes it was! His excitement began to grow as he felt himself getting hard again. He probed, just a little, and he felt her respond to his movement immediately. Missy was still needy and had not yet been satisfied. As that thought washed through him, he began to really feel fully aroused and once more he began to move rhythmically inside her.

Missy felt Mike's rapid recovery and her body instinctively moved, adjusting so her sensitive places were getting the maximum benefit for each of his strokes. Missy had already learned, when Mike had given her that mind blowing orgasm last Thanksgiving … her first ever … that her ability to experience pleasure was enhanced way beyond what any normal human might feel. Her body could feel things to a far greater extent and for much, much longer … if she allowed herself to do so. If she relaxed and released all her controls, giving herself fully to the whole experience. She did that now.

As Mike's renewed strength and energy allowed him to stroke in and out, at first at a much more relaxed pace without all the frenzy that had accompanied his first time inside her, Missy's body began to completely enjoy every part of their lovemaking and her excitement began to build, bringing her higher and higher, closer and closer to … something! Her entire being began to throb and pulse and she began to release energy waves she'd never experienced before. These somehow helped Mike as he began to pound his body into hers, harder and harder, increasing the tempo of his movements to keep up with the wild bucking that her body was now doing.

She reached some final threshold and she screamed with pleasure, her release starting but then somehow her body was seeking an even greater release, hovering just out of her reach, driving her to scream for more. As she demanded that he bring her to even greater heights, her fervor and excitement finally triggered his orgasm and he ejaculated once more, this time somehow lasting much longer and being a much more powerful experience. As he gradually was able to think once again, he realized his big moment had finally brought her completely over the edge, enabling her to experience that tremendous release that had been building in her for so long.

Missy indeed had finally felt her entire being disintegrate, completely coming apart as her body was wracked with convulsions so powerful and so pleasurable she didn't know how she could survive. These had begun even before she'd felt Mike exploding inside her and only grew stronger and stronger, going on and on and on ... long after Mike had stopped moving, she continued to feel herself shiver with little spasms of pleasure. She was completely spent and it felt so good. So, so good. Once again, she found herself sobbing, tears of such complete joy at the incredible fulfillment she'd found this time, bonding with and making love to Mike.

When his flaccid member finally slipped outside and they were no longer joined as one, Mike felt suddenly vulnerable. He noticed Missy was completely out, unconscious, and he took a moment to admire her beautiful naked body. Yes, this was much better than those nanoseconds when she'd allowed him to see her being naked before. This was total saturation as he drank his fill, glorying in what a magic moment they'd shared. He pulled down the covers and picked Missy up, sliding her under the sheets. He then climbed under those sheets and snuggled up close, pulling her body into his, her back against his chest, his arm going around her to cup one of her breasts, his leg squeezing between her thighs, and he cradled her head against his neck. He drifted off to sleep, with his body as entwined with hers as he could possibly get, continuing to enjoy how happy it made him to hold her in his arms.

Chapter Eight
Feb 2018

When Missy woke up the next morning, she felt wonderful. Better than wonderful. She was still entwined with Mike, whose big limbs were encircling her and whose bare flesh felt so great everywhere it touched her bare flesh. Being naked like this, together, was amazing. Sweaty, their bodies were sticking against one another in several places. With the very strong scent of the sex they'd had still permeating everywhere, she started getting excited all over again.

Mike felt Missy moving, cuddling up against him and he slowly woke up from a very satisfying sleep. Nothing felt as right as this, holding her, having made love the way they'd done the night before. Suddenly, before he was fully awake, he could hear her inside his head. *Mike? Can we do that again? Please?*

Before he realized she had not actually spoken out loud, he said, "Of course! Missy, you can have me anytime you want! Always!" He reached for her, pulling her close, cupping her breast and tweaking her nipple. His erection was pressed up against her lovely rear end and he became fully awake. He also realized he probably needed to go empty his bladder. "Okay if I go take a leak first?"

Missy laughed and focused once again. This was fun. Was he really able to hear her in his head? She felt as though the bond she was feeling with him was so strong, this had to be possible. She waited to see him react.

Mike was slowly sitting up when he again heard her voice inside his head. *Ladies first, Mike. I actually have to pee really badly. Can I go now?*

He started to respond, saying, "Sure, sure, go ahead …" Then he stopped and looked down at her, still lying there with her back to him. "Did you just tell me you have to go pee or am I imagining that?"

Laughing, she turned and looked at him. He was staring right at her and in his head, he definitely heard her words. *You're such a gentleman, Mike! Thanks!* With that, she hopped out of bed and raced to the bathroom. Watching her lovely rear was a special sight but he was still trying to process what had just happened.

"Missy, tell me you're not saying things inside my head." Mike looked at the closed bathroom door and then, once again, he could hear her words in his mind. *I'm telling you that I'm not saying things inside your head.* This made him fully wake up. Then, more of Missy's words. *Only, I really am saying things inside your head. Ha, ha! I think it's because we have this bond now.*

She emerged, still completely naked and walked back to their bed, without any embarrassment whatsoever. He hopped up and went in, relieved himself, and came back out. She lifted the covers, inviting him to join her. He decided they could postpone any further discussions until later. He slipped in next to her and pulled her into his arms. As they kissed, the sexual heat between them was once again building and it was a long time later before they got around to talking about anything. Their lovemaking was slow and leisurely but once again built to very satisfying climaxes for both of them. Mike's staying power had been helped by the previous night's lovemaking so he lasted for a long time. And, this time, he laid on his back and let Missy ride on top. She actually had three orgasms before he finally released his seed inside her.

Missy could have multiple orgasms. Wow! How nice! This time, with her energy spent, she managed to remain conscious. Time to get going, back to the real world. They couldn't just lie around all day, making love. Could they?

Mike asked her, "Tell me about this not being fertile. You said you can't get pregnant right after you Shift. Why not?"

Missy explained, "When I had my first period, it was twenty eight days after I finally managed to Change back. I told you how that took me more than two years, right? Well, since I'd never had my period before, I was naturally very curious and I kept track. And, for the first few months, I was so busy adjusting to being back home, I didn't get to be a cat. Twenty eight days after my first period, I got my second. Twenty eight days after that, my third. Pretty regular, right?"

"Sure, I get that. So?"

"So, when I eventually Changed again? No more periods. Not unless I didn't Change for twenty eight days. Then, right on schedule, I'd get my period. It's pretty obvious to me what's happening. If I Change before I get my period, everything gets absorbed. Then, when I Change back to human, it's day one all over again. I read about the female cycle and how, if you check your temperature first thing every day, you can actually tell when you ovulate. Sure enough, for me? Fourteen days after I Change back, my temperature rises. That's when I ovulate. So, if it's been maybe ten days since my last Shift, I'd better abstain. Your semen might still be there four days later when I ovulate and I'll maybe get pregnant."

Mike thought for a moment and then asked, "What happens when you get pregnant? Can you still Change? If you do, how does that affect the baby?"

"All really great questions, Mike. Unfortunately, I just don't know. I doubt those "P" Branch guys can even tell me. I'm the only female werecat they know of, in recent times. And, as for any werecats back two hundred years ago? They haven't found any documentation. If I know I'm pregnant? To protect the baby? I just won't Shift. I can go nine months without Changing. I think. But, I'm not planning on any pregnancies for quite a few years yet, so I'm not going to worry about it."

"Okay, I get it. Makes sense. So, next time I'm getting you all worked up ... with your raging enhanced hormones all begging for my special attention? If it's been ten days or maybe a few more? Just as I'm about to …? Ah, jeez … I guess you'll maybe Change first, huh? Then, I'll have to wait around for two hours …?"

Missy broke out laughing. "Very funny, Mike. But sure. Exactly. Except for the part about my raging enhanced hormones … they don't really *beg*. Do they?"

"Oh, they beg all right! In fact, I think they're in need of some attention right now." Mike had been getting ready to take a shower. Now he looked at her and raised his eyebrows. "Join me in the shower, Missy, and I'll see what I can do."

Missy laughed. "When does one's enjoyment of being ravished change to outright debauchery?" She did, however, end up joining him in the shower.

When Les and Marsha were joined at their table by Robert, they all wondered a little about how Missy and Mike had spent the night. When they were joined a bit later by the two teenagers, freshly scrubbed and obviously so satiated from their night of lovemaking, it was indeed hilarious. Was it that obvious? Oh, yes. It was that obvious.

Then Missy decided to share the news about her now being able to push her thoughts into Mike's head. Evidently, she could not only push her energy out there where anyone around her might feel something, but she and Mike were now bonded. She delighted in having them write down several messages, out of Mike's sight of course, which she then would look at. After merely a glance, she'd tell him … without saying anything out loud or even looking at him … and he'd immediately quote the message, word for word, as though he were reading it. They even had her do this with Mike out of sight, in the next room, and she had no problem communicating with him.

"How far away will this work, Missy?" asked Robert. This was a new ability no one at "P" Branch had ever heard of.

"Probably as far away as I can still feel him," Missy answered, without thinking. Then, realizing what she'd just said, she explained, "I can feel where he is. I'm just noticing this. Wow!" They then experimented a little with that, having Mike walk around outside the hotel, and they learned she was indeed able to know exactly which direction Mike was at, relative to where she was, and approximately how far away. She and Mike agreed to test this later, when they could be a lot further apart.

When Missy suddenly broke out laughing, they asked her what was so funny. She wouldn't tell them but she did tell Mike later. She wanted to test how these new abilities might improve, the more they had sex with one another. Mike agreed that was a test program he was for, one hundred percent, and then thanked her for not sharing that with the others. At their brunch. It had been embarrassing enough that everyone knew how thoroughly Missy had enjoyed *bonding* with Mike. What made him swell with pride, however, was the fact that Missy wasn't at all embarrassed. Not the least little bit. She had sat there and glowed, obviously very happy, throughout the entire brunch.

Once they'd all finished eating, they eventually did get around to discussing more serious matters. While Marco and his boys would not be telling any tales, other than the testimony that four of them would eventually be giving, the fact that all five of them would disappear would surely be a concern to the East Boston criminal organization, both those in prison like Frank and Ramon and those on the outside. Especially to the new leadership team headed by Carlos Mancini.

Missy decided she needed the further support of "P" Branch, now that she'd seen how Mike could have been attacked. She also knew once she went away, hopefully to West Point, that her ability to monitor Sal's organization would be difficult. It was time to ask for help. She trusted Robert and so far, Lester and Marsha Goodding also had impressed her. This "P" Branch hadn't tucked her away in any lab but seemed to be genuinely on her side.

She'd learned during their conversation at brunch that Les and Marsha had both gone to the same college here in Boston, where they'd met and then had married right after graduation. This explained why they'd picked Boston for their vacation weekend, in February. They'd also been able to get a great rate at the hotel and had wanted to see the play they'd gone to earlier in the evening, prior to getting Robert's call. They'd both been recruited as research technicians by Drew Martinson, after only two years working at a company in Boston, and they had moved to Washington

D.C. It had been six years now and they had nothing but good things to say about Drew and his organization. They loved their work and had been thrilled when Missy had been assigned for them to watch, two years ago. That assignment was partly because they were from Boston and partly because they both were young.

"Watching the various Missy McCrea activities has definitely been a fun assignment," explained Marsha. "None of the other *supernatural's* seem to heal the way you do. They don't seem to need all that extreme physical stuff, either. Of course, maybe it's your spending two years in your cat form ... or, maybe it's those special genes you have ... whatever it is, you've been very exciting for us to keep track of. Meeting you like this is really just blowing our minds, and I don't mind admitting that."

"Well, thanks ... I guess!" Missy laughed. "I've talked about this with my family a lot and they all agree with me. We think I'm some sort of genetic anomaly. Until Robert talked to me last month, I didn't even know there might be others. You called us *supernaturals* ... I suppose this Paranormal Branch gets to investigate lots of spooky stuff, huh?"

Lester explained, "We get to investigate a lot of things, yes, but most of those things just don't check out. Congress and all the other government agencies all think our organization exists to debunk all the claims about paranormal activities, alien abductions, etc. That's why we get funded and have such great resources. We keep it a well guarded secret that, indeed, some of those activities are real."

Missy said, "And, for those activities that are real, there are some supernaturals involved. Others like me, right?"

"Yes, there are some cases ... which we can't talk about. But werecats? We only know of twelve others, Missy. Carlos and three others from South America. Four from here in the US, including you. Five others around the world. Not that it's spooky, but you are the thirteenth person we've identified as a werecat."

Marsha added, "Even your birthday ... am I the only one who thinks it remarkable you were born exactly at midnight on the summer solstice?"

Mike said, "Gosh, I didn't even know that! What was that old TV Show from the 1950's ... Twilight Zone? Maybe Missy's from there!" Everyone broke out laughing.

"Okay, okay ... have your fun, guys!" Missy looked at everyone and smiled. "Since you all think it's so interesting to keep track of me and everything ... learning all my secrets ... I guess this is as good a time as any for me to share a few more of them." With a deep sigh, she looked at Mike. Then she looked at the others and told them all about Salvatore D'Amato and his two hit men, Billy and Donny. She didn't hide the fact that she'd forced them to kill Tony Gonzales. Now that Mike had accepted what she'd done, she really wasn't concerned about what the others might be thinking. She didn't think she'd be arrested. And, her cat nature was very comfortable with the justice that had been meted out.

"Wow! We all had our suspicions, Missy. But, never in our wildest dreams did we imagine all that. Robert told us he thought you had to be using that FBI surveillance software for something related to Sal, and not just the Frank McCarthy organization." Lester looked at his wife. They'd had many conversations, speculating about this. "We'll be glad to take over monitoring those cameras for you. We might even be able to go in and change all the batteries on your video equipment, once the time comes."

"You actually went back during Christmas vacation and did that?" Marsha was shaking her head. "With your sister and your friend Alice?"

"Oh, sure! Of course we did. But ... please ... just don't start with the lame cat burglar jokes, okay? I got enough of those from Heather and Alice." Missy was feeling very relieved that she had friends now who were willing to help. And, these "P" Branch friends had unlimited resources.

Marsha looked at her husband and started laughing. "Wait until we tell Drew. We have to change our name now. Instead of "P" Branch, we should call ourselves Nanny-Cams-R-US, right?"

Chapter Nine
Mar 2018

"Missy, it's here! Come quick!" Missy's Mom had just gone through the mail and there was a letter for Missy. From West Point. When Missy came down from her bedroom, her Mom handed her the letter and watched as her daughter tore open the envelope. Then she watched how Missy's face lit up with joy and she knew, before Missy even said anything. Her daughter was going to West Point. It was a very proud moment.

An hour later, Missy was back in her room and had called dozens of people. Friends, relatives, Robert Ulrey, the Stratton's in Washington D.C., even Senator Maxwell's office. She was pretty excited and everyone was congratulating her and telling her how sure they were that she would do great. She'd told Mike, of course, sending him the message by pushing it directly into his mind. He'd called her back on her cell phone and they'd talked for several minutes. Then they'd agreed to get together that weekend, for sure, to celebrate.

They'd not been together since that weekend after Valentine's Day when she'd not only enjoyed having such wonderful sex with him but had mysteriously bonded with him as well ... he could easily get her words in his mind and she could feel him there, in Medford, about twenty miles from her home in Salem. Now she wanted to spend another full night with him. Waking up that morning in Mike's arms had just been the nicest experience and she wanted to do that again. Making love in the morning, after having fully sated her needs the night before? Priceless! Since this would be day twenty one since her last Shift, her female cycle was cooperating; she wouldn't be fertile now and didn't need to Change, just to avoid the risk of getting pregnant.

At school, her basketball team had finished and her softball team had not started up yet. And, there were no conflicts with her karate and martial arts activities either. She was feeling really great and had put on about five pounds, lifting some extra weights at her gym just because she felt so good doing it. Even though this was solid muscle that she'd packed on, it made all her body's curves somehow that much more noticeable. She felt sexy as hell and knew she looked really good right now also.

Now that she knew it was definite -- in late June she'd be starting at West Point -- she thought about how she wanted to manage her physical conditioning. Her focus now was to get in shape for Cadet Basic Training, two months of cadet preparation that is reportedly the most difficult experience of the whole four years -- emotionally, physically and psychologically. She wanted to arrive at her best for that. She probably wouldn't be able to Shift during those months and she wasn't sure how much food she'd be allowed to have. Trusting her instincts, she decided she'd continue to bulk up over the next three months. She'd lift heavier weights and gradually add more and more muscle mass until she was up around 150 pounds.

She'd be adding a lot of calories, mostly lean meat and some protein drinks. It was great to have some goals to strive for and the fact that this one would allow her to eat lots and exercise lots, both of which she loved doing, was all the better. She'd be faster and stronger than anyone else there, even without adding any of her supernatural cat powers which would always be there for her, if needed.

Drew Martinson called Lester and Marsha into his office and gave them the good news. "Robert just called ... Missy's going to West Point. She's really showing some great potential and I want you two to continue supporting her. Whatever is necessary; use the full resources available here. I like the way she handled that last incident. No one got killed and she took out four of those guys before she finally Changed. Only that guy Marco knows she's a werecat, right?"

"Yeah, the others hardly know what hit them. Or, at least three of them don't." Lester looked at his wife and back at Drew. "That guy Hector is actually having worse problems. He claims she somehow messed up his head. He keeps seeing these flashes with her suddenly popping out completely naked. He knows that couldn't have really happened and doesn't understand how she got the drop on him, first stabbing him and then somehow knocking him out. That sedative

114

I gave him while he was out probably helped, adding to his confusion when he finally came to."

Marsha added, "She actually did that, of course. When I was talking to her afterwards, she even joked about it. She said it was her "shock and awe" time, a strategy she considers appropriate since she wants to go into the military. Since she figured she'd have to Change, she had started getting ready and had removed her clothes. But, she figured she could get Hector first before actually Changing and it worked. She actually said she was curious ... wanted to see what time advantage it might give her. She seemed quite pleased. Apparently, it was even better than the old "deer in the headlights" look. She jumped out naked, he froze and she was able to throw that knife. He dropped his gun before getting to fire a single round."

"Well, like I said, she's showing great potential. Not everyone would have gone up against professional gangsters like that ... and these were some big guys with knives and guns ... even if they did have her supernatural abilities. That took some real courage. What kind of information have you been able to get from them? Will they make good witnesses?"

Lester said, "Except for Marco, we've turned them over to the FBI. Armando Sanchez up there is saying two of them don't really know that much but Hector and Pedro were in McCarthy's organization for years and are willing to talk. As long as they get immunity and are kept safe in witness protection, they'll testify to several extortion incidents and a few murders. They've already given information about where three bodies were buried, which has proven to be accurate. Armando's team was able to locate and identify the remains. Three mystery disappearances have now been solved and two additional arrests are being made. No one is rolling on McCarthy yet, but as Armando's team grills everyone he has evidence against, someone may be willing to talk. We'll see."

"We're closely watching the new guy, Carlos Mancini. He's in quite a panic and all this activity has him scrambling." Marsha knew Drew was very concerned about Carlos, both because he was a werecat and also since he might be a problem for Missy someday. "He now knows these missing guys are in custody and are talking. While all the talking is not about him or the guys he brought up here, he can't trust any of the old organization. Those not already in jail or missing are of no use to him now."

Drew asked, "What about this guy Marco, who knows about Missy? Does he have any information that helps? I know he won't be testifying but … anything?"

"Marco might be a problem. Now that he's had time to think … and doesn't have a huge cat chewing on his arm … he's wondering if he might have some leverage." Lester looked at his wife and then back at Drew. "Our threat to expose him as an informant isn't all that strong, since he knows we're trying to hide the fact that Missy's a werecat. He also doesn't think we'll prosecute him for attacking her in that garage. Do we want him to stand up in court and tell everyone she's this wild animal? While he knows that's not very credible, he doesn't think we'll take any chances. And, he's right."

"He thinks his gangster buddies will believe the government's framing him to protect supernatural creatures, huh?" asked Drew. "Maybe we should tell him about Carlos being a werecat. Then again, I guess that would only give him a different kind of leverage. He'll know we want to avoid Carlos hearing about her."

Lester said, "We are worried about that since Marco already told his buddy Ramon that he was going to get Missy. He and Ramon were doing a lot of talking about Missy, even before Frank got arrested. They figured she had some sort of hold over Frank. Then, with Frank in prison, his "hands off Missy or else" threat wasn't a deterrent any more. Obviously, since all those other guys were with Marco, there had to have been a lot more talk. So, with all the talk, it's quite likely that Carlos will eventually hear something about her."

Marsha then pointed out the risks, saying, "Yes, and if he puts two and two together? Missy shows up and asks about Tony Gonzales, Frank won't talk about her, Marco disappears after saying he would get her ... Carlos will probably want to check her out. Even if he only learns what she did to Ramon? That alone is probably enough for him to go check her out."

Drew nodded and added his own worry. "Even without all those concerns, once he hears about those two guys she actually killed? As a cat? We can't hide all that info. It'll definitely make him suspicious and the timing ... Missy showed up that same day, kicked Ramon

the way she did and then disappeared with Frank ...
Robert and I discussed this. Carlos will definitely want
to check her out. That's why we agreed to tell her
everything the way we have, when we've never done
that with any of the others. We'll see. That's why I'm
asking you both to give her all the support she needs. I
don't know what else we can do, besides keeping Marco
on ice, at least for right now."

Chapter Ten
Apr 2018

Alice had been talking to Missy on the phone for several minutes, catching up on things and sharing things, as they'd been doing for the past two and a half years, ever since she'd opened up to Missy about Tony. The way Missy had rescued her back then had completely changed her whole life. When she later was kidnapped and Missy again rescued her -- as a cat -- her life changed even more. Having a werecat as her closest friend was pretty special. But, it was Missy's human attributes and qualities that mattered most. Now that Missy was being as open with her as she'd been with Missy, they'd grown even closer.

Alice asked, "Are you at all worried about so many people now knowing you're a cat?" Missy had explained about Robert Ulrey and had mentioned he was somehow a member of the government, in addition to his FBI role. Some mysterious branch that Missy wouldn't talk more about, other than to say there were others in that organization who all knew. But, they were actually helping her, like the way they'd made those guys all disappear after that parking garage adventure. Missy called it an adventure; Alice thought it had to have been pretty scary.

"Well, they haven't locked me up in any lab yet, so I'm getting more and more relaxed." Missy giggled, thinking back to the many conversations she'd had with

Alice when she'd actually been worried about that happening to her. "You can't talk about this, of course, but there apparently are other *supernaturals* out there. They do think I'm sort of special though ... apparently, I'm the only female werecat in at least two hundred years."

"Well, *I* know you're special, Missy!" Alice laughed. "Actually, that does bring up something I've been meaning to ask you about though. You know how you and Mike are ... you share everything with each other, now that you're *bonded* and everything." Missy had told her all about that, of course, including how she'd revealed to Mike that Alice had been abused by Tony. He didn't really know all the details but Missy had needed to include some of it, just so he could understand why those guys had wanted to attack the two of them that night. Alice was okay with that and was actually thrilled about Missy and Mike now being so close. And, the mysterious bonding? Only Missy could manage something like that. As though all the great sex hadn't been enough? Jeez!

"Yeah, I know how we are ... and no, I'm not sharing any more details about all the positions we've tried now. I've already told you far too much." Missy giggled, thinking back to some of the things they'd talked about. She'd even joked how "her cat really liked it doggy style" and was determined to avoid any further conversations in that direction, if that's where Alice was trying to go.

This broke Alice up and she howled with laughter. Finally, she said, "No, no, I wasn't going to ask

… but, now that you mention it? Oh, never mind. But, later for sure! Okay?" She was still laughing and it was hard to talk. She then managed a big sigh and said, "No, I was hoping you could relate to the problem that I'm having, keeping your secret from Mark."

"Oh!" Missy paused and considered this issue. She was seeing why Alice had asked if she was nervous, now that so many knew about her. Mark was her soulmate and this secret was probably the only one she hadn't shared with him. Her being so completely open with those she loved, after years of secrecy forced on her by Tony, had been very important to Alice. It had really helped her to heal and fully recover. Missy knew how beneficial that was, sharing and being open with loved ones, and she hadn't suffered three years of abuse like her friend Alice had. She also knew she could trust Mark. "Okay."

"Okay? Just like that?" Alice giggled. "Missy, you know he won't actually believe me … not if I'm merely telling him about you. Can I … umm … can you *show* him?'

Missy had fully realized what she was agreeing to when she'd said okay, and now she added, "Yeah, you can bring him tomorrow morning. To the State Forest in Andover. I was already planning to spend the day out there. You know it's my favorite place where I can run around for hours and hours and even indulge myself, find a deer, you know …"

Laughing, Alice said, "Yes, I know … raw meat. You're so predictable, when it comes to eating. Thanks,

121

we'll be there. And, I really appreciate it. How's the *dieting* going anyhow?" She knew Missy was actually bulking up for her summer training at West Point.

"That's why I'm going to spend hours and hours out there. It's been such a long time since I've been wild and furry, with all my other activities. I've plumped up to 150 pounds but now I need to run off about five pounds. My goal is to reach 150 pounds but with only eight percent body fat. I've still got two more months, so it shouldn't be difficult."

Alice said, "Well, you could just stay with Mike a couple of nights. I bet he can help with that. Just be sure you tell me about any new positions you two might invent. Of course, I haven't had a chance to ask Mark about that one, you know, where you and Mike ..."

Missy quickly interrupted her and said, "Hey, quit while you're ahead, Alice! I said you can bring Mark. Be there at ten. And, bring a blanket, okay? I am not going to strip my clothes off and get naked in front of your boyfriend."

Missy sprang from the tree branch she'd been laying on, easily landing on the deer's back. She quickly broke its neck with her powerful jaws and then dragged it over to some underbrush where she could conceal her kill, after she'd eaten her fill. She'd waited patiently for this one, an old doe, which she'd scented upwind of where she'd been prowling. Once she'd realized it was headed in her direction, she'd climbed the tree and had settled herself out on the branch. It was so great, just being a cat for awhile once again. She had two distinct natures which she'd now melded into one being, herself. She loved being a werecat.

Her Changing for Mark that morning, allowing yet another person in her life to know her secret, had gone well and been lots of fun. Alice had almost convinced him with her very detailed explanation. But, when Alice was holding up the blanket and Missy was taking her clothes off ... which she tossed out for Mark to see ... he was still equally as ready to believe the two of them were merely teasing him, pulling some new prank. He did remember that energy pulse she'd recently pushed at him at Mike's swim meet. And, he had always wondered about Missy's disappearance for two years, just as so many others had wondered. Just what had really happened?

So, now he knew. It still had been somewhat of a shock, which she and Alice had thoroughly enjoyed. Only after he'd watched Alice actually go up and scratch behind her ears ... this giant mountain lion proudly standing right there in front of him ... had he let himself really believe it was Missy. Of course, Missy's eyes were Missy's eyes and she even had those same scars on her left shoulder and back, just like he'd seen many times before on Missy.

Alice was so happy! That's what really mattered to Missy and filled her heart with joy. Her friend was bursting with emotions, babbling to Mark about all the things she'd been forced to keep quiet about. And, Missy could tell that Mark was seeing a lot of things all fall into place. He now had answers to many of those questions he'd previously not even asked about since he'd been willing to just accept things without knowing -- all because of how deeply he loved Alice. This full disclosure was indeed a good thing for the two of them. Alice didn't want to keep any secrets from Mark ever again and Missy was certain that wouldn't happen. She was also certain the two of them would guard her secret and never reveal anything to those not fully aware of just what she was.

Once she'd finally left the two of them and raced off, she'd put all her human thoughts away and allowed her cat instincts and cat needs to fully manifest. She'd long ago learned how to compartmentalize things in her mind and considered this to be just one more of her special abilities. Her enhanced senses allowed her to experience things in ways that went far beyond what any human or cat might experience, but she could also control herself and go places in her mind and deal with all of it. Pain? She could ignore it. All her wild, predatory instincts? She could control them as well.

Until recently, of course, she had always restrained her huge sexual appetite, something she had noticed getting stronger and more demanding as each year had gone by. She'd reached full sexual maturity at fourteen, while living as a cat. Now, with Mike, she was complete and fulfilled, and that carried over to both her natures. She was the happiest she'd ever been and today, she was really enjoying everything.

That is, she was until she suddenly scented another big cat. A male mountain lion had been in this same area and not that long ago. Since she knew there weren't really any mountain lions in this region that could only mean one thing. Carlos. The other werecat who'd moved up here and who must have come out to this State Forest for the same reason she did. To have a place where he could be a cat.

There really weren't that many areas in and around Boston. She'd been to most of them and had found this one suited her needs the best. It was 3,000 acres and the only places this large in Massachusetts were further away, west and south of Boston. So, it wasn't all that surprising that Carlos would find his way to this place. And, now that he had? He certainly knew about her, a female cat who'd been running wild and free. Since he'd quickly do some research and verify there really weren't any mountain lions -- he'd know. Strange as it might seem, he'd know there was a female werecat who occasionally roamed this State Forest. How long would it be until he was able to track her down?

Carlos Mancini had indeed noticed. When he'd scented a female cat, he at first had assumed she must be a normal mountain lion that had somehow managed to migrate down from further north. But, her scent was a bit unique and it made him very curious. He'd spent extra time exploring the area and he'd noticed she was an infrequent visitor, rather than any animal that had actually moved in and made this her regular territory. This was not the behavior of any normal animal. But, a female werecat? Was that even possible? Then again, why not?

He'd grown up in the mountains, with his family ranging back and forth from Colombia to Peru, and he had an Uncle who had warned him how being a werecat might be possible. It was in their family. Every few years, someone in the family would show they too had inherited this strange affliction. When he'd hit puberty at fourteen and had Changed that first time, he'd been very upset. Why him?

Then, because he'd already known it was possible to Shift back to human form, it hadn't taken him much time … in just a few days, he'd Changed back. After that, he'd tried to avoid Shifting. But, for the first year or so, if he didn't Shift, it would be forced on him. As he got older, he could avoid it and go for months at a time but, eventually, he'd feel the need so strongly it was just easier to give in and Change. He needed to satisfy his cat nature. He considered it an affliction, a family curse, but he learned to live with that.

As an adult, he'd kept his two natures separate, never really growing comfortable at all with being a cat. He did, however, appreciate the enhanced abilities which being a werecat had given him. His strength, speed and agility had been a huge factor in his rising to a position of leadership. He was six feet tall, weighed two hundred pounds and was very fit. He hardly needed to exercise at all and managed to stay fit. Going furry every two or three months, running as a cat for a few hours each time, seemed to help with that in addition to satisfying his cat nature's need. He didn't really enjoy it

126

that much and definitely kept it a secret from almost everyone. He doubted the criminal organization in which he'd thrived and prospered would trust him if they knew he was a werecat.

His ferocity had helped him get where he was, as much or more than his enhanced abilities. Most people had learned to fear him and he had a reputation for dealing violently with anyone who got in his way. He had the ability to control his temper, though, and this had helped him avoid making mistakes. Rather than strike out in anger, he'd always been very careful and would bide his time. But, eventually, he would always find a way to take care of those who had opposed him. His rise in power had been steady. He'd earned respect for being a cool head and his willingness to do whatever was necessary in order to get things done had impressed a lot of the right people.

He'd migrated to the US and had quickly found a place where his contacts with various drug lords up in the mountains back in Colombia were valuable and appreciated. In a few short years, at the age of twenty eight, he'd taken over a huge organization in Miami. And, he'd run that very successfully for ten years. He'd never been arrested and had not spent any time in prison. But, he'd known the FBI was watching him. He'd been looking for a way to move on. He'd wanted to get out of Miami and away from a number of associates whom he no longer trusted.

Carlos had never married anyone and had no intention of doing so. He had perfect teeth and was rather handsome, with his dark hair and hazel eyes, swarthy complexion and overall good physical appearance. His prowess in the bedroom was legendary and a lot of girls had been very willing to be his consort. His appetite for women was insatiable, however, and he never allowed anyone to stay long or get too close. He was careful and, even though he'd forced himself on a few young girls, he'd always avoided being accused of anything. Most of the time, he'd simply paid them off or else he'd paid off their families. There had been one incident, however, when he'd accidently killed one girl. He had buried her where she'd never be found and had not been a suspect for her disappearance.

He had supplied Frank McCarthy's organization with drug shipments on several occasions and had met with several mob members in and around Boston who were all well connected. When the FBI had arrested Frank and eight others, he was quick to make his move. After a couple of meetings and some negotiations, he was being welcomed up in East Boston with open arms. At first, that had all seemed pretty good.

As it was turning out, it had maybe been a little too good. Suddenly, five guys just vanished? They all had been long time members in the East Boston organization and were trusted associates of Frank McCarthy. Soon afterwards, it was obvious the Feds had them, probably in some kind of witness protection program, since there were bodies being dug up and two more guys had been arrested. Even the guys he'd brought up here with him from Miami were getting nervous and jumpy. He'd been working his ass off trying to hold everything together.

But, discovering a female werecat was probably somewhere in the area? That was the first good news he'd had since coming up here. There were a lot of things he'd be interested in finding out once she was located. Now, all he had to do was find her.

Chapter Eleven
May 2018

It was after midnight and Aaron and Michelle were driving through Lynn, returning to Boston. Saturday had been fun, a nice break from school, but they would each be studying all day Sunday. Final exams were coming in just a few weeks now and those were typically worth half the grade for the whole semester. They were taking different courses but were both at the same university.

She'd followed him there after they'd been dating for most of their high school years. Aaron and her brother had first met as Freshman at the Prep in Danvers. She'd gone to a different high school, since the Prep was for all boys, but what had started out as occasional dates with her twin brother's best friend had ended up being exclusive for the last two years they were in high school. Being at the same school in Boston had enabled their relationship to reach several more levels and they'd been intimate since last December.

While Michelle still had a roommate, Aaron's roommate had dropped out after the first semester and no one had replaced him. She now found herself sleeping in his room for more nights than she was spending in her own room. What had been an experiment, living together, had actually been working out very well and they were already planning to get their own place off campus next year.

As Aaron braked for the red light, Michelle said, "I'll be so glad when this semester is over. College is a lot harder than it was in high school and days like today, when we didn't spend all day in the library or else doing some paper, have been few and far between. I can't wait for summer vacation."

Aaron glanced over to look at her and then looked back ahead, waiting for the light to change. "Yeah, today's our last free day. I'm going to be so busy from now until the end of exams, I don't know if you'll even be seeing that much of me. I'm so glad you insisted we take time out for enjoying ourselves today, though." They'd actually just relaxed at his house, with his parents away for the weekend, so it was just the two of them. Getting away from school and just watching TV in familiar surroundings had been nice. Chasing her around his bedroom, without worrying about some classmate barging in on them, had been even nicer.

The light turned green and he slowly accelerated forward, after glancing both ways. He never saw where the other car came from; it raced out of some side street, turning onto the street perpendicular to theirs, and then accelerated straight towards them. It never even slowed down for the red light and only at the last moment was there the screech of tires on pavement as it tried to stop. The police never did learn what the driver might have been thinking, since he died on impact. They did determine that his blood alcohol level was way over the legal limit, however.

The impact was on the passenger door of their car and it pushed their car all across the intersection.

131

Aaron was okay but when he looked over at Michelle, she had smashed her head on the passenger door window and it was obvious she was badly injured. She was out cold and the window glass was broken where her head had impacted. He knew this was serous and was afraid to even more her. He kept calling her name, hoping she'd respond, but to no avail.

It only took about ten minutes before a police car showed up but by then Aaron was frantic with worry. He'd managed to get out of his side of the car and had come around to her side, but her door was completely crushed in and wouldn't open. When he'd looked over at the other car, it was obvious the driver was hurt pretty bad. He didn't actually realize the guy was already dead but he could see there was no movement. When he couldn't get Michelle's door open he'd raced back around and scrambled inside through the driver's side but then he didn't know what else he could do. He'd gently started to pull her up in her seat but then had stopped, realizing there might be neck injuries that he'd be compounding. Just as he climbed out of the car again, the police car drove up.

Missy woke up and knew immediately that something was very wrong. She could feel it inside but didn't recognize what she was feeling. She only knew it was bad. Then, she thought of Mike, without knowing why. She immediately pushed her thoughts out, desperately hoping he'd respond. Her instincts were somehow telling her this was related to Mike and the panic that realization caused to well up inside her was something she'd never experienced before. She was very frightened. And, very worried about Mike.

What seemed an eternity but was actually only less than a minute later, her cell phone rang and it was Mike. She was so relieved and she cried out, "Mike, are you alright? Please tell me you're okay?"

Mike said, "Yeah, I'm okay ... but what's happened? You woke me up and I could practically hear you screaming inside my head." His head was actually aching now and he couldn't believe how forceful her words had felt inside his mind.

"I don't know what's happened, Mike. I only know something bad has happened ... and, I think it's related to you. This crazy bond that I feel with you ... I just don't know. I can feel you there but I can also feel ... something. Something else. Are you sure everything's really okay?"

Mike was now fully awake and he was trying to think. His head was still really hurting even though she wasn't pushing her words into his mind any more. It was all on the right side of his head, almost as though ... Michelle! Without knowing how he knew, he just knew. Something must have happened to his twin sister. "Missy, I think my sister may have injured her head. Could that be what you're getting, somehow? Maybe because she's my twin and you're now bonded with me? I really don't understand any of this supernatural stuff but ..."

Missy asked, "Where is she? Can you call her? Or, call Aaron? Hang up and then, after you reach them, call me back. Okay?"

Mike had already disconnected before she'd finished talking and was dialing his sister's cell phone. When it went to voice mail he hung up and called Aaron's cell. After four rings, he heard Aaron's voice come on the line.

"Mike? Where are you? Why are you calling?" Aaron then went on to say, without waiting for any response, "Mike, it's bad. Michelle's hurt. We were in our car and we got hit. The police just came and they've called for an ambulance. She's unconscious and ... I just don't know. I'm so worried."

Mike talked to Aaron for only a couple of minutes and then assured him that he was on his way. He knew where the hospital was in Lynn and he didn't want to waste any more time talking. He called Missy back and told her what he'd learned. She agreed to rush right over there. She was closer than he was and could get there even before he did.

Two hours had passed and Missy was really concerned. She'd arrived right after the ambulance had brought Michelle in. Then, Aaron and a policeman had arrived right after that. Since there was a fatality, the police were doing a thorough investigation. However, they had agreed to bring Aaron over to the hospital, sending along the policeman to take his statement there, once Aaron had calmed down enough about Michelle to even think straight. Mike had shown up not long afterwards and they were now all waiting for news concerning Michelle. Since Mike was family, the hospital staff were directing all their reports to him first. Mike had insisted on waiting until they had some prognosis before calling his parents.

Michelle's condition was still unknown. She had never regained consciousness and they'd already given her an MRI examination. It had taken the rescue team several minutes to get the car door ripped off so they could treat her at the scene. But, other than the massive head injury, nothing else was apparent. Still, her head had sustained a severe blow and everyone was very worried. Aaron had finished giving his statement to the police and, now that he didn't have any specific task, he was slowly going crazy. He kept second guessing his own actions, reviewing the accident over and over. His concern for Michelle had him agonizing over every detail and there was nothing anyone could say that would console him.

Mike had learned from the policeman that another car had been behind Aaron's car and the couple in that car had seen the whole thing quite clearly. They'd stopped and had given their statements at the scene. They were excellent witnesses and once the police had understood how the other car had run the light, their attitude towards Aaron had been very understanding. There would not be any charges pending for him since he'd clearly been exonerated.

Missy was growing more and more concerned and wanted to do something. She kept asking if they could see Michelle but no one had been allowed to see her, as yet. They were waiting for the neurosurgeon to review the MRI results. Finally, a Doctor Arvin Messina came out to see them and looked for Mike. When he asked where Michelle's parents were, they knew this was not good.

"I'm really sorry, Mike, but your sister's condition is critical. We want to operate sometime very soon … can you have one of your parents come in to sign some forms?" Doctor Messina was not very encouraging and would not say whether or not any brain damage had occurred. He wouldn't even say whether Michelle would survive. So, this was serious. Mike called home and broke the news as gently as he could. His parents said they were both on their way to the hospital.

Mike asked, "Can we see her, Doctor? Please, just let us go in to see her? While we wait for my parents to arrive?"

Doctor Messina frowned but then, since it really wouldn't matter at this point, he agreed. At first, he wanted to limit the visiting to just Mike but when he saw how insistent all three of them were, he said okay. They could only stay a minute and were not to touch her but they could stand next to her bed and see her.

When they entered Michelle's room and saw how pale she looked, Aaron went to pieces. After only a minute, Mike took him outside and had him sit down. Missy stayed and looked at her friend. Inside, her feelings welled up and … suddenly, she just knew. Without knowing how or why, her instincts were convincing her. She could help Michelle and she was absolutely certain of her ability to do that. Just then, Mike returned and she turned to him.

"Mike, I'm going to try something. I feel pretty sure it'll help but I may need you here. I'm going to give Michelle my healing energy. I've never done this before and I don't know why I believe this is possible. But, I just do. Let me try, okay?"

Mike looked at her and could only say, "Sure. Anything you can do, Missy. Go ahead. How can I help?"

Missy gave him a kiss on the cheek and said, "You'll know what I need when the time comes. Just stay here with me." Then she turned and looked at Michelle. And, she focused. She went to a place in her mind that she really hadn't gone before. Not like this. And, she exercised her will. It was almost as though she were Shifting only instead, she was pushing out her energy. While she'd playfully pushed out energy pulses before, this was different. This was something she felt inside that started slow and built and as she pushed this at Michelle, she wasn't sending any mere pulse.

The room was suddenly being filled with Missy's energy, with almost all of it going directly at Michelle. Mike recognized the burst of energy as being similar to what he'd noticed during her Changes only instead of this being a burst or a pulse, it was steady. And, it gradually was increasing, growing stronger. There was no shimmer of light or anything visible. But, Mike could sure feel it and, when Doctor Messina and a nurse came rushing in, it was obvious they were feeling something also.

Mike was a big guy and he stopped them from approaching Missy. "Leave her alone, leave her alone." He turned back and looked at Missy and he could see that there was clearly something happening to her. She was looking as though she was being drained and he quickly realized that was exactly what was happening. Missy was pouring all of her supernatural energy and power, somehow, into his sister. The energy continued to pour out from Missy in a steady flow and this was something no one had ever experienced before. Both Doctor Messina and the nurse stopped and were just staring at Missy and looking back and forth, from Missy to Michelle.

After more than a minute of this, Mike could see Missy was going to pass out. She wasn't stopping while she had anything left to give and he now understood why she'd asked him to stay with her. He quickly went over and put his arms around her, just as the last of her energy seemed to flare in a final burst. Missy collapsed and he swooped her up into his arms and held her tightly to his chest. "Doctor? Can we find a bed for my girlfriend? I think she's passed out."

The room felt strange, now that her energy had stopped flowing. Aaron had stepped back in just moments before Missy's collapse and was looking from one person to the next, looking for an explanation. He'd felt the energy too and had come running.

There were several people in the corridor outside the room. They had all felt the strange energy and had tracked it back to the source, the room Missy was in. Michelle's room. Now that it had stopped, the ones in the corridor were just standing there, waiting to learn what might have happened. When the nurse came out, with Mike following behind carrying Missy, they stepped back. Another room was found where Missy could be set down, lying on a bed. Mike gently sat down beside her and didn't know what else to do. He was concerned about his sister but he wouldn't leave Missy for even one moment. He kept holding onto one of her hands, squeezing it tight. He sat and just waited.

Doctor Messina went up to Michelle to check on his patient right after Mike left the room. Aaron followed behind him and stared down at Michelle as well. He noticed right away that she somehow looked better. She was no longer so pale and, without understanding why, his heart was suddenly filled with hope. "Michelle? Michelle? Can you hear me? It's Aaron."

The doctor turned to him and said, "She can't hear you, I'm afraid. She …"

He was interrupted by a voice from the bed. Michelle said, "Aaron? Is it you? Where am I? What happened?" She had her eyes open and she looked around, quickly focusing on Aaron. "Are you okay? I think I remember a crash … did we have an accident? Where am I?"

Aaron rushed up to her and, at the same time, Doctor Messina turned back to stare at her in shock. He told her, "Try not to move, yet, Miss. You've been hurt and we don't want you to experience any further injuries. Can you tell us how you feel? And, can you tell us your name?"

Michelle answered, "My name is Michelle Ryan and I feel very strange. My head hurts. Aaron, come hold my hand." She slowly looked around and then asked, "Was Missy in here to see me? Somehow, I have this feeling that she's here." Aaron immediately reached out and began holding onto her hand as though he'd never let it go again.

"Michelle, our car was hit and you were knocked out. Please take it easy. I'm sure you're going to be fine, right doctor? This is Doctor Messina. And, yeah ... Missy was here with Mike a minute ago. They've just stepped outside for a moment. And, your parents will be here soon."

Later, after a lot of people had all milled around outside Michelle's room, getting the story in bits and pieces until finally everyone had some idea of what had happened, Doctor Messina finally came out. He'd talked with Michelle and had observed how she'd greeted her parents when they'd arrived and how alert and coherent she now appeared to be; he'd ordered up another MRI. The previous one had definitely shown probable brain damage, no matter what treatment she would have received. Now, if he was going to recommend any treatment, he needed a new MRI. She just no longer seemed like a candidate for surgery but he was not about to assume anything.

Mike's parents came in to Missy's room and gave him the good news about Michelle regaining consciousness while he continued to sit there with Missy. He wouldn't leave her side and told everyone to simply leave her alone. He was sure she'd wake up when she was ready. A lot of people had come in asking about her and he told them all the same thing. Missy would be fine. She just needed some rest. He told his parents how thrilled he was about Michelle and asked them to tell her he'd be in sometime soon. When he heard she had been asking for Missy he wasn't at all surprised.

Aaron was now refusing to leave Michelle alone and the hospital staff ended up just letting him stay with her. When the time came for her MRI, he accompanied her down and stood outside the room while this was administered. Michelle remained awake and alert but admitted she was beginning to feel tired. No one wanted her to go to sleep until the results of this latest MRI could be evaluated. Finally, a half hour later, back in her room with Aaron again by her side, Doctor Messina came in. Since the news was good, he didn't have to ask anyone to step outside to hear this.

There was clear evidence that Michelle had suffered a concussion but that was all. No other damage was apparent now and once the swelling went down, she should be okay. Of course she needed to stay in the hospital for observation for a day or so, but things definitely now looked very good. He could only

141

comment this was indeed some sort of a miracle and he'd leave it at that. He really had no other explanation and he wasn't about to speculate at all with regards to what he'd seen Missy doing. He truly just didn't know anything about that and was kind of hoping Missy herself might talk about it later.

Missy did finally wake up. Mike heard her words inside his head before she even opened her eyes. *Hey, am I still alive? What about your sister? Did I help?* Then she looked up at him and smiled. When she saw tears streaming down his face, she reached up and pulled him down, squeezing her arms around him. They both held each other for a long moment and then Mike sat up.

"Yeah, Missy, you helped. We think Michelle is going to be okay now." Mike looked at her and didn't know what else to say. There were a zillion things all competing inside his mind that he wanted to say, but he didn't know which to say first. Finally, he said, "Michelle's actually been asking for you. Do you feel up to checking in on her now?"

"Sure, I'd love that." Missy went to sit up and Mike pulled her into his arms once again. After a huge hug, he got up and helped her get up. She wobbled for just a moment and then seemed to get her bearings. Her color had returned and she almost looked her normal self again. Yeah, she was a little drained. But, she was back and he was now so relieved and also so proud of her, he just didn't know what to do. He figured it was probably time to go out there and pretend like it was no big deal. His girlfriend had feinted. Girls did that in hospitals all the time, right?

Michelle was resting comfortably when Mike and Missy came in but, without anyone saying a word, she roused herself and looked at them both. Her twin brother and the girl she'd grown to really love, at first because of how much her brother loved her but then, just because Missy was such a great friend to her as well. "Well, look at you two lovebirds ... can't quite keep your hands off one another, huh? Had to sneak off together for a quickie, maybe?" She laughed and suddenly realized their parents were still there in the room. Opps!

Missy chuckled and then looked right at Mike's parents. With absolutely no embarrassment at all she turned to Michelle and said, "Actually, Mike and I are hoping to do that a bit later on, now that you've brought us both rushing in here tonight. You've been trying to get us together for so long now ... especially since you and Aaron ... umm ..." She paused and looked around, with the most innocent expression on her face, and then continued, "This was a rather extreme way, though. You have to admit that, right?"

Mike's Dad coughed and decided this might be a good time to go grab some coffee. He insisted on his wife showing him where they could find coffee this late at night and dragged her out of the room. There were a couple of nurses in the room but they suddenly decided it was getting too crowded and they left also. Then it was only the four of them.

They spent several minutes enjoying one another, teasing and bantering back and forth, but soon it was obvious Michelle was really tired and Mike and Missy said goodbye. Aaron crawled onto the bed and was lying next to Michelle. He had no plans to go anywhere and, before Mike and Missy even left the room, they could see that he was falling asleep also.

Once outside, they slowly walked down the corridor and took the elevator down. Mike didn't think he needed to say goodbye to his parents and he walked with Missy back out through the exit doors and into the parking lot outside. *Drive me home, Mike. Okay? And, just stay with me tonight?* Missy didn't have any energy left and was glad Mike was there to take care of her.

He drove her home and they went up to her room. She told him to stay right there and she stripped out of all her clothes and, with one final glance at Mike, a look that was filled with love, she Changed. Then she lay down on her bed and closed her eyes. Mike went over, locked her door and came back. He crawled onto her bed and curled himself around Missy, now this huge cat who had fallen asleep. Soon he drifted off to sleep as well, thinking how he was maybe the luckiest guy in the world.

Chapter Twelve
May 2018

"So, what more can you tell me about this Carlos?" Missy was back in the coffee shop with Robert Ulrey and had asked for this meeting. She'd explained how she'd been out in the State Forest and had noticed Carlos's scent out there. She was pretty certain -- since he now obviously must be aware of her -- that he'd be searching everywhere to find her. "How does "P" Branch even know he's a werecat, anyway?"

Robert could understand her concern. "Well, without giving away too many classified secrets, I think I can tell you that the US Government recognized the need for our Paranormal Branch about forty years ago. Things started slowly but, as resources were provided and with the help from one special individual who joined the organization, our worldwide database was established identifying all supernaturals. That one individual was a supernatural herself, a witch. I can't share much more than that but she's gone now, so I can at least acknowledge how she helped us."

"A witch? So, besides werecats ... and, maybe other wereanimals ... there are witches too?" Missy raised one of her eyebrows, and then moved it up and down, quietly grinning about this news.

"Yeah. Witches and wereanimals and a few others. But, no vampires or demons. Not that we know of, anyways," Robert answered. "No aliens, either. Just some people that have supernatural abilities or paranormal abilities. Psychics, clairvoyants, people who can see and communicate with ghosts. People with telekinetic abilities. Some who can start fires. Lots of interesting stuff that I'm not going to talk about. The point, however, is that long ago "P" Branch was able to identify most of these people and their families. There seems to be a genetic component so all these families are now being watched. That's how Carlos was identified. He was being watched because of his family."

"Hmmm. So, now my family will be getting watched too, huh?" Missy sighed, realizing that made sense. From now on, all her cousins and nieces and nephews would be monitored, not to mention if she herself were to have any children. Oh, well. At least the government wasn't trying to lock anyone up in a lab. "From what you've told me already, Robert, it sounds like all this monitoring and watching is pretty much hands off. I suppose I should be really grateful you guys have agreed to tell me anything and have helped the way you have with Marco. How is Marco, anyway?

"He's being a real pain in the ass so we're keeping him locked up. Maybe I should let you have a chat with him. We'll see." Robert had been briefed on how Marco thought he had some leverage and had been refusing to cooperate, but he didn't want to discuss all that with Missy. "But, you're correct about our non interference policy. We've made an exception for you because of Carlos. Then too, after what you did to those

146

two guys that grabbed Alice -- even though it was justified -- we'd rather help you avoid any more incidents like that."

Missy said, "Yes, I appreciate that. Having our Plan WP did make the difference this time. So, now you have Marco. I can't say there was any other option last time ... those guys were going to hurt Alice and I just couldn't let that happen."

"Yes, we understand that." Robert had to agree with her. Then he said, "It was decided long ago that we didn't really want to take any actions beyond monitoring, unless absolutely necessary. The layers of complexity, once we get involved, are very troublesome. As we're now finding with you and Marco. And, Carlos. Those other guys with Marco were not a problem; turning them over to Armando was easy since they're not really witnesses to anything supernatural. Business as usual for the FBI."

Missy said, "Other than how I kicked their butts, of course, but that at least can be explained. Sort of. Since I have all that karate and martial arts training which is not exactly a secret, right? Anyone who reads the local papers can find out all about that."

"Yes, exactly. And, I understand you'll be going up for your third degree black belt in karate next month so there will be even more news articles. I hear there are a few reporters out there who have been closely following all your activities ever since that martial arts trophy you won at the Expo in New York. So, I guess "P" Branch isn't the only organization keeping track of you."

147

"Very funny." Missy smiled at him. "Getting back to Carlos, how were you able to confirm he really can Shift?"

"You mean get all furry with claws and fangs the way you can? Become a cat?" Robert laughed. He still was amazed at what Missy could do, in spite of actually seeing her do it. "We don't have any eye witness accounts but the circumstantial evidence was pretty conclusive. From back when he was younger, in South America. On two different occasions that we know of, there were guys who got in his way and they were attacked and killed. He slaughtered their entire families, each time, and those kills were obviously done by a cougar or some large cat. He was never a suspect for the local authorities, who of course don't know werecats exist, but that confirmed things for us."

"Yes, since you were already watching for behavior like that … Hmmm, sort of similar to how you confirmed I was a werecat, I guess."

"Yes, Drew had already determined you were something supernatural, showing up like that after two years with all that super strength and athletic ability, plus the way you could heal yourself so quickly. Tell me more about this healing energy you used for Mike's sister, Michelle. You were starting to explain about that before asking me about Carlos." Robert had researched their wereanimal database and there was no one else with any healing ability like Missy's. When he expanded the search to all supernaturals, a few witches did show up. Now he was hearing she could use that for others?

"Well, I already knew my healing was accelerated by Shifting and I had figured it was because of those energy bursts. I'd been playing around, pushing my energy out, as you know. When I saw how hurt Michelle was, lying there in the hospital, I just knew. I knew I could help her. While I've never understood how or why I have this energy -- or how or why I can become a cat -- once I finally managed to use it and Change back? It's been part of me and I've been drawing on it more and more ever since. I can use it for more than just Changing. I guess it's all about control. I've worked so hard, learning how to control all my senses, abilities and instincts."

Missy had already tried explaining all this to Mike. How, for her, it was all just part of her essence. She was both cat and human, and in either form, she was now completely herself, one person. Using her energy bursts to heal Michelle rather than for Changing forms was merely an exercise of her will. Her mind could go to special places and she could draw upon her energy, her essence, and use it. She could use it now for all sorts of things. And, she knew she was growing stronger and stronger. Somehow, her energy was increasing and the more she used it, the more she found she had available. She also was finding the time required for her recovery and recuperation was less and less.

She was now able to Shift and then Change back after only one hour. Her total time before Changing a third time was three hours rather than six hours. She

149

never before had experienced that complete energy drain like what had happened when she'd healed Michelle. But, when she had awakened that next day? Still in her cat form, with Mike's arms and legs entwined around her? She'd just known. Her powers had increased and had multiplied. Maybe love was the source for her energy and the more she gave, the more she got. All she knew was she was suddenly bursting with power and energy, all thrumming throughout her body and completely filling her soul.

After waking Mike up that morning, licking his face with her huge cat tongue, she'd really enjoyed teasing him. She had refused to Shift back and had kept talking to him, putting her words in his mind. He'd found himself having this long conversation with a cat and after several minutes, when it was obvious she wasn't going to behave, he'd gone over and unlocked her bedroom door. He'd then yelled for her parents to come and discipline her, which of course meant he'd had to explain why he was even there, why she was in her cat form, why he could understand what she was saying, and all this while Missy came out and then ran around the house, leaping onto furniture and acting as naughty and outrageous as she possibly could.

Hours later, after she'd finally Changed -- and had devoured two huge breakfast portions -- they both had gone back to visit Michelle. As soon as they had walked in, several hospital staff members had come up to Missy. This was the same hospital where Missy had been brought in by ambulance a year ago, with her broken leg. The one she'd then healed in four days.

She'd never explained to anyone how she'd managed to do that but had merely flaunted herself, posing for photos in her lifeguard bathing suit and had insisted they take x-rays to prove her full recovery.

Someone had recognized her the night before and had spread the word. Not only had Doctor Messina been there, asking for an explanation, but several others had all been crowding around hoping to talk to her as well. She'd been very gracious and had joked about *"not being a normal girl"* but had stonewalled them all, not giving them anything at all.

Her EMT friend James Murray had shown up; he'd heard about her being back the night before, once again making magic. That's what the doctors, nurses and interns had all been saying about the way she'd healed Michelle. Doctor Lisiewski, who had been the one to set her broken leg, had also been there. Missy had gone up to these two, planting a kiss on the Doctor's cheek and whispering something into James Murray's ear, making him laugh. When Mike had looked at her, she'd told him silently, in his mind. *I told him not to tell on me being an alien, Mike.*

Then, they'd gone up to see Michelle. Aaron had just left, finally, and she'd been sitting up and had been very happy to see them. When her eyes had met Missy's, something had passed between the two of them. Missy had then gone over and they'd hugged each other for a long while, without anyone saying a word. Mike had finally cleared his throat, getting their attention, and Missy had backed away so Mike could hug his sister. They'd enjoyed a nice visit and had talked about a lot of things. But, as for how Missy had done what she'd done, which Michelle had by that time fully learned all about, Missy would only smile and shake her head. She had explained to Mike ahead of time that, unlike with Alice and Mark, she had no intention of sharing her werecat identity with Michelle and Aaron. Let them just think of her as having some sort of mysterious abilities and leave it at that.

Missy knew her bond with Mike was special and that he didn't need to share her secrets with anyone else. She had a very different bond with Michelle. For her, she somehow didn't feel any need to explain any of her mysteries. They were just fine together and Michelle seemed willing to fully accept Missy just the way she was. Michelle wasn't hiding anything from Aaron since she just didn't know any answers. She didn't need any answers. Missy was simply her very close friend. And, she was very thrilled Missy and her brother had managed to magically bond together. She was quite comfortable believing in magic.

Rafe Santiago knocked on the door and when Carlos told him to enter, he went in to see his boss. "There's this girl on the phone, asking for you, insisting she'll only tell you about her reason for calling. She also says to tell you she's the one from the State Forest in Andover. Does that mean anything to you, Carlos?"

Rafe was the only one that Carlos completely trusted and he was number two in the East Boston organization that Carlos had taken over now that Frank

McCarthy was in prison. Rafe had been one of the ones to come up with Carlos to Miami from South America and he'd managed to fully earn his number two position, which he'd held for the last seven years. He was also the only one to whom Carlos had revealed his werecat identity.

"I don't know any ... wait! Wait. Did you say State Forest? That might be her, Rafe. The one I told you about. Put her through to my private line here and make sure no one else can listen in." Carlos looked at Rafe and smiled. This might be a very interesting phone call, if it was really her.

After the call was put through, he answered, "Hello? This is Carlos. Who is this?"

"I think you know exactly who I am, Carlos. But, I've arranged for a package to be delivered ... why don't you check with your guys? It should be there already. I'll just hold on and wait until you've opened it." Missy was using one of the throw away "burner phones" that Robert had provided her with. He'd also provided her with the phone number for reaching Carlos and had arranged for the delivery of her package by messenger service. Delivery had been timed to coincide with her call and, of course, was at the correct location. Having resources was indeed nice.

Carlos called Rafe back in and then had him go check. Sure enough, there was a small package being delivered outside. It took a few minutes while his security guys examined this but then Rafe brought it in for him to open. When he did, it was merely a cotton

153

handkerchief. What was she up to? Then, he caught her clear scent on that handkerchief and he knew. Yeah, this was from her alright. The mysterious female werecat he'd been wanting to locate for a few weeks now. Very clever.

"Okay, you definitely have my attention, whoever you are." He didn't know if she was recording this call and he didn't want to say anything more than that. He did switch his recorder on, of course, so he'd have his record of this conversation.

Missy laughed. "Good! Now that we've established who I am ... can I ask if I'm on speaker phone? Can we talk freely? You know ... about stuff?" She also was recording this call.

"Sure, go ahead, you can talk freely. I'm not planning to give you any information but you can feel free to give me information. How about your name, for starters?" Carlos was amused at her tone and he appreciated her caution. She wasn't just blurting things out that might embarrass him but was checking first.

"Okay, then. As one cat to another, I thought we should talk. Since you recently moved up here and have invaded my territory and everything, you probably have been wondering what my reaction might be. I'm sure you had to have noticed, right? That you're in my territory?" Missy was hoping to draw him out a little, poke and prod him, so she could get some measure of just who he was.

Carlos said, "You're trying to claim *territory*? Since you've managed to find me and get my phone number and deliver this little package of yours ... you obviously must know who I am. So, let's not play games. You'll have to forfeit all claims for any territory. Why don't you come see me and we can discuss what I might be willing to *share*?"

"You mean, come see you before you find me? Forfeit my territory? Those sound like threats, Carlos. I don't like threats. You're in my territory and I want you to leave. Go back to South America." Missy was figuring her best defense was to now go on the offense and challenge him.

"You dare to make demands? To me? What the hell ...!" He then sputtered angrily in Spanish with what she assumed were expletives.

"I don't want you here, Carlos. I don't want you causing problems for me. So, leave. Or, I'll find ways to cause problems for you. You've got three weeks. If you're still here after that? You'll regret it. Are we clear?" When Missy started hearing more expletives from Carlos she hung up on him.

Missy had explained to Robert the only way she now could be comfortable was to force Carlos to leave. She wouldn't risk going off to West Point in a month, with her family vulnerable to whatever whims Carlos might have. He was a threat she just couldn't live with. She was even willing to fight for this, if that became necessary. If "P" Branch wouldn't interfere, arrest and

155

hold Carlos the way they were now holding Marco, she would somehow force the issue.

Carlos was not happy with how that phone call had gone. Not happy at all. When she hung up on him, he got really upset. "Rafe, I want that woman found. This is unacceptable." He'd played the tape for Rafe to hear, three times. "What have you come up with so far?" He had assigned Rafe the task of finding her right after he'd first noticed her scent and it had been weeks now. Getting this call from her was indeed rankling. He now wanted her found, top priority.

Rafe explained, "I just don't have anything to go on. Some mysterious female. Somewhere on the North Shore. She might even be coming down from Maine or New Hampshire. You say she must be young, based on her scent. Her voice sounded young, assuming it's not been disguised. Still ... she seems to have some very good resources, to find you. And, those didn't sound like any idle threats. So I'm not so sure that really makes her all that young. That girl sounded very experienced."

Carlos said, "It's really pissing me off that she has those resources. All the more reason for finding her. Before? I was only curious. I figured she might be interesting ... I just never heard about any female werecats. Now? She's a threat and I don't like it. What if those resources of hers can create problems for me here? You already know how crazy things have been since Marco and those other guys disappeared."

"Yeah, the Feds have been all over us. It's obvious someone's been talking. That's why we haven't been able to focus on finding her. We've been too busy handling all these other problems, keeping guys in line and making sure no one else rolls over. And, it's not like we can tell our guys who we're trying to find, exactly."

"Okay, okay. I understand." Carlos was very frustrated. But, he didn't intend on going back to South America. Maybe she'd show up in three weeks. He'd deal with her then.

Chapter Thirteen
May 2018

Missy was really excited and her sister Heather was losing patience with her. Heather had come home for the weekend, just so she could do Missy's hair and help with any last minute adjustments her dress might need. Senior prom. Yes, it was a big deal. Missy would be saying goodbye to a lot of her friends. The remaining school days would be much too hectic for doing that. They'd all be graduating in a couple of weeks and there were now so many activities with so little time remaining.

Missy wanted to wear her hair cascading down its full length with only a few tiny braids crisscrossing at her crown, something Heather was an expert at making look really nice. Missy's gorgeous red hair now reached all the way to her waist when she let it down. And, she wanted to show it off this one last time. She planned to have her hair cut just before reporting to West Point; either a short pixie cut or maybe a page boy cut. That way, she wouldn't need to pin it up to meet the Army's requirement for hair not extending below her collar.

Tonight, she just couldn't manage sitting still long enough for Heather to complete her special touches and Heather finally called for their Mom to come up. Missy was not wearing any slip since the dress had one built in. She was seated on a stool in her bedroom, wearing thong panties and a pushup bra, waiting for Heather to be done. When their Mom came in, that calmed her down. Finally, Heather declared her task was done and said Missy could pull on her dress.

Missy's body was definitely at her voluptuous best and this dress had been fitted for her accordingly. She'd bulked up during her gym workouts, as planned, increasing her weight to 155 pounds. She'd get down to her 150 pound goal by Shifting a few times later on. The energy bursts for those would strip away mostly body fat, leaving her ripped and shredded with all her muscles clearly defined. But those extra pounds she was now carrying on her tall sturdy frame were in all the right places and she was really looking great.

Her dress was black and strapless. Her pushup bra combined with the low cut of her dress to reveal all her luscious curves up top to full advantage, with some marvelous cleavage. The way the dress flowed over her wide hips, flaring from her narrow waist, was showing off her curvy body down below in an equally flattering manner. Her movements, walking on four inch heels, were mesmerizing. Missy was looking more stunning and beautiful this night than ever before.

Her Mom and Heather watched as she now strutted around, flexing various muscles as she got used to the feel of her gown and how it hugged her in some places and flowed freely in other places. "Does my ass look too big?" she asked. "I can Shift and Change back in an hour now, if I need to … there's still time, right?

Heather immediately exclaimed, "No!" in her most exasperated voice. "Your butt looks absolutely perfect and especially in this dress. I told you it would, as long as you wore the thong panties, right? Everything that shows through this filmy black fabric is one hundred percent Missy McCrae flesh, firm and taut from hours of running and working out."

Her Mom laughed and said, "Mike's not going to wait around if the only reason you're not ready is something silly like that. Now, put on my pearl necklace … I want to see how it goes with the dress." She was loaning Missy her necklace and her matching pearl earrings, definitely the most valuable jewelry she owned. Seeing how lovely Missy looked wearing these items was special and filled her heart with pride.

Her Dad yelled, "Mike's here!" and her brother Patrick chimed in right after, mimicking him in his best voice imitation, only an octave higher, saying the same thing. "Mike's here, Mike's here!" This was followed by lots of muted male laughter.

"Okay, okay. I'm making my grand entrance now! Mike, here I come! Patrick? You'd better hide!" Missy walked to the top of the stairs and then started down, stepping slowly and regally, holding her gown out with both hands to avoid catching and tripping on any portion of her hem. Halfway down, she paused and looked around, a queen surveying her subjects. The ooh's and aah's of appreciation from below made her preen and, to show her audience that she was pleased, she pushed out an energy pulse which everyone felt. That caused an even bigger reaction and made her laugh. Sometimes, it was such fun being a girl.

Mike greeted her with a chaste kiss on the cheek, not wanting to mess up whatever makeup she might have applied, and he presented her with the corsage he'd selected for her, special. A black orchid. Now it was Missy who ooh'ed and aah'ed.

Then he stepped back to look at her closely, from head to toe and back again. "That dress looks fantastic, Missy! Wow! I really love those ruffles." Although the gown closely hugged her figure all the way down, showing all her curves, it then had large ruffles starting at mid thigh that flared out and made it appear as though she was rising from a large black mist swirling around her legs.

Missy was happy that Mike liked her dress and was thrilled at how handsome he looked. Mike was wearing an all white tux, just to show off her gown that much more. With his height and wide shoulders, they certainly would make a striking pair. He had a black flower for his boutonniere and a black cumberbund. Missy slid her arm inside of his and hugged it close, brushing it up against the side of her breast and clinging to him. She noticed him react and a little thrill spiked right through her body, warming her insides. They then had to get through posing for photos, both inside the house and outside by Mike's car. The weather was cooperating and it was a glorious day. Missy had a shawl but only carried it across her arm, leaving herself exposed.

Then, at last they said goodbye and drove away from her house, heading for the hotel where her prom was being held. Mike had booked them a room for later and Missy was looking forward to once again spending the night with his arms around her and waking up in the morning, cuddled inside his warm embrace. Their lovemaking had become such a wonderful part of her life now and she just loved opportunities like this, when they could truly be a couple.

So much seemed to have happened for her in the three months they'd been bonded. She just felt so much more complete with her energy always right there, strong and powerful. Her constant awareness of Mike, whether he was close by or far away, was now another part of her and who she had become. She was constantly sending her thoughts out, pushing them into his mind. It made her happy, being able to touch him even if he was miles away. She'd fine tuned this experience for herself and could now receive some feedback. Not his thoughts but instead, his emotions.

She had always been affected by his emotions and had also been able to affect him, right from their first times together. This all began when she finally had started actually dating him. After all those months when she'd ignored him, once she'd opened herself to Mike, they'd both begun to really feed off one another. This had never happened for her with anyone else and she doubted it ever would. Somehow, her entity had recognized Mike and things had continued to grow stronger and stronger between them ever since. She now realized she'd never once doubted him or the strange resonance they seemed to have. She looked at him and smiled.

Mike was watching the road and carefully driving along, making sure they'd get there safely. The recent scare with his sister was still fresh in his mind. Then, Missy's words were there. *Mike, I love you. In case I forget to say that later, I'm saying it now. I love you.* These words definitely required a response and he quickly glanced at her and then looked back at the road. "I love you too, Missy. You know that. Thanks for telling me how you feel. That means the world to me."

He glanced at her again and marveled at how lucky he was. She was such a unique, wonderful person, a creature so beautiful in every way it made his heart ache, anytime he was separated from her. Thank goodness for the strange way she was now constantly inside his mind, sharing her thoughts and feelings throughout the day. What initially had seemed a bit of a distraction had quickly evolved. She was a drug for him, an addiction he'd never get enough of, and experiencing her in this special and magical manner was something he now depended on. Whatever he could give her in return, he would always be striving to give. He knew she really did need him and could always tell when she was drawing strength and sustenance from him, something she seemed able to do even when he was miles away.

After parking the car, he went around to help her get out and -- just as when he'd brought her to his senior prom a year ago -- he pulled her into his arms and kissed her. That had been their first kiss. This time, they both were anticipating the gratification they knew would come later and after enjoying a long kiss, with their bodies pressed together, they broke apart and smiled. For Missy, the next few hours would all be foreplay and her eyes were filled with gold sparkles, showing Mike how aroused she was. Then, she stepped back for a moment and carefully checked their surroundings.

She took several deep breaths, drawing air across her tongue and the roof of her mouth as well as into her nose. With her enhanced senses, she was able to register all the scents and sort through them, categorizing them. This wasn't even a conscious effort, but something she merely would do now, quickly sensing if anything might be wrong. Her subconscious and her instincts would alert her if there was any danger or anything else she should be concerned about.

After Marco's attempt to attack them and with Carlos somewhere out there, Missy was being careful. Fortunately, everything tonight seemed normal and safe and she stepped forward, letting Mike take her arm. He had noticed her scenting and raised his eyebrows, glancing at her. *Everything is good. Let's go in.* Reassured by her words, he led her up to the hotel entrance and they went in. People stopped to stare at them, which they both enjoyed. This was indeed a special night.

Once they found the ballroom and worked their way to their table, stopping at several tables on the way to exchange greetings with Missy's classmates, things got very busy and the time began passing quickly by. It seemed everyone wanted to say things to Missy and guys kept coming up and insisting on her giving them one dance. Mike still managed dancing with her more than half the time and everyone knew they were a couple, but Missy had been very popular and had a lot of friends. Tonight, she was in her glory and Mike was very happy for her.

Missy glowed, enjoying how everyone kept coming up, complementing her and just wanting her attention. She was happy to be there, showing off her big handsome boyfriend, and yet also giving back to all her friends. She had a knack for knowing the right thing to say and, since she truly had always taken an interest in the lives of those around her, she found it easy to focus on each person in a meaningful way. Her words of encouragement and support were obviously appreciated. Missy had touched a lot of lives in the three years since she'd returned from the mountains.

With her enhanced hearing, of course, she couldn't help but overhear the many comments being made about her, even by groups sitting several tables away. There was a group of guys who had been admiring her all year, watching her work out at the gym and going over to her martial arts club to watch when she'd be sparring with the guys there. Usually, she wore her karate gi but, recently, she'd been checking herself out at the gym and been only wearing shorts and her sports bra. All the effort to bulk up her body had been paying off and she'd wanted to see if she needed to pay more attention to certain areas. Hearing the comments from these guys was now making her smile.

"Can you believe how *big* Missy is now? I don't know how she does it …" "What do you mean? You've watched her workout, right? Talk about extreme. She goes for forty minutes, non-stop, never resting, and mostly free weights." "She runs five miles every day too, first thing in the morning." "She was bench pressing close to two hundred pounds …" "What about those squats she was doing the other day? She was only wearing skimpy shorts and those thighs of hers …" "Forget the legs, guys, I can't stop studying her perfect ass …" "Yeah, that too … but, her boobs are just about the most perfect set of tits I've ever seen …" "That Mike is such a lucky guy!" "Yeah, she hasn't looked at anyone else for more than a year. They're definitely doing each other now, you can tell by how they look at each other." "What I wouldn't give to be doing her …" "Hey, she'd kick your ass for just thinking like that. Have you seen her spar with those big apes at that club she goes to? She's still the only girl there. Kicks ass big time every week."

On and on the comments went. Missy knew how she affected all these guys since she was always hearing talk like that, every day in school. There were a few girls who were somewhat jealous but even they couldn't help but admire how Missy handled herself. She had never lorded things over anyone or put anyone down. Instead, she'd always been very sensitive to the feelings of others. She was the first one to stand up to any bully; that was always to protect someone else, since no one dared try any intimidation against her. She was fearless and had earned the trust and respect of everyone around her.

166

She had helped others so often, usually without looking to take any credit for herself, that her reputation for that had actually become legend. So, all the good wishes she was hearing tonight, as she kept saying her goodbyes, were truly sincere. She was well liked and her friends were going to truly miss her. High school graduation was an end of an era for them all, of course, and a new beginning. It was just that everyone would be going off in different directions and that made for a bittersweet evening, especially as the prom was finally ending. Then, they called for the last dance.

Mike swept Missy into his arms as the music started for that, the final dance of the night. He could feel how happy Missy was, her emotions spilling out and filling him up. As he pulled her close, she seemed to completely let go of everything around them and give herself now to just being there with him. Her body pressed against his and her movements became fluid, following his lead. Her energy began to seep into him and he was, once again, sensing how aroused she was getting, just dancing with him. When Missy relaxed her controls like that, it was overwhelming. His response was immediate and he definitely was experiencing a familiar aching in his balls as his hard erection once again reared itself. Missy shamelessly pressed her pelvis against him, hugging him even closer, and it was intoxicating.

Missy indeed had relaxed her controls and was now allowing all her senses to experience Mike and how wonderful it was to be in his arms, dancing like this. She'd talked to everyone she'd wanted to see, satisfied her need to wish them well and say goodbye, and was now opening herself to this moment, tuning out everything else and focusing on giving herself to Mike. Wherever he led, she followed. She knew she was turning him on and that filled her with joy. Her body flowed to his, moved with his, wanted to be united with his. Gliding across the dance floor with him as the music played out the last song, an ending not just for the prom but for all the years that had gone before and had led up to this moment, Missy felt a sense of completion.

Somewhat later, after they'd gone up to their room, they eagerly began undressing. Mike had already brought up their suitcases when he'd checked in earlier that day, just before going over to her house to pick her up. They were not feeling at all tired and enjoyed taking their time now. No need for frantic fumbling. The hours of foreplay had them both burning with desire, desire which they knew they could now gratify. Mike helped Missy climb out of her dress which he then hung up in the closet. As he stepped out of his pants, he had to comment on what a sight she was, standing there in her black bra and wearing that incredibly tiny triangle of black silk that supposedly was her panties; it didn't quite cover her curly red pubic hair.

"Thong panties, huh? Don't those bother you, Missy? Of course, you've no idea how bothered I am, seeing you wearing those. Wow! What a vision!" Mike laughed.

"Heather insisted on them. So my ass wouldn't be marred by any panty lines or whatever. I almost wish I'd simply gone naked under the dress. I pretty much felt naked all night and the way the guys were staring, I don't think they needed to use their imaginations much." Giggling, Missy added, "Of course, you make me get so wet, it's probably a good thing I had this on. Otherwise, someone might have been slipping on the dance floor … you know … from the huge puddle I'd have made."

Mike was now down to just his underwear and stripped off his tee shirt, exposing his huge chest. Flexing his pectoral muscles, he came over and said, "Well, really, now … inquiring minds are all wanting to know, Missy. How wet are you?" He reached over and unhooked her bra, which he tossed across the room. Right away, her nipples perked up and she giggled.

She stepped back and hooked her fingers under the thin waistband and began to slowly peel her panties down, wriggling her hips back and forth. Stepping out of them, she presented them to Mike and pushed her words into his head. *You tell me, Mike. How wet am I?*

Mike groaned and couldn't help but inhale the musky scent of her very wet panties. To end any further teasing she might want to attempt, he picked her up and tossed her onto the bed and then crawled up on top of her. As she reached for him, he pressed his body down on top of hers and began kissing her, slowly and deliberately, with his tongue spearing into her mouth to take control and show her how he felt. She responded by thrusting her tongue against his until she finally managed to push her way into his mouth. She kept making mumbling sounds and he realized she really was a very vocal person, always managing to make various noises whenever they made love.

Mike began to slide down her body, planting wet kisses all along her neck and the top of her chest. Pushing down further, he carried his weight on his elbows and began circling first one nipple and then the other with his tongue. Missy wriggled her body under his and her obvious pleasure was a sure incentive for him to continue. He began tweaking her left nipple, already erect and proudly poking up from her pink areole, which also had several little bumps. He began to lick those little bumps as well and then began sucking on her nipple, all to the lovely sounds of her gasps and groans.

Missy was feeling herself become completely and thoroughly excited, blood racing through all her veins and making her pulse hammer as her heart rate increased. Mike's tongue on her nipple was sending sensations to her body that reached out everywhere, as nerve endings began to sing and she felt her energy thrumming. She began quickly climbing from one plateau of pleasure to the next, pausing for only moments to enjoy how that felt before continuing onward and upward. Her skin was alive and she began rubbing herself against Mike's skin wherever possible, seeking more contact with him; her hands began massaging his shoulders and back. As she reached higher to his neck, he shifted his position and switched over from her left nipple to her right nipple, nibbling on it with his lips.

Missy's body shivered underneath him and he then felt her spasm a couple of times, so he didn't actually need her words to tell him how much she enjoyed what he was doing. *Oh, that feels so good. Ummm. More, more. There! Again, ohhhhh!* Her words were expressing her feelings anyway, encouraging him and guiding him. He was able to find places to caress and spots to touch with his hands all while his mouth and tongue continued driving her to greater and greater heights. Neither one of them were experienced lovers but they had been learning and experimenting on one another and had tried several interesting positions.

Mike knew Missy was pretty open with her friend Alice and he'd kidded her about that several times. He also had done some research, reading all about how to please a woman. He wanted to please Missy, of course, and what he was now finding was that he could learn more from her responses, reading her body language, then all the things he'd read or heard about. Missy was showing him exactly what she liked and how she liked it and he only needed to follow along, taking direction from her. He began to slide down much lower, moving first one hand and then the other, reaching under her legs to cup her buttocks as she willingly spread her thighs far apart.

As she felt Mike slide down and grab her ass, holding each of her butt cheeks in the palm of his large hands, she indeed spread her legs and brought her heels up behind his head. This feeling of being so completely exposed was absolutely wonderful and delicious quivers of anticipation began working their way through her body, bringing her to an edge where every sensation was now one of both pleasure and pain. The pain was the terrible longing for even more sensations. There was now a need building inside her that demanded more. More and more of what her Mike was now doing and just the fact that he was doing these things to her was driving her wild.

Mike began kissing his way all down her abdomen, until his chin was rubbing her pubic hair. Her tummy was making these little involuntary movements, and she sucked in breath after breath, gasping and making some whimpering sounds he'd never heard her make before. He then focused on her inner thighs, first the left and then the right. Using his lips and his tongue, he kept touching and teasing her, getting such a wonderful reaction he almost didn't notice that she'd finally stopped saying things in his mind. Missy was now way beyond any words and unable to think coherent thoughts.

Now he began to lick his tongue all along the folds of her sex, up and down, this area so sensitive and so anxious for even more attention. Her hands grabbed his hair and he could feel how she was wriggling her fanny, squirming where he held her with his hands. He saw the way her clit was hiding just under its little hood, but poking up and begging for his touch. He blew some air across her flesh and she actually jumped. His tongue darted out to stroke along one side of her clit and then he began to lick at it directly, not stopping but now following and chasing after it as her body began violently bucking. She screamed her pleasure and that only made him get more forceful. He kept moving it side to side, back and forth, which seemed to really drive her crazy.

He knew she could endure this for a long time, with her enhanced senses and abilities, and he continued to apply more and more pressure with his mouth and tongue, constantly pushing and prodding. His hands pulled her ass up in the air and he began to suck on her engorged clit as her orgasm exploded, the intensity increasing and her movements becoming more and more violent. Mike backed off from her clit to begin lapping all along her slick folds, which opened up to his tongue as her lubrication flowed out, covering his chin and lower face. He pushed his tongue inside her and could feel the way she was pulsing, clenching and releasing. He moved back up to her clit, now also pulsing and he began to lick as hard as he could.

Missy had been shuddering for so long -- jerking and twitching as wave after wave of such intense sensations wracked her body, forcing her to spasm and convulse, at times providing a wondrous release only to then drive her higher yet, seeking an even greater release -- that when at last her final release happened and her body allowed her to gradually subside, spent and satiated beyond anything she'd ever dreamed possible, she truly wasn't sure she could recover. She squeezed her thighs together clamping them on Mike's head and forcing him to stop. Then, those delicious aftershocks began and she just knew she'd died and gone to heaven. Her tears were flowing and the sounds

173

she made were incoherent. She was completely drained and unable to move a muscle.

Mike knew how thoroughly satisfied Missy was since her energy had been really flowing into him all this time, driving him on during the height of her passion and now, it was quickly ebbing away as that lassitude that always overwhelmed her was making her limp and boneless. Once she managed to achieve her incredible release of all her sexual energy, she always disintegrated. But, this time, it was beyond epic. Never had he seen her climb so high, cry out for so long, and collapse so completely.

Her final throes had almost made him come, just from how excited it made him get. Now, he pulled his head out from between her thighs and sat up. Slowly, he stood up and then peeled off his underwear. There was a huge wet spot on the front of his shorts from all his precum. He tossed the shorts away and climbed back onto the bed, pulling Missy into his arms and holding her close. *Mike, that was amazing. Beyond belief and out of this world. Now, it's your turn. Please.*

He wasn't sure he was actually getting her words. She still seemed completely out of it and he was thinking it was much too soon for her to have recovered. Then, she began to move within his embrace. She clambered up, pushing him onto his back and she looked down at him. *I know I'm beyond satisfied but, if you can do it with a limp body, I'm all yours. Just use my limp body anyway you want, Mike. I love you so much that I just can't even talk about it.*

Missy then wriggled down and positioned herself where she could slide up and down, rubbing all along his now throbbing erection, coating him with her slick and slippery fluids. Before he could react, she'd slipped the head of his male member into her wet opening and then she slid herself down further so he was fully penetrating her, all the way in.

When he felt her pubic hair mashing his pubic hair, her pubic bone pressing against his pubic bone, he indeed was in heaven. She didn't move, probably couldn't move, but she didn't have to. Her limp body was still providing him with such a wonderful sheath for his hard member, wet and warm and tight around him, that no movement was necessary. This really felt great! Slowly, he began to move.

Missy was slowly recovering, now at least able to think, and she really enjoyed being able to just give herself to Mike. Her body was still beyond feeling any sensations but having him inside her was wonderful, nonetheless. She had no energy and was laying there, dead weight, but maybe that was okay. This time. She thought it might be enough and, as Mike's strokes and thrusts began to increase, she was more and more convinced of that. Soon, his powerful body was pounding and hammering into hers and she simply clung to him, riding along.

They were joined together and Missy was feeling a true sense of fulfillment. Each time was different and each time, their bond grew stronger yet. This time, just as she finally began to feel some sensations once again, Mike's orgasm swept her up in his explosion of passion.

She felt him ejaculating, his seed pulsing inside of her and her contentment was complete. She was able to share his emotions and she could actually experience his pleasure. She allowed herself to lay on him, letting every muscle in her body relax once more, and before he slipped out of her, after gradually growing soft inside her body -- she was asleep. She never noticed when he eventually pulled back the covers and then tucked her underneath, folding her completely within his warm -- and very satisfied -- embrace.

Chapter Fourteen
Jun 2018

Missy was feeling really frisky, all her energy right there inside her, ready. Ready for what, she wasn't sure. But, she was ready. Her readiness for something was driving her crazy. She'd been exercising to extremes, had actually been thrashing her martial arts opponents so badly they were now asking her to find a new hobby, and her karate Sensei was suggesting she take a few days off. She was going for her third degree black belt in another week but had already demonstrated her proficiency in all the requirements to such an extent that her test was a mere formality.

She'd graduated from high school and would be going off to West Point at the end of the month, just after her eighteenth birthday. Her body was toned and ready, now at 150 pounds of powerful, formidable, supernatural muscle. Her sexual romps with Mike, now that he was also out of school and back home for the summer, had become frequent and highly satisfying.

She suddenly realized she did know what the problem was. Carlos. She couldn't continue until somehow resolving that situation. He had to go.

She had been running out at the State Forest almost every day now, with school over and no summer job. Being a cat. She'd wanted to get as much cat time as possible before reporting to West Point, since her opportunities would then be very limited. With the way she was eating and exercising, these cat runs fit right in and helped her maintain herself at what she believed was her peak condition. She'd also been checking for Carlos but hadn't scented him being out there again.

Not wanting to risk his identifying her during any of these runs, she was having someone drop her off and pick her up each time rather than drive her own car and leave it parked there. She also wore minimal clothing with nothing that could trace back to her. She knew all the cars that Carlos might be using, thanks to her "P" Branch friends. So, she was always on the lookout and before going into the woods, she would check to see if any of those cars were there. All of this caution was adding to how antsy she was now feeling.

Alice arrived and honked her horn. Today, she was dropping Missy off for her run. Alice was home for the summer and, not really needing a job, was spending time with her best friend while she could. Missy bounded outside and raced up to Alice's car, quickly opening the car door and plopping herself in the passenger seat. "Hi, Alice! Thanks for the ride today! I'm *really* in need of a run and can't wait to Change out there. Can you feel my energy?" Missy pushed some at Alice which made her friend start giggling.

"Yes, I can feel that, you crazy cat! Obviously, you're not getting enough lately ... shall I call Mike?" Alice laughed and then had another thought. "Or, maybe you're doing it with him too much? Is that your problem? I'll definitely be calling Mike. He's turning my best friend into a wild animal. It's all the wild animal sex, right?"

"Stop with the animal jokes. Ha, ha. My sex life with Mike, which I'll not be discussing with you at all today, since you're making fun of me, is absolutely perfect. And, I had turned into a wild animal long before I met Mike, remember?" Missy was enjoying this banter with Alice and knew she'd really miss her when she went off to West Point. "How's everything going for your wedding? Anything I can help with?"

"No, thanks, there really isn't anything right now. My Mom is having the time of her life with all the arrangements and I'm letting her have her way, most of the time. It keeps her busy and her ideas are actually pretty good so there's not much that I've asked her to change or do differently. We're hoping you can get home Labor Day weekend for my bridal shower and bachelorette party. From what you've told me, that might work, right?"

"Hopefully, if all goes right, I'll get a pass and can come home then. Yeah." Missy smiled, thinking over what she'd read about her schedule for the first few months. "Did you know they refer to Cadet Basic Training as Beast Training? Assuming my wild animal nature can manage getting through Beast Training without too many problems and I can stay out of trouble for the month after that, I should get a weekend pass. That will be my first one and I'm definitely looking forward to it."

Alice laughed, "Yeah, so you can see Mike again, right? Then, you'll want to go be a cat. Hopefully, you'll Change back before showing up at my events, right?"

"Very funny. But, yeah. Both of those actually complete me, Alice. Being with Mike and being a cat. It's really helped me these last few months and I know it's why I have all this energy now. I don't know if you can relate to that or not, because you aren't into all the extreme physical activity stuff the way I am. The way I have to be, actually. I just can't help it." Missy then laughed and added, "Then again, maybe what you and Mark have been up to lately would actually qualify as some extreme physical activity."

Alice giggled. "Now who is making fun of whom? But, I think I get it. Mark really does complete me and I certainly can relate to that part of it. The cat part? You're unique, Missy, and there's no one else like you. I'm just happy you're my friend. And, that you have Mike. If he's helping you with all the amazing, crazy things you do, that's great. A girl's gotta do what a girl's gotta do and a cat's gotta do what a cat's gotta do, right?" They both laughed at that.

They drove into the parking area and circled around. After Missy checked all the cars, she had Alice drop her off and she went into the woods. After a short climb, she reached a small cave on the hillside that was off the normal trails. She stripped off her clothes and placed them under some brush inside the cave. Then she Shifted. With the added weight from all her eating and exercising, she was now a very large cat and it felt wonderful to be in such great condition. Female mountain lions normally didn't grow to be 150 pounds but Missy was not a normal cougar any more than she was a normal girl. She was a werecat and went off to prowl and run and expend some of that special supernatural energy she was so filled with.

Hours later, as she stepped out to survey the area below from her position high on a hill, she sensed him. Carlos. Looking downwind, since she'd not yet scented him so he couldn't be upwind, she searched. Somehow she had sensed him and her instincts had all gone on high alert. Finally, she saw where he was, way across a valley with a small river, and up on a hill, probably about a half mile away. She realized he had to be following her scent, since he was downwind from her and would obviously have noticed her.

She climbed to the very top of the hill and let out one of her most powerful cougar screams, clearly challenging him and expressing her displeasure with his being in her territory. He looked over and saw her and their eyes met. Missy stared at him and considered her situation. He'd probably parked somewhere near where Alice had dropped her off and had been trailing her. That meant, since she was now actually closer to that parking lot than he was, having been on a return route after enjoying her day in the woods, that she could possibly race back and find his clothes. Then, maybe she could steal his car.

This was going to be fun. She'd promised him that if he didn't leave, she'd be causing problems for him. This was indeed perfect, an opportunity too good to pass up. Giving him one more piercing scream to remember her by, she began to run. Cougars aren't meant for long distance running but this was merely a sprint for her, which was exactly what her body was made for. Once she came back to the path she'd been on when she'd left the area hours earlier, she easily scented him. As she'd guessed, he'd been following her scent.

Following his scent back down, she easily found where he'd stashed his clothes. She Changed right there and dressed herself in some of his gear, delighting in the set of car keys she found in his pocket. Grabbing the rest of his gear, she went down to the parking lot and using his key fob to identify and unlock the car that belonged to him, she soon was driving away with her prize.

She stopped at a convenient shopping mall several miles away and searched his car. There was nothing special on the seats or in the trunk. She did find his cell phone and wallet along with a gun in the glove box. Interesting! The cell phone needed a password which prevented her from using it but she was pretty sure Robert and his buddies would manage to get past that and download whatever was on the phone. Hopefully, they'd learn some new things that might help with the FBI case Armando's team was hard at work putting together. As for the gun, it was too much to hope that it might be traced to any prior criminal actions but, even if it was, her stealing the car like this was probably not the way to gather evidence.

She went in the mall to find a phone. She was pretty sure Robert would use those "P" Branch resources of his to dispose of all this stolen property. She planned to abandon the car right there and simply tell him where to find the key, which she would leave on top of the right front tire. She would have Mike bring her some clothes and then take her out tonight. She wanted to celebrate. Being a car thief was such fun! Even more fun was wondering how long it would take Carlos to get home. He'd probably find the clothes she'd left behind but would certainly look pretty ridiculous in those, wandering around out there and trying to find someone to lend him a phone. She didn't think her shoes would fit but he'd probably manage to squeeze into her warm-up pants and jacket. She hoped he liked pink.

Carlos had indeed been furious. It had not been a good day for him at all. But, that was yesterday and now he was in his office, talking to Rafe. "You can't believe what a magnificent sight she was. Big, bold and beautiful; she looked right at me. Then, she screamed at me. Twice. Her territory. Then off she raced and her movement was a blur. So fast. She was mostly this tawny, reddish color and the way she moved ... Rafe, she must have lived as a cat somewhere and not just been Changing into one, now and again." Carlos realized he was no match for her as a cat. And, he probably would never be able to intimidate her. He'd been able to see enough while she'd raced down from that hilltop to convince him she was indeed something special.

183

Rafe said, "You know I don't understand any of this werecat stuff, Carlos. How would that make any difference?"

"Well, when I was young and spent some time as a cat, up in the mountains? Sometimes I'd get challenged by other mountain lions, you know? The regular ones, not werecats but real animals. There was a huge difference. I knew it and they knew it. I had no chance, even though I was usually bigger. I never messed with them."

"And, you get the sense she's like that? Like a real animal that you shouldn't mess with?" Rafe really wasn't seeing the point. "If we can find her, you won't have to mess with her as an animal. She's a woman, right?"

"I don't know what she is. She's a threat and she's causing me problems. So, I definitely want her found. You're right. We'll deal with her as a woman." Carlos was still thinking how much he had to admire her, though, as a cat.

"Your car has disappeared. My guess? You'll never see it again. Good thing that gun was clean. What about the phone? Are you worried she now has all your phone contacts and your email address book?" Rafe had already arranged to have Carlos's email account closed out as well as all his credit cards. There wasn't anything on his emails which could be used against them, but still. They weren't happy knowing she now had access to people he had been dealing with.

And, it was damn inconvenient getting replacement credit cards, driver's license, etc.

"Yeah, I'm worried. I don't understand all this electronic crap. Emails and stuff. Who knows what she can do with any of that info?" Carlos also wasn't sure if he had any codes or passwords that would show up on his phone. He hated all the complicated security crap he now had to put up with. It seemed you couldn't order a pizza any more without having to know some code or password. Jeez!

"Well, on the bright side, we've been getting some useful stuff from our guy Jerry Masterson on the police force," said Rafe. "Did you know one of McCarthy's guys already in prison has asked for protection in there? He's telling the cops everything he knows, all about Frank, just so they'll protect him. He's not asking to get out or anything. But, he's convinced Frank might now want to kill him and he's willing to roll over first, before that happens."

"Yeah, so? That just means Frank goes away forever, right? The more his guys are willing to testify … isn't that better for us?" Carlos had negotiated with all the other bosses up in Boston and the less influence McCarthy now had, the stronger the new alliances he had with these guys would get.

"Well, the interesting part is why this guy Ramon is suddenly so worried about Frank. How much do you know about the problems that got Frank and his guys arrested, anyway?" Rafe had met with several different

185

guys now and had finally put together what he thought was an interesting story.

"The money laundering and tax evasion? He was careless, right?"

Rafe explained, "Not as careless as you might think. It apparently all went to hell when some guy died. He had this money guy, Tony Gonzales, some guy he grew up with, who took care of everything for years. After that guy died, the Feds somehow managed to put together all kinds of stuff and then make this really strong case. From what I hear, none of the lawyers working for Frank are saying he has any chance."

"Okay, bad luck. His guy Tony dies and the Feds get lucky. Frank loses. We win. Why are you telling me all this?" Carlos knew Rafe was going somewhere with this stuff and was actually paying close attention. Rafe had proven his worth, over and over again.

"It's because of what a lot of different people have been telling me. Apparently, a couple months before all the arrests? Some girl shows up at Frank's place. A kid in high school, okay? Maybe sixteen or seventeen? She says she wants to see Frank. Ramon and Marco were the guys out front who met this kid. She says to tell Frank she wants to talk about Tony. Now, this is more than six months after Tony died. And, not a lot of people even knew about Tony and Frank. For some reason, when Frank hears this? He says okay, send her in." Rafe was watching Carlos and could see he was following along, so far.

Rafe continued, "There were witnesses who saw all this, see? She shows up, asks for Frank, mentions Tony and then when Frank says to send her in, Ramon goes out, gets her and brings her in. No big deal so far. Just a little strange that Frank would waste any time on some kid. Here's the interesting part, though. The girl was a real looker and it turns out that Ramon felt her up on the way in. Supposedly checking to make sure she wasn't wearing a wire or hiding any weapon, right? They even have all this on video; they saved the surveillance tape because of what happened after. So, then they go into Frank's office. She doesn't come out. Nobody sees her again."

Carlos was definitely curious. "She disappears? Why would Frank … wait, you're holding back now. I can tell by looking at you. What happened?"

Rafe laughed. "Marco finally broke into Frank's office two hours later, when no one could get any response. They didn't have any surveillance in there, only outside his office. Frank and the girl are gone, out the back way. And, Ramon? This guy is huge, probably close to three hundred pounds, mostly muscle. He's laying there out cold. That kid kicked him in the balls and then broke his jaw with another kick. His jaw was wired up for weeks after that."

"What the hell? You saying some girl did that?"

"Yep. There was never any doubt about that. Everyone figures she didn't like the way he groped her. Ramon was really pissed and then, when Frank told him "hands off", he got even more pissed. Frank came back late that night and wouldn't say anything about it. Only that everyone better stay away from Missy McCrae or else. Obviously, that kid has something pretty big that she's blackmailing Frank with."

"That's the girl? Missy McCrae?" asked Carlos.

"That's her. I've actually got a really interesting folder on her. It turns out she's this martial arts supergirl or something. Lots of trophies. But get this. Why do you think Ramon suddenly decides to worry about Frank? He's in prison and everything, so what suddenly happened to change things?" Rafe was now really enjoying his story.

"What? Don't drag this out, Rafe. Hurry up!" Carlos was still trying to process all the information and wasn't seeing anything significant, yet.

"Marco disappeared, that's what happened. Marco and those four other guys. You heard how we traced their arrest to some incident at that parking garage, right? The police had one level all blocked off for two hours and that guy Jerry we have with the police, he thinks it was our guys getting grabbed for something. Guess what they were doing that night?"

Carlos said, "This better be good, Rafe, because you're talking in circles and I'm getting a head ache. What was Marco up to?"

"He wanted to get some revenge for his buddy Ramon. They figured it was worth the risk, in spite of Frank's orders. So, they were going after that girl, Missy

McCrae. And, when Ramon learned Marco disappeared? He decided he didn't want to risk whether or not Frank was the reason for that. He's demanding full protection in return for his testimony."

"Well, if they attacked her, was it in the papers or on TV? What happened to her, anyway?"

"Oh, nothing happened to her that anyone knows about. She just graduated from high school last month. It's right here in the newspaper. I only found out Marco was planning to grab her by getting the story from some of our own guys. They all knew because Marco bragged how he was going to make a little video he could show Ramon. They were wondering if Frank somehow did manage to interfere, since he was so adamant about hands off her or else."

Carlos asked, "So, it was hushed up. But, there had to be a complaint, right? What does this guy Masterson say?"

"There was no complaint," said Rafe. "Jerry checked and there's no crime report or complaint or anything. The police at that parking garage were providing security and traffic control but don't know what happened; they were only following orders. But, Jerry did learn one of the cops was pretty sure he recognized Marco. He spotted him being put into an unmarked van. Just like the two other unmarked vans that were there that night. Jerry says it has to have been the Feds grabbing our guys."

Carlos said, "Yeah, okay, that makes sense. And those guys -- aren't they now talking to the Feds? We figure they're in witness protection, right? But, not with the cops? So, it has to be the Feds that have them. That explains why the police don't know shit; the Feds were in charge that night." Then, Carlos asked, "Why would this girl not file a complaint, if they attacked her in that parking garage?"

"What I don't get is what the hell was she doing earlier, that day with Frank?" Rafe had gone over everything and a lot of things just didn't add up. "I went to see Frank yesterday and asked him that. That's where I was when you tried calling me. I didn't have my phone with me while I was in seeing Frank."

"So, what did he say?" asked Carlos.

"Nothing. He told me to go fuck myself. But, her name definitely registered with him. Whatever she has on him, he's still worried about it. I don't think he's worried about the cops the way he's worried about her. Ramon ratting him out, maybe getting him charged with murder? Not a concern. Missy McCrae being messed with? Big concern. He's still worried. I asked around about exactly what he told everyone and it's not just her. Nobody's supposed to mess with anyone in her family either. How do you figure that?"

"Let me see that folder on her. Are there any photos?"

"Sure, here take a look. She's a knockout. Some of these show a pretty girl that looks all sweet and innocent, right? Then, look at this one someone took last month at her senior prom? Gorgeous and all grown up. Long red hair, black gown, incredible body. But this one? Right after she won some martial arts trophy in New York? I even found video clips on the internet showing the championship match for that, which she won easily. Look at her body in that photo. And, her face. That's the face of someone I can see taking down a guy like Ramon."

"Wow." Carlos was studying the photo and noticed all the scars on her shoulder. "How'd she get those scars? That almost looks like she was mauled by some wild animal."

"I don't see anything written up about how she got those. She sure has a lot of articles that were written about her, though, when you do a search. Athletic events, karate tournaments, lots of stuff. Oh, and look at this article. Missing teen returns home. Hey, get this? She disappeared from soccer camp and then, two years later, she just shows up. That was three years ago." Rafe was sifting through his folder, glancing from one article to the next. He'd had two of his guys pull everything together and hadn't gone through it all himself yet.

Carlos was staring at him and the expression on his face changed several times. "It's her! It has to be. That girl must be the werecat we're trying to find, Rafe. Don't you see? She suddenly turns into a cat when she reaches puberty, then goes off somewhere for two years? Even those scars; she probably did get mauled. And, that explains why there's no complaint about that

191

parking garage attack. When those assholes tried to grab her, she turned into a wild mountain lion. Surprise!" He began chuckling.

Rafe nodded his head. "Yeah, I can see that, now that you're putting it that way. But ... she must be getting help, right? There's nothing in the paper about any wild animal attacking anyone in that parking garage. And, if the Feds have those guys? They're helping her. Does the US government know about werecats, Carlos?"

Chapter Fifteen
Jun 2018

"Robert, I'll be okay. He only wants to meet me, one time, and then he's leaving. He and his buddies are really going back to South America. He says I've actually helped him out. He had no idea the Feds were watching him so closely. And, he wants no part of the US government grabbing him, identifying him as a werecat … maybe experimenting on him in some lab. Same thing I was worried about, remember?" Missy was once again sitting across from Robert at their favorite coffee shop.

"He called you and said all that? And, you believed him?" Robert was worried and not at all happy at this latest turn of events. He thought Missy might be getting in over her head and was being way too trusting.

"Yes, he called me and that really freaked me out. He could tell that, too, and he laughed. He said freaking me out was payback for my stealing his car and everything. By the way, did you get anything useful from it? He didn't seem very worried about that." Missy hadn't talked to Robert since letting him know where she'd abandoned the car. It had only been a few days and Robert actually had thought this meeting she'd asked for was to discuss that.

"Nothing really of much use in the car and the gun was clean. Not much in the wallet but some cash and credit cards; they're still reviewing the contents.

But, I hear the phone has some interesting stuff; contacts and addresses and maybe even some codes or passwords. I haven't heard any details yet. I gave the wallet and phone to Armando since it's his team working to make a case. We've already talked about why "P" Branch doesn't go after organized crime; that's for the FBI." Robert had tried explaining all the politics involved. He knew Missy still wasn't happy they hadn't simply grabbed Carlos for her.

"By the way," Robert added. "Armando still wants me to convince you to forget West Point so he can recruit you. When I told him you were the one who stole the phone from Carlos, he got a big kick out of that. And, no, he insists he definitely does not want to know any details. Just like last time, with your other *FBI Freebies*? He's fine now with getting whatever stuff you can get for him, without knowing details. Since it's only information and not actual evidence, he *definitely* doesn't want to know details."

"Yeah, I know, I know. He's making sure there'll never be any scandal for his team regarding informants." Missy knew Robert had been asked by Armando to be her contact, rather than having anyone from the FBI's Organized Crime Division do that, since he'd worked her kidnapping case and wasn't actually on Armando's team at all. That was after getting all the info on Tony Gonzales that she'd brought them. Not to mention the ten million dollars, her earlier FBI Freebie.

"Tell him sorry, though. I'm still going to West Point. What about Lisa and Marie? How are they working out?" Lisa and Marie were at the same university as Heather and, like Heather, would graduate in one more year from the five year, co-op program their university specialized in. Lisa was studying criminology and came from a family with several members already on the police force. Marie's specialty was computer science. The girls were also beautiful models which had paid well enough so they didn't have any school loans.

Robert said, "They're doing fantastic and Armando thanks you for insisting he give them co-op assignments, which have been going great. He's bragging how they both will be joining the FBI after graduation a year from now. Then, once they finish the FBI Academy, they've agreed to join his team. Marie is actually the one who hacked into Carlos's phone. She's been telling Armando some of the ways they can mess with emails, all without anything tracing back to his team. Those email addresses Carlos had? Even though the account was closed she ..."

Missy interrupted him by bursting out laughing. "Oh, you don't have to explain, Robert. I know all about what Marie can do, messing with emails. I just think it's too funny she'll end up doing it for the FBI." She had helped Lisa and Marie over a year ago by breaking into the apartment of a guy named Jonathan Baxter who had sold videos of them to a porn site.

Jonathan had managed to install spy cameras in their Boston apartment, which they had alternated using with Heather, whenever attending school rather than doing co-op work assignments. Missy had tracked him by his scent and had dropped down a rope from the roof, getting into his apartment through a window. She then had let Lisa and Marie come in and that had ended his days selling stuff to porn sites. They had accessed his computer, had learned all his codes, passwords and personal information, and then had turned on file sharing.

Leaving the way they'd each come in, so he never knew they'd been there, they went home and accessed his computer remotely. Marie installed her own software on his system and stole his identity. Missy was amazed at all the different ways the two girls had then messed with his life, sending emails out from his account, wiping out his bank accounts, destroying his records at school and ruining any chances he had to get hired anywhere.

They also had learned which porn sites he'd contacted, allowing them to get everything showing the two of them deleted. They were together as a couple, having met on a photo shoot back in high school. It didn't matter that they were lesbians but their modeling would definitely have suffered, having videos on the internet showing how wild and uninhibited their sexual activities had been. Fortunately, they'd not suffered any further embarrassment, after one of their friends had alerted them about the problem in the first place. They felt indebted to Missy for enabling the quick actions that saved them from what might have been disastrous.

Missy decided she could let Robert know a bit more. "Lisa and Marie are the ones who helped me set up my surveillance system, checking on Billy and Donny."

Robert laughed and said, "Ah, I'd wondered about that. Your system, using that FBI software you had me provide you with? From what I've learned, now that Les and Marsha have taken it over ... it's rather complicated and sophisticated, even for you. By the way, you'll be glad to know all the batteries were replaced. It wasn't easy. The guys we had do the break-ins for that weren't cat burglars ... just normal humans."

Missy laughed and said, "Please, stop with the cat jokes! And, since we're back to talking about cats, can I give Carlos some assurances that he's asking for?"

"It's never easy with you, is it? I guess I'm not surprised. So, he wants more than just this meeting with you ... you know ... so he can kiss you goodbye? What else does he want?" Robert was shaking his head, not sure he wanted to hear whatever terms Carlos might want.

"Well, he knew the Feds were watching him in Miami. That's why he came up here and only brought guys with him he could trust. He thought he could avoid them here, easily enough. When he figured out who I was, which was probably inevitable ... that's why you guys decided to break with all your super secrecy crap and actually tell me about him in the first place, remember? Well, he knew I had not handled his five guys in that parking garage all by myself. Not with the guys just disappearing, no complaints being filed about any attack, and even the police being on the scene. Then, too, the police were all in the dark as to what had happened there. Once the FBI started digging up bodies and arresting more guys?"

197

"Then, he figured you must be working with the FBI or some government agency, and that they had to know you were a werecat." Robert was connecting the dots, just as Carlos obviously had. "I suppose if we'd never helped you with Marco, making guys disappear who then obviously were talking to the FBI ..."

"Exactly. That, and I clearly had some great resources no high school girl would have. I found him, thanks to you. But, I don't regret my calling him and challenging him. You should be happy. He's leaving. He only wants assurances the US government will let him go and not chase after him. Or, identify him as a werecat to any other governments or countries. I can tell him that, right?"

Missy drove into the huge mall parking lot in her Toyota and cruised around until she found the spot Carlos had designated. She'd agreed to his picking the place and to her coming there alone. She even had agreed he could search her for any wire, provided he used electronic equipment and didn't try actually touching her. He'd laughed and explained how they'd watched the video and knew what Ramon had done. No, he said his guy Rafe didn't want to end up like Ramon and had no intention of making any inappropriate moves whatsoever.

She got out of her car and waited. After only a minute, a big Cadillac limo pulled up. She'd seen their photos so she recognized the two guys who got out. Carlos and Rafe. It was a beautiful June day, hot and a little humid, but there was no shade where they were, out in this parking lot. She came up to them and smiled. She was wearing white shorts and a simple sleeveless tee shirt, also white. She wasn't showing any cleavage or exposing any part of her breasts but there was no disguising what a great figure she had; she looked great. She had a pair of strappy white sandals on with no socks. Her hair was up in a high pony tail, similar to how she'd worn it that time she'd visited Frank. She somehow knew they'd appreciate the irony of that. She sent a mental message to Mike, who was not far away, but parked at the other end of the mall. *They're here now. So far, so good.*

Carlos said, "Missy McCrea. Very nice to meet you. This is Rafe. He knows what we are so you can talk freely." He studied her and was definitely impressed. "You're a very beautiful young lady. In your cat form, you're also very impressive. Okay if he checks you with this wand?"

Missy smiled and said, "Sure, go ahead. Did you go out and buy that special, just for me?" She recalled how she'd asked Ramon if he was going to use a wand to check her just prior to their entering Frank's office. Ramon had liked fondling her instead and she knew they had seen all that on the video tape. She raised both arms and watched as Rafe came forward, slowly and carefully. After he checked her, not touching her at all, he stepped back.

Carlos was still studying her and she saw him take some deep breaths, clearly enjoying her scent. Then, he raised his eyebrows and said, "You're already

199

mated? I can smell him on you, deeply embedded, and no one else. Ahh, but you are so young. Such a shame for all the other men. Does he know about you?"

Missy actually relaxed and laughed. "Oh, yes! He knows all about me. Can we talk about you leaving? That's why we're here, right?

Carlos smiled and nodded his head. "Yes, but let's go inside, where it's cool. And, I promised that you could get something to eat. There's no need to be out here, baking in the sun." He waved for her to go ahead of him, and she turned and led the way. He loved watching the way she moved. To distract himself from how lovely her rear end looked in those shorts, he said, "Those scars ... did that happen up in those mountains? I read how you disappeared for two years. I can't imagine what that experience must have been like."

Missy turned to look back at him and answered, "Yes! I was thirteen then and not quite as wise about how to handle things. Today, I'd probably avoid fighting that bear ... he only wanted what was left from a deer I'd only half eaten ... from the day before. It was mine, though, and I warned him to leave. He wouldn't leave, at first."

"So, you fought him. How did that go? Those scars look like he badly mauled you before you gave up. Was he very big, this bear?" Carlos was enjoying everything about this amazing girl, walking in front of him. He could see the play and definition of all her muscles, yet she was as feminine and curvy as anyone he'd ever met.

"Oh, I wasn't the one who gave up, Carlos. He was an average size black bear, maybe two hundred pounds ... probably just about your size. I was much smaller four years ago, of course. I've maybe put on about thirty five pounds since then." Missy smiled at him. "I did let him slink away, once he gave up ... he saw I wasn't going to let him have what he wanted." Missy knew Carlos was getting all her double meanings. They weren't just talking about how she fought that bear.

"Missy, you don't have to keep warning me. I'm going." Carlos looked at Rafe and shook his head. "Maybe under different circumstances, it would have been interesting to stay here. But, you now have those government friends up here. They know about you and yet, here you are, free and acting all pissy with me. Tell me about your friends."

"No, sorry, I'm not sharing information like that. I agreed to meet with you. And, I have obtained those assurances you wanted. I hope you'll take my word for that since there's really nothing else I can give you." Missy was not really sure why Carlos had insisted on meeting her.

They'd arrived at the mall entrance and went in, but then walked to where a restaurant was located not far inside the mall. They eventually were seated, off in a corner booth where they had some privacy. Missy ordered a huge steak, rare, which Carlos had agreed to pay for when first setting up the meeting. Then, she made them wait. No more serious conversation until she'd been served her food. They'd asked for this meeting and had picked the place, right? Carlos actually got a big kick out of this. He just wasn't used to watching girls eat the way she did.

After watching her devour half her steak, Carlos said, "How you can you eat so much and yet look so fantastic, Missy ... is it because you run so much as a cat?"

She decided to allow this question. "No, it's because I train so hard as a human. But, I love being a cat whenever I can. Don't you?" She wanted him to be the one to provide information.

"No, I don't like having to Shift. It's always a problem for me but I have no choice. I am surprised to hear that you love being a cat." When she didn't say anything, he then asked, "Why do you train so hard?"

Missy decided to share some things and see if he then would explain himself more to her. She really only knew what her own dual nature was like. Perhaps other werecats were different? "When I first Shifted, I didn't know if I would ever be human again. It took me a long time but I accepted what I was and I became a cat, only I was an enhanced cat ... plus, of course, I still had my human mind. Finally, I Changed back. But, now I am an enhanced human because I am a werecat. I have two natures which I have melded into one. I have special needs and I train to satisfy those. Don't you have special abilities and instincts, Carlos? Why is being a cat a problem for you?"

"Well, that's actually quite interesting ... two natures, melded into one. Hmmm!" Carlos studied her for several moments. Finally, he said, "My uncle had warned me of our family curse. When I Shifted … well, it was very difficult for me to accept that I must live this way. I appreciate having enhanced abilities but I don't think I'm like you, Missy." Carlos again studied her. "You took some big risks letting your government friends learn about you. I was never willing to risk that. It's why I'm leaving, now that I realize they know my secret."

"But, you came here and replaced Frank McCarthy. You have chosen a life in organized crime. That's not been a secret. What about those risks?" Missy was reviewing all she'd been briefed about him.

"I know the rules in organized crime … and, I know the rules for the Feds, the cops and everyone I deal with. So, those risks I can manage. But, I don't know the rules when it comes to werecats. You indeed seem to have been lucky. I don't trust that my luck will be so good, if I stay here. That's why I'm asking for information about your government friends."

Missy said, "I didn't want the government to learn about me. But, I was willing to use my abilities to help people. And, to defend myself and my friends. I accepted the risks to protect my friends and my family. Luckily, after the government learned about me, they agreed to help."

Carlos said, "Growing up, where I come from, I really had very few choices. Like you, I did things to protect my family. And, our family business … the only one that pays … we export drugs. But, enough about why I'm what I am. How did they know you were a cat, Missy? And, how did they know about me?"

"I'm not at liberty to explain how they know about you. But, they've known for some time now and have been monitoring your activities. Since you're heading a criminal organization, they are looking to help the FBI make a case against you. Your time here would have been limited, regardless of my existence. Me?" Missy smiled. "They figured out that I was a cat when I took care of those two guys, Luis and Jose, and left my cat tracks everywhere, so a wild animal would be blamed rather than me. That night I saw Frank. He's my alibi, or at least I thought he was. Isn't that how you learned about me?"

Carlos looked at Rafe and asked him, "Who were Luis and Jose? Why don't I know anything about them?" Then he looked at Missy. "No, I already explained it was because Marco and his guys all disappeared, going after you. We heard he'd bragged to several guys about how he would be helping his buddy Ramon. Payback for what you did ... why is Frank protecting you, anyway? What do you have on him? We never understood why you showed up that day. Or, why Frank agreed to see you."

He studied Missy but he could see she wasn't going to respond. So, then he asked her, "And, who were Luis and Jose? You took them out and left cat tracks behind? Damn!"

Missy realized they knew a lot less about her than she'd thought. "Well, those were associates of

Frank's and, since you scented me out there in the State Forest, I knew it was only a matter of time. Once you heard how they were killed by some large cat animal, you'd find me. There were a lot of witnesses who saw me at Frank's place that night."

Rafe looked at Carlos and said, "If they were only associates of Frank's, that's probably why we haven't heard about them. If their deaths were reportedly caused by some wild animal, no one in the organization is seeing any connection. And, Frank isn't talking. I tried asking him about Missy and he wouldn't say a thing. But, she has him worried. I told you about that."

Carlos now looked at Missy. "What is it with you, anyway, Missy? You've got something on Frank which has him more worried than being charged with murder. He knows that's very likely, now that Ramon has rolled over. And, you're telling me you killed some guys? In your cat form? Jeez! Maybe I'm seeing why you have these government friends after all. You're really only now getting out of high school, right?"

Missy laughed. "I have you to thank for them being my friends, Carlos. They only told me they knew my secret so they could warn me about you. They'll let you leave the country and the FBI won't know anything. But, they'll continue to monitor you wherever you go. It's what they do. Monitor us."

Carlos stared at her, as this really was more information than anything else she'd given him so far. "They monitor us. Well. What would have happened if they didn't tell you about me? From what you're saying,

I'd have found you out because of Luis and Jose. You actually killed those guys, huh? Maybe ... damn, we would have made a great team." He looked at her and brown speckles suddenly flooded his hazel eyes.

Missy scented his sudden arousal. Or, rather, his sudden increase in sexual awareness which his eyes were now showing. Both guys had been lusting after her the entire time, checking her out constantly, but she was used to that. It had only been the normal interest that all males typically took in her. But, now Carlos was getting all turned on and this was definitely a much greater interest. "Hey, don't start thinking about me being on *your* team. Especially when it's triggering your arousal that way. I can scent you getting all excited, Carlos." She stared at him for a moment. "Hey, you know those clothes of mine you wore after I stole your car? That's the only damn time you're ever getting into *my* pants!" She giggled.

He laughed and said, "Damn, Missy ... but the thought of you killing those guys? I admit that's a trigger ... how many did you kill the night Marco and the boys went after you?" Seeing her now, not as merely a high school girl, but instead as a very complex, desirable, powerful woman was definitely causing his sexual arousal to surge.

Missy said, "None, but only because my government buddies had already told me they knew my secrets. And, that they'd work with me to avoid my killing anyone else. Otherwise ...?" Now Missy let her cat energy flow into her body and she stared at Carlos while her eyes filled with sparkles and blazed back at him. Then, drawing on her bond with Mike to help harness and control her energy, she released one large pulse and pushed it at the two of them.

Carlos and Rafe were slammed back against the seat back in their booth. The dishes had mostly been cleared away by this time, since Missy had finished her meal as they'd been talking. But, what few remaining items were still on the table all moved, as though a sudden wind had blown through; some fell off onto the floor and others dropped into their laps. Heads turned and looked in their direction as others in the restaurant clearly noticed something. This had been an energy pulse much stronger than anything she'd done before and even Missy was surprised.

"What the hell was that?" asked Carlos. "What *are* you, Missy?"

She smiled at them both. "I'm enhanced, like I said. And, I've been training really hard. Haven't we just been talking all about that?"

Robert called her the next day. "They're gone. We tracked them all the way back to Bogota and they're now returning to the mountain region where he still has family. So, at least for now, things are good."

Missy said, "Yes, he has plenty of money and he prefers to be back there now. I assured him you guys will leave him alone and stay out of things, even if he continues doing what his family has been doing for years. Exporting drugs. He wasn't giving me any excuses but he did explain his reasons. Apparently, for people like his family, making a living has really depended on that for years. No other crops up in those mountains compare to that. Otherwise, they never would have survived."

"Well, Armando is happy. He doesn't understand why Carlos just took off like that, but whatever causes trouble for organized crime in Boston definitely works for him. He is curious, though. Why does this happen so soon after his office gets that wallet and cell phone? From you, no less. Why does your name keep coming up, always with something strange going on? He already was asking me that question after getting those four guys from some mysterious government agency. He now has them in witness protection and they're providing him with some great stuff. But, each of those guys is telling a different story about you. And, their buddy Marco has disappeared."

"Well, does that mean he'll be happy I'm away at West Point?" Missy giggled. "No more me, messing around with his gangsters. Life will get pretty boring, now, huh?"

"Very funny. I'll tell him you said that." Robert laughed. "Just think how he actually knows less than half of what you've really done to various gangsters, messing around the way you have."

"Well, I'm glad you appreciate me so much, Robert." Missy also laughed. "You're still coming to my going away party, right? And, Les and Marsha will be coming up too?"

"Absolutely, we wouldn't miss that," said Robert. "Marsha wants to know what you're going to do with all your hair, after you get it chopped off so short. She's guessing you're maybe going to have extensions made for later, whatever those are."

"She's right, I am. My sister knows someone who will do that for me. Clip-in hair extensions using my own hair will work great. One day, I'll have short hair and the next day, I can have long hair again. All the celebrities are doing that. Presto! Magic!" Missy considered it very appropriate that she'd now be using a bit of magic once in awhile, which she told Robert to explain to everyone at "P" Branch.

Chapter Sixteen
Jun 2018

Missy was really excited and it took all her incredibly strong controls to tamp down her energy and just stand there, in formation. She'd just finished raising her hand and reciting her oath of allegiance, promising to support and defend the Constitution of the United States, and to obey all legal orders given to her. She was now a New Cadet and had officially started Beast Training.

The day had been a blur, West Point's Reception Day or R-Day, and after saying a quick goodbye to her family that morning she'd marched off across the field at Michie Stadium with the rest of the Class of 2022. There were a total of 1240 members in her class of which 236 were women. She'd dutifully reported to various "Cadets in the Red Sash" for instructions and then had been incredibly busy with all the various in processing activities.

Everyone had been anxious to follow orders and not mess up. That, of course, had led to a lot of fumbling around, scrambling from one place to the next, running in circles as they went from line to line. She'd been fitted and issued her clothing and then had received more uniforms and supplies until eventually she'd filled up two large duffel bags which she'd dropped off in her assigned room.

Finally, they'd all gathered behind closed doors in several of the classrooms, faced the American flag and had just been sworn in. Then, they got to repeat receiving this oath in front of all their families by going outside on "The Plain", the huge grass field between the Hudson River and Washington Hall. She knew her family had been touring West Point throughout the day and had listened to the Superintendent speak. She was able to see them in the crowd out there, but only from afar, as she passed in review and then went marching off with the rest of her company over to her barracks. She wouldn't see them again for seven weeks.

She was assigned to "Charlie" Company, or C Company, and was one of ten members in the second squad, second platoon. She was paired with another girl while the other eight members of her squad were men. Normally, each platoon had four squads and each company had four platoons. There were eight companies in her regiment, four each in two battalions. The 236 women in her class had been assigned in pairs to 118 of the 124 squads.

This would only be for Beast Training and would all change during Reorganization Week, right after Beast Training was completed. Then, the rest of the West Point classes would return and rather than just the one regiment, there would be four regiments in the Corp of Cadets and each company would be made up from members from all four classes. Sophomores would be team leaders, juniors would be company NCO's or non-commissioned officers and seniors would hold all the company officer positions.

For right now, Missy's whole world was her squad, since they'd be doing everything together throughout the summer. And, for Beast Training, all the leadership positions for her squad, platoon and company were held by upperclass cadets in their junior year.

The other girl in her squad was Tracy McGonagle who was also one of her roommates. They'd be living in the same building as the guys in her company but they had a separate women's latrine and showers. Supposedly, the roommate assignments had been completely random and were not alphabetical. She knew there'd be three girls in her room but didn't yet know who their other roommate would be; she only knew that girl would be in one of the other squads in her platoon.

Although she'd met Tracy during all of this in processing, Missy still hadn't had a chance to say anything to her. She hadn't actually talked to any of her fellow classmates but had only spoken to the various upperclass cadets using one of the allowed four responses whenever they'd spoken to her. If the cadet was male, then she could say:

"Yes, Sir"

"No, Sir"

"No excuse, Sir"

"Sir, I do not understand"

If the cadet was female, she would substitute Ma'am for Sir. To ask a question, she first must say, "Sir (or Ma'am), may I ask a question?" Or, to make a statement, she first must say, "Sir (or Ma'am), may I make a statement?" Anything else would result in her being corrected, severely.

She'd known this from studying ahead of time, as had all her classmates, but throughout the day she'd constantly been hearing one classmate after another getting reprimanded for speaking out of turn or for not quite getting their wording out the way they were supposed to. She'd managed to avoid being corrected herself but only because she'd hardly spoken all day. Having enhanced hearing helped her a lot since she didn't have to ask about a lot of things; she'd already been able to hear many of the answers being shouted to some other New Cadet as part of the verbal dressing down they'd been getting.

The requirement for always responding in this fashion was not limited to Beast Training but would continue for her entire first year as a plebe. Freshmen at West Point were fourth class, also known as plebes. Sophomores were third class and yearlings, juniors were second class and cows, while seniors were first class and firsties. In spite of all her preparation and studying, the new terms and acronyms were mind boggling. And, when she didn't know them or know any of the other cadet slang expressions? She figured the response she'd be giving the most would be, "No excuse, Sir!"

Her biggest worry had been about all the rules and requirements during meals in the Mess Hall. She

213

was concerned she'd not be getting enough to eat and her fear seemed well founded, based on this first day's experience. Her squad had all sat at the same table, under the watchful eye of her squad leader, Cadet Harold Jamieson. He'd instructed them on how to eat, sitting at attention and using the slow motion method that was required for every meal.

Jamieson had said, "Start with both hands on your lap, eyes straight ahead, then pick up your fork, raise one bite to your mouth, but do not chew until returning the fork to your plate and putting your hand back on your lap. Don't move your eyes during any of this but keep them looking straight ahead. Then chew, but if more than three chews are needed before you can swallow, your bite was too big. There will be no unauthorized big bites in my squad. Understood?" Ten voices had all answered, "Yes, Sir."

Missy had barely managed to finish the meager portions she'd gotten and only because she'd taken some unauthorized big bites while others in her squad were being yelled at by Cadet Jamieson. She had a huge advantage; with her enhanced senses both for scents and peripheral vision, her eyes never seemed to stray while she did this. Yes, it was all a game and she'd have to work really hard at every meal, playing this game, in order to somehow get enough food to eat. She knew this was going to be her biggest challenge but she was determined to make the best of it. It was one of the reasons she'd bulked up so much ahead of time.

After entering the barracks and finding herself finally free from the scrutiny of any upperclass cadets,

Missy paused to register each of the many scents. She took several minutes to parse them all, drawing in air across her tongue and the roof of her mouth as well as into her nose. So many new and unfamiliar scents; she took her time to experience and categorize them. Then she went up to her room on the third floor, opened the door and greeted her two roommates.

Tracy was about two inches shorter than she was, and at least thirty pounds lighter. She was attractive and athletic, with dark brown hair and dark brown eyes. She had a really pretty smile but seemed a bit standoffish when Missy came in. Perhaps what she'd been telling the other roommate just before Missy opened the door had something to do with that. Even though their door had been closed, Missy had heard Tracy's words as she'd approached the door. "... the way she kept sneaking food off her plate, whenever Jamieson wasn't watching her. I only got to eat half of mine but she ate every bit of hers. She looks like she's a really big girl, too, so I only hope our squad isn't going to suffer because ..." Missy's arrival halted the rest of that sentence as both girls looked up at her when she opened the door.

Taking everything in at a glance, including how the girls had already selected bunks, with Missy apparently the one to get the upper bunk above Tracy, she said, "Hi, everyone, I'm Missy McCrae. I guess we're roommates, right? Glad to meet you both. I already know your name, Tracy ... we're in the same squad ... but we didn't get to talk earlier." She looked at the other girl, who was Asian, and a classic beauty. She

215

looked fit enough, but probably only weighed a hundred pounds and wasn't much taller than five feet.

Tracy said, "Yes, we sat together at lunch and again at supper. I was just telling Kelly what a difficult time our squad leader gave all of us today. This is only our first day, too. I can hardly wait to see what he has in store for our squad during the rest of Beast Training. Ugghhh!"

"Hi, Missy, my name is Kelly Wong," said Kelly. "I'm a California girl. I was born in Mountain View, right in the middle of the Silicon Valley region, and this is my first time our here on the East Coast. Tracy's from Texas but has been telling me how she's really been all over everywhere. Where are you from?" Each year there were classmates from all 50 states plus several international countries.

Now that Missy was up close and personal with the two of them, she couldn't help but notice how each girl had their own special scent, their unique signature scent. For Kelly, however, she could also notice at least three male scents, all from guys she'd definitely been having sex with in the last couple of months. Frequent, consensual sex. For their scents to linger like that and be combined so strongly with her own scent, she obviously had been a player. Wow. Hopefully, there wasn't some underlying issue.

For Tracy, however, it didn't smell as though she'd ever had sex. There was, however, a very different scent for her ... Missy could only categorize it as "other". All this, of course, was merely her initial

216

impression which she hardly gave any thought to. She answered Kelly's question by saying, "Massachusetts. Salem, Massachusetts. But, I've been through most of the mountains, from New Hampshire down to Virginia. Does that count?" Then she looked at Tracy and asked, "Where in Texas? Everyone's always saying what a big state that is."

Tracy said, "My family now lives in Arlington, not too far from Dallas. But, I'm an Army brat … my Dad dragged us all over before he retired as a bird colonel. I'm an only child so I get to carry on the tradition. Not only did my father come here, but my grandfather did too."

Both girls had already squared away all their stuff and Missy emptied out her two duffel bags and quickly put everything away. She didn't want to be the one to fail any inspections and was glad to see that both her roommates seemed to be very familiar with how things were supposed to be done. Tracy had been well prepared and had helped Kelly a little. Now she showed Missy how to arrange some of her gear, which was nice. Suddenly, she stepped back from Missy, almost as though sensing something that clearly was bothering her.

Tracy asked, "Did you say you were from *Salem*, Massachusetts? Really?"

"Yeah, sure. Why?" Missy looked at her, not sure what could be the matter. She removed most of her clothes, getting ready for bed, and was now standing there in only her panties and a tee shirt, similar to how both her roommates were already attired. She wasn't self conscious any more about showing any of her body, and didn't think twice about this.

Before Tracy could say anything, however, Kelly exclaimed, "Holy shit, look at you. Are you some kind of body builder or something? Tracy, look ... she's all muscle. Jeez, no fat anywhere at all ... even I have more body fat than you do, Missy."

Tracy still hadn't said anything. Missy didn't know what might be bothering her, but she didn't think it was how her body looked. She said, "Well, I did kind of bulk up a bit, getting ready for this place. I'll probably lose most of it during Beast Training, though, since I know my rations in the Mess Hall won't be enough."

Tracy finally said something that surprised both Missy and Kelly. "I can't believe I've ended up in here with *you*, Missy. It can only mean the Fates are really pretty fickle after all. Or, maybe they just have a really huge sense of humor."

Kelly said, "Why would you say that, Tracy?"

Missy was still trying to process what might be "other" about Tracy. But, it had been a very long day and she was tired. She said, "Let's all get some sleep. That five AM wake-up call will be coming before we know it. We'll have to talk about all this stuff some other time." She hopped up onto her bunk and let her mind go to one of her many places; places with no stress. She was asleep before one of her roommates turned out the lights.

Chapter Seventeen
Jul 2018

It was morning of her third day and Missy was feeling very happy. Right after this reveille formation was the daily physical training or PT. She loved doing PT, of course. First there were the various calisthenics exercises, just to warm up. She had no problem doing them all exactly right, just the way the Army wanted them done. Some of her classmates were having difficulty and the squad leaders were quick to correct them, barking out orders that only added to their difficulty. If you didn't show perfect form, you were doomed to failure. All part of "The Game" that Missy now considered this Beast Training represented for her.

Then, after enough pushups and sit-ups and jumping jacks had been done, they'd go for a run. She'd already been put into the fastest group, or black group, due to her performance on the initial APFT, the Army Physical Fitness Test. This consisted of doing pushups for two minutes, sit-ups for two minutes and then a two mile run. Missy had done 50 pushups and 100 sit-ups, well above the requirement even for the men. Her time for the two mile run had been just over ten minutes, earning her a spot in the black group. Her scores were the highest for any female and only a few of the men had higher scores. She was right where she'd wanted to be.

Her squad leader Jamieson was quite pleased to have a woman from his squad do so well, so he wasn't getting in her face quite as much, criticizing her the way he'd been doing all the others. There was clearly some competitiveness between squad leaders and she knew she was playing right into that. She had played on a lot of sports teams and had always worked to contribute whatever made the team do best. That's how she viewed her squad and, by making her squad look good, her squad leader would benefit. All part of "The Game", right?

Tracy was in the normal group, or gold group, and only one of the guys in their squad was in the slow group, or white group. Three guys were in the gold group with Tracy and two were in the grey group, or fast group. There were two guys in their squad also running in the fastest group with her. Missy thought, overall, her whole squad ought to do well enough on any physical challenge tasks. She knew there would be a lot of those in the weeks to come.

Today's run was on a course with a lot of steep hills. Missy was staying just behind the leaders, which didn't require much effort for her. It did allow her to think back over the hectic days just before finally coming down here to West Point. The highlight, of course, had been her birthday party. That had also been her going away party and the huge turnout had been overwhelming. Family and friends, all wishing her well. Relatives she didn't even know, coming up to talk to her. Her "P" Branch buddies -- Robert, Les and Marsha. Senator Maxwell and his wife Jennifer, recently returned from their honeymoon. The Stratton family, up from D. C. Mike, of course, was by her side the entire time.

She was still getting used to her short hair. It was just a little longer than a pixie cut and gave her just enough to put up in a pony tail, which was how she liked wearing it for running. But, for all the other times, it didn't go below her collar when she had it hanging down straight. While she appreciated how easy it was now to take care of, it was still quite an adjustment to make. Of course, making adjustments was something Missy did really well.

There were two other girls from Charlie Company running up here in this group. Both were obviously runners and had been on their high school track teams. They were thin, without either the muscles or all the curves that she had. Even in her black shorts, not at all form fitting, and her simple grey tee shirt, her body looked great. She had those large, solid hips, flaring out from such a narrow waist; then, her wide shoulders and prominent bustline; finally, her movements -- so fluid and graceful. She was a sight to see and few were able to just ignore her. They actually made an effort to not watch her since they didn't really want to get distracted. Not while coping with all the other challenges they faced this first week of Beast Training.

Missy ignored the effect she was having on all the guys and just focused on the pure enjoyment of running. Gradually, as the group raced up and down the hilly terrain, the two guys in her squad found themselves staying with her, one on each side. She was their squad member and somehow, that mattered. By taking these positions next to her, everyone else was forced to stay that much further away from "their girl". They also found it less distracting, having her at their side. That way, their eyes weren't constantly checking out her backside with their thoughts then focused on her lovely ass the entire time.

By the end of the run, as the three of them sprinted together for the last lap, they all somehow knew without saying anything that this was how these runs would go from now on. Tony would run on her left and Marcus would run on her right. Once they stopped and caught their breath, they introduced themselves while the rest of their group finished the run and caught up with them. They had a few minutes before needing to get back in formation and march back to the barracks.

Anthony Fugia was from New York, out on Long Island. He was Italian and looked it; dark hair, brown eyes, prominent nose and a good sturdy frame, just under six feet. Marcus Brown was black, from Philadelphia. He was an inch taller but probably weighed ten pounds less than Tony. The three of them all agreed that runs like this one would help them get through the rest of the day, which Jamieson would surely be making stressful. When Missy suggested they take turns at the dinner table, distracting Jamieson in order to each get a few more large bites of their food, that had them all laughing. They agreed to try out her plan and see how much success they'd have.

Soon, Missy was in taking a quick shower, before dressing and getting into formation for breakfast. She'd managed getting in and out of the shower a couple of times now, without anyone actually paying attention or noticing her. This time, however, another girl was in there and stopped her before she could leave.

"Hey, aren't you one of Kelly Wong's roommates? I'm Angel Meriwether, and Kelly is in my squad. She told me about you. Bodybuilder, right?"

Missy said, "Well, not exactly. I mean, I'm Missy McCrae and I'm in the same room with Kelly all right. But, I wouldn't really call myself a bodybuilder. I just work out a lot. I like to play sports and ..."

"Whoa, look at yourself, girl! You are totally ripped." Angel was a black girl about the same height as Missy but weighed only 120 pounds. She was fit and athletic but had more of a runner's body. Except for her huge boobs. Now she added, "Ripped, shredded and scarred! How'd those happen, Missy?" She had been staring, studying Missy's naked body while Missy had dried herself off.

Missy wasn't really looking to talk about her scars or any of her history during those two years she'd spent in the mountains as a cat. She hoped she could joke about it and get away quickly. "Well, my secret's one of those cases when, if I tell ya, then I gotta shoot ya, you know? Gotta go now. Don't want to be late for formation. Later, maybe?" She wrapped her robe around herself and headed back to her room.

At breakfast, she decided to be the first one to try out her distraction plan. After only a few minutes, she turned to look right at Jamieson and said, "Sir, may I ask a question?" Tony and Marcus were seated on the opposite side, so when Jamieson looked at her, right away they both managed getting larger bites onto their forks and into their mouths, unnoticed.

"New Cadet McCrae, what is your question?"

"Will there be tables in here for special diets? I heard there would be some diet tables, maybe sometime soon?" Missy gave him her most innocent expression and then, as though suddenly remembering the rules, she turned and faced straight ahead, sitting at attention with her hands in her lap.

Jamieson continued to stare at Missy, allowing her two co-conspirators time for even more large bites. "The diet tables will be for New Cadets who are overweight and need to lose some body fat. Do you think you need to lose any body fat New Cadet McCrae?"

Missy was well aware that having anyone from his squad be assigned to the diet table would make him look bad. "Sir, may I make a statement?"

"New Cadet McCrae, what is your statement?"

"I think I need to *gain* some body fat, sir. I thought perhaps there'd be diet tables for … you know …" Missy stopped and waited.

Sure enough, Jamieson quickly yelled at her. "Are you trying to be funny, New Cadet McCrae?" He began closely examining her, noticing that indeed she was a big girl. He could see her face appeared thin but he had no idea as to what the rest of her really looked like. He knew she was in running group black. He had actually been amazed at her high APFT scores, which was the only reason he wasn't thinking she might be too big.

Missy said, "No, Sir!" She somehow managed keeping a straight face but several of her squad members were now having great difficulty suppressing their laughter. Was she actually messing with Jamieson?

Jamieson decided he'd teach her a lesson. "New Cadet McCrae, I want you to report to the DPE for a body fat test this afternoon at 1600. Understood?" The DPE was the Department of Physical Education and 1600 was military time for four PM.

Missy said, "Yes, Sir!" She then continued to eat her breakfast.

Marcus decided it was his turn, so he spoke up. "Sir, may I ask a question?"

With an exasperated voice, Jamieson asked, "New Cadet Brown, what is your question?" Once Jamieson was looking at Marcus, Missy began sneaking her large bites. Today's breakfast actually included ham and she'd put several pieces on her plate which she'd already sliced into decent size bites. Now she was moving them up to her mouth, one at a time, as fast as she could.

Marcus said, "Is it true the female cadets are allowed more body fat than the male cadets? I thought there was no discrimination here. A policy for no special treatment …"

This was too much for the rest of the squad and they all broke out laughing. When they quickly tried to stop themselves, that only made it worse. Some were snorting loudly as they tried to contain their laughter. Meanwhile, Missy managed to finish everything on her plate and was now just sitting there, quietly at attention. Before Jamieson had a chance to yell at Marcus, which he clearly was planning to do, the end of meal announcement was made, followed by over a thousand chairs being moved back as everyone rose from their seats and prepared to march out, in formation.

Not wanting to have his squad get noticed or draw any more attention than what their laughter might already have done, Jamieson allowed them to form up and fall into place, and then march out along with the rest of the class. He definitely planned to yell at each and every one of them. While he was marching them out, though, the realization hit him that his squad had actually just now come together and that, after this incident, they would most likely be a real team. That bond that is always desired but not always achieved, even after weeks, had already started to form for this crazy group.

Of course, notwithstanding the pride and satisfaction that he now felt about that, he'd make certain they were all appropriately punished. Each and every one of them. Just to further strengthen that bond they were now forming.

Missy reported at 1600 hours, just as she'd been ordered to, for her BFT -- the body fat test. But, after weighing her and taking her measurements -- height, neck, chest, waist, hip -- the DPE officer wanted to confirm his results by using skin fold calipers, pinching fat areas at various places. Only, Missy had no fat areas. Her muscular definition was far beyond anything he'd ever seen. She had twelve pack abs and, in spite of all her curves, any measurements using calipers were not possible. He realized that only hydrostatic weighing would provide any accurate determination for someone like her who had obviously done some extreme bodybuilding.

She learned this procedure would be performed in the swimming pool and that she needed to bring her black Speedo swimming suit. When she returned, the DPE officer was waiting for her at the diving board, where a body harness had been attached. Once she changed into her suit and then climbed into the harness, she was instructed to blow out all the air from her lungs. They would completely submerge her under the water and take a reading. Three times. Then, they'd average these readings and compute her body fat index. Missy had been a lifeguard the previous summer and had no problem with doing all this.

Missy had maybe lost a pound or two since she'd arrived and she knew she'd not gained any fat. Even so, she had prepared for this test by calling on her cat and pushing out some energy, sending harmless pulses out where no one would notice. Doing this was just enough to drain any residual fat that wasn't essential fat. Sure enough, her BFT measurement was only eight percent. She had determined long ago that this was as low as she wanted to let herself get. Anything less would just not be healthy for her.

As it turned out, the DPE officer was very concerned. He considered this much too low for a healthy woman, even if a top athlete. He advised her to ask for additional food rations and then return in two weeks for a retest. She asked if he'd put that in a note for her squad leader and he was glad to oblige. She couldn't wait to present this note to Jamieson at dinner -- after all the hazing her squad had received from him all day long, she was quite sure this would definitely make it all worthwhile.

Not surprisingly, when she did present him with the note, which she'd managed to show each squad member beforehand, he acted very annoyed. Even though he refused to discuss it, and only barely acknowledged it, the attitude of the entire squad during that meal was clearly triumphant. Jamieson would be hearing references to the "body fat incident" for the rest of the year as word gradually spread throughout all of Charlie Company and then went out even beyond that.

He would even hear jokes being made with Missy's request to gain body fat being compared to Oliver Twist's request for a second bowl of porridge. All the rumors continued to make the story become more and more exaggerated and, with Marcus Brown's complaint about discrimination being included, there was just no way to make the story go away. Since it wasn't so much a joke at his expense but was really just highlighting the audacity of the members in his squad, he secretly was proud.

For Missy, she was happy to see how well "The Game" was going. She definitely was admired and respected by her squad members, especially Tony and Marcus. Even Tracy seemed a bit less standoffish. She really wanted to get a chance to talk to her alone but there never seemed to be any opportunity for doing that. She sensed that Jamieson was really okay with her, also. And, since he was not about to risk losing control of his squad by correcting Missy for eating too much, she benefited by that as well. She had less and less difficulty after that with sneaking her unauthorized oversize bites and in spite of always serving herself heaping amounts of food, she usually was able to finish each meal with nothing left on her plate.

Chapter Eighteen
Jul 2018

It was their first Sunday at West Point. Missy had learned all about how to be a cadet, what the Honor Code was, how things worked at West Point, how to report to officers and upperclass cadets, how to recognize ranks and insignias, how to properly wear all her various uniforms, how to "ping" everywhere she went (walk at 120 steps per minute, arms moving purposely, eyes straight ahead), how to square all her corners (abruptly change direction using 90 degree turns), and had practiced drill and ceremonies with her squad until they now all moved and marched in near perfect unison.

She no longer thought in terms of one day at a time. Now her focus was one meal at a time. There were more than enough tasks that all needed to be accomplished during each of these time periods to keep her fully occupied. So, she didn't bother to look beyond the next meal. Prioritizing things, so she could complete what really needed to be done, was very important. Her time management, of course, was always being interfered with by various upperclass cadets who constantly stopped plebes to correct them or assign them some new task.

With her enhanced senses, she could scent or hear the approach of an upperclass cadet and would always manage to present herself in perfect form, with little for them to criticize. That reduced her problems but being dressed down by those upperclass cadets could not always be avoided; often, they'd have her stand at attention anyway and get in her face, yelling about some non-existent infraction. Her response was always, "No excuse, Sir" or, when appropriate, "No excuse, Ma'am".

Without consciously doing it, she would somehow manage to always react ahead of time, trying to avoid situations and dealings with those upperclass cadets. Soon, she found her squad members paying more and more attention to her reactions. Whenever she'd snap to attention, often stopping in mid sentence to do so, they would follow her lead. When this resulted in avoiding those hated confrontations, making things go just a little bit easier for them as well, that reinforced their paying more and more attention to Missy. In addition, Missy always just seemed so competent and confident. That really influenced all her squad members.

She was genuinely interested in each of them, looking to be helpful whenever possible; she never did anything at their expense. She didn't seek credit for herself and she never made anyone else look bad. These were small, subtle things, but over the first few days of intense activities that she spent with her squad, these character traits of hers were noticed. She also was quick to stand up to anyone who either bullied or put down any member in her squad, including other squad members. She could be very intimidating at times like that and no one really wanted to mess with her.

Somehow, she and Marcus were always the ones the rest of her squad would look to. They both always seemed to be on the same page and everyone else followed their lead. Missy was also very comfortable being around guys; she had overcome all of her shyness for a couple of years now and instead, she could be very relaxed in their midst, joking and bantering. The three years of sparring with guys at her martial arts club had enabled her to feel at ease and fit in with guys, without any sexual hang-ups. Her attitude in turn made it easy for them to accept her.

Tracy was really the only one she wasn't able to be relaxed with. Tracy also did have some sexual hang-ups and wasn't that comfortable with the guys. This only further alienated her from Missy, who was fitting in so well with everyone. While Tracy was clearly a good squad member and was more knowledgeable about military things than anyone else, it was obvious she really wasn't that comfortable yet at West Point. And, she still kept her distance and was standoffish with Missy, in spite of being her roommate.

Her other roommate, Kelly, seemed to be getting along well enough with her own squad and had really bonded with Angel. Since Angel wasn't too happy with her two roommates, she was always visiting Kelly back in their room whenever possible. Angel's roommates were paired together in a different squad so, in addition to Angel being black while they were white, Angel was the odd girl out. She had a really bawdy sense of humor which both Missy and Kelly really liked. Tracy was friendly enough but didn't seem to enjoy Angel's humor quite as much.

The four of them were taking advantage of actually being free for the first time since R-Day and had all been relaxing in Missy's room. Since it was the easiest, most comfortable clothing to be wearing, they all were in their PT uniforms -- shorts and tee shirts. Missy was sitting on her upper bunk while Angel was telling them a story about the bus ride home from an away game at her high school.

She and several cheerleaders had gone with the football team and had celebrated the big win by drinking beer and raising hell in the back of the bus. The coach had turned a blind eye to this and was known to be rather permissive as long as "the kids" didn't get too out of hand. After an hour of everyone drinking, one of the guys had insisted that all the girls put on a "Girls Gone Wild" show for them, exposing and shaking their breasts. Angel had countered by saying they'd only perform any shows like that after the guys had first dropped their trousers, exposing their rear ends.

Angel had figured that would stop things and also put the guys in their place. Instead, she and her friends were suddenly confronted with half a dozen bare asses shaking back and forth in front of them. "You never saw guys move as fast as they did that night, all racing to drop their pants and bend over for us once I said that," she explained, laughing.

Kelly asked, "You didn't really put on a show for them, though, did you? I mean … you know …"

233

Angel laughed even harder. "Of course we did, girl! What the hell, my tits are my best feature. Why not have some fun with them? No one did anything besides look. There wasn't any touching or anything. Not that I'd have minded all that much. I mean ... don't you just love it when a guy plays with your nipples?"

Kelly laughed and said, "Now you're opening up a very interesting topic of conversation, Angel. My nipples are aching right now, just thinking about this." She looked around at Missy and Tracy. "You girls willing to share stuff like that? You know ... sex stuff? I mean, if you're not comfortable with this, Angel and I can do this another time."

Missy could sense that Tracy was actually *very* uncomfortable. Rather than have her be embarrassed, she said, "As much as my nipples love being played with, I've explained to each one of them they'll just have to wait until Mike gets here in seven weeks. They told me that I'd better cool it until then, so they don't get in the way while I'm trying to get through Beast Training."

Kelly laughed and said, "Fair enough, Missy. We'll change the subject. We don't want your nipples to suddenly go crazy or anything, right? Angel, distract me ... what else can we talk about?"

Angel said, "We can ask Missy to tell us about that scar on her thigh. I'm pretty sure that was from a bullet, right? Or, do ya really have ta kill me if ya tell me?" She laughed and glanced at the other girls, who obviously were not aware Missy had any scars. "What? Haven't you girls seen all her scars?"

Missy laughed and rolled up her shorts to expose the one scar on her leg, a straight gouge about six inches long. "I suppose I can *show* you, without having to actually *kill* you. This really was just an accident that happened five years ago. But, I really don't want to talk about it."

Kelly and Tracy both came up and studied her scar, which neither had noticed before. Then Kelly asked, "What did you mean when you said "all her scars", Angel? Does she have more anywhere else?" Looking at Missy, she said, "Show me, show me!" Then she actually began hopping up and down, making fun like a little kid.

Missy laughed and said, "Okay, okay, but this is *not* show and tell. This is show and no telling." She hopped down from her bunk and peeled off her tee shirt. With only her bra on her upper body, all the scars on her shoulder and back were very visible.

Kelly exclaimed, "Holy shit! Those are some seriously scary scars, Missy!"

Tracy was also looking and added her thoughts by saying, "I don't think those had any stitches, did they?" She stared at Missy with a very intense expression, showing both wonder and concern. "When did that happen? You can't just say you're not telling."

For some reason, Tracy's reaction was getting to her and Missy was no longer able to lightly pass the whole thing off the way she had intended. Instead, she said, "Look, if I tell you girls, I don't want you talking about me to anyone else. Okay? I mean, it's really no big deal but I'm already hearing people talk about me after that body fat incident the other day. Please don't feed me to the upperclass cadets. I don't need that."

After all three girls promised they'd keep her secrets, Missy said, "This also happened five years ago. I was mauled by a black bear. I was up in the mountains when it happened. You'll probably find all this out about me later on anyway. I mean, it's on the internet if you Google my name. I disappeared five years ago from soccer camp in New Hampshire."

Tracy asked, "You disappeared? And, your story was in the papers? And, on the internet?"

"Yes, but I didn't explain about things when I came back, so you won't find out much. I mean, I came back. I lived up in the mountains and then came back. End of story." Missy was already feeling she'd opened up about all this way too much.

"Missy, come on … you can't just leave it at that. You haven't even explained about the bear. Why didn't you get any stitches? How long were you gone, anyway?" Tracy was finally showing some actual interest and was no longer being standoffish.

With a long sigh, Missy said, "Two years. I was gone for just over two years. That much is in those stories about me. Oh, and I may as well explain something else. I heal really, really fast. Hopefully, nothing will happen here but, if it does? You'll have my back, right? If I need you?"

Kelly and Angel both said, "Two years?" Then Angel added, "Fuuuuuck!"

Tracy asked, "What do you mean have your back? How would you need us to have your back?"

"Well, if I get injured or anything. I won't be going on any sick call. I'll just heal myself." Missy realized she really wasn't explaining things very well. But, she wanted to move on from her being gone for two years in the mountains. "Last summer, I broke my leg. I fractured my tibia and I broke my fibula, right here." She pointed to her left leg and showed them the areas. "They had to set my fibula. They wanted to put a cast on but I didn't let them. And then? I healed it up completely in four days."

This was met with silence for several moments. Angel finally said, "Fuuuuuck!" which make everyone laugh.

The girls tried to get Missy to talk more but she told them she'd said enough and reminded them not to talk about any of this. A little while later, Angel decided to go back to her own room and Kelly agreed to go with her. They thought Angel's two roommates would be gone and they'd be able to relax there, just the two of them.

Missy looked at Tracy and decided to push, now that she sensed an opening. "Hey, are we good now?"

Tracy said, "Sure, Missy. What do you mean, anyway?"

"I know you're bothered about something, Tracy. I just don't know what." Missy studied her. "I really want us to be friends but … well …" Missy stopped because she could see that Tracy wanted to say something.

"I know that you're a supernatural, Missy. I noticed that right away. At first, I thought maybe you were a witch, especially when you said you were from Salem and everything. I guess you've just admitted that, right? That you're a supernatural? Only, I don't know what kind. You're quite different from any of the other witches …" Tracy suddenly stopped herself, obviously flustered.

Missy stared at her and then smiled. "I'm different from any of the other witches?" She quickly made the connections. Tracy's scent was "other" and Tracy had recognized Missy was a supernatural. Didn't Robert tell her that "P" Branch had used a witch to help identify many of the supernaturals all around the world for their database? "Relax, Tracy. I promise your secret is safe with me. I'll never tell anyone about you being a witch. I actually have never met a witch before. You're my first one!"

Tracy looked visibly relieved. Then she asked, "What about you, Missy? If you're not a witch … what *are* you?"

Missy laughed. "Are you sure you really want to know? Or, is it enough for you to just know I'm enhanced? And, can heal rapidly?" She now let her cat energy come flooding in, surging everywhere inside her body and making her eyes sparkle, glowing from green to gold to green. Then, she pushed out a small energy pulse, just enough for Tracy to experience some of her energy.

Tracy was really shocked for a moment. Then she laughed and -- mimicking Angel's voice -- she said, "Fuuuuuuck!"

Missy began to laugh with her, and it felt really good. She and Tracy were going to be good friends now; she felt sure of that. "I'm just your normal, everyday werecat, Tracy. Now, you'll have to tell me all about you being a witch."

Tracy McGonagle was a witch because her mother was a witch. Her Mom had fallen in love with her Dad while visiting her college roommate over the summer; while there, she'd found herself next door to this handsome guy from West Point. He was home for a few weeks that summer and then was going back for one more year. The chemistry between them was so strong that by the time he needed to leave, she was completely and totally smitten. She'd then told him how she was a witch, but was willing to leave her coven and follow after him, if he was willing to accept her.

He was equally into her and they made love the night before he went back. It was her first time having sex and after that night, she never looked back. She dropped out of college and followed him, getting a job and living in a small apartment just outside West Point.

He managed to see her several times during his last year and right after he graduated, they were married in the chapel at West Point.

For years, she'd gone with him when he'd had assignments that allowed families to come along. Then, when he'd had unaccompanied tours overseas, she'd lived on various Army bases in the States. Tracy was their only child. Tracy's Mom was very content with the life they'd had. She'd never been concerned about having to leave her coven and no longer participating with other witches. She'd been happy enough just being a "latent witch" who wasn't practicing any of her spells or using any of her powers.

That all had changed when Tracy hit puberty and it suddenly had become obvious that she indeed was also a witch. Heredity had gifted her with powers and abilities that required some very strong guidance. For whatever reason, Tracy was a strong witch, much stronger than her Mom. It was very clear that being a "latent witch" was not really an option for Tracy. Her Mom then located and joined a coven in the Dallas area and brought Tracy in for the help she needed.

Tracy was actually quite happy to meet other supernaturals and became really close to one witch in particular who became her mentor. Her high school years were normal enough and she enjoyed athletic activities but never went out for any varsity teams. She was busy with her studies in school but was also learning all about her legacy, being a witch, by spending lots of time with her mentor and the other witches in the coven.

The one area of her development that she really was not very experienced in was dating.

She was definitely interested in boys and there were several who had wanted to date her. She went on a few dates and attended both her junior and senior proms. But, she was not comfortable with going beyond mild petting and the guys she'd dated all broke up with her, calling her a prude. One exasperated date had accused her of being frigid. The truth was, she'd had such a beautiful example of what true love might be like, because of her own parents, that she'd just really wanted to someday have that. Plus, she was not about to explain to any of the guys she knew that she was a witch.

Then, there was the whole West Point thing. Her Dad and his Dad had both graduated from there and it was somehow part of that beautiful love story that she was hoping might somehow happen for her as well. Things just seemed to come easy for her and without ever really considering anything else, she was accepted to West Point. After that, she really got excited and focused all her energy towards getting ready and preparing herself for her first year as a plebe.

R-Day had been really exciting for Tracy and, as Missy had experienced, that first day went by in a blur. Then, when Missy came into their room that night, she felt the incredible energy that Missy was bringing in with her and she just knew. Missy was a supernatural. When she heard her mention being from Salem, where one of the strongest covens in the US was located, she figured that had to be it. Her roommate was a powerful witch.

What did this mean for all the hopes, dreams and aspirations that Tracy had for her life? What had those fickle Fates done to her, with Missy actually being assigned to the very same squad that she was?

Now, suddenly she was seeing things in a whole new way. Missy was a werecat? Maybe, just maybe, those Fates knew what they were doing. Maybe, having Missy be in her squad and be her roommate was really meant to be. Rather than being a risk or anything bad, this was a wonderful blessing. They could help one another. So far, everything she'd seen from Missy had been very positive. And, that energy bolt. Wow! She thought only witches could throw energy bolts. Of course, she really had no idea at all about werecats. She was now rather looking forward to finding out all about them. And, to maybe finding a true friend, right here at West Point.

Chapter Nineteen
Jul 2018

It was 1600 hours and, once again, time for mass athletics. Missy loved this period even more than PT in the mornings. Every day, there were sports activities for her to participate in and for an hour and a half, she could go all out. She'd already tried out for soccer, lacrosse and judo and had impressed everyone so much that each of these clubs now wanted her. Of these, only soccer was available as a varsity sport for women, so she figured that's what she'd probably end up doing in the fall season.

For now, it was fun to try out every day for various activities. Some of them provided an opportunity to compete against the upperclass cadets, turning the tables on the squad leaders. It was especially nice to kick the butts of those leaders who were constantly hazing plebes all of the other times. Unfortunately, they wouldn't let her do any boxing against any of the men. She'd have liked going up against Jamieson. But, she was able to watch Tony Fugia actually get to do that, while she and Marcus cheered him on.

Today she asked if they'd let her put on an exhibition, highlighting some of her karate skills. This was initially met with both cheers and jeers, but once they finally did let her get out there and she began putting on her show, a large group quickly gathered around. She knew exhibitions weren't really what the mass athletics program was designed for but, when her request for a "one time thing" got approved, she took full advantage. She'd been very persuasive. And, after all, she did have her third degree black belt and was pretty sure there'd be a lot of interest.

Missy was fun to watch and she knew just how to please the crowd. About twenty minutes into her demonstration, she invited any of the audience members who might have some karate experience to join her. This was merely an exhibition, with no sparring or contact. And, there were some guys out there who knew a few things; they were all quick to volunteer.

Missy had always made a point of not damaging what she considered to be the very fragile egos which most guys had, especially concerning any physical prowess competitions. So, as each guy came forward, she managed to choreograph an entertaining display that somehow made each of them look pretty good. She knew how to move in ways that suggested she was barely able to escape at the last minute from some skillful attack from her male opponent and, surely had this been for real, that guy would have indeed kicked her ass. Some of her movements drew laughter, at the way she danced and cavorted out there. There were very few who truly recognized what she was doing, how she was manipulating things and how incredibly skilled she herself really was.

Tracy knew, though. Missy was constantly surprising her and they had been getting along really well since sharing their secrets on Sunday. Most of their squad were gathered around now, all watching Missy. They'd sort of gotten used to keeping an eye on her at these mass athletics sessions, waiting to see what she'd do next. She and Marcus had clearly been stepping up as their leaders, but they both were always encouraging everyone else to strive harder also. They made sure that everyone's input was included before any decisions affecting the squad were made. Even Gary Sabre was now showing a lot more confidence in himself.

Gary was their one member running in the white group and, at first, he was even having trouble keeping up with that group. Lagging any further behind was not an option, though, and he had really made an effort to avoid that. He was a bit of a nerd and was not in very good shape. He had a brilliant mind but had never really been athletic. In the beginning, he was even a little pudgy. Then, Missy started helping him.

She had noticed him and had decided to see what she could do. When she had first approached him at PT, he clearly was very much in awe of her. He did not consider himself very attractive to women and was usually very timid with girls. He was not unattractive, but not being athletic and being somewhat soft and pudgy, he had no confidence in himself. With Missy, he was unable to think straight. She was an inch taller than he was and clearly in top physical condition while he was just a wimp. The fact that she was also such a beautiful girl was way too much. He wouldn't even look at her but kept his eyes cast downward instead.

Missy had explained that he needed to work his way out of the slow group and had told him she'd be helping. Then, she'd asked him to look into her eyes. The first time she'd said that, he'd ignored her and kept his eyes downcast. But, then she'd insisted so he'd finally looked up. He'd watched as her eyes began to change, with lots of yellow and gold speckles appearing. She'd said that his goal for that day was to stay ahead of at least five others. Do that, and things would improve. Then, she'd walked away. During that day's run, he somehow had managed staying ahead of at least six others and by the end of the run he was feeling rather proud of himself.

Missy had then come up again each day and always had him stare into her eyes. He'd gotten used to doing that, no longer feeling self conscious about it, since she'd really seemed so nice and was so easy to be with. Her eyes were incredible. But, it was her encouragement that had mattered more. She'd insisted he stay ahead of at least ten others the second time. Then, it was fifteen. Then, twenty. Two days earlier, he'd been up with the leaders the whole run. In another day or so, he knew he could be retested and would qualify to advance to the gold group. His whole squad had started paying attention to his progress every day and their encouragement had really helped. He had even lost that pudgy look as his level of fitness steadily improved. All of a sudden, he just felt so much better about himself and was excited at the way his squad was behind him and pulling for him. Not a single person was criticizing him. Even Jamieson was no longer yelling at him.

Missy had actually been doing even more, which only Tracy was aware of. Each day, while Gary was staring into her eyes, she'd been pushing some of her energy into him. He couldn't feel that, since it wasn't a pressure pulse or anything he could feel. Instead, this was more like the healing energy she'd pushed into Mike's sister, Michelle. Tracy had only noticed her doing this the day before but, being able to sense Missy's energy with her abilities as a witch, she immediately had recognized what Missy was doing. And, she then knew that Missy must have been doing this right along which helped explain Gary's very significant progress and improved fitness.

When Tracy had asked Missy about it that night, while Kelly was out of the room, Missy had said, "Sure, I've been giving Gary a little push and feeding him a little extra. Isn't he doing great? We need every member of our squad to be giving one hundred percent, right? So we can win top squad later on? Gary seemed a few percent short of that, so I figured I'd give him a boost. He probably won't even need my help much longer. Haven't you noticed how much stronger he seems now? A lot of it's just the mental attitude and Gary's now really getting with the program."

Today, Tracy watched as Missy concluded her karate exhibition and insisted on having each of the guys who had joined her go back and take a bow. The bantering back and forth was really entertaining and Tracy once again marveled at how Missy seemed to make things happen with no apparent effort.

Earlier that day they'd been learning first aid. When their class instructor had asked if anyone out there had any prior experience, of course Missy's hand had gone up. Her squad was used to this now. Did being a certified life guard count? Oh, yes, indeed that was excellent experience. Could Missy come forward? Be an assistant that day, helping the instructor demonstrate various key things? Sure. While the instructor was clearly the one up there teaching, once again it was Missy participating in a way that not only demonstrated how proficient she was, but was somehow making things look simple and easy for others to learn. Instead of this being a boring class, which many might not have benefited from, it suddenly became an interesting class. Everyone paid attention and ended up learning something.

It wasn't just Missy, though. Each day, their squad found more and more reasons to be proud of itself as a unit and proud of each of their squad members as individuals. Inspired by what Missy and Marcus were doing, everyone else began contributing more and more. They also were getting bolder and bolder, giving poor Jamieson more and more nonsense to deal with. It had reached the point where he absolutely refused to allow anyone to speak a single word during meals. Too many times it had been obvious that someone was messing with him.

He had indeed lost control of them ever since that "body mass incident" with Missy the first week and now he'd found it far easier to get through the meals by pretty much ignoring them. He pretended not to notice all the unauthorized big bites. To their credit, they were now very skilled at how they would sneak their food. No blatant behavior but they were getting to eat all the food they wanted at each meal, no problem. On the positive side, it was becoming very obvious that his squad was definitely one of the top squads in the whole company. Since that made him look good, he really didn't mind. All part of "The Game", as Missy had described it to everyone else in the squad.

That night, when they once again finally had a few minutes of free time, Angel came in and the four girls all relaxed while they talked about the day's activities. This had become routine now. The squad that Angel and Kelly were in was also gaining a reputation as one of the stronger squads. More and more, the guys from both squads were dropping by to check with the girls about one thing or another, often standing in the hallway since there wasn't enough room for everyone to crowd inside.

Then, as it became more and more common for Angel to make one of her naughty comments, the comic relief that provided became an even bigger draw for them to stop by. She had such an easy going manner, always very open and in your face, which she combined with a blatant sexuality that was impossible to resist. She wasn't really inviting any sexual advances but somehow managed to always get the guys stirred up. No matter how outrageous her suggestive remarks would get or how deliciously sinful she'd hint that her behavior could be, she was never coming on to any of them. They were *not* being invited to join in or participate in such awful behavior.

Tonight, when Marcus had started to make a comment about something, she'd actually outdone herself. He had only gotten as far as saying, "You wouldn't want me to be indecent ..." when Angel had interrupted him.

She'd said, "Oh, but I actually insist that *all* my men be indecent." She'd paused and looked around, making sure everyone was listening and that no upperclass cadets were nearby. "When they're long enough, hard enough and in far enough, that's when they're *in decent*." Marcus never did get to finish whatever he had intended saying, due to all the raucous laughter.

A few guys had stopped by after that, but the girls had bantered with them and then chased them off, finally leaving their door closed for a bit of privacy. Kelly decided to bring up a subject she'd been curious about for awhile now. "Tracy, I know Missy has this incredible boyfriend back home. She even claims she can sense him back there, using some of her woo-woo powers. Of course, Angel and I recognize the so called bond she's bragging about is really just Missy's huge radius of lust, keeping her on that perpetual edge. But, what about you? You haven't told us about any of your boyfriends. Time to share, Tracy."

Missy jumped in first and said, "Whoa! Not fair, Kelly, you first! Leave Tracy alone. You and Angel are clearly the ones with some tales to tell when it comes to boyfriends."

Angel laughed and said, "Yes, but you already know we're just a couple of slutty whores so our stories don't count. We want to hear about all the guys Tracy's been banging. Those stories will be much more interesting."

Kelly said, "Very funny, Angel. You're always kidding and I never know when you're serious. But, yeah … I admit that I've slept around. So what? I really like having sex. And, guys like having sex with me. Of course, I'd never consider marrying any of those guys. But Tracy? We all know you're not one to bang a lot of guys. You probably only did it with one or two special guys, right?"

Missy once again tried to come to Tracy's rescue. "I don't think you should be putting anyone on the spot, Kelly. Tracy might not really be comfortable …"

Tracy interrupted and blurted out a quick statement. "I'm a virgin. There haven't been any guys. Okay?"

There was a long pause, and then finally Kelly spoke up. "Oh! Okay. I'm sorry if I've made you feel bad. I really didn't mean to, Tracy. Honest. I … we … umm …"

"It's okay, Kelly. Really, don't worry." Tracy looked at each of them. "There just hasn't been anyone that I'd … you know. I'm sure my guy is out there, somewhere. In a way, it's easier for me right now. I'm not really missing anyone."

Missy said, "Hey, it's late. Let's all go to bed. And, trust me girls. After the day I've had, Mike could be standing outside that door and I still wouldn't care. Absolutely no being on any edge tonight. Nope, not me!" Everyone laughed, as Missy had hoped, and then Angel left and they all climbed into bed. Kelly turned out the light and, a little later, Missy knew she'd fallen asleep.

Missy knew Tracy was awake, though, and she remained awake herself for a long time afterwards. *Mike, I really miss you!* Then, as she sensed an emotional response coming back from him, thanks to her wonderful bond with him, she did drift off to sleep. She'd definitely been on edge, though. Her nipples had been aching and her clit had been throbbing. A little more than four weeks yet to go -- she couldn't wait.

Chapter Twenty
Jul 2018

Missy and her squad had learned Close Quarters Combativeness. They'd all had some Bayonet Training. They'd done road marches carrying full packs and their weapon. They'd learned lots and lots about their weapon. How to strip it down, clean it and reassemble it. Soon, they'd get to learn how to actually fire their weapon which she was looking forward to. She had never fired either a pistol or a rifle.

They'd all learned about Nuclear, Biological and Chemical matters. Very scary stuff. If they ever really needed to do any fighting while wearing all the Army's protective gear to avoid being exposed to any of those, it would be extremely difficult. Just wearing a gas mask was a challenge. They were all actually tested in a gas chamber, filled with tear gas.

First, they'd entered wearing the mask. That was to give them some confidence about how good the protection was. To reinforce that, so they'd experience what tear gas was like *without* the mask, they'd been required to remove the mask and recite a few things. Then, they'd been allowed to walk, not run, to the exit. Even though they'd all taken a deep breath and held it, prior to unmasking, this exercise was designed to be very unpleasant. And, it was. Tear gas, of course, wouldn't kill them. But, a lot of the stuff they might someday have to deal with on the battlefield could be very, very lethal. And, they'd die a slow and agonizing death from that stuff as well. Ugh!

On the fun side, Missy had gone back for her body fat test once the two weeks had passed. Although she'd managed to eat a lot of food, the content wasn't as high in lean protean as her werecat body really needed. So, her total weight was down. And, since there were a lot of carbs and fat in the food she was eating, no surprise, her body fat percentage had increased. So, she now weighed 144 pounds and her body fat was ten percent. Her DPE officer still thought that was low but congratulated her on making progress. He wanted her to again be checked after two more weeks.

At dinner that night, she'd given Jamieson the note she'd received but she didn't say anything about it. No one had said anything but every single squad member somehow had found a way to display the number "ten" during that meal.

Jamieson knew he was actually going to miss this squad. At the end of the fourth week, all the leadership positions would change. Some other poor upperclass cadet would then have to deal with this crazy bunch. But, he felt pretty good about turning over a squad that had demonstrated itself as the best in the company and, possibly, might just be the best in the whole regiment.

There had been Warrior Competitions out in the field where squads climbed over logs and various obstacles, navigated from place to place, performed runs and demonstrated their teamwork. Jamieson's squad had really bonded with one another and almost seemed to enjoy these tasks. Their enthusiasm never lagged, no matter how difficult and frustrating the circumstances. They had consistently been in first place. Jamieson was positive this squad would do very well for the final challenge exercise out at Camp Buckner during the last week of Beast Training.

Missy had grown very close to Tracy and, while not sharing any info about either her "P" Branch friends or any of the difficulties she'd had with mobsters, she'd been able to explain a lot of what it meant to be a werecat. She'd explained all about her enhanced senses, her super strength, her energy and her rapid healing. She'd even talked about her mysterious bond with Mike. At first, she hadn't mentioned how she had helped Mike's sister Michelle but Tracy had already seen how she'd helped Gary, which was merely a scaled back example of how she could push her energy into others.

She'd told Tracy how she had melded her two natures into one and now felt really complete and balanced. She'd explained how much easier all the physical demands were at Beast Training compared to how hard she'd been driving herself during the past three years. She'd discussed how her body *needed* to train hard. And, how so far, she was thoroughly enjoying every bit of this West Point experience. For her, "The Game" was all just great fun. She also wanted to help Tracy, Kelly and Angel, all the guys in her squad and several other new cadets she'd gotten to know.

After hearing all this, Tracy then finally opened up about being a witch. She'd been very reluctant, at first, but after Missy openly shared so much with her, earning her trust, she began to share as well. Real witches did not openly admit to the rest of the world that they were witches. Too often, over the centuries, that had turned out badly. Even though none of the witches convicted in Salem back in 1692-1693 were real witches, those trials and executions clearly illustrated how hostile and prejudiced many people could be, and those same sentiments still existed today. There weren't really that many true witches and they were careful to keep their covens very secret.

Tracy explained there were twelve covens in the US, located near major cities. Salem was of course near Boston. Her coven was near Dallas. Others were near New York City, Atlanta, Miami, San Francisco, Chicago, Washington D.C., New Orleans, Seattle, St. Louis and Las Vegas. There were at least three witches in a coven and never more than thirteen. There were just over a hundred witches now actively participating in these covens. And, there were several more latent witches, of course, who were not participating.

Witches were male and female. Male witches were witches. Not warlocks and not wizards. Witches. Although there currently seemed to be a higher percentage of female witches -- the ratio was maybe sixty-forty -- that wasn't always the case.

As far as what powers and abilities these real witches possessed, Tracy explained it varied, from witch to witch, but was always about energy. Telekinesis, where objects were moved, was a well known power. Being able to use fire or light, creating it and throwing it, was also fairly well known. Many witches could use energy to camouflage themselves or others, by hiding, cloaking or blurring. What else? Sensing and finding others, sometimes called scrying. Controlling the weather. Creating illusions that altered what others might perceive. Binding others. There even were defensive abilities including deflecting the powers of other witches.

Even though Missy was a werecat, Tracy told her that she might also be a witch. She seemed to be doing more than just shapeshifting. What witch abilities did Missy have? Sending out energy bolts in waves or pulses, sometimes in blasts were definitely what real witches might do. And, there was regeneration, healing herself, which Missy had admitted she could do. Tracy wondered -- could Missy also heal others? She suspected this might be possible, based on what Missy had done for Gary. When Missy confirmed it, telling her about Michelle, Tracy was convinced. Missy was also a witch.

As Missy considered all this, she suspected that Tracy might be right. The surprised reaction she'd gotten from Carlos to her energy pulse certainly had suggested he wasn't familiar with that. And, Robert had likewise been surprised when she'd done that to him. Also, he'd told her she was the only werecat that "P" Branch knew about who could heal the way she did. And, for witches, being a witch was passed down from one family to the next. While it might not manifest in every generation, it definitely was genetic. Since Missy already believed she was somehow a genetic anomaly, this certainly seemed possible. It was all in her genes.

What could Tracy do? While she couldn't do any of the things that Missy could do, Tracy could harness and use fire and light. And, she could control the weather. Was she powerful? Well, she could conjure up a severe storm, even on an otherwise clear day, and send down lightning bolts. She could direct those onto targets with great accuracy. She'd only practiced doing this on trees and old car wrecks, but from what the others in her coven were saying, she apparently was quite gifted.

How had Tracy's powers first manifested themselves? Fortunately, her Mom had been tuning in very closely, as Tracy had approached puberty, and she'd still been enough of a witch herself to recognize her daughter was definitely a supernatural. So, Tracy had learned from her Mom about witches and that, indeed, she was likely to have certain powers. With her Mom's help, she'd tested herself, always in private. First, it had been light. Then, fire. While none of the other abilities seemed that apparent, she definitely was able to create and use these. As her powers in these began growing, year after year, her Mom brought her to the Dallas area coven for help and training.

Within two years, Tracy was conjuring up thunderstorms and sending down lightning bolts. That had been at age sixteen. Her powers were continuing to get stronger every year. She'd learned how to control her powers and how to keep them well hidden. Being exposed as a witch and then maybe seeing an end to all her West Point dreams had been her biggest concern. She believed it was her destiny to graduate from West Point and that, by doing so, she would then find her greatest happiness and fulfillment.

By pairing now with Missy, Tracy could see her goal being that much more attainable. And, as her confidence increased, she became a lot more comfortable with everyone in her squad. Including all the men. While not yet enjoying everything as thoroughly as Missy was, Tracy really began to fit in and make her own contributions. As the others realized just how knowledgeable she was about the military, she became a more and more valued member of the squad. She was especially knowledgeable about the Honor Code and able to help clarify things whenever any questions came up on that. By the end of those first four weeks, she was included with Missy, Marcus and Tony as one of their key leaders in the squad.

Then, Jamieson moved on and all the upperclass cadet positions changed. Maureen Winslow, a female cadet, was the new commander for Company C. This, however, did not sit that well with the new second platoon leader, Ronald Quigby. Quigby tolerated women at West Point, since he didn't have much choice in that, but he definitely believed men were far superior. This was the first time he was actually forced to report to any female cadet and, even though it was only for the next few weeks, he was not happy about that. Martin King, who replaced Jamieson as squad leader, not only was a close friend of Quigby's but also shared the same low opinion about women at West Point.

Quigby and King considered it their duty to force out those female New Cadets whom they did not consider worthy of being there. They'd heard about New Cadet McCrae and that body fat nonsense and had decided they'd be making an example in her squad. Jamieson had obviously been pussy whipped and that wasn't going to happen once they took charge. Jamieson had lucked out by having his squad somehow perform so well, which was how he'd probably avoided being written up as a poor leader. Since almost every squad had two females, the performance by Jamieson's squad wasn't all that impressive. They were certain that his squad's performance had been in spite of, rather than because of, any contributions from either of its two girls.

Right from the start, King had been very quick to criticize each squad member, correcting anyone who was not following all the required eating procedures. There would be no unauthorized big bites, which he'd learned this squad had been getting away with. He paid particular attention to New Cadet McCrae. He noted that she actually would move her eyes the least of anyone. He was suspicious about her. He had been surprised to see her APFT score for pushups and sit-ups. Some girls could run fast, having less weight to carry and excellent lower body strength in their legs to do that.

But, she'd scored 50 pushups and 100 sit-ups. He decided to challenge her on that a couple minutes into Monday's lunch. "New Cadet McCrae, is it correct that you scored 50 pushups and 100 sit-ups on your initial APFT?" He also wanted to interrupt her meal, just by forcing her to talk rather than eat.

Missy stopped and, without moving her eyes, she answered, "Yes, Sir." Then, without moving a muscle, she waited. She could sense this Cadet King was trouble.

King said, "Why those *exact* numbers, 50 and 100? Those almost seem as though you selected those numbers and paced yourself. Did you do that, New Cadet McCrae?"

Missy answered, "Yes, Sir!"

"Well, what is your intent when you take this APFT again later this week? Do you intend to pace yourself and repeat those exact same numbers again?" King was actually surprised to hear her admit to pacing herself.

Missy said, "Yes, Sir!"

King pounced on that answer and said, "So, you have no intention of improving those scores, is that right New Cadet McCrae?" He noticed that everyone else at the table was obviously growing uncomfortable with all this. Good.

Missy said, "No, Sir."

"Well, why not, New Cadet McCrae? Aren't you capable of better scores than that?" King wanted to rattle her but, so far, she'd been sitting there like a rock, not moving and not looking at him.

Missy asked, "Sir, may I make a statement?" She wanted to avoid answering his questions without first using the specified responses required for a New Cadet being corrected. She knew he was baiting her.

"New Cadet McCrae, what is your statement?"

Missy said, "My APFT scores are acceptable, more than twice the minimum even for males, and there is no requirement for me or benefit for my squad to my achieving any higher scores. In spite of my loss of muscle mass since that first week, I hope to again achieve those same scores." She knew he was harassing her because of that body fat incident. Now, her squad members were smiling at her. She was messing with King, just as she'd done with Jamieson.

King was not happy with her response or her attitude. Quigby had shown him those notes from the DPE concerning her and he knew she'd gained two percent body fat. She appeared to be a big girl and he'd assumed she had to have *gained* weight, getting fat on all the food Jamieson had allowed her to eat. But, if she was claiming to have *lost* weight, he so wasn't going there. He could easily check this information and, if indeed she'd gained any weight, he'd be all over her about it. He decided to try a different approach.

"Well, you obviously are sliding backwards rather than making any progress and that's not very helpful for your squad. What training will you be getting this afternoon?"

Missy said, "Rifle marksmanship, Sir."

"And, will you be helping your squad in marksmanship, New Cadet McCrae?

"Yes, sir!" said Missy. She still hadn't eaten a single bite since he'd started asking her questions. And, since yesterday had been day twenty eight since her last Change, she had gotten her period, right on schedule. Perfect timing. She was really not in any mood today for all this bullshit.

"Have you ever fired any weapons, New Cadet McCrae?" King was fishing now, but he knew his questions were keeping her from eating.

Missy said, "No, sir."

"Well, how exactly will you be helping your squad, then, New Cadet McCrae?" King was thrilled to discover this. She'd probably be dragging down the squad average scores quite a bit, just starting out.

"By achieving the highest scores in the Company, Sir." Missy was willing to pick up the gauntlet which he'd just thrown down in front of her. Her squad members were definitely reacting to this; she was totally messing with King now.

King did not appreciate her attitude one bit and did not like the way all her squad members seemed to

263

be supporting her. But, had she just dug herself into a hole she couldn't possibly climb out of? She'd said highest in the Company. "Why not try for best in the Regiment, New Cadet McCrae?" That was putting her in her place.

"Yes, sir! By achieving the highest scores in the entire Regiment, Sir. I will be top shot. Sir." Missy was now slapping him with that gauntlet and was going way, way out there on a limb that might be a bit too far, even for her. Oh, well! All part of "The Game", right?

The end of meal announcement was made, which ended any further questions from King but also ended any further eating. Missy was leaving the table hungry this time. Somehow, she didn't think this little pissing contest would end well, no matter what she did. But, regardless, word of her claim to become top shot would now quickly get all around, both to her classmates and to all the upperclass cadets as well. Even the tactical officers, or TAC officers as they were called at the academy, would all be hearing about the brash and bold manner that she'd responded to King with.

Cadet Quigby pulled Cadet King aside, asking him to stay for a minute. He'd just finished a short meeting with his squad leaders; they both waited until the others were gone. Then he asked, "What's this I'm hearing about New Cadet McCrea in your squad? Did you actually get her to say she'd be top shot?"

264

King proudly answered, "Yeah, I sure did. That was after I tried to rattle her about not making any effort to help her squad. At first, she was giving me attitude. She even brought up how she's losing muscle mass, which is supposed to be her excuse for why her APFT scores won't be improving."

"But, she's the one who tricked Jamieson into getting her body fat tested ... didn't she *gain* body fat when they tested her a week ago?" This was why Quigby had suggested that King start in on her in the first place.

"Oh, she gained body fat all right, but it turns out she's some kind of muscle freak. Here, look at this photo. I found this on the internet, along with a lot of interesting stuff about her." King showed Quigby the photo of Missy, looking fierce in her most intimidating pose, right after she'd won the amateur trophy at the mixed martial arts Expo.

Quigby said, "Holy shit! That's her? Wow. When was this taken?"

King explained, "Two years ago. She's playing us, Ronald. This bitch came here four weeks ago weighing 150 pounds but obviously in very similar shape to that photo. Not an ounce of fat anywhere, except maybe for those nice boobs of hers. And, I checked. Now she's *lost* weight in spite of increasing her body fat. I almost fell for her bullshit, too. When she mentioned losing muscle mass as being why her pushup scores wouldn't increase, I was this close to calling her out on that. But, I could see by the looks I was getting from her squad members ... that was going down the rabbit hole. You know?"

"Good job, then. So, you changed the subject to marksmanship. And, she's saying she'll get top shot? Do those internet stories talk about her being an expert, in addition to being this ... what? ... freaky fighter chick?" Quigby began studying the photo, examining it very closely. "Hey, did you notice these scars? Are those real or just some makeup for her act?"

King said, "She claims she's never fired any weapon. Those stories don't say anything about her doing that, either way. Or, about her having those scars. I don't think that really matters, anyway. When I asked how she expected to be any help to her squad, she gave me this crap about maybe getting high scores in her Company. I then pushed her and she announced she'd be the top shot in the whole Regiment. I think we're going to be having some real fun, messing with her now."

"Great. We don't need any freaks here ... especially if they look as hot as this girl does. Women are nothing but a distraction in the military." Quigby paused, and then asked, "What else do those internet stories say about her, anyway?"

Chapter Twenty-One
Jul 2018

"Clear on the right?" The range safety officer had just yelled out the standard question over the PA system, asking if all the weapons had been cleared on the right side of the range. He waited until he heard the appropriate response being yelled back at him, "Clear on the right!" Then he yelled out, "Clear on the left?" Again, he heard the appropriate response, "Clear on the left!" Now he yelled out, "The firing range is clear. New Cadets, you may go down and retrieve your targets."

Missy got up from where she'd been lying in the prone position, having fired her M4 rifle for another group of three rounds. The M4 carbine was the Army's latest combat unit rifle and she was learning how to zero her weapon. The M4 was similar to the M16 that the Army had used earlier for many years, but shorter and lighter. This was her weapon, issued for her use during marksmanship training. Each weapon was issued out and checked back in by serial number and she would now be the only one using this rifle. Once she had it zeroed in, which meant the sights would be adjusted as needed for her use, she then would be firing this same weapon in all her later training exercises. Eventually, of course, there would be the marksmanship qualifications and competitions when she'd again be using it.

To zero the weapon, a series of rounds were fired, three at a time. Although the rifle was capable of automatic firing, and the entire magazine could then be fired in just a few seconds, most of her firing would be only one round at a time. Her very first shot group had resulted in all three rounds hitting her target, which was certainly a good thing, but they were somewhat scattered and all were off to the right and a bit low. Likewise, her second shot group had also been low and to the right. But, she had placed all six rounds within a four centimeter circle and been ready to make her sight adjustments.

Per the TAC officer's instructions, to move the shot group up, down, left or right was a matter of adjusting her sights so many clicks one way or the other. Then, after making her adjustments, she had fired her next shot group of three rounds.

Missy had enhanced eyesight, of course, and now that she'd been able to "get the feel" of her weapon, experiencing how it kicked back against her shoulder and her cheek following the discharge of each bullet, she was easily able to aim, breathe, squeeze the trigger while holding her breath, and after the recoil, return to position her rifle for the next round. In order to minimize the recoil, it was important to always keep her cheek and her shoulder pressed firmly against the weapon. This was merely another physical task and she was having no difficulty. Her later groups of three rounds had all been within a small circle, just larger than a quarter. She had only needed to make one click more to move the group down and two clicks to move the group to the right.

Now, she'd just fired her final shot group and she didn't even need to walk down the 25 meters to retrieve her target. She could see all three rounds were in the center and they now could be covered by a quarter. She walked down with the rest of the class, of course, and retrieved her target. Sure enough, she had her weapon properly zeroed in. There would always be a small variation, one shot to the next, since each bullet was different and the atmospheric conditions were slightly different each time as well. These differences were extremely minute but resulted in her rounds not all going in the exact same spot.

Now that her rifle was zeroed in at 25 meters, it supposedly was also accurate out to 300 meters, using the same settings. A cone of fire within a circle of four centimeters, or one and a half inches, would be within a nineteen inch circle out at 300 meters and hit the target. The targets she'd be shooting at were all nineteen inches wide and a little bit taller than that. With her eyesight, she'd be able to actually notice any variation and, if needed, she'd then merely make slight adjustments to her aim. Marksmanship was all about making her body perform the same task in the same manner, consistently, over and over again. She was a very quick study and found she could actually "tune herself", adjusting each little aspect of her position, her aim, her breathing, how she squeezed the trigger, and where she would allow her mind to go.

She soon had begun to "feel" when she was tuned in and ready to fire. She'd then gradually squeezed the trigger, with the actual firing always coming as a surprise. She never twitched or moved, never anticipated but always just let the round be fired straight and true, with the recoil all after the fact. She knew she would need to find just where her "sweet spot" was for each of the firing positions. She had already found it for the prone position. The Army also had kneeling, sitting and standing positions and these would be used for some of the firing she'd be doing later.

She'd had several classes, all leading up to live firing, explaining all of this stuff. She knew her qualification targets would be "pop up" targets positioned out at various distances. If she hit the target, it would go down. The more targets she knocked down, the higher her score. She was thoroughly enjoying herself, once again. With the unique werecat skills and abilities she'd been gifted with, she just felt this was right, her being in the military. She was good at this. It was what she was meant to do. And, she felt really, really good doing it.

Tracy had learned to shoot years earlier, from her Dad, and was also an excellent shot. Whether being a witch was helping her or not, she had no idea. But, like Missy, she felt really good about herself while accomplishing all her various training tasks and was growing more and more comfortable. This was her dream come true.

As it turned out, none of the guys in their squad were quite as comfortable as the girls were with firing their weapons but they all did reasonably well. Even Gary. When they checked with Missy, anxious to see how she was doing, and saw her big, happy grin, they all were greatly relieved. She'd gone out on that limb, messing with King, and they were all rooting for her to somehow pull off what would truly have to be a miracle. Yeah, they all knew she was pretty good at just about everything. But, to earn top shot, without ever having fired a weapon before coming to West Point?

That night, several guys were standing outside Missy's room while the four girls were once again laughing about the day's activities. Kelly and Angel had been shocked when first hearing about Missy and her audacious boast. They'd heard about her crazy top shot announcement long before seeing her that night. The word had gone out and everyone had quickly heard about this. They'd also heard how Missy hadn't been able to eat at lunch. Food kept showing up all night long, even though Missy had eaten plenty at dinner.

That meal, her squad members had all pestered King with questions, never allowing him to interfere with Missy. They'd purposely positioned Tracy right next to him on one side and Missy on the other. Neither girl said a word but merely ate their meal following all the rules while their squad members asked question after question. Missy had sat there, eyes straight ahead, and devoured a huge portion while King became more and more frustrated with what was going on. But, each of the guys knew exactly how to properly do things, giving him nothing to correct or find fault with.

Now, as the girls began turning away food, the mood was definitely festive. When Missy pulled out her final target, from zeroing her weapon, which showed such a tight shot group in the center, they all whistled in amazement. Soon, the excitement level began to ramp up and so the girls insisted they be given some privacy.

After sending everyone away and closing their door, Angel turned to Missy and said, "Girl, you're gonna get yourself a real reputation now. Just be careful ... I hear that guy Quigby is a real asshole. He hates women in the Army and especially here at Woo Poo U. His buddy King is only following his lead. You guys all seem to be handling King all right, but ... you know? Watch your backs!" Then, she slipped out and went back to her own room.

A little while later, Kelly decided to talk to her roommates and get their advice on dating. Kelly had noticed how close Missy and Tracy now were. Whatever problem had existed in the beginning for them had now totally evaporated. "Hey, can I run something by you girls? I mean ... what Angel said just now. You'll have my back, right? If I need you to cover for me or anything?"

Tracy and Missy both assured her they did indeed have her back and they definitely would always cover for her, as long as Kelly wasn't asking them to violate the Honor Code. She wasn't, was she?

Kelly sighed. "I don't know. I mean, I know the rules. No fraternization with upperclassmen. No fraternization with guys in my squad. But, I think it's okay to date other plebes, right? Especially if they're not even in my company?"

Missy had noticed that Kelly no longer had any residual scents from the men she'd been having sex with prior to coming to West Point. Four weeks of abstinence had done that for her. Apparently, it had also been driving her crazy. She knew Kelly wasn't really looking to just date.

Missy said, "You want to have sex with someone? Jeez, Kelly ... I mean, it's not lying, cheating or stealing. So, I guess since we're not tolerating you doing any of those, it's not really an Honor Code thing. But, still ... aren't you taking a pretty big risk? If you get caught? I mean, it's almost impossible to find the time or the place without breaking some rule. At least, right now, while we're going through Beast Training. Tracy, what do you think?"

Tracy said, "Missy's right, Kelly. The point isn't that you're dating some plebe. It's that you'll end up lying about it, or about where or when, you know? Or, are you planning to wait until Acceptance Day? Like Missy? She's been telling us every day how she almost doesn't even want to see her parents. She's planning to shack up with her Mike from the time we get released in the afternoon right up until we have to report back here that night."

This was a huge exaggeration and Kelly knew that. Missy was hoping to see Mike then, of course, but whatever time they'd have -- in her parent's hotel room -- would be limited. Shacking up the whole time would not be possible. She'd actually been telling her roommates how she was hoping to somehow manage a "quickie" at least once during his visit. She was also

273

hoping to maybe Change, which needed at least an hour, but she hadn't shared that with Kelly.

Acceptance Day would be on a Saturday, a few days after completing Beast Training, when they'd formally graduate in a ceremony in front of family and friends. It was the first time they'd be seeing any visitors. They then would be allowed to leave with their parents and could actually go to any hotel within 75 miles. And, yes -- friends were allowed also. But, this was only a Walking Privilege, with lots of rules and cadets must return before taps that night. They'd be allowed to leave again the next morning, but would need to return much earlier, sometime in the early evening.

"I don't think I can wait another three weeks!" cried Kelly. "My little solo sessions just aren't doing it for me anymore. I need to feel a man touching me, doing me, you know? I'm not like Angel. All her stories? All those boyfriends? She's only had a few real boyfriends. Most of the time, her boyfriend has actually been battery operated."

"Ewww! *TMI*, Kelly. Please!" Tracy looked at Missy. "Now you guys understand why it's really not such a bad thing, me being a virgin and everything. Right?"

Missy felt bad. Yeah, too much information all right. About Angel and about Kelly. "Tracy, I think the problem for Kelly is that none of her ex-boyfriends are going to be here for her that day. And, trying to meet some random guy then? Not really a good idea." Missy looked at Kelly and asked, "What happens if you ask this guy to wait until then. Just three more weeks?"

Kelly said, "His girlfriend will actually be meeting him then. She's coming with his parents and … shit, this isn't gonna work, is it?"

Missy said, "I see, now. He's only asking you to be his fuck-buddy? And, if you don't agree, he's got a few other girls he'll go to instead? Damn, Kelly, you don't have to be that desperate. And, no. That definitely won't work. You'll only regret it, even if you don't end up getting kicked out for some Honor Code violation."

"The ratio here is better than five to one, guys to us girls. I bet you can find someone … you know … for more than just sex." Tracy looked at her. "Why are you really here, Kelly? Is it to be an Army officer? Or, only to get some guy?"

"Arrggh! Can't I have both?" Kelly was obviously frustrated but after listening to her two roommates, she resigned herself to just gut it out. New Cadet Jeremy Hanson could just go fondle some other girl's breasts and nipples, press his great big hard throbbing erection up against some other girl's swollen, aching, slippery wet … "Arrgghhh!"

Field exercises. While Missy's period had been right on schedule over a week ago, it seemed many of the girls were finally getting their periods now. And, many of those periods had been very late. Apparently, this was not unusual -- the stress from Beast Training was known to cause a lot of girls to be late or miss their periods altogether.

Tracy suddenly spoke up, complaining, "As if personal hygiene wasn't difficult enough out here, with no hot showers, lots of grime and dirt, sleeping in tents, all this miserable heat and humidity, and now I get my period? And, no pads and no tampons. Damn!" Since she actually shared that with the entire squad, and not just with Missy, her comment was met with several complaints from the guys. The complaints were all good natured, however, since the guys now really had grown to appreciate Tracy.

"Really, Tracy? I gotta hear that news? Let me check ... nope! Sorry. I left all my tampons home. Guys, anyone wanna help poor Tracy out?" Tony was not a happy camper today either and actually enjoyed this excuse to be sarcastic. Their squad had been working their ass off for two days, dealing with one frustrating problem after another. And, this exercise would continue for one more day.

"Relax, everyone," said Missy, laughing. "Tracy, I brought some ... just in case." Then she smiled to herself, thinking how all this training together as a squad had helped Tracy overcome most of her sexual hang-ups. She was finally able to just really fit in, do whatever they needed her to do and not give a damn about whether they might be judging her, finding her lacking because of her gender. She knew her value and was pitching in one hundred percent, all the time now. They

276

all were and no one was concerned about males versus females. They'd grown to depend on each other, adjusting for all the various strengths and weaknesses each of them brought to the table. And, as a squad? They were awesome!

Marcus came up just then. "Hey, Missy, I hear you qualified today at the range. Expert, huh? You and Tracy both? I bet King and Quigby are starting to worry big time. Isn't the final marksmanship competition tomorrow morning? Your big day has arrived at last?"

Missy said, "Yep! I got expert all right. Perfect score too! I'm ready." To qualify as expert required hitting thirty eight out of forty targets; she had hit all forty. "Tomorrow will be fun. Even more fun than my note from the DPE three days ago."

Tony laughed. "Yeah, I heard about that too. You've dropped to 140 pounds and your body fat has gone back down to only eight percent, right? Any reaction from King?"

"Hell no, of course not!" Missy laughed. "He can't handle this at all. There are no secrets around here. So, he's now getting blamed for my losing my body fat and for his harassing me about my poor performance on the APFT ... even though my 50 pushups and 100 sit-ups are still the highest female scores in the regiment. Did you see how pissed off he got when I stopped at those exact numbers each time, even though there were still a few seconds remaining before the two minutes were up?"

Marcus said, "Cadet Winslow knows how he and Quigby have been messing with our squad and with you in particular. She's not happy about that at all. We're still getting best squad in her entire company, in spite of those two assholes. Her words, and I quote: 'those idiots would fuck up a wet dream.' I got that from my buddy over in first platoon."

"Be sure and guard that weapon of yours tonight, Missy," said Tony. "I wouldn't put it past those guys to try and sabotage your rifle ... fuck with the sights, you know? We're all going to try keeping watch tonight, just in case."

"Don't worry guys! I'm sleeping with it. As Charlton Heston once said, 'when you pry it from my cold, dead hands' -- right?" Missy laughed but knew she really did need to watch out for something. This would be the last chance for them to mess with her. Then, only one more week to go until the end of Beast Training.

She'd been sending Mike more and more mental messages and had also been able to sense his growing excitement. She'd been really filled with energy lately, feeling it go thrumming through her whole body. She'd been sending out lots of this energy, pulse after pulse, trying to maintain her controls. That, of course, was why her body fat was back down to eight percent. Being so highly charged had really worked out okay. Sometimes, it was good to just be a witch.

Quigby asked, "So, you're telling me she actually has a chance? Top shot? Over twelve hundred other plebes here and yet she might actually score highest?" King had just explained how New Cadet McCrae had qualified expert, with a perfect score no less.

King said, "I told you she was playing us. There's something really freaky about her. I told you how she's making me look bad. And, the whole squad just thinks it's funny, her messing with me. Even Cadet Winslow is criticizing me now for supposedly hazing everyone too much. No matter what I've tried, that bitch McCrae somehow turns it around against me. I'm getting blamed for starving her when the truth is she's been eating huge portions at every meal. You can't believe how much food she eats. And, then, she goes and loses weight? I really wonder if those body fat readings of hers are bogus, you know?"

"I've been checking her out and you're right. At mass athletics, she does some pretty amazing things but always makes it look easy." Quigby studied King for a moment and then added, "I hate to even admit this, but watching her movements is weird ... mesmerizing even. She's freaky all right. Wherever she goes and whatever she does, there now seems to be a lot of guys just following her around, watching her. Just proves my point about how women can be such a huge distraction in the military."

King smiled and said, "Well, now that she's out here in the field, away from the barracks? Exposed? Not safely locked in her room all night? For insurance, I've arranged a little surprise for her. My insurance so she'll be in no shape tomorrow for any top shot competition."

Quigby said, "You made that call? To your friend, like we talked about?" King was from New York City and had promised Quigby he could round up some local guys, if and when needed.

"Oh, yeah. Nothing that can trace back to us. But, there might just be a few intruders out there tonight, wandering around on academy property. And, if they happen to assault some females, who are sleeping in tents? Won't that be a shame?" King had explained things to his high school buddy, former captain of their football team. He'd even warned him to bring several friends along, since one of the girls was a real freak. Just Google her and read all about what they'd be dealing with. Be sure and also check out her photos. Then, enjoy!

Tracy woke up and had to pee. Damn! Getting her period wasn't enough? Now she had to wake Missy up. They'd agreed to this ahead of time. Since you weren't supposed to bring your rifle into the Porta-Potty and since you didn't dare leave it behind, you always had a friend go with and hold your rifle for you. All part of their training.

King's buddy saw the two girls emerge from their tent and couldn't believe his luck. It had taken them several hours to sneak in here and find which squad area their targets were supposedly located in. All these tents looked the same, of course, but King had marked the area for him. He wasn't able to actually mark which tent the girls would be in but his map was clear enough to get them close to the marked area. It was after midnight and all was pretty quiet.

Now, rather than having to check any of the tents, all they needed to do was follow these girls. He saw they were headed for the Porta-Potty's. Perfect! He signaled his three friends to follow him. He'd promised them that they'd have a good time tonight and it looked like the fun was about to begin.

Missy and Tracy didn't talk while they walked over to the Porta-Potty area that had been set up. There wasn't any need for that. The day's heat had finally dissipated but it was still in the eighties and muggy. Missy was able to scent all the tired, dirty bodies out there, sleeping in their tents. There were a lot of scents to deal with which is why she didn't notice the four guys following her right away.

Then, when she did notice their scents, she wasn't alarmed or concerned. Just some of the guys, needing to use the toilets, same as Tracy. Going in pairs was normal for them, for the same reason. No one wanted to leave their rifle behind or bring it inside the Porta-Potty. Rules were rules. They reached the area, stopped in front of one of the Porta-Potty's and Tracy handed her rifle to Missy and went inside. Tracy had a fresh tampon that Missy had provided and would be busy for a minute or so.

Missy's senses suddenly all went on the alert. Somehow, although she wasn't sure if it was their scents or their movements that had alarmed her, she was certain these guys were not military. And, they had no business being on academy grounds. Her first thought was that protecting their rifles was no longer merely a training exercise. And, she didn't want Tracy to come out. It was better if she locked herself inside the Porta-Potty. Since the guys were still several paces away, she quietly alerted Tracy.

Missy whispered, just loud enough for Tracy to hear her. "Tracy, open the door and take our rifles. Quick! There are four guys out here from outside the academy. Intruders. Hurry!"

Tracy didn't question her but opened the door, even though she wasn't dressed and was mostly exposed from the waist down. Missy's voice had convinced her to act quickly. When Missy handed her both rifles, she grabbed them with one hand and then closed and locked the door with the other hand. She trusted Missy and would wait there, in spite of how difficult that was.

Missy spun around and moved forward, away from the Porta-Potty and toward the approaching men. It was not very bright out, with only a partial moon and a slight haze that prevented the stars from shining through all that much. This was definitely an advantage for her. Various scenarios were racing through her mind as she considered the situation. She did not want to risk any adverse consequences that might affect her being at

West Point. Obviously, Changing to her cat form was not an option.

Although it was dark, the guys all saw Missy approaching them. Alone. They figured they'd grab her first and then look for her friend. They fanned out just slightly as they continued moving forward. It was obvious she had spotted them, since she continued walking right up until only a few feet away. They weren't sure which girl they were dealing with as both looked similar in height and had short dark hair. Then Missy spoke to them and identified herself.

"I'm New Cadet McCrae. Are you assholes looking for me or are you just lost out here?" Missy had decided it was too much of a coincidence for them to have merely wandered in. She suspected King and Quigby might be trying to mess with her because of the marksmanship competition. This was their last chance to get her and she'd been hearing plenty of warnings. She hoped they'd confirm this and, sure enough, they did.

"We know all about you, Missy. We've been reading all sorts of interesting articles about you and studying your photos. We've decided we want to get up close and personal. Really get to know you. What do you say?" This was spoken by the big guy, second in from the right.

Missy had been checking each of them for weapons. She noted two were carrying large flashlights, but otherwise nothing obvious. Now she said, "If you've been studying all about me, then where's the rest of the group? You can't possibly expect to subdue me with only these three bozos. Seriously?"

Her words had the desired effect and one of the bozos decided to make a grab for her. She spun and met him with a solid kick to his jaw, faster than any of the others could even react. Now there were only two bozos, since the guy she'd just kicked dropped like a stone, out cold.

The three remaining guys finally reacted and all came charging right at her. They'd played football and tried to tackle her, as though she were the opposing team's quarterback. One went low and two went high. But, Missy went back three steps and then darted to the left, just beyond any of their grasping fingers. The guy who had dived low was now flat on the ground but the other two made quick adjustments and came after her. She dropped and placed one hand on the ground, which she used to pivot herself with as she brought both legs forward and connected solidly with one of these guys. The other went stumbling past, missing her once again.

The guy she'd kicked tried to grab her as he went down on his knees but Missy was very, very fast. She wanted to end this as quickly as possible. First she jumped up and away and then she smashed her right elbow down and connected with the side of his head. That set him up for a quick rabbit punch and she hit his carotid artery with one of her knuckles. Two guys now out cold.

The guy who'd landed on the ground after diving at her and the big guy who'd done all the talking so far were still there. They were both up and coming at her once again. They wanted to grapple. Missy didn't. Their flailing arms again came up empty as she cartwheeled herself out of reach, off to one side. Then she rushed one of them, surprising him with a series of kidney punches that sent him to his knees. She smashed one of her knees up and broke his nose. He didn't actually pass out but he dropped and was no longer interested in grabbing her.

Three bozos down. She looked at the last guy standing who was also the one who'd spoken to her. She assumed he was their leader. He had stopped and was now just standing there. She smiled at him and said, "Is this close enough for you? Personal enough? Do you know me well enough yet?"

He said, "Oh, fuck! He said you were a real badass. Shit." He looked around at his three friends and back at her. "Look, enough already. We don't want to get in trouble. You're way more than we bargained for, lady. Sorry! Damn!"

Missy looked at the guy with the broken nose, who was now slowly standing back up. She said, "You guys even know where you are? I can't just let you wander back out of here. Sorry, but I'm not getting criticized for not reporting this. You want to make this easy or hard?"

"What's easy?"

"Easy is you grab your two friends still out cold there and wake them up. Then, I'm getting my friend up there to join us and we're all going to walk down there, where you're going to give yourselves up." Missy looked back and forth at the two of them. "You won't say anything about knowing me and targeting me. You won't say Martin King sent you in here. You'll claim you were all drinking earlier and just thought it would be fun to spy on the student soldier boys. And, the student soldier girls. Especially them. You were hoping to get lucky with some soldier girls. But, that didn't happen."

Tracy walked up, having heard Missy explaining things in a calm voice, so she'd figured things were now under control. She handed Missy her rifle.

Missy said, "If you're wondering what hard might be, let me explain that too. If you try to say that I was your target or discuss King sending you after me? If you don't treat this whole affair as simply the four of you all being incredibly stupid? I'll find you. If you don't treat this as merely a whim? Wandering in here like this? I'll find you."

"Okay, okay. I get it. We want easy. Fuck! He told me you were a freak. We shoulda listened. Fuck!"

"I didn't finish easy yet. The rest of easy is you assholes did all this damage fighting amongst yourselves. We did not fight. And, we do not know you. Us girls found you stumbling around in here, after you'd finally sobered up. Can you handle all that? Can your bozos handle that?" Missy was now putting some real iron in her voice and she let just a little of her cat energy make her eyes begin to sparkle. The glow was apparent in the dark and both guys backed away from her. She added, "Don't make me come find you."

She and Tracy went off to the side to review everything while the guys worked at rousing their two friends, still out cold. Tracy asked, "Are you sure this is best, Missy?"

Missy said, "I think so. My big worry is our Honor Code. The part about not tolerating those who lie, cheat or steal. If it comes out that I knew King sent these guys in here to mess with me and didn't turn him in? What do you think? We can still insist these guys sing a different tune if you'd rather go down that whole road." Missy didn't want to pressure Tracy or make her feel compromised in any way.

Tracy considered things for a little while, turning various alternatives over in her mind. Finally, she said, "I guess there's not much risk these guys will name King or admit to targeting you. If all they say is this was a prank, after a night of crazy carousing, they'll surely end up without any criminal charges, right? But, if they admit to anything else, things get a lot more serious for them. Even without you scaring the shit out of them the way you just did." She laughed. "You really should see how your eyes look, Missy. You know, when you get all pissed off and everything? Wow!"

It was long after two in the morning before Missy and Tracy finally crawled back inside their tent. But, they'd pulled it off, extricating themselves from what could have been a lot more complicated. Their story was simple. Tracy had to pee and after that, they noticed these guys wandering up. They'd reported them immediately, of course. And, the guys were all acting very apologetic. What had sounded like fun, back in the bar, had not been such a good idea by the time they'd wandered up to where the girls found them. No harm, no foul, right?

Since the academy was not keen about stories getting around concerning intruders, the four guys were quickly whisked out of the training area with a minimum or commotion. After being escorted to a local police station, outside of West Point, there was the taking of names and statements and so forth. But, at the end, no criminal charges were filed and the guys were all allowed to leave, with the threat of charges later being filed should any of them step out of line and come back anywhere near West Point or its students ever again.

Morning came and Missy and Tracy went on about their business. Tracy admitted she'd not been able to fall back asleep but Missy had managed. She had all those places in her mind that she'd trained herself to go to. Over the past few years she'd become very capable of controlling herself and could block out extreme pain, if needed. For her, it was all part of the melding she'd done, bringing her two natures together so she was one person, in either form. If her body needed rest and sleep? She'd focus on making that happen and within minutes, she could be off in dreamland.

A few short hours later, she was glad she'd grabbed that little bit of rest, as she now really needed to be sharp and at her best. She'd been selected to compete with the other experts in her class for the marksmanship award. Top shot. This was what she'd bragged about doing. Now she needed to step up and earn this. Time to win.

They would all be tasked with shooting from the four basic positions, and would be presented with several targets each at ranges of 50, 100, 150, 200, 250 and 300 meters. These targets would pop up in various groups but, after several seconds, any targets not hit would then drop back down. Thus, of course, their time was very limited. Whoever hit the most targets once the shooting was over would be declared top shot.

Missy was convinced she had the advantage because of her speed. No one could move as fast as she could. She was able to quickly tune into her own sweet spot for each position and could then fire round after round at a rate that was not humanly possible. With precision accuracy. So, she was confident. Even so, she still had to actually do it. There were always things that could change, things that might mess things up for her.

But, she had already dealt with the guys that King had sent to mess her up. She was comfortable with how that had turned out and so was Tracy, her Honor Code expert. They'd done nothing wrong and really had no proof that King had done anything wrong either. While she may have had enough to suspect King, which of course she did, she didn't think anyone could claim she had enough evidence to really bring charges up against him before any board. She and Tracy did not believe they were required to report things they only suspected but could not prove.

And, for the competition firing, Missy's superhuman speed did indeed make the difference. When all the smoke had cleared, and the last round had been fired, she was the top shot. She'd won by a clear, decisive margin, hitting every target. This was a dozen more targets than anyone else. Being best in the whole regiment was indeed a big honor. And, of course, she had helped her squad.

Her squad, her platoon, her entire company. Cadet Winslow made a big deal about it and declared a free period that night for everyone in the company. It was only a three hour period, but coming just when they all got back to the barracks, finished with the three day field exercise they'd all been through, it was a very welcome event. Spirits were definitely soaring, as there now were only a few more days remaining. The end of Beast Training was less than a week away. And, Acceptance Day would follow a few days after that.

Chapter Twenty-Two
Aug 2018

The encampment out at Camp Buckner for their final field training exercise was where it all had come together. The squads had all trained hard for various tasks involving patrolling, convoys, land navigation and dealing with obstacles of all shapes and sizes. They'd worked as individuals and then as squad members. They'd charged through the bayonet assault course and had rappelled down steep cliffs out at the mountaineering site. They'd gone on marches and on runs, mile after mile. They'd thrown live grenades and fired their weapons. So, this final exercise, based on actual conditions they might experience in a Middle East theater, had been met with great enthusiasm.

There'd been several days of again working their ass off, again in miserable heat and humidity, but this time there were goals in sight. Each person was all in. One hundred percent. All ten members in each squad had bonded with one another in ways they'd never have dreamed possible. No prior experience even came close compared to how they now played "The Game", more excited and motivated than ever before.

The squads had all competed against one another for this final "Beast Challenge" and Missy's squad had performed the best in their whole company. They'd really been determined to do well and their teamwork and creativity in problem solving, combined with all the physical skills and mental abilities from each member, had definitely earned them top honors.

And, that last day, as they marched back twelve miles, they were jubilant. They'd learned more about themselves and about life in their six and a half weeks of Beast Training than during the entire eighteen or so years leading up to it. Beast Training was over. They were going to graduate and become Cadets, no longer being referred to as New Cadets. Now they'd be full-fledged members of the United States Corps of Cadets.

They'd also be reorganizing, getting assigned to new squads. Once again, the upperclass leaders would change. Missy was looking forward to no longer having Cadet King watching every bite she ate during her meals. He'd been very distant, clearly avoiding her since she'd won top shot. So had his buddy, Cadet Quigby. She knew they'd probably be looking to mess with her sometime later, but for now, she'd clearly won the day and had put them in their place.

As Missy marched back with her squad, she thought about each one of them. How much they'd all grown and all the changes each of them had made. Tracy was much more comfortable being with guys and, although she probably didn't realize it yet, even more attractive. Her confidence, now that her earlier hang-ups were not affecting how she interacted with everyone, was indeed making a difference.

Perhaps the most dramatic change, however, was in Gary. His whole appearance had changed. He now was physically fit, no longer soft or pudgy, and his self confidence had given him a whole new personality. He'd not only been able to keep up with the rest of his squad but had now made several contributions which the others had clearly appreciated. He'd done well in marksmanship, missing expert by only a few targets. As he'd seen his dream of becoming an officer appear more and more realistic, he'd become more and more relaxed. And happy about life.

Gary had never been one to gripe and had often been the one everyone else would go to, whenever they wanted to complain. Gary's standard response had always been, "Tell me about it!" Then, he'd smile and he'd listen. He was easy to talk to and Missy had noticed more and more of her classmates all sharing their frustrations with him. Even Kelly. Gary had often been one of the guys stopping by their room at night and, lately, she'd noticed how Kelly would step outside into the hallway and somehow end up in one-on-one conversations with Gary.

Poor Kelly! Missy knew she really had struggled with her temptation to have sex but had accepted the advice she and Tracy had given her. The real low point for her had been just a few days after that conversation and after Kelly had then explained to Jeremy Hanson, the guy who'd propositioned her, that regretfully she was going to pass on his wonderful offer. Apparently, New Cadet Irene Hwang -- also Asian, which was probably not a coincidence -- had been quite happy to step up in her place. Or, as Kelly lamented, to lie down.

Kelly was hardly a woman scorned but her constant references to "that slut Hwang" had finally made even Kelly start to laugh. So, she'd gotten over all that. And, she'd managed to keep going and somehow had gotten to the end of Beast Training without getting into any trouble, resigned to no sex other than her solo sessions, which she wouldn't discuss at all with her roommates. Missy would have noticed right away by Kelly's scent if there had been anyone else.

"Tracy, look at her eyes, will you? I've seen her get those yellow and gold specs before, but never like this! Missy, you're amazing, you know that, right?" Kelly and Tracy had stopped at Missy's new room on their way to breakfast formation. Missy had waited for them, letting her new roommates go on ahead.

Tracy giggled and said, "She's in *lust* mode, Kelly. She can't help it when that happens. How far away is Mike now, Missy?"

"About forty eight miles, in that direction, and he arrived there maybe twelve hours ago. It's been driving me crazy all night, feeling him this close." Kelly figured this was just Missy knowing which hotel Mike was at. Tracy, of course, knew Missy really was able to feel exactly where Mike was and how far away he was. Today was Acceptance Day and everyone was pretty excited. Missy hadn't realized she'd let her eyes show how filled with energy she was so she tamped down some of her cat, hoping to keep things under better control.

The last few days had been very stressful, since this was Reorganization Week. Yes, they'd finished Beast Training but, suddenly, the cadets from all the other classes were there. Instead of the academy population being mostly plebes with only a few upperclass cadet leaders to watch out for, the plebes were now outnumbered three to one. The hazing and harassment had more than doubled since plebes were constantly coming in contact with all of these upperclass cadets.

The plebes all had new squad members after being reassigned. No longer were there only eight companies in one regiment. Now, there were thirty two companies in four regiments. And, each company had members from all four classes. Missy's new company would be her home for the rest of the academic year. She was in Bravo Company, third Regiment or B-3. Tracy was in D-2 and Kelly was in E-4.

They also had been assigned to new rooms with new roommates. These would all change again in December for the second half since roommate changes were made twice a year. Missy was good at making adjustments but that didn't mean she wasn't experiencing a lot of stress. She didn't know either of her two new roommates although they both claimed to be well aware of who she was.

Missy had been issued more equipment, more books and her laptop computer. That, at least, enabled emails and contact once again with the outside world. There was also a landline phone in her room. She hadn't even attempted making any phone calls during Beast

Training, preferring to focus all her time and energy on the many day to day activities at the academy instead. She'd always known where Mike was and had been able to experience emotional responses from him to the many mental messages that she'd sent. That had been enough.

Later on, sitting at breakfast, she realized she'd once again relaxed her controls. She was staring straight ahead, like always, but suddenly realized all her new squad members sitting across the table from her were staring back at her, obviously noticing how her eyes were sparkling. She hardly knew any of them and now they all probably thought she was crazy. Oh, well! Soon she'd be seeing Mike and her family. She'd be a lot less crazy after that.

Missy's family had found their spot in the B-3 section of the bleachers on the Plain. They were all there and Mike was also with them. He'd explained that B Company, third Regiment was where Missy had been assigned. So, they knew that's where she'd end up after being accepted into the Corp of Cadets. Her class would march out separately, after the rest of the Cadets had paraded onto the field and taken positions. Then, after being accepted, she'd march over to take her position in Company B.

John looked at Heather and said, "I'm still trying to get used to Mike getting all these messages from Missy in his head. And, this bond they have? Mom and Dad are really okay with that? Missy hasn't even called any of us since she got here. He's really getting her exact words?"

Heather said, "Oh, yes, it's the same as if she were talking to him out loud in person. And, she also knows how far away he is and in what direction. She told me all about it last May, right after that night she healed Michelle. You heard that whole story, right?"

"Patrick told me everything, yeah. Including how she brought Mike home afterwards and he spent the whole night in bed with her. But, that was *after* she'd Shifted. Then, the next morning she wouldn't Change back and ran around the house as a cat for over an hour, acting really silly. Mike had to do all the explaining, not only about her healing Michelle but also about his now having this bond with her, including how he was hearing her inside his head."

Heather giggled. "Leave it to Missy to make her boyfriend tell our parents about that. Mom had guessed they'd already been having sex but Dad was clueless. It took him a while to figure out what their having that bond *really* meant. As far as their being okay with it? And, with her not calling anyone? Hey, Missy is Missy. What else can they do but just go along with her?"

John smiled and said, "You're right, of course. For two years, we all thought she was dead. These last three years since she's come back? It's all been good. Really, really good. Oh, look! It's starting. Here come the cadets."

They all watched as the Corp of Cadets paraded
out onto the field, looking so impressive in their
uniforms and moving with such orderly precision. Over
thirty three hundred upperclass cadets wearing short-
sleeve white shirts, white cross belts with polished brass
breastplates, grey trousers, white gloves and white hats.
They carried M14 rifles and the band played while they
all marched out. The ceremony had started and it
wouldn't be long now. Soon they'd see Missy out there,
part of all this.

Anxiously they waited for the twelve hundred
New Cadets to appear. And, finally, out they came.
They were also impressive, all wearing those same
uniforms and moving with that same orderly precision.
Not surprisingly, Mike was the first to point out Missy.
There she was, in her cadet uniform, marching out there
on the field. Carrying a rifle. They all were really proud
of her.

Missy was feeling very proud of herself, of
course, but she had many other emotions all flooding
through her as well. She could hardly contain them all.
She was thrilled to be marching in front of everyone like
this and part of such an elite institution, the oldest of
the country's military academies with so many famous
graduates that had gone before her. She truly believed
it was her calling now. She'd been gifted with so much
and felt it was her responsibility to now use those
enhanced skills and abilities in the best way possible.
She was going with her instincts on how to do that. So,
she was going to be a warrior.

But today? Today she was going to be with her family. And, with Mike.

It was a great ceremony, with several speeches and all the typical military fanfare. Finally there came the merge and all the new cadets marched over in groups to join their companies. Once they'd all taken their positions there were some more speeches and music by the band. Then, forty five hundred cadets all began marching back off the field. Thirty two companies in four regiments all paraded past the huge crowd in the bleachers and eventually disappeared back into Washington Hall.

An hour later, after finally being released, Missy went out to join her family. She was still in uniform, as that was required during Walking Privileges. And, being in uniform, she was very reserved and proper with Mike as no PDA was allowed. PDA was the Army's acronym for public display of affection. She gave Mike a quick hug and a kiss, similar to how she greeted the rest of her family. Then, she pushed out a little of her energy and laughed at everyone's reaction.

Missy and Tracy had discussed things ahead of time. They each wanted to meet the other's family and Missy of course wanted to introduce Mike. Missy was not going to tell anyone that Tracy was a witch. Tracy was not saying anything to her parents either and wanted to see if her Mom would sense what Missy was. So, after all the initial excitement of greeting her own family and Mike, Missy soon walked them over to get introduced to Tracy and her folks. Mike had explained ahead of time how Tracy had been Missy's roommate, had been in her squad and was now her closest friend at the academy.

Tracy was proud to introduce her Dad and her Granddad, both graduates from West Point. Her Dad was very interested in meeting Missy and said, "So this is the other girl in Tracy's squad, who not only helped win best squad in the company during Beast Training but also has some individual honors as well? I have to say I'm very impressed, Missy McCrae. Highest APFT score for any female and top shot as well?"

Missy said, "Tracy has told me so much about you also. Growing up a military brat, with you teaching her how to shoot her rifle and so many things about West Point ... that made her a huge help to our squad. Plus the inspiration you and your father here have been for Tracy. She was always talking about that and it really helped not just her but all of us." She could see how pleased Tracy was and it was obvious how much Tracy's family loved Tracy.

Tracy's Dad beamed as he looked at his daughter. "Tracy has made us all so proud. Coming back here and watching her march out on that field, where both my Dad and I once marched? The McGonagle tradition is being carried on and we couldn't be happier!" He looked over at his Dad, who was nodding his head in full agreement.

Tracy's Mom had been very gracious and had greeted everyone warmly during these introductions. Suddenly, she looked closely at Missy and then stared at Tracy, raising her eyebrows. Tracy had been waiting for this and laughed. She pulled her Mom aside, out of normal hearing range from the others. Missy, of course, was able to still hear them talking. Missy had scented the same "otherness" about Tracy's Mom as she had about Tracy. She now had categorized this special scent as that for a witch.

Tracy said, in her most innocent voice, "What is it Mom?" She was really curious since, although her Mom wasn't all that powerful a witch, she had lived with her coven years ago and had learned a lot about the supernatural.

Tracy's Mom said, "Your roommate over there … you do know she's a supernatural, right? Some kind of a witch but also something else, something even more than that. Wait … is she also a Shifter? She's very rare, whatever she is. And, powerful too. Tremendous energy." She studied Tracy and could see the laughter in her daughter's eyes. "Does she know about you, Tracy? Can you trust her?"

"Very good, Mom! You guessed right and I'm impressed. Missy is a werecat. Her other form is a mountain lion. And, I think you're right about her being powerful. And, maybe also being a witch too. She didn't know anything about witches but she guessed about me after awhile. She can definitely be trusted, so relax. And, now she's interested in hearing what you can tell her about witches and covens."

"I'm not sensing anything supernatural for any of the others over there. Is she going to tell them about us?" Tracy's Mom was still a bit worried. Suddenly, Missy approached the two of them.

"No, Mrs. McGonagle, I'm not planning to tell anyone. Not unless you first say it's okay. But, they all do know about me and they are very good about guarding my secret. That is, they know about me being a cat. Tracy thinks I might also be a witch." Missy sent one of her little energy pulses out and let her eyes suddenly fill with gold specs. "We both are curious to know what you think."

Tracy's Mom said, "Please call me Harriet. And, I honestly don't know what I think, Missy. This energy of yours is amazing."

Tracy said, "Oh, she's barely letting you feel it, Mom. And, she can regenerate. But, even more impressive than that, she can heal others too. She thinks it's all some sort of genetic anomaly. But, we'll have to talk about all that later. Everyone's anxious to get going."

Tracy had told Missy which hotel her family would be staying at which Missy had told Mike about ahead of time. So, of course, they were all now going to the same hotel and they agreed to not waste any more time just standing around. Everyone suddenly wanted to leave the academy grounds and take advantage of the hours away that Walking Privileges allowed. So, they headed to the parking lot and climbed into their cars.

Missy's Dad had rented a minivan just for this weekend so all seven of them could ride together. Once inside the car, Missy snuggled up next to Mike and squeezed tightly against him, letting his arm wrap around her. She ignored everyone for a full minute and just scented his wonderful smell, allowing herself to bask in his closeness. She sent him several mental messages and Mike actually got embarrassed and laughed. "It's really great to see you too, Missy! Now, pay some attention to your family. Patrick's making those faces again and I know John has a question. I can see he's dying to ask you about something."

John laughed and said, "Thanks, Mike. But, yeah ... I wanted to know more about that girl you introduced us to back there. Your roommate, Tracy? You seemed to be really good friends. I guess you were lucky getting her in your squad, huh?"

"Oh, you might say it was actually Fate that brought us together, John. Yes, we're BFF's now, even though we're not roommates anymore." Missy smiled and raised one eyebrow. "She's really a wonderful person. Besides being really attractive, of course. In case you hadn't noticed that about her." She giggled.

"Oh, I noticed that all right," said John. "But, there's something more, something else." John didn't know when he'd been so impressed by and drawn to a girl before, just by meeting her. They'd not even said anything to each other but he'd shaken her hand and had felt a connection. "We're meeting them again at the hotel, right?"

"That's why I asked Mike to have you guys get rooms there. I wanted everyone to get to know her and her family. Somehow, I feel pretty certain that will help during the next four years. Her Dad and her grandfather both went to West Point."

Heather said, "What she really means, John, is she wants us to have some interesting people we can spend time with at the hotel when she and Mike disappear." She looked at Missy and asked, "Do you need to Shift, Missy? I know it's been almost two months, right?"

Missy smiled. While she'd love to Change and be a cat for awhile, she'd done the math. She wasn't fertile right now, and would be getting her period in another week. So, no ... she didn't *need* to Shift. What she *needed* was a couple hours alone with Mike. Before she could reply to Heather, her Mom spoke up.

"We're going to give Missy and Mike some time alone this afternoon and I think it's a wonderful plan to meet with other West Point families. Then, we can all have dinner together tonight right at the hotel."

Missy told stories during the rest of the ride about her West Point experiences and had them all laughing about the way she'd been manipulating her body fat. She was afraid she was probably better known for that than her winning top shot. Oh, well. At least they were now letting her get enough to eat. Her new squad leader hadn't said a word about how much food she'd been serving herself. And, she'd become really good at somehow getting to finish with an empty plate, in spite of never moving her eyes or even taking large bites. All part of "The Game" which she told them all about and how she'd really become very skilled at it.

At the hotel, she pulled Tracy aside and suggested they plan on dinner together. Tracy liked the idea and was sure her family would agree. She also liked the idea of maybe spending a couple of minutes with Missy's brother John. When she learned he was indeed interested in talking to her, she blushed.

Then, after being social and relaxing with everyone for as long as she could stand it, she and Mike finally slipped away. Her Mom had promised they'd not be disturbed and Mike had a room there of his own. They got on the elevator and headed up to his room. Missy began relaxing all her controls and before they even reached the room, she and Mike were both getting very aroused.

Once inside the room, they didn't waste any time. They tumbled onto the bed completely naked and crawled under the covers. Then, Missy insisted on some "alone time" with Mike's penis. He groaned but she was adamant. She'd been dreaming of this for weeks and was not to be denied. She considered it hers now and wanted to experiment. Before letting him distract her, she forced him to lie still while she explored the different ways that she could play with this marvelous male appendage.

It certainly seemed to appreciate all her attention and remained very hard and erect while she stroked its velvety soft head. She began nibbling with her lips and her teeth, all up and down the magnificent length of his manhood. Soon, several drops of precum were visible, oozing out while Mike groaned and writhed at her constant touching and rubbing. She delighted in tasting those drops with her tongue and soon followed by putting her mouth on the tip of his throbbing member, sliding him deeper and deeper into her mouth and then to the back of her throat. She cupped his balls with one of her hands and gently bounced them up and down. His response to all of this was getting her very excited. His musky scent was adding to her excitement. Nothing was quite as arousing as having Mike so completely hers with his pleasure totally hers to control.

After he'd allowed her to gratify her urges and satisfy her sexual curiosity about his reactions and responses, he finally said, "Enough!" She'd been bobbing up and down with his sensitive shaft in her mouth and he wasn't going to let that continue. He grabbed her and after forcing her onto her back, he laid on top of her, his aching member well out of her reach. Now his mouth began to explore her special places and his fingers began rubbing and touching her body, with his chest pressing firmly on her abdomen and pelvis, crushing her under his weight.

She moaned just a little and wriggled underneath but when his tongue began lavishing attention on her nipples, she stopped and let him have his way. She began making involuntary movements as her hungry body reacted in shudders and spasms, starving for more. Mike's forceful assault was awakening every nerve ending. He slid further downward, cupping her breasts with his hands, using his fingers to tweak her hard nipples while his tongue traced its way all across her abdomen. She groaned, spreading her legs wide apart and raising her knees. Sliding further downward, Mike brought his hands down and slid them underneath her, cupping her buttocks while he began licking her inner thighs.

Missy grabbed his hair with her hands and thoroughly enjoyed each wave of sensation her body was experiencing. Feeling him grab her ass like this was heaven. He was now in control and as he continued to do things with his tongue and his mouth to her exposed female parts, those female parts became swollen and achy. Her slick lubrication was making things very slippery and Mike seemed to really love that. He began probing inside her with his tongue, tasting her juices which soon covered his lower face. His enthusiasm only increased and he finally began sucking on her throbbing clit.

Missy's ability to experience pleasure was greatly enhanced, just like all her other senses, and her excitement began to climb from one height to the next, higher and higher. Mike had learned what she liked and how she liked it. Now, he was doing all those things, noting how she was rising to these greater heights. Her body was telling him just what it wanted and he was thrilled to provide her with sensation after sensation, each driving her closer and closer to that point of no return.

He'd learned, though, that by pausing and backing off just a bit, her body would become wracked with need and desire and suddenly require that much more stimulation just to return to that point. Playing with her was like performing on a finely tuned instrument, and he'd become an expert. He used that expertise now to drive her completely crazy, bringing her to new places, new pleasure plateaus where he'd linger. The more she wanted to come, the more he'd tease. He'd bring her so tantalizingly close and then do something, anything to keep her just on that edge but unable to reach that incredible release. Blowing softly on her tender places would often cause her to squirm and gasp but, each time, force her body to begin yet again on another upward climb.

Mike knew how close he'd brought Missy to reaching her ultimate place, beyond which she couldn't bear more pleasure, and each time he'd backed away. Four times he did this and as he was getting her there for the fifth time, he decided to let her take control. He stopped completely and flipped over on his back, next to her, while raising her hips high above. After positioning her wet entrance over the head of his hard shaft, he slowly lowered her down. Once he'd penetrated deeply inside her, he released her hips and brought his hands up to squeeze her breasts.

Missy felt herself being filled and as Mike relaxed his firm control, she at last was able to move. Now she was in control and there would be no stopping, no backing away. She began to ride him, slowly at first, feeling the pressure and fullness and delicious sensations from each movement. Then, once again sensing her approaching release, she increased her pace until she was thrusting so hard and so fast that nothing else mattered. She could only focus on those wonderful sensations and the anticipation of that final explosion. When her orgasm began, her bucking became that much more violent and she screamed. This time, her build up had been so intense she was completely out of control. She yelled and cried and screamed once more, oblivious to everything else. And, her convulsions continued to wrack her entire body, again and again. She was completely engulfed by waves of the most wonderful and amazing feelings, beyond any she'd ever known before, and this lasted for close to two minutes.

Mike's orgasm happened somewhere in the middle of all that, with the delicious sensations from his seed pulsing inside her just adding to everything else. She was boneless, completely spent. All her energy was gone. And, there had been so much energy being released that Mike had even groaned. She'd been unbelievable this time and he'd experienced things he'd never known before and had no way of relating to or describing. When she finally subsided, he was surprised the bed was still under them and hadn't somehow been obliterated.

He stayed firmly inside her for a long time, only gradually becoming flaccid, and noticed with deep satisfaction all the quivers and little movements her body continued to make, signaling how thoroughly she'd been satisfied by all their lovemaking. Once again, he realized she was off in never-never land, no longer conscious. She was, however, supremely happy and satiated. Her limp body now felt so good, just lying on top of his body. He knew he'd never get tired of having her be like that, so completely his. He wrapped his arms around her and held her tight, marveling at all the ways she made him love her.

A long time later, perhaps a half an hour or so, Missy finally stirred. Wow. Now she felt good. By expending all her energy in such a total way, giving all and everything, her body recuperated and replenished itself with even greater reserves of energy. She awoke, still spread-eagled on top of Mike, fully recharged. Her lovemaking with Mike continued to amaze her as each time, she felt more and more empowered. He was somehow her source for energy and, after going crazy this time, she'd now been supercharged. She crawled up to where she could bring her lips to his and began kissing him, slowly and lovingly. Her passion was spent but her energy, what she believed was her essence, had been fully restored and this time, perhaps with an added measure.

Mike of course began kissing her back and, not really any surprise considering she was lying there naked, rubbing herself on top of him, his erection was quickly obvious. Awareness of his arousal was all she needed to once again become wet and ready. She rolled over and invited him to mount her. As he slipped inside her once again she wrapped her legs around him, firmly holding him while she tilted her pelvis to meet his thrusts. Mike placed his huge hands on her breasts and that excited and aroused her even more. Soon, they were rocking in a wonderful rhythm that went on for several minutes. No rush this time and no teasing either. Just a long, slow buildup that inevitably brought them both to another climax, first his and then hers.

But, now she was fully awake and her body felt great in every way. She climbed out from under Mike and laughed. "I'm taking the first shower. You need to pull back the covers to air out the sheets underneath, since we really made a mess. And, open the door out to that balcony, so the scent of all the sex we've enjoyed having will fade. My sensitive nose is overwhelmed right now with what we've done here."

The room was Mike's but since he wasn't going to have any visitors he wasn't all that concerned. He did pull back the covers and opened the balcony door and decided that was adequate. He followed her, climbing into the shower to join her. He rubbed her body with his soapy hands and got a kick out of how much she enjoyed his doing that. Then, they both rinsed off and got out. Twenty minutes later, freshly scrubbed and with Missy back in her uniform once again, they took the elevator down to join the others. They'd been gone just over two hours but, for Missy, it was like she'd been on vacation for a month. She felt really, really good.

Sometimes, being sexually satiated was such a wonderful experience.

Chapter Twenty-Three
Aug 2018

Missy settled in to the new routine with her life as a plebe and her focus now more on academics. Each morning there were chores to perform, such as delivering newspapers or laundry to the upperclassmen rooms. And, it was required that plebes memorize the next three meals which they'd be asked to recite constantly by the upperclass cadets. They also must know the exact time until the next meal. Missy had no problem with either of these since meals were always her favorite parts of the day and she still marked time from one meal to the next.

There was a great deal of required knowledge for a plebe. Each week, additional facts needed to be learned and any time they messed up, when tested by upperclass cadets, they earned demerits. This required knowledge was called "poop" and the list of poop went on and on. There was the Code of Conduct, General Orders, ranks and insignia, the location and significance of every monument at West Point, dozens of songs and lots more Army and West Point trivia. Testing plebes was the favorite past time for upperclass cadets, their single most enjoyable task.

Once a plebe accumulated enough demerits, the punishment was to spend what otherwise would have been free time doing walking tours. They'd walk for hours at a time on Saturday afternoons in full uniform and carrying their M14 parade rifles on their shoulder, walking back and forth in the Central Area.

There were still the morning exercises and runs, which Missy loved. And, she was playing on the women's varsity soccer team, the Black Knights. Her skill in both scoring goals as striker and in making assists was quickly noted by her coach, Kristen Cassalia. Kristen was a civilian, totally focused on soccer, and it was refreshing for Missy to interact with her. She, in turn, was excited about Missy. She'd researched Missy's high school soccer background and knew Missy had been a big part of her team's winning the state championship the year before. When she observed Missy out on the practice field and saw what a strong player Missy truly was, she was thrilled.

Then, there were the inspections. Cadet uniforms always had to be perfect and so did their rooms. Or, more demerits. Being able to depend on one another was important for every roommate. Missy's roommates soon learned they could always count on her. She sometimes would ask them to step outside their room for a few minutes and then she'd move with accelerated speed, putting everyone's things in perfect order. This, more than anything, helped her win their trust.

She indeed had earned herself a reputation during Beast Training and not everyone knew just what they could expect from her. Some worried she was only out for herself at the expense of others. Thus, when Sharon and Kelsey first met Missy, they were worried. And, because of the body fat incident stories which continued being updated each time Missy went back for a body fat test, they wondered if they'd be targeted along with Missy by upperclass cadets. Missy's boldness, which she'd somehow gotten away with so far, was definitely not anything they wanted any part of. They'd heard how she'd definitely made some enemies. Cadets King and Quigby made no secret about how much they disliked her. They both had lost face and been badly criticized, which they blamed on Missy.

Sharon Manton was a tall girl, five eleven, and a good athlete. She'd been a star basketball player in high school and had no problem with athletic requirements. She was slender with small breasts but that had not affected her self image. She'd been a tomboy for many years and then, suddenly, her easy manner with guys had worked very well as they all finally caught up to her in height and began asking her out on dates. She'd found a really great guy that she'd been dating for over a year and he was absolutely crazy about her. She had dark brown hair and bright blue eyes and was attractive. Not beautiful and not pretty but attractive in her own way, nonetheless.

Kelsey Powers was blond with brown eyes and a round, pretty face. But, she was always struggling to keep her weight down. She was five four and not really athletic; she still hadn't passed the APFT. Her hips were broad and she had huge boobs. Keeping her uniform properly squared away was almost impossible. She truly was always busting out somewhere and had accumulated many demerits already because of that. Boys had been coming on to her for years but she still was insecure and unsure of herself. The upperclass cadets terrified her. But, she was determined to get through West Point and had been second in her high school class academically. She came from a large family who could not afford college tuition and this was her big opportunity.

Missy had hardly spent any time getting to know her new roommates prior to Acceptance Day weekend, with everyone scrambling and adjusting to all the changes and getting ready to finally get away for a few hours each day with their families. That Sunday, when she'd returned from another wonderful time which had again included lovemaking with Mike, she'd been both refreshed and exhausted. And, there'd been a lot of preparation necessary for the next day. She'd focused on her homework and her roommates had both done the same. They'd have time for getting to know one another later.

Then, over the next week, Missy's happiness had been contagious. She made no secret about why: sex with Mike had really helped her, even more than seeing her family. She knew by their scents that Sharon had also had sex with her boyfriend but that Kelsey had not been with anyone. Neither of them talked about it so Missy didn't press. And, she didn't make either of them jealous of her and Mike. She kept all details of their lovemaking very private and simply acknowledged that she had a boyfriend who completed her. She considered herself extremely blessed to have him and since he was such a huge part of her, fulfilling her needs in ways she truly could never explain, she simply could not hide how important he was. She sincerely wished they'd each find their own soulmate someday.

She was good at everything and as she continued each day to help her roommates, making sure their uniforms were squared away and taking care of their room so it was always ready for inspection, both Sharon and Kelsey began to relax. As they realized Missy was truly looking out for them, all their earlier concerns and worries rapidly disappeared. They noticed that Missy had an awful lot of loyal friends and they no longer worried about being targeted. If anything, they learned Missy had a way of intimidating others. She'd made it very clear to everyone. They could target Missy but they'd better not mess with any of Missy's friends or roommates.

Missy not only had a lot of friends in her own plebe class but she was getting many upperclass friends as well. Her being selected to play first string on the soccer team was only one of the reasons. She had also been invited to try out for the Combat Weapons Team, due to her winning top shot during Beast Training. Since the team fired both the M4 rifle and the M9 pistol, she'd been brought out to the pistol range for some training with that weapon by some enthusiastic upperclass cadets. She'd done extremely well and was sure to be selected at the team tryouts as a candidate for the team. Tryouts would be just prior to the Labor Day weekend. Her new cadet friends were highly optimistic she'd then prove herself during the follow on three week assessment and evaluation period.

Since Missy was such a promising athlete, potentially helping West Point teams compete and win, it was only natural that many upperclass cadets were interested in her. That in turn helped Missy avoid being targeted since no one wanted to interfere with what might bring honor to the academy. Cadets King and Quigby had quickly found themselves in a very small group. Only those other cadets who resented women being at West Point were willing to side with them.

Missy approached Kelsey about a week after Acceptance Day when the three of them were sitting around their room, finally actually able to enjoy a bit of free time. She knew how worried Kelsey was about passing the next APFT. "Hey, Kelsey, which part of that test do you have the most trouble with?"

Kelsey said, "All three parts, but probably running is what I find the most difficult. Maybe if I could run faster and lose some weight, my scores in pushups and sit-ups might improve. I wish I could just give you some of my body fat, Missy." She'd heard how Missy supposedly had gained a couple pounds and was up to eleven percent body fat. Jeez! Her own body fat was more than double that and she was not really eating that much. It wasn't fair; Missy had a reputation for eating huge quantities of food but yet had no fat on her.

Missy laughed. "I'd only burn off whatever fat you gave me. But, maybe we can work on things so you can burn off some of yours as well. I helped a guy in my squad and I think I can help you too. Come over here and look into my eyes. Tell me what you see."

Kelsey thought Missy was crazy but figured she'd humor her. Then, after a minute, she realized Missy's eyes were actually changing. "Hey, where did all those yellow and gold speckles come from? I never noticed those before."

"Those only show up at certain times, Kelsey. But, tomorrow morning when you go for your run? You'll run a little faster. Okay?" Missy had given her some energy, just as she'd done with Gary. "You can't really give me any of your body fat but maybe I can give you some of my running speed."

Sharon decided to offer some encouragement also. "Go ahead and take whatever Missy can give you, Kelsey. Maybe if you believe she's doing something, it will make a difference. I'd like to help too but I don't think I can make my eyes sparkle like that." She had walked over and had looked at Missy's eyes. Now, she giggled. "Hey Missy? What can you do for me?"

Missy said, "Right now, Sharon, you don't need a damn thing. But, if you ever need my help, I'll be there for you, sparkly eyes and all. Don't worry!" She laughed and the others laughed along with her.

Ironically, Sharon's needing help ended up being sooner rather than later.

Two days later, Sharon tripped during their morning run and badly twisted her ankle. She was running in the fast group with Missy and her legs got tangled up when one of the other runners stumbled in front of her. Missy heard the commotion and raced back. Sharon was rolling on the ground, holding her ankle with tears running down her face. Most of the others came back and crowded around her, asking if she was okay.

"No, I'm not okay, dammit! I've sprained it. This happened to me three years ago and I missed the rest of the season playing basketball. Fuck!" Sharon was hurting but even more than the pain she was concerned about how an injury like this might affect her West Point activities.

Missy told the others to just give Sharon some room and that she'd take her back to the barracks. She was Sharon's roommate, after all. They all stepped back and Missy knelt down, next to Sharon. After looking at the ankle closely, she told the others not to worry, it probably wasn't that bad, and asked them all to keep on with their run. Once the rest of the group had left the two of them, Missy turned back and smiled at Sharon.

"Why did you say that, Missy? About this not being so bad? This is going to ruin everything for me!" Sharon was still in a lot of pain and not at all happy with Missy. Her ankle had already swollen to the size of a grapefruit and she figured she'd probably torn some ligaments as well.

"Hey, Sharon, right now it's just the two of us. I can see it really is badly injured but no one else really knows how serious this is. So, when you're better by lunchtime? They're not going to know. They saw you fall and no one will claim you were faking anything. But, you're going to be running on this again tomorrow."

Missy reached out and grabbed Sharon's leg. Then she looked deeply into Sharon's eyes. "I'm going to do my sparkly eyes thing now but you have to promise you won't tell anyone else about this. Not even Kelsey. Okay?"

Sharon was really starting to get mad at Missy. "Why? What the hell can you do?" Then, she noticed Missy really did have eyes that were almost glowing because there was so much gold in them. She realized Missy was still waiting for an answer. "Okay, okay. I promise." Then, she began feeling something coming from Missy. And, suddenly the ankle wasn't hurting so badly. She looked closely at Missy and realized Missy was really focused on her; it made her feel strange. This was truly weird.

After three minutes, Missy suddenly stood up. "I think that'll do it, Sharon. See if you can stand and then try to put some weight on it."

Sharon wasn't sure she really could believe this. Her ankle was still very sore but something had definitely happened. And, a lot of the swelling was gone. When Missy reached out her hand, she grabbed it and let Missy pull her up. Then, she gingerly transferred some of her weight to her injured leg, testing her ankle. She stared at Missy, who nodded her head. She put more weight on the ankle, expecting to suddenly feel sharp pain but instead, the ankle held and still only felt sore. She let go of Missy's hand and took a step forward. Then, she took another step and another step. "What did you do, Missy? This is unbelievable -- I know I really sprained it bad … but, did you really do something?"

Missy smiled and said, "Yeah, I did. We can't have you hobbling around on crutches for the next six weeks. Not when I can fix you. You're my roommate and I figure I can trust you to keep quiet about this, right?"

"But, this is incredible! I … I can walk on this. It only hurts a little bit. Is this temporary or did you heal me for real?" Sharon was now walking around, pausing to wiggle her foot back and forth and then walk on it some more.

"It's healed, Sharon. You'll be able to run again tomorrow, if you don't mind it still being a little sore. I'm guessing you're okay with that, right?" Missy came over and looked into Sharon's eyes. Missy's eyes were back to deep green with only a few yellow specs showing. "Let's get back to the barracks. We don't want to be late for formation, now that you're not hurting enough to give us any excuse."

Sharon was deeply moved. "Missy, you really did this for me? I don't really understand it but thank you. Thank you, thank you! This would have been a disaster for me." She started walking back with Missy but was still thinking about what Missy had done, healing her like this. Another thought occurred to her. "You really are helping Kelsey, aren't you? For real? She's going to run faster?"

Missy smiled. "Yeah. And, you're going to see her lose at least ten pounds over the next few weeks too. And, she'll pass her APFT. Her level of fitness will keep improving and her body will firm up nicely. But, you're going to keep all my secrets, right? You promised."

"Oh, yes! I won't tell anyone -- they would never believe me anyways. I'm still not sure I believe this." Sharon continued walking and then she had another thought. "Hey, can you give me bigger boobs? Not that my boyfriend is complaining or anything, but still ...?"

Missy broke out laughing and said, "Gee, Sharon, I've never tried *that* before. But, I doubt it. And, if you and your boyfriend are enjoying them the way they are, then I'd say that old saying definitely applies. If they ain't broke, don't fix 'em!"

Two weeks had gone by since Acceptance Day and Missy finally had a chance to stop in and check on her old roommates. They'd agreed by email to get together at Kelly's room that night, since Kelly's roommates would be out for a little while. They all had a lot they wanted to share and it was great being together again. When Missy arrived, Tracy already was there chatting with Kelly.

Kelly jumped up, hugged Missy and said, "Hey, Tracy's been telling me all about your super hunky brother. How come you never told me about him?"

Missy laughed and was about to reply when she noticed Kelly's scent. She stepped back and looked at Tracy and then back at Kelly. "Never mind about my brother, Kelly. What's going on with you and Gary?" Gary's scent was embedded with Kelly's and they obviously had been having sex. Frequently.

Kelly blushed and said, "Oh, well ... I was planning to explain about that. How come you always know stuff, Missy? Jeez!"

Tracy asked, "What's this about Gary? I haven't heard anything."

Missy giggled. "Kelly is no longer starving for sex, that's what. Start explaining, Kelly -- we want all the details!" Tracy started laughing and was obviously surprised at this news.

"Okay, Missy is right." Kelly looked back and forth at the two of them. "You know how I had started talking to Gary more and more the last few weeks at Beast Training, right? I mean, he stopped by our room almost every night. At first, it was just because he was so easy to talk to. My other relationships with guys haven't exactly included much actual talking. Those were all about having sex and when would we have sex again and was I having sex with other guys. I just never ... whatever. Gary is different."

"When did it change to more than just talking?" asked Missy.

"Acceptance Day. Did you know Gary's Dad is a Brigadier General?" Kelly could see this was news to both Missy and Tracy. "Well, he's stationed in Germany right now and Gary's Mom is there with him. So they didn't come to visit Gary and I invited him to come out with my family. The first day was really nice and we just relaxed at the hotel and then had dinner together. My parents never had dinner with any of my other boyfriends. They really liked Gary."

Tracy said, "Well he is really smart and, as you say, very easy to talk to. His only problem was talking to girls but I guess you helped with that since he was talking to you so much; obviously, you got him to relax and just be himself."

Missy giggled and added, "He's actually changed a lot in appearance since that first week. I don't suppose Kelly noticed that ... or, maybe she did. Come on, Kelly! Details, details!"

"Well, actually, I hadn't really noticed that when I first started talking to him. But, you're right. He really got himself into great shape and lost weight and, well ... I had started checking him out, actually, that last week. That's kind of why I invited him. And, I invited him to come back with us that second day. I told my Mom how I wanted to spend a couple hours alone with Gary and she thought that was a great idea." Kelly giggled. "Gary was clueless. But, I had decided to seduce him and let's just say I was successful. That was Gary's first time, too."

Tracy and Missy were both getting a huge kick out of hearing all this. Kelly explained how she'd never stopped taking her birth control pills and how during that nice dinner with Gary and her parents, the idea of seducing him suddenly just seemed like such a wonderful idea that she began planning it right then. She went on to explain how surprised she was at what a wonderful lover Gary turned out being. He was totally into following her direction and wanted to know all about giving her orgasms. She said no one had ever been as focused on her pleasure as Gary. They'd managed getting together several times since returning to the academy. Gary was really clever at finding times and places. He was now head over heels in love with Kelly and she realized she was really in love with him now also. She never had had a relationship like this before.

Tracy summed it up by saying, "So, you started out seducing him just to satisfy your horny sex starved libido and then you realized how fantastic he was to have sex with and then you noticed how crazy he was about you and then you realized you actually loved him back just as much? Wow! That is crazy!"

Kelly smiled and said, "I probably should thank you both for stopping me when I wanted to have sex with Jeremy Hanson. You heard how he dropped out after Beast, right?" There had been 42 New Cadets who'd decided West Point was not for them and Jeremy had been one of them. Seeing her friends obviously knew about this already, Kelly went on with news they probably hadn't heard yet. "Did you hear about Irene

Hwang? She's leaving now also. She's just learned she's pregnant and wants to keep the baby even though she's already heard from Jeremy. He wants nothing to do with her or the baby. I actually now feel sorry for all the times I called her a slut."

Missy laughed, "Wow! That's a shame. But we're happy for you, Kelly. Truly, we are. Just continue being careful so neither you nor Gary get into any trouble."

"Oh, we will be, we will. We're even careful with all our emails." Kelly looked at Tracy and said, "Speaking of emails ... does Missy know you and her brother are emailing each other?"

Now Tracy blushed. "This isn't as exciting as you and Gary, Kelly. I mean ... we're just telling each other stuff. Nothing romantic or anything; he's not my boyfriend. He asked if he could email me and I said sure. So far, it's been really nice. He's really interesting and has been sharing a lot of things and encouraging me to share stuff. I've been telling him about how it is here at West Point and he's been great. I'm sure it's because Missy doesn't tell him anything."

Missy was staring at Tracy as she listened to all this. She doubted John was at all concerned that she wasn't telling him anything. If John was sending Tracy emails then he really had felt a connection. "How long did the two of you talk to each other that weekend, Tracy? I really had no idea about any of this!"

Tracy said, "Oh, well, we actually did end up talking quite awhile. Especially that second day. Of course, you and Mike were in your own world." She looked at Kelly. "You wouldn't believe how the two of them were so into each other. Even my parents noticed. We all had dinner together that first night and when Missy and Mike came back after disappearing for two hours? Let's just say there was no doubt what they'd been doing."

Missy said, "Enough about what Mike and I were doing. That indeed was out of this world but I'm not sharing anything about that at all. Tell me about you and John."

Tracy laughed. "Sorry, Missy. There's not much to tell. But, he really is a pretty nice guy and I'm enjoying our emails. You know I don't have any experience with guys. But, for some reason, I'm able to just be open with your brother. I think it's because he's being open with me, even though he doesn't know me that well. It's different, telling him stuff in emails. We're not talking about sex or anything. Just stuff. Things I don't think I'd ever say in person. Thoughts and feelings about life and everything going on from one day to the next. I don't know … at first I hardly said anything but he kept sending me these nice messages."

Kelly said, "And, now you're sending him back some nice messages. That's really sweet, Tracy. Watch out though … look what happened to me after I found it so easy telling stuff to Gary."

Missy was seeing a whole different side of her brother John. He'd had a lot of girlfriends but had always moved on for one reason or another. That he was finding a connection with Tracy was indeed amazing. Maybe those fabulous Fates were having even more fun and had put Tracy and Missy together those first few weeks for more than one reason. Interesting!

Chapter Twenty-Four
Aug 2018

Ben Marchitto was sitting in first class, watching the Boston skyline slowly disappear as his flight headed back to New York. He'd talked to all the Boston guys and things there were definitely a mess. Sal was right. Ever since the Feds had arrested Frank McCarthy eight months ago the situation up there had just seemed to go from bad to worse. First, they'd let that guy Carlos from Miami take over in East Boston. An outsider? What were they thinking?

Next, in February five of Frank's guys had disappeared. Then, it turned out the Feds must have them in witness protection since they had to be talking; bodies were getting dug up and more guys were being arrested. Sal was concerned since Marco was one of the guys who had disappeared. He and Ramon had often come down to New York, whenever Sal had asked Frank to loan him some guys. Just as Sal had loaned his guys to Frank. At the time, they both had figured that further insulated them from the various jobs since these loaner guys didn't actually know who was calling the shots. They'd show up, get their instructions and later get paid, all without anything that could be traced to either Sal or Frank.

Now, Frank and Ramon were in prison and Marco might be in witness protection with the Feds. Worse, when Marco had disappeared, Ramon had then asked the cops for witness protection and had implicated Frank in several murders. Sal was not very comfortable but, so far, the Feds had not appeared to be looking at anything in New York. So, Frank wasn't talking. At least, not yet.

Ramon and Marco couldn't directly connect Sal to anything as long as Frank kept quiet. But, if they talked about the jobs they'd done in New York, when on loan from Frank to "somebody down there", that indirect connection was still a worry since the motive for many of those jobs did point to Sal.

Next, in June, Carlos up and goes back to South America? No one knows why but they suspect the Feds might have been too close to grabbing him for something. If so, did they know anything that Sal should know about? That was one of the two reasons Sal had sent Ben up to Boston. Although no one had anyone inside the FBI, there was this guy on the police force … Jerry Masterson. Jerry had been one of Frank's informants and then had been talking to Carlos and the guys he'd brought in. Jerry was very concerned about Carlos up and leaving, as that had left him somewhat exposed. Sal wanted to know everything Jerry might know and might have been talking about to Carlos.

The other reason for this trip was Ramon. Someone had managed to stab him to death with a shiv, in spite of the cops having him in witness protection. So much for witness protection, right? Although, the Feds seemed to be doing much better at that than the cops. So, Ramon wasn't going to testify about anything now. It seemed obvious that Frank had managed to get someone to kill him. All those murder charges against Frank were now going nowhere. But, even so, there were still rumors there might be even more to it. Hence, Sal wanting a thorough investigation.

Why had Ramon rolled over against Frank in the first place? They were only being charged with money laundering and various "while collar" crimes. Something had to have triggered some of these events, which then seemed to cascade one after the other, and Sal wanted to know what that might be.

So, Ben had talked to everyone and had interviewed Jerry Masterson. He'd even learned how Frank had managed taking care of Ramon; he'd used the carrot and stick options on some lifer. The carrot was taking care of the lifer's family so they'd never have any financial worries. The stick was taking care of the lifer's family so they'd all be dead. The lifer had opted for doing what Frank wanted.

Ben had even talked to Frank. That had not resulted in learning anything but at least Frank had assured him that he was not talking to anyone about anything. Frank had said, "You be sure to report that, in case there are any interested parties who may be at all concerned." Yeah, right. Frank knew Ben was Sal's troubleshooter and that, indeed, Sal was both interested and concerned.

So, Ben had documented everything he'd learned. Maybe Sal could make sense of things from Ben's report, since he knew a lot more than Ben did about Frank and things in Boston. Ben had included every wild rumor, including Jerry's latest theory that a high school girl had somehow been mixed up in some of this. Apparently, it was no secret Frank had a strange "hands off" warning concerning her. And, Jerry claimed he'd finally learned that's who Marco was going after, in spite of Frank's edict, when Marco and the guys disappeared. The high school girl. Why? To get some revenge for what she did to his buddy Ramon.

According to Jerry, it was right after Marco disappeared that Ramon decided to maybe worry about Frank's edict after all. That was when he'd demanded witness protection -- supposedly to get protection from Frank. Jerry had thought that was pretty funny, since what had started out as a kick in his balls had ended up being a shiv in his back. Sorry, Ramon!

But, Frank couldn't really be tied to the hit on Ramon and now that all the murder charges were being dropped, it was less likely Frank had any reason to talk. So, Sal could probably relax. While the organization in Boston was in a real mess, none of the turmoil up there should be causing Sal any problems. Hopefully, Sal would agree.

Marsha and Les looked at their boss, Drew. Now what? They'd just finished briefing him on their latest review of the surveillance tapes they'd been checking ever since Missy had turned that task over to them. Billy Martin and Donny Delgato. Checking that neither of these guys would do anything to harm Missy or her family.

While Billy and Donny had often referred to Missy in their conversations with each other, they'd been very careful to never say anything in front of anyone else. From listening to these frequent conversations about Missy, Les and Marsha learned how Tony Gonzales had not been killed right away but had talked to these two guys first. All about that "witch bitch" Missy McCrea who had managed to put a spell on him and had escaped the handcuffs he had her in, using even more witchcraft. She'd even convinced him she could become a wild animal with claws and fangs. Some spell, right?

That hadn't mattered to Billy and Donny very much since they were not about to risk Missy sending her video tape to Sal -- showing them naming Sal responsible for murders they'd done -- so they'd gone ahead and made Tony's death look like an accident in his car, just as she'd ordered them to. But, their favorite reference to her now was as the "witch bitch". Missy, of course, had already programmed the surveillance software to key on that phrase so every time either of them called her that, Les or Marsha would listen to see whatever else these two guys were talking about.

And, that's how they managed learning about this ongoing round up that was apparently one of Sal D'Amato's latest ventures. His guys were rounding up several girls, all to be shipped over to Brunei, a small oil rich Muslim nation where forcing girls to become harem sex slaves was still happening. The country was the richest per capita in the world and, in spite of the scandals years earlier when the royal family had been caught doing this, the demand for girls continued to be very high. As did the payments.

The girls needed to be young and beautiful. More important, they needed to be girls that wouldn't easily be able to escape their fate. Runaways were usually good, since they often were more afraid of going home than of life in some billionaire's harem. Some due diligence was needed to assure the girl wasn't someone with either family or friends seeking to find her. The girls were often held in New York for weeks until it was certain they'd not be missed. Then, with false passports and ID's, they'd be shipped over to Brunei.

Very few of these girls ever returned. And, those who did were not likely to identify anyone back in New York. Typically, they'd been lured in one way or another, or else blackmailed. In any case, there wasn't any evidence of kidnapping and all of the real crimes against these girls happened once they arrived overseas. Arranging for the export of these girls was a very lucrative enterprise and Sal's organization had been doing this for years.

From the comments Billy and Donny were making, another roundup was in process for a shipment later in the year. They were very vocal in how much they wished they could include Missy in one of these shipments, but of course they knew her tape would then get sent to Sal. Missy's well being was their biggest worry since, should anything actually happen to her, they had no way to stop Sal from seeing her tape. She'd told them how it was somewhere on the internet and Sal would get an email with instructions on how to access and watch the damn thing. He'd also be getting a DVD in the mail and there were other methods for getting him to see the video as well.

If nothing else, since it would also be going to the FBI, Sal would see it as part of the evidence against him after his arrest. The only way to avoid all that from ever happening was to make certain Missy was safe. They'd followed her activities which, due to the frequent news articles about her, had not been very difficult. When they'd learned she'd chosen West Point and at least five years after that in the Army, they were not happy. They were still trying to figure out some way to deal with her. They wanted her assurance that if she ended up getting killed in the Army rather than from anything they did, that wouldn't trigger whatever arrangements she'd made for sending the tape to Sal.

Oh, well. Banishing her to Brunei was certainly something they could only dream about. Meanwhile, they did have all these other girls to deal with who would actually be going to Brunei.

And, that's why Les and Marsha had gone to Drew. While they didn't know enough details about this venture to interfere and rescue the girls, assuming any of the girls even wanted to be rescued, they were not comfortable ignoring the fact they now did know about this plan. The whole non interference policy that "P" Branch had was at question here. So, after briefing Drew, they waited for his guidance.

Drew said, "Although we have our non interference policy, we also have to accept our responsibility to Missy. Which, by the way, only reinforces why we have this policy in the first place. See how complicated it gets when we interfere?" Drew smiled at the two of them and then continued, "Missy set this surveillance system up, right? And, we agreed to do this for her. Otherwise, since she couldn't continue doing it at West Point, she'd have involved someone else. Bottom line is we agreed. So, we have to share with Missy whatever we learn."

Les said, "I think I get it. We're not required to listen to all the stuff on these tapes, which might indeed reveal various crimes. But, we've agreed to listen to those parts which the surveillance software identifies as having her key trigger words and phrases. So, whatever we learn from that, Missy would have learned. She's entitled to know about whatever she'd have heard if she was still doing this. If we don't share, we're compromising ourselves."

"Exactly," said Drew. "We don't interfere but we do need to share the info with Missy. If she is okay with ignoring it, then so do we. If she wants to do something about it, then we probably need to support her. That doesn't mean we agree to everything she wants and I think she understands that. But, it's in our interest to support her. Especially since she might take action anyway, even if we don't support her."

Marsha giggled and said, "May Luis and Jose rest in peace."

Sal D'Amato had read Ben's report. Then, he'd been discussing it with Ben to be sure he understood all the details. Sal was only fifty years old and the youngest currently heading any of New York's five families. He hadn't gotten where he was by missing details. He looked like a banker, with average height and weight, and he was starting to go bald. When anyone looked into his eyes, however, they did not think he was a banker. Sal was a predator and his dark brown eyes expressed that very clearly.

Now he wanted to know about something strange that caught his eye in Ben's report. "This high school girl who took out Ramon ... you mention here that Frank agreed to see her but nobody up there even knows why. She shows up out of nowhere and everyone says she's not connected. But, Frank says to send her in. He stops whatever else he had going to make time for this nobody. Why?"

Ben paused a moment and then said, "She told them at the door to tell Frank it was about his friend, Tony Gonzales. That's really all she said and then she sat down and waited. She seemed pretty confident he'd see her. Apparently, that guy Tony had been a friend of Frank's. They grew up together. But he'd been killed months earlier in a car accident. See, I've explained all that over on page twenty two."

Sal stared at Ben for a moment and then looked back at the report. "Okay, I see you mention this on page twenty two. In a fucking footnote. Don't you know who Tony Gonzales was?"

337

Ben shifted uncomfortably as he realized Sal was pissed about something. "No, I never heard of him. The guys in Boston didn't say much and that cop, Jerry -- he didn't know anything about him. Just some dead guy Frank knew ..."

"Tony Gonzales was the guy who handled all Frank's money," snarled Sal. "Yeah, they grew up together and Tony wasn't part of the organization. Frank kept him a big secret. But, that's how Frank got to where he did -- Tony helped launder all their money. Frank told me about Tony when he had me send my guys up there a few times. Tony had a wife he wanted taken care of. Years later, it was his daughter. But, you want to know what's really bugging me right now?"

Ben asked, "Sure, what's the problem, Sal?"

"All the times I've sent my guys up to Frank on loan? Never a problem. Right? Same for all the times his guys Ramon and Marco came down here. But, my guys were up there the weekend Tony had that accident. They came back and said no one left them any folder at their hotel. So, no job and no payment afterwards. When I checked with Frank, he explained how Tony was supposed to do that but had that car accident. He also said he had no idea what Tony wanted done."

"I guess I don't see any connection," said Ben.

"That's my fucking point, Ben. There isn't any connection. Why would some girl be wanting to talk about Tony? Months later? And, be confident Frank would see her." Sal stared at the report and paged back and forth. "It says here that after she took out Ramon, she and Frank then disappeared for hours. Then, Frank comes back and all he has to say is that nobody should bother this girl or her family? Even after she did that to Ramon?"

Ben nodded his head as he began to see Sal's concern. "Frank still won't talk about that girl. But, a lot of folks up there are saying maybe that's why Ramon is dead now. He had his buddy Marco going after the girl, in spite of Frank. You want me to see if I can find out why she mentioned Tony's name?"

"You're damn right I do. And, find out what else happened that night she went off with Frank," said Sal. "Where the hell is she now, anyway?"

"Well, I know she graduated from high school -- that's in my report. I have it in my notes somewhere ..." Ben went through his folder looking at various scraps of paper. "Here it is ... there was a big article in the newspaper. She's at West Point now."

Sal stared at Ben with a quizzical expression. "I thought she was this fighter, doing karate and shit. West Point? You don't get in there unless some senator or congressman is pushing for you. You better go research this girl. If she's got something going with Frank and knew enough about him and Tony being friends ... I don't want to overlook anything. But, be careful how you approach her with any questions. We don't want any congressional investigations being started now, do we?"

Chapter Twenty-Five

Sep 2018

Labor Day weekend finally arrived and Missy was granted a pass. This wasn't automatic but she'd done well, with hardly any demerits. She'd indeed been accepted at the Combat Weapons Team tryouts and things had been going along very well for her. She loved being at West Point.

She signed out Saturday morning and Mike was waiting. First on the agenda was to head for the hills. Missy needed to be a cat. She really wanted to Change and let her wild predatory animal nature have a chance to once again go free. She wanted to kill a deer and had been dreaming about this for several nights. Eating a fresh kill and enjoying the taste of blood -- this was now even more important than her lovemaking with Mike. If she didn't satisfy her animal needs she was concerned she'd start having trouble with the controls she'd worked so hard at for the past three years.

Lovemaking with Mike, of course, would come later. Mike always satisfied not only her human needs but some of her animal needs as well. He really seemed to understand her. And, when there were things about her that he didn't understand, he simply accepted her. Today, he had insisted on going with her; he wanted to really see her while she was in her cat form.

He brought her to a state forest in Connecticut encompassing 24,000 acres and after parking in a secluded area, he walked with her into the forest. She scented they were alone and took off all her clothes. Cavorting naked in front of Mike was fun but she was so anxious to Shift that she didn't waste much time. She Changed. After all the stress from her first two months at West Point, being in her cat form was now just such a wonderful experience. She came up to Mike and leaped into his arms, knocking him to the ground. There, she continued to play, licking his face and rubbing herself against him, all the while purring loudly.

Mike was laughing at her antics and getting a huge kick out of seeing her like this. Then, she had to hunt. She leapt up and raced off, leaving him to follow behind. At first, she just reveled in being in the outdoors, scenting the forest and clean fresh air. Experiencing how different everything was for her in her cat form and yet how familiar all this was as well. She'd lived as a mountain lion for over two years and loved now being able to move as a cat, once again running on four paws. She was in no hurry and enjoyed prowling through the hills and ravines, just as she'd done so many times before.

After an hour, she circled back and climbed to some higher ground. Within minutes she scented a large deer and tracked it to a small river winding down through the hills. She stalked it for awhile and finally charged, leaping onto its back and breaking its neck. Doing this was primal and she let out a cougar scream, announcing her joy and letting Mike know where to find her. She also sent him a few mental messages as well, just because she could.

By the time he arrived, she had feasted and half the deer was gone. She wasn't staying and so didn't bother hiding her kill; she'd leave it for scavengers to find. She came up to Mike and rubbed herself against his leg. He laughed and sat down on a nearby log. She stretched out next to him and went to sleep.

After napping for about forty minutes, she stirred and found him studying her. She bared her fangs at him and yawned, letting him truly get a sense for how she was in this form. He seemed really impressed with her long tail and started making jokes about it. She chuffed and after parading around him for a minute, clearly exhibiting regal behavior, she loped away and headed back towards their car. Mike followed and rather than racing ahead, she circled back and kept pace with him all the way back. They actually talked, Mike using his voice and Missy sending him mental messages.

Returning to where she'd left her clothes, she Changed. Once again, being exposed and naked in front of Mike was exciting and she sensed how aroused he started getting. But, it was a cool September day and she decided to get dressed. She wiggled her bare ass in front of him, no longer having any tail, and pulled on her panties. He laughed and promised to punish her later, which she assured him she was looking forward to. Then she finished putting all her clothes on and they went back to his car. Not surprisingly, she slept for most of the way home after that. A very content and happy werecat.

That night, after a very busy afternoon with family and friends, followed by an evening that had been really special -- Alice's bridal shower -- Missy finally was able to crawl into bed with Mike. They were in Mike's home, alone. He'd planned ahead and had arranged to spend this weekend with Missy without having his parents there. They'd been very understanding about that and had gone away on a vacation cruise. Michelle, of course, was with Aaron.

Missy had spent the night at Mike's home a few times before, but -- like tonight -- always with his parents away. Having the place all to themselves allowed them to freely frolic and they both really liked that. Especially after being separated for two months. Their lovemaking at the hotel during Acceptance Day weekend had been wonderful but they both missed being together all night long. Falling asleep in each other's arms after making love, waking up together and making love all over again ... those were really special times. Since such opportunities were now so rare, they both really enjoyed it whenever possible.

And, tonight, it was possible. Missy had returned with Mike from the bridal shower which he'd gone to merely to keep Mark company. While all the ladies were oohing and aahing over each gift, as well as nibbling on delicious goodies, the two guys had strolled outside on the walkway along the ocean. Alice's Mom had done a fantastic job and the restaurant where the shower was held was in Gloucester, not far from the famous memorial statue to all the fishermen who had lost their lives at sea. The shower was a huge success but the guys stayed away for most of it, returning only at the end of the event. Mark could barely fit all the gifts into their car. And, the guys helped pack up all the decorations, whatnots and dodads that Alice's Mom had brought.

Since Mark was one of the few whom Missy had revealed her werecat identity to, Mike had been able to discuss that with him openly. Mark now knew most of what Missy had done for Alice and was deeply grateful. He'd even provided Mike with a few details Mike had not actually heard from Missy yet. But, most of their conversation had been about other matters, such as life at college and various friends they had in common. It was Mark who explained to Mike about Missy's brother John. Apparently, John was getting more and more involved with that girl Tracy he'd met that weekend at West Point.

Mike had told Missy all about her brother as they'd driven back from the shower. She'd told him what little she'd learned from Tracy and had been amazed to find out that John was actually at West Point, seeing Tracy, right at that very moment. Tracy had not taken a pass for the weekend since going home to Texas was too far away. Instead, she had planned to merely enjoy Walking Privileges. Since so many upperclass cadets were gone, the plebes who stayed behind were actually able to freely enjoy themselves right there at the academy and many had visitors.

From under the covers, Missy asked, "Tell me again what Mark said." She looked at Mike who had just

344

joined her. "About how John told him that Tracy was different from anyone he'd ever met."

"Well, he was very impressed with meeting her. He told Mark he knew she was shy and inexperienced but that, for some strange reason, he found it very easy to talk to her. Then, he came home and has been sending her emails ever since. He said he's really feeling a connection with her and told Mark he hadn't been able to think about any other girl since. Reminds me how I felt about you, remember?"

Missy laughed. "Yeah, but I ignored you for months. Thank goodness that didn't stop you. So, John is down there visiting Tracy, exploring whether this connection he's feeling might lead to something more?"

Mike pulled Missy up against his chest and was delighted to find that she was naked under the covers. Her breasts were pressed against him and he slid one hand down to caress her lovely rear. "He told Mark that he just wanted to spend more time seeing her, face to face. She's going to show him around West Point and he'll only be visiting her there during the day and evening, but still. He thinks by Monday he'll know one way or another. If she's the one."

Missy giggled and, getting turned on by Mike's hand on her ass, began wriggling on top of him. He was wearing undershorts which were restraining his erection, now noticeably pressing against her right leg. She wrapped both her arms around him, hugging him tight. She pulled herself upward so she could plant a quick kiss on his lips and then slid back down placing her head back on his chest. "If she's really the one, then John better be prepared for making a lot of sacrifices over the next few years. Look what you're going through, putting up with me ..."

Mike laughed and rolled over on top of her, keeping most of his weight on his elbows. He stared into her eyes, which were definitely filling up with golden specs. "When the girl is the one, the right one, then any amount of sacrifice is more than worth it. Plus, there are those occasional *benefits*." He began slowly nibbling on one of her erect nipples. "Ummmm! Like this!" Moving over to her other nipple, which he began licking and teasing with his tongue, he murmured, "And, this!"

Missy quickly forgot all about John and Tracy as her body began to throb with that wonderful achy reaction to Mike's attention. She grabbed his underwear and began pushing that down and between his wriggling and her assisting with her feet, they managed to get him free. While he was kicking his underwear off to the side she began kissing him and wrapped her arms around his neck. She was getting very turned on in a sudden rush of desire. Then, she relaxed all her controls and completely opened herself up to Mike. Her passionate emotions suddenly flooded her with an excitement which also overwhelmed Mike with an equally passionate reaction.

Suddenly, she was so wet and ready. "Hurry, Mike! I want you *now*. Please ... ohhh ...OOHHHH ..." Mike had moved into position, just as she was spreading her knees wide apart, and he easily entered her and smoothly penetrated deep inside. She wrapped her legs around his rear and began thrusting, eagerly seeking more sensations. Feeling the pressure and fullness of him hard inside her was wonderful but her body was on fire. Mike responded by moving side to side, rather than in and out.

Wow! How he knew that was just what her body wanted, she didn't bother thinking about. Instead, she ground herself against his hardness and began bucking wildly as an "almost" convulsion somehow happened. She was "almost" able to experience her orgasm which only drove her to thrash and squirm under Mike, seeking to bring herself over the edge. Mike responded by taking control, forcing her body to follow his lead, and soon they were moving in a mutual rhythm that caused her to climb even higher. The climb, however, was one of certainty with the ultimate release no longer in doubt.

Then, finally, she felt the explosive convulsions begin and wave after wave of pleasure consumed her. She began shrieking and yelling, screaming for more and more and more. Mike soon went over the edge and she felt his body convulse and his seed being spurted inside her; this only added to her pleasure and brought her to even greater heights. Missy's enhanced senses were especially sensitive, causing several involuntary contractions and spasms for each of her convulsions. Whether she was having one long, continuous orgasm or several multiple orgasms, one after the other, she didn't know and it hardly mattered.

Mike stopped moving and Missy finally felt her body relax and subside, her release total and complete. This time, there weren't even any of those aftershocks she usually found so delicious. No, this time she was totally spent and satiated and felt absolutely wonderful. She squeezed Mike and began slowly returning back to earth. She could hear herself making unintelligible noises and her face was wet with tears. That had sure been great!

And, to her great delight, she suddenly realized Mike was asleep. This time, he'd passed out first. He was still semi-erect inside her but his huge body was lying on top of her, limp and spent, and he was definitely sound asleep. She inhaled deeply, enjoying the strong scent of all their sex and lovemaking and slowly slid herself out from under Mike. Then, she wrapped him around her so he was hugging her back and rear and their limbs were entwined together. She pulled one of his hands to her chest and he cupped her breast in his sleep. Less than a minute later, she also was sound asleep.

The bachelorette party Sunday night was several hours away yet and Missy was indeed looking forward to that. But, once again, she was walking into her favorite coffee shop, meeting Robert Ulrey. He'd called asking for this meeting and she was actually happy to see him.

Today, of course, she was pretty happy about everything. She'd awakened with Mike still there, cuddled closely against her sensitive body. Her super

348

sensitive body, filled with an amazing amount of energy. She'd inhaled deeply and began getting aroused right away. It hadn't taken her long to realize how wet, slick and slippery she was feeling inside her thighs, with her insatiable libido once again taking advantage of things with Mike right there.

Before Mike had fully awakened, she'd already been astride him. She'd grabbed what he'd later explained had merely been his "piss hard-on" and had climbed right on, mounting him. She leisurely had continued to ride, feeling quite satisfied with herself as he grew firmer and harder inside her, gradually joining in the fun. His hands had reached up and grabbed her breasts, which had spurred her movements more towards the fast, furious and frantic side of things and it didn't take long before they both were engulfed yet again in blissful climaxes, first his and then hers. When he'd then rushed into the bathroom to relieve his bladder, joking how she'd taken unfair advantage of him, she'd giggled with delight and been very pleased with herself.

For Robert, she'd dressed in a nice pair of slacks with a bright yellow sweater. Not having to wear her cadet uniforms was especially fun and she enjoyed being out and about in normal clothes. Her shortened hair was up in a high pony tail. She was wearing her favorite earrings and had applied just a touch of makeup and lipstick. She knew she was looking pretty good, which was confirmed when she entered the coffee shop and every eye in the place looked her way. She found

Robert in a booth in the back and gave him one of her dazzling smiles.

Robert said, "Wow, you really know how to amp up the excitement in this place." He laughed and said, "Of course, you're radiating that glow you seem to exude now whenever you've been with Mike. Do I dare ask how military life is treating you?"

Missy laughed and said, "Life is good. And, yes, Mike is great. You know I'm not at all bashful about that. He's the source for all this energy I have." She sent him an energy pulse and was delighted at his reaction.

Robert said, "You know, I've been researching our archives ... not many of you supernatural types are capable of pushing out energy the way you do. Have you figured out yet why you can do that?" He was really pleased to see how happy she looked.

"Well, my guess is that all those others your research has turned up are probably witches, right?" Missy sighed. "When were you planning to tell me there was a witch in my class, Robert? Surely you guys know about Tracy McGonagle. Did you think we wouldn't notice one another?"

Robert laughed. "Actually, we weren't sure. We figured she'd notice you ... we really had no way of predicting how things would go after that. She, of course, knows nothing about us stodgy folks in "P" Branch. You haven't been telling her any tales, have you?"

"Of course not. You know me better than that. I'm really good at keeping secrets, remember?" Missy laughed. "Tracy is my best friend at the academy. We actually were paired together during Beast Training. I know you guys didn't arrange that. We both figure it's those Fates, having fun. Fortunately, we really like each other. And, she's pretty much convinced me. I'm also a witch. That's why I can heal myself and heal others and push out these energy pulses."

Robert smiled. "I didn't want to say anything but that's pretty much what Drew and most of the experienced guys on his team have been telling me. Werecats can Shift form but it takes a witch to do those other things you do."

"Interesting. Not that I'm about to join any covens but it does help me better understand what I am. I think." Missy giggled. "Now that I know I probably am one, I have a whole new world of supernatural activity to learn about. Being a supnat is not all fun and games … lots of work, work, work involved too!"

"Well, as much fun as all this supnat stuff might be to talk about, I do have a couple of reasons why I asked to meet with you today. For one, Ramon is dead. He was stabbed to death in prison by one of the lifer inmates. We're pretty sure Frank was behind that, but no one can prove it."

"Wow! Does that mean all those murder charges against Frank will get dropped?" Missy asked.

"Yes, without Ramon's testimony, getting any conviction would be difficult," said Robert. "What's interesting is the complete turnaround this has caused for Marco. He's now fully on board with staying in witness protection and is quite happy to talk about everything. Unfortunately, we probably will never let him testify so all his information is just that: information. No one is being charged with anything."

"Interesting, indeed! I suppose he figured if Frank could get to Ramon, his chances back on the outside were not looking so good, huh? At least you're able to confirm a lot of things as fact, even if you can't act on that unless you can find other sources."

Robert nodded and said, "Yes on both counts. He figured Frank would get him and we're glad to know a lot more about things. Knowing those things might help us find those other sources. By the way ... Marco thinks Frank might actually have had Ramon killed for ignoring his edict about leaving you alone and encouraging Marco to go after you. Not that it really matters but that thought was what tipped the scales for Marco. No way was he interested in finding out the hard way. Frank knows a lot of people and obviously can still influence things."

Missy asked, "Does that make it easier for you "P" Branch guys? Holding him? I realize your holding him was only to support me and when he was not cooperating, I know that had you all rethinking your policies. Maybe regretting you didn't just stay with your non interference policy unless absolutely necessary due to dire, drastic situations. And, I don't flatter myself that my situation was dire or drastic. I mean, obviously, it was for me. But, not for you guys. I bet you could easily have found a way to cover up something simple like a little massacre in that parking garage." Both Missy and Robert broke out laughing at that.

"Regrets? What's done is done and I'm not going there, Missy. Nope, not at all." Robert shook his head side to side. "To answer your first question, though, it indeed is much better that Marco is fully cooperating. He's quite happy to sign paperwork for us, saying his long incarceration for all these months has been voluntary. But, while that solves one ethical dilemma for us, we now have another."

Missy raised one eyebrow and studied Robert. "Oh?"

Robert said, "Yeah. We learned a few things using that surveillance system you had us take over for you. Ironically, it was the phrase "witch bitch" that you programmed the software to key on that led to this. While we don't want to interfere, Drew insists you have a right to know about these things. You'd have learned them if we hadn't taken this over and we realize we can't withhold things from you without compromising this whole arrangement."

Missy nodded her head. "True, I'm glad you guys understand that. We didn't actually talk about it but, Drew is correct. If we had discussed this, he knows exactly where I'd have stood on the issue. I'm actually wondering about him. He knows so much about me and I haven't even met him yet."

Robert smiled and said, "Oh, I'm pretty sure the two of you will meet someday. Probably when those Fates you mention think that might be fun. Meanwhile, Les and Marsha have learned about this one scheme you probably wouldn't ignore. And, I agree with them. We all know you pretty well, too, you know." He laughed.

"Well, this must be interesting. I have willingly ignored all the murders, gambling, prostitution, loan sharking, extortion and various other day to day activities for Sal's organization. Interfering with any of that would be like trying to boil the ocean." Missy stared at Robert. "What's he doing now? Hurting innocent kids?"

"Well, not exactly. Not kids and I don't know how innocent they are. But, a couple of times each year he rounds up several young girls and then, after making sure no one will be looking very hard to find them, he ships them over to Brunei. There are several very rich clients over there that will pay big bucks for these girls."

Missy thought about this for a moment. "Brunei? I've never even heard of that place. And, are you saying these girls will maybe become sex slaves or something?"

"Brunei is one of those oil rich Muslim nations. It's a small country located on the northern part of Borneo, an island in Southeast Asia. They have a Sultan who runs the country. And, these girls would end up in some billionaire's harem. Since that's maybe only part forcing them and part luring them with riches and a life of luxury, the sex slave part isn't exactly clear. But, yeah

… we all figured you'd be a little concerned and unhappy about that."

"And the girls? What can you tell me about them?" Missy was indeed concerned and unhappy.

"Young. Pretty. Natural blonds are very much in demand. Then, maybe redheads. That's why Billy and Donny keep talking about you, their redheaded witch bitch. It's only wishful thinking about you, of course, but they have been helping with this scheme and there are probably going to be a dozen or so girls in the next shipment. Mostly runaways. Fifteen, sixteen years old."

"Ugh. I can definitely relate." Missy thought back to those two years when she was all alone. "Once they get way over there, there's not much chance for their coming back is there? Who are they gonna call?"

Robert said, "Exactly. They enter the country with false ID's and passports and no money or resources of any kind. By the time they might ever manage getting money of their own, they will have lived in a harem for months. Maybe years. And, trying to escape only exposes them to things probably much worse than being in the harem, which I'm sure is clearly pointed out to them."

Missy took a minute to process all of this. "If I'm okay with ignoring this, what happens? You have made a career in the FBI trying to solve and prevent kidnappings, right?"

Robert nodded. He knew she'd understand how he felt. "If you say to ignore it, then "P" Branch will ignore it. Their non interference policy. And, I'll ignore it also. Even though it kills me ... there are many open cases in my files which might very well be for girls this has happened to."

"And, if I say not to ignore it? What then?" Missy was now curious. After all, the government didn't work for her.

"Missy, we won't act on this information. But, if you take action, we'll support you. Just as we supported you when Marco and his guys went after you in that parking garage." Robert realized this was putting the whole moral dilemma squarely on her shoulders. The subject had been discussed at great length by everyone at "P" Branch.

"Okay, okay. I get it." Missy was not happy but this was probably the way it had to be. The government couldn't suddenly go charging in and make any arrests. The surveillance they were doing for her was not even legal. They'd merely agreed to help her and support her because it was keeping her safe. And, only because she was a supnat. A supnat they'd already accepted some responsibility for helping. "You guys will clean up after me but I need to handle it. Or, ignore it."

"About all I can offer you is more information. It's probably what you'd be doing if you didn't want to ignore it and you were still doing the surveillance yourself. Get more information, right?" Robert paused for just a moment. "We still don't want you out there being a vigilante. You do understand that, right? You can't save the whole world, Missy. And, running wild out there won't really help much. Rescuing Alice the way you did was one thing. We really don't need to have this conversation, do we?"

Missy sighed. No, they didn't need to discuss it. She'd been lucky the government had been willing to ignore what she'd done, killing Luis and Jose. And, arranging for Tony's death. A year ago, she'd been afraid the government might lock her up in some lab. Hell, they still might. She looked at Robert. "Okay. Keep feeding me with information. Just as though I were the one doing the surveillance. I'd probably tweak the software to key on a few additional words and phrases, right? I'm sure Les and Marsha will know what to do."

Robert nodded. It's what they'd anticipated from her, after all. Missy had demonstrated her willingness to merely sit and wait. Several times. That, and her ability to stalk her prey. She was a predator who only took direct action when forced to do so and no other options were available. She'd handled that parking garage attack pretty well. Maybe she'd find a way to handle this. "Good luck at West Point, Missy. We'll send you emails about this Brunei harem girl thing. I'm guessing you'll let us know how we can help you, when the time comes."

Chapter Twenty-Six
Sep 2018

Missy had been back at West Point for three weeks and was now totally focused on her life at the academy. Her family and friends were not forgotten but her thoughts about them were in a different compartment of her mind. She'd thoroughly enjoyed her weekend home, Alice's bridal shower and bachelorette party and of course her time with Mike. But she was dedicated to being the best possible cadet and to all her activities at the academy. She also was helping many of her classmates.

She was keeping her weight at 140 pounds and her body fat at twelve percent, which actually made her clothes fit more snuggly in a few places then when she had weighed 150 pounds. Since those places were her curvy hips, ass and breasts and only made her appearance sexier than before, she really wasn't concerned. She was at an optimal level of fitness for her athletic activities, which was all she cared about.

She had helped her soccer team a lot and they'd only lost one game so far. Her coach, Kristen, was excited about this year since they were clearly headed for one of their better seasons. Kristen was not only pleased with how well Missy played, scoring goals and making assists, but with how much Missy was helping her teammates. Somehow, each of them was playing much better also and Kristen realized those improvements were definitely because of Missy.

It had taken Kristen almost three weeks to see it, but once she finally sensed it was because of Missy, she was able to notice all the little things going on after that. She realized that many of those assists that Missy had made were incredible. The girl who actually scored the goal had gotten all the attention but, as Kristen reviewed the game video tapes, she began to realize just how amazing Missy's play really had been. Even more, Missy's attitude and leadership was affecting the others. They all grew more confident and began playing as a team rather than as individuals.

Missy never wanted any credit but was always encouraging the other girls, pointing out what they'd done right and quietly helping them see where they could improve without making them feel bad about any of their shortcomings. She also had a knack for keeping it fun, inspiring them to work harder and never get discouraged. Missy really tuned into each of the other players and, whatever problems they were having, on or off the playing field, Missy was offering her help.

Missy was very quick to get right into anyone's face if they bullied or belittled others. Kristen had seen a couple of instances where things had gotten quite scary. Missy was so physical that everyone else would always back down, even those who hadn't heard of how badass a martial arts fighter she truly was. When Missy's eyes blazed with anger there was never any doubt who would win any argument. No one messed with either Missy or with anyone else that Missy wanted left alone.

Fortunately, Missy didn't hold grudges and the entire team was now really all on the same page. Even Barbara. Kristen smiled at the way the two were now getting along. Barbara was a fiery Latin American girl, born in New Orleans but her parents were both from Brazil. She was a big, powerful girl and very athletic -- almost as fast as Missy and a couple inches taller. She and Missy were always facing off during the first couple of weeks, mostly because Barbara had such a short fuse and would lash out at others in her frustration. Whenever that happened, Missy was immediately right there, even though she wasn't the one Barbara had lashed out at.

Only once did Barbara ever attempt pushing Missy. She was used to always being able to cower others and when Missy objected to the way she was yelling at a teammate during practice for some mistake, she turned around and brought both hands up, preparing to shove Missy aside. Suddenly, Missy was holding both of Barbara's wrists and Barbara couldn't move. She was completely immobilized by the iron grip Missy had on each of her arms. Missy never said a word but her eyes were glowing and those standing around said later they could feel some sort of energy force.

Then, it started to become a team joke. Barbara would get pissed off, start yelling at someone else and Missy would be in her face. Missy never yelled and would let Barbara vent, streaming one expletive after another until running out of steam. These incidents happened less and less as Barbara herself began realizing how ridiculous her rants were becoming, with everyone else finding it amusing.

Kristen didn't see what happened back in the barracks but apparently, there were incidents when some upperclass cadet was really making Barbara's life miserable. Every time she turned around, she was getting demerits and with her short fuse, she was headed for some serious trouble. And, suddenly, that upperclass cadet was no longer bothering Barbara. Missy had some of her Combat Weapons Team buddies put the fear of god into that guy and he totally lost all interest in Barbara.

Missy never even acknowledged doing anything but everyone knew. She was making such a huge impression with those Combat Weapons Team upperclass cadets that clearly she was behind this. Barbara and Missy now seemed like they'd always been best friends and the rest of the team now joked about that.

While Missy loved playing soccer, it was her participation on the Combat Weapons Team that was really bringing her some fulfillment. She had quickly learned how to be both fast and accurate with both the M9 pistol and the M4 rifle and the others on the team were very excited to have her help at the competitions they'd gone to so far. She rarely missed any target and no one else could shoot as fast as Missy could. She loved competing and her performance was so outstanding that it didn't take long for the whole academy to hear about her. Her reputation as one of

West Point's finest in marksmanship was something everyone became aware of.

The Combat Weapons Team was both men and women and all that mattered was how well you fired your weapon, not what sex you were. Life at the academy was difficult for everyone but at the firing range, Missy was able to focus solely on shooting and that really provided a fabulous release for her. Nothing else mattered. And, no one was concerned about whether she was a plebe or a firstie, a male or a female. As she practiced and her skill continued to improve, her satisfaction carried over into all areas of her life at West Point.

She not only loved shooting weapons, she loved learning about them. She studied everything available and her thirst for knowledge about pistols and rifles even carried over to field artillery pieces, both modern and those used in earlier times. If there was a gun that could fire a projectile, Missy wanted to know about it. After only a month of studying, she was hardly an expert but her ability to assimilate facts, figures and miscellaneous data about weaponry was amazing.

She told her friends she'd added a compartment to her mind just for weapons that could be fired. She claimed to have another compartment for other weapons, such as knives and swords and battle axes -- weapons that could be wielded. And, yet another compartment for bows and arrows, crossbows ... even blowguns ... primitive weapons. She'd actually started those mental compartments years earlier in her karate classes. She was not just knowledgeable about wielding and using such weapons but was also proficient as well, although she hadn't trained herself in those the way she had in martial arts and was now doing at the firing range.

Her roommates Sharon and Kelsey were now close friends and part of a gradually increasing group of close friends that Missy had at West Point. Sharon never told anyone else how Missy had healed her ankle but continued to be grateful and feel indebted to Missy for that. Kelsey had indeed lost ten pounds and had passed her APFT with no problem. She no longer was having as much trouble keeping her uniform properly squared away. Her only problem was how all the guys now seemed to notice how great her ass looked and how perfect her boobs were. She was still insecure and unsure of herself with guys but Missy had promised to help her with that. Just knowing Missy was going to help somehow made Kelsey feel more at ease.

Kelly and Gary were now definitely a couple. They kept things strictly according to all the rules, which Gary was an expert with, but managed to still find many opportunities to be together. They really loved each other and just being together was often all they needed. Of course, as Kelly had explained earlier, Gary was indeed clever at finding times and places and he had continued way, way up the learning curve on how to give Kelly some rather spectacular orgasms. She was definitely now a very happy girl which had translated to her doing very well with all her studies and activities at the academy.

Not everyone was happy. Angel was really struggling and in spite of having a lot of friends, she was constantly finding herself getting demerits and into trouble. Her study habits were poor and her academic ability was not that good, resulting in her really floundering in most of her courses. Having a few upperclass cadets that seemed fond of picking on her didn't help and wasn't anything Missy could do much about. Angel just seemed to have a knack for messing up. She was now complaining how all this military shit wasn't really her thing. Her friends reminded her how she was good at a lot of things -- she had no problem with all the physical stuff -- and to just keep her head down and try harder at her studies. So far, she was hanging in there.

Most of the others that had been in Missy's squad during Beast Training were doing well enough. Marcus and Tony continued to stay in touch with Missy and Tracy. The four of them were looked up to as the natural leaders by all the others in their group of friends. Their combined knowledge and talents made them always the ones everyone else sought out for advice and help.

Life at West Point was difficult for everyone but those who took things in stride, one day at a time, and who had a real desire to become an officer in the Army were able to manage. Each week seemed to bring a new crisis but somehow, that hurdle would be gotten over and then it was a new week, and a new crisis. What happened last week was old news, quickly forgotten, and the focus was always on whatever new challenge was being presented.

Tracy was not having any problems and continued being Missy's closest friend. She was actually very comfortable with all the "military shit" and being a good athlete and an excellent student, her progress as a cadet was going well. Her interacting with guys had really improved and that was the most noticeable change for her. She now had an inner confidence and self awareness that was special. She told Missy this was all due to her emails back and forth with John.

Missy had quizzed her right away, of course, upon returning after Labor Day. How had things gone with John? He had visited all three days and had spent every possible moment in her company. Tracy had enjoyed showing him around and had been amazed at how the time had just flown by, without their actually doing anything. They'd talked for hours and she simply had never had anything like that happen before. Being with a guy and just talking. John had wanted to know everything about her, going back to first grade; she couldn't really remember much before that. Where she'd been, what she'd done, what she liked and didn't like, what did she get excited about.

No, she didn't say anything about being a witch. No, she didn't let on that she knew Missy was a werecat. And, yes -- he did kiss her. Not until the last day, but Tracy was ecstatic over how nice that had been. They'd been walking on Flirtation Walk, the rocky foot trail along the Hudson River that had so much history. It was inevitable that their conversation would finally bring them to would it be okay if he kissed her. Tracy had been anxiously waiting for that the whole three days and of course had said yes.

When John had taken her into his arms and began kissing her, she'd almost melted. He had been so sweet with her, somehow knowing just how to make her relax and enjoy being kissed. She told Missy that kiss made her feel willing to do anything he wanted and give him anything he wanted and she truly couldn't believe it. She'd gone totally gonzo over him by that point and was definitely experiencing things she'd never known before.

Apparently, John had been fully aware of how vulnerable she was and was very careful not to take advantage. He'd kissed her and he'd made sure she knew she'd been kissed. But, he'd stopped and had explained how this visit with her had changed his life and he was not going to rush anything. Tracy of course was all the more ready to abandon everything and run away with him, if that's what he wanted. Or, at least that's how she'd felt at the time. She and Missy had had a lot of fun talking about all that.

Was John now her boyfriend? Oh, yes! Tracy explained that wasn't the issue, as she'd never really had boyfriends before. A few dates, yes. Boyfriends? No. So her being serious about John was easy. The issue, of course, was whether John was serious about her. She really couldn't believe he'd be willing to consider her as his girlfriend and not continue to date other girls out there "in the real world". But, all of his emails since then had been very convincing. He was interested in her and in seeing where things with her might go. And, he was willing to go slow, and knew full well how difficult it would be trying to have a relationship with someone like her, a cadet at West Point.

Missy of course was thrilled and had promised she'd not interfere in any way. Whatever the two of them were telling each other in all those emails was definitely having a huge effect on Tracy. She was now much more open and comfortable with guys around and was not having any problems in class or out of class. She was even okay listening to all the talk about sex which was constantly going on all around her. Her inexperience didn't matter now because she had this guy out there who was convincing her that she was his whole world. She wasn't yet ready to believe that but it definitely was making her feel pretty good about herself.

Missy tried to stay in touch with her friends outside but it was difficult. So little time. She did exchange emails with Alice and Mike's sister, Michelle, but she just couldn't find time to respond to any of her other friends. She didn't even send Mike all that many emails. He sent her wonderful messages almost every day, which she loved getting. She replied more with mental messages she'd send him at odd moments throughout her day. Since he always acknowledged them in his emails to her, she had no doubt about his getting them. She could feel his emotions also when she stopped and tuned in to him. She considered Mike to truly be a part of her and that was that.

She was getting updates from "P" Branch, and that was her only real worry item. She had no idea yet what to do about Sal, the New York mob organization and this Brunei harem girl venture thing they had going. She began considering a few options and decided she wanted more info on Sal's home. She knew the address of course, along with all sorts of things about Sal and his entire organization. She'd traded for that info back when she'd given the FBI all those documents showing how Tony Gonzales had laundered money for Frank McCarthy. Sal had a nice estate just outside of New York City. She decided she needed to know a lot more about that estate. Just in case she ever needed to pay Sal a visit.

It was the last Sunday in September, the football game the day before had been at home and Army had won, 35 to 16. Life for plebes was definitely a little better the week after any football win. Missy was relaxing in her room, lounging in her gym shorts and a tee shirt, when her phone rang. She learned there was a visitor who wished to see her. No, he was not a journalist and he didn't think she knew him, but he had a private matter to discuss with her. It shouldn't take long. His name probably wouldn't mean anything to her. A Mr. Benjamin Marchitto. A lawyer. Was she willing to come out to the Visitor Center and maybe give him thirty minutes?

Wow! Missy knew exactly who Ben Marchitto was but she didn't know anyone in Sal's organization had ever heard anything about her. Billy and Donny hadn't said anything or she'd have gotten an alert from Les and Marsha. Obviously, her name had finally come up somehow and it probably was that visit she'd made to Frank. She was pretty sure Frank hadn't talked but maybe they were probing, now that Ramon had been killed. She said she'd come out to see Mr. Marchitto. Give her fifteen minutes.

She only needed ten minutes to get dressed and she used the other five minutes to check up on her internet storage site for the latest info on Marchitto. She had uploaded all her files on Sal and his organization. In addition to monitoring her surveillance system on Billy and Donny, she had asked Les and Marsha to keep updating all those files for her. Since they had access to all the FBI files and many other sources as well, the info she'd originally obtained on Sal was now a lot more detailed and complete.

There was some new info that she'd not seen before. And, they even listed Marchitto's latest mistress with the address in the Bronx where he was keeping her. Missy smiled. Who called themselves Minerva these days, anyway? She was from Russia and that of course wasn't her real name but Minnie, as she liked having Ben call her, had been going under the name Minerva Rollinson since coming to the US five years ago. There was even a photo showing a small, blond woman with a very nice figure and an interesting face. She had green eyes which Missy thought was ironic; maybe Ben had a thing for girls with green eyes.

Missy dressed in her full dress grey uniform, a grey wool coat with "swallowtail" coattails over grey

369

pants. The coat had ball shaped brass buttons in three rows down the front plus three brass buttons on each sleeve, with more buttons on the back and even two buttons on the collar. There was black braid embroidery that went with the buttons but she was not wearing the starched white cross belts and polished brass breastplate she'd have also worn if this was for a parade. Even so, she was very impressive. This uniform was basically the same as that adopted for cadets at West Point back in 1816.

She wore her hair straight down in her pageboy style which reached to just above the collar, per regulation. She now had bangs over her eyes and their dark red color made those deep green eyes of hers that much more noticeable. With her natural coloring and glowing good health, she didn't need any makeup to look really great -- she didn't even bother with any lipstick.

When she entered the Visitor Center, she was directed to a small conference room where Marchitto was waiting. He stood up as soon as she entered and introduced himself. He was in his late forties, five-ten and about a hundred and eighty pounds. He had dark brown hair and brown eyes, which were checking her out and very clearly liked everything he was seeing; she could see he was very impressed seeing her in uniform like this. He was only average looking but had a pleasant enough smile. The smile seemed a bit forced, however, as though he wasn't all that comfortable actually using it and it didn't match what was happening behind his eyes. Missy didn't trust him at all.

"Ms. McCrea … or, should I call you Cadet McCrea?" Marchitto looked around and gestured for her to take a seat, which she did on one of the lounge chairs. He seated himself on a similar chair with a small table next to it. The chairs were at about forty five degrees to one another and at the end of the room, beyond the small conference table. Missy could see the Hudson River out the window behind him.

"Cadet McCrea is good. I don't know you, sir … what is this about?" Missy was seated with her back straight and her hands folded in her lap, knees together and feet side by side; very prim and proper. She smiled briefly and waited.

"Well, I've come here today on a rather delicate matter … allow me to show you a photo?" When Missy nodded her consent, he opened a small leather briefcase and pulled out an eight by ten glossy and handed it to her.

Missy wasn't all that surprised. It was a still photo taken from the video footage of her being frisked by Ramon outside of Frank's office. This photo clearly showed her face. She was holding her arms out to the sides and Ramon was behind her, with his hands merely touching her hips. He hadn't yet reached up and grabbed her breasts, which she knew the video also clearly showed him doing. She looked at Marchitto and raising her eyebrows, she said, "This was taken outside of Mr. Frank McCarthy's office about a year ago. Why are you showing me this?"

Marchitto nodded and said, "Ahh, yes ... and, I'm sure you recognize that man behind you in the photo?"

Missy smiled sweetly and said, "Ramon? Oh, yes. I remember him. I'm quite sure he remembers me also. I heard he was arrested when Frank was arrested and is in prison now. Some sort of tax thingy, right?"

Marchitto stared at her, trying to size her up. He had no idea what she really knew and had decided this approach might be the best way to get some sense of how things were, sounding her out but being cautious. "Actually, Ramon was attacked last month in prison by another inmate. Unfortunately, he did not survive. That's actually what brings me here to see you, Cadet McCrea. I work for the law firm handling his estate which is quite sizeable. There are several million dollars but, of course, the government has filed claims against that estate due to alleged tax evasion charges."

Missy put on a confused expression and asked, "Why does that bring you here to see me, Mr. Marchitto?"

"Well, the law firm handling the estate ... they somehow ran across the video tape from which that photo was taken. And, ah ... there is concern that possibly you might yet wish to bring charges for ... ah, well ... Ramon took some liberties that day that were inappropriate. It's not at all clear what your visit was about and if you were to bring any charges ... especially now that he is deceased ... well, let's just say that I've been asked to discuss this matter with you." Marchitto looked directly at Missy, hoping she might say something that would give him a direction to continue going with.

Missy knew he was fishing and that Sal probably wanted to know why she'd been to see Frank. "Well, I guess I can see how that might be a concern to whoever is handling the estate. Yes, I see. If I should sue, and perhaps even ask Mr. McCarthy to testify in my behalf? Would my claim have precedence over the government's claim? If the court agreed that I'd been wronged, of course."

Marchitto said, "Well, that's really not at all clear right now. But, the firm handling the estate was concerned. In order to avoid any such issue, I've been authorized to offer you a small settlement. In exchange for your release of all claims, of course. Then, everything would be clear; no loose ends. I'm sure you can appreciate the firm's position on this?"

Missy looked at him and nodded her head. Then she asked, "And, if I don't agree to signing any release? What then?"

"Oh, well … err, that's complicated, I'm afraid," said Marchitto. "This incident might then become something more … how shall I put this? Questions might be raised concerning why you were associating with Mr. McCarthy. I can't promise that your reputation might not then be tarnished …"

Missy laughed. "You mean, am I concerned about West Point learning I was there? Please … does that video show anything to suggest I was there as a hooker, propositioning Mr. McCarthy?"

Marchitto now wanted to press, just a little. "Oh, of course not, Cadet McCrea. I didn't mean to suggest anything of that nature. Of course, it's not exactly clear just why you were there visiting Mr. McCarthy, a known criminal. There's mention in one report that you stated you had some matter to discuss concerning a Mr. Tony Gonzales, a friend of Mr. McCarthy's?" He left that question hanging, hoping she'd provide an explanation.

Missy knew this was his real purpose -- finding out what she had going with Frank. She decided to use this visit as an opportunity to put Sal on notice. "Well, let's see. I don't believe you really have any information about my visit, do you? But, I'm guessing you have done some research all about me. So, I'm going to give you several possible scenarios, Ben. You don't mind if I call you that, right? Oh … first, please turn off that tape recorder you've got going in your briefcase."

When he merely stared at her, she just waited. She was still giving him her prim and proper behavior, very formal and military. But, she began to draw on her energy. Lately, she'd noticed how she could harness more and more of it. Finally, he nodded and opened up his briefcase and turned off the recorder.

Missy said, "First scenario, which Frank would actually support one hundred percent, if he were talking -- which, of course, he isn't -- is that I was merely there to chit chat with him about his poor childhood buddy

374

Tony. My connection is that I knew Tony because he was the stepfather to my best friend, Alice Morris. Your research surely shows all that, right? So, first scenario is I was riding around for several hours that night and Frank and I were reminiscing about Tony. I, of course, had already kicked the shit out of Ramon for feeling me up, but you must know that. There's no evidence that you can prove that I did that to Ramon, by the way, so I'm not too worried. I know Frank won't tell on me." She smiled and gave him a moment to digest that.

Now for some fun. No more prim and proper -- Missy shifted her position and suddenly looked at Ben with a very sexy, sultry expression and lowered the tone of her voice an octave, sounding breathy and husky to go along with that. "Second scenario is that I was there, all dressed up like a schoolgirl because I figured Frank might be just like his buddy Tony. You do know about Tony's proclivities, of course ... for young girls? And, then I indeed seduced poor Frank. I was well paid but Frank was *very* satisfied -- I totally fucked his brains out and he definitely considered our little adventure worth every penny. Ahhh, but he'll never tell you about any of that." She laughed and the way Marchitto was staring at her was indeed fun to see. He had not expected anything like this from her.

Then, she continued in yet another tone of voice which now was quite hard, with some steel in it. "Third scenario, which no one will ever be able to prove, is that I actually was talking to Frank about all the evil things Tony had done. That, by the way, included trying to have me killed. Oh, yeah ... first he had planned on raping me. That actually bothered me a lot more than Ramon's grabbing my tits. So, I arranged to have Tony killed instead. Then, I stole all his money."

Marchitto was clearly shocked at both this information and the matter of fact manner in which Missy was presenting him with it. He was also noticing the atmosphere in the room had changed. It felt charged with energy. "You ... but ..."

Missy interrupted him and went on. "Fourth scenario, which also cannot be proved, is that I was rather upset with Frank. He had his good friend Salvatore D'Amato -- your boss, Ben, when you're not too busy screwing your mistress Minnie over in that nice Bronx penthouse apartment you're paying for -- does your wife know about Ms. Rollinson?" She paused to enjoy the horrified expression on his face, and then continued. "Salvatore sent up some loaner guys to kill Tony's wife for him and then a few years later, to kill Tony's daughter Roseanne. I actually liked Roseanne, Ben. So, I explained to Frank how unhappy I was about that."

Now Missy began harnessing her energy in earnest and the way Marchitto shifted uncomfortably, it was obvious he was experiencing an awareness that something was happening all around him.

"But, Ben. I see you're wondering why I know all this stuff. Especially about you and Sal. Actually, about Sal's entire organization." Missy began letting her cat energy come rushing in, with gold sparkles in her eyes suddenly becoming very obvious. "It's because I'm a witch. Do you believe in the supernatural, Ben?" She sent him a small energy pulse, which he definitely was taken aback by.

"You can't prove that, of course. In fact, even if you could, I really doubt Sal will want to admit to the other four families there in New York that he has this witch that's all pissed off at him. So, you know what? Just so I'll continue to not bother him -- and, so far I have kept my distance, Ben -- I want you to tell Sal to do something for me. I'll give him until the end of October. I want each of those girls he has collected -- for that shipment to Brunei? You know about that, right? I want each of those girls to be sent back home to their family. With enough set up in a little trust fund so they can go to college or hair dressing school or wherever they want. Let's call it the Roseanne Trust Fund, okay? Just so they don't end up in any harem over in Brunei or anywhere else. I don't think they'd really like being sex slaves, do you?"

"Cadet McCrea! You can't be serious!" Marchitto sputtered. "I don't know where you're getting your information ..."

"Exactly my point, Ben," snapped Missy. "And, I assure you ... getting information isn't all that I do. See, I'm not the type of witch that merely casts mamby-pamby spells and shit. No, I'm the type of witch who can get really pissed off and arrange for people to die mysterious deaths. In case your research didn't yet turn this up, go check the news for that night I was with Frank to see if anything else interesting happened that night. You'll find that a couple of guys Frank sometimes associated with met with an untimely end that same night. Luis and Jose, over in Boxford." She noticed he recognized those names immediately. "Oh? I see you already heard about them. That was my demonstration to Frank -- I was showing him just a few of my witchy powers."

Marchitto now stared at Missy, with both confusion and amazement in his eyes.

Missy said, "First, I arranged for some large cat to kill those two guys and then their place burned to the ground, leaving them as crispy critters. I only mention this, Ben, since you can't possibly connect me to those deaths. Even though I'm responsible for them, just as I'm responsible for poor Tony having his accident. Are you seeing a trend here? Piss off that witch Missy McCrea badly enough and you might die a horrible death. That's why Frank leaves me alone. Tell Sal to take care of my little request and I'll back off and leave him alone also. At least, until I learn he's maybe doing something else that really pisses me off."

Marchitto was still trying to process all this. Seeing her eyes and feeling that energy pulse she'd sent him was definitely making him extremely uncomfortable. He couldn't move at all and just sat there, stunned. She claimed she was a witch? What the hell? Who was she? He indeed had researched her thoroughly and had a huge dossier on her. But, this? This was unbelievable.

"Oh, and Ben?" Missy asked. "I want you to know that if anything should happen to anyone in my family … anything that's even the tiniest bit unpleasant? Well, I'll be holding *you* personally responsible. *You,* Ben. You understand me?"

Marchitto was speechless. But, he nodded his head to acknowledge he understood.

"Tell Sal that I'll be waiting to hear all about the Roseanne Trust Fund. Tell him he'd better not make me come out there to his place to see him about that. Can you do that, Ben?" Missy stood up and smiled. "Thanks for coming out today, Ben. I don't get out all that much, you see. So, you've saved me from wasting one of my passes. Now I don't have to explain all this to Salvatore. You be sure to do that for me. Just know that I'll be watching, of course. I have my witchy ways you see." Her eyes blazed and she looked down at him, still seated in his chair. She pushed out an energy pulse that was so strong it actually moved him and his chair back a foot. Then she turned and walked out, without a backward glance.

Marchitto slowly pulled himself together, gathered his briefcase and the photo she'd left behind, and slowly walked out. He was not looking forward to relating any of this to Sal. And, he doubted Sal was going to believe in anything supernatural. He had no idea how to convince Sal that Missy was a witch. Marchitto, however, was thoroughly convinced. He believed Missy was a witch, all right. He had absolutely no doubt about that at all.

Chapter Twenty-Seven
Oct 2018

A week later, Missy wished Tracy luck and waved goodbye to her and John. Tracy had Walking Privileges and John was there visiting her once again. He'd been back once before since his Labor Day weekend visit and that had gone really well. But, Tracy was very nervous about this visit today. She had discussed things with Missy and had decided it was full disclosure time. Tracy needed to tell John she was a witch. And, all week long she'd been tormenting herself about that.

When Missy had returned to her room after meeting that lawyer, Marchitto, Tracy had already been there, waiting for her. Missy's roommates had been out so the two of them had been able to talk freely. Tracy had noticed the big energy pulse and had rushed right over to find out what was going on. She had known that had to have been Missy, doing something. Missy, of course, had wanted to know how Tracy had even known about it. That had led to a discussion all about what witches could and couldn't do, what they could feel happening in the world around them and various other witchy related matters, all to do with energy.

Missy still had so much to learn! Tracy had explained how Missy's energy came from inside herself and how amazing she really was. Missy had more energy than any witch Tracy had ever heard of. Most witches, like Tracy herself, harnessed energy from outside themselves rather than from within. Earth, wind, water, light, fire ... the sun, the moon, the atmosphere. All sources of huge amounts of energy which witches were able to tap into, harness and control. Being a witch was all about using energy. That was why they could sense other supernaturals and why they could sense whenever energy was being used.

Their conversation had covered some new ground for Missy. Apparently, witches could even reinforce one another, which was why they typically joined covens. A witch could magnify his or her power by drawing from other witches. Missy could relate to that -- she believed some of her power actually came from her bond with Mike.

Then, the conversation had changed to how Tracy felt about John. Tracy blurted out how deeply concerned she was -- she knew she couldn't continue her relationship with John unless he was okay about her being a witch. And, she was well aware that he didn't know anything at all about witches. Being insecure and inexperienced, Tracy had been driving herself crazy. John had become very important to her; she'd be absolutely devastated and heartbroken if they broke up.

Missy had reassured her. Whatever feelings John had for her would only increase. She had advised Tracy to actually demonstrate her powers. That's what she'd done, after all. John had been very skeptical of her werecat claim until actually seeing her change into a cat. So, today Tracy was bravely venturing forth with John, very nervous about the show and tell that she had planned for him.

John was excited to see her and after saying goodbye to Missy, they headed off on the path along the road, walking south along the Hudson River. He had been writing email messages to her every day since they'd met and he knew he was slowly winning her heart. He really had never been drawn to any girl the way he was affected by Tracy, especially when actually in her presence like today. Writing to her had become a compulsion, sharing all his innermost thoughts about things -- his goals, his views, his own history and little tidbits about his everyday life. His writing also included several gently probing questions, seeking to learn whatever she was willing to share.

Being with her was so easy and at first they talked back and forth about things they'd already shared in their emails. Tracy had opened up to him quite a bit, responding to all his prying and probing -- she'd found him quite irresistible, as he typically asked things in a very humorous manner. So, being able to now discuss these topics they'd already written about was fun and exciting for them both. After awhile, however, John noticed their conversation was more one sided, with he being the one doing all the talking. Sensing how nervous she was today, he asked, "Is everything all right, Tracy? My crazy sister hasn't said or done anything, has she?"

Tracy tried to relax and smiled. "No, Missy has been wonderful. Um ... did you know she's actually more than just a werecat?"

This caught John off guard as he hadn't realized Missy had shared her secret with Tracy. Sure, he knew they were best friends but still … he laughed. "She told you about that, huh? I'm almost afraid to ask what else she's been telling you. That's a pretty big secret but Missy keeps a lot of secrets."

Now Tracy laughed. "Oh, I know. Your sister is really something. And, I'm sure there's a lot she's not telling me. You know how protective she is, right? But, actually, I think she has a lot she hasn't been telling you. For example, she is also a witch. That's why she can heal and push out energy pulses the way she does." She stared at John to see what his reaction would be to this news.

John said, "I don't really claim to understand any part of what my sister is and what she can do. Does it really matter what labels you use? She's unique, right?"

"Actually, she's extremely rare. But, no, she's not unique. Or, at least there are other werecats and other witches. I don't know of any others who are both a witch and a Shifter, the way she is, but anything is possible. Right?"

Now John stopped to look at Tracy. They'd been walking for almost a mile and had reached a nice spot that looked out over the river, well away from the academy. He sensed this conversation was going somewhere and that he really needed to pay attention. "There are *others*? Other werecats? And, witches? Tracy, you're way ahead of me with this stuff. Missy hasn't told me or anyone else in our family any of this, although we certainly do know anything is possible. Once I saw Missy Change that first time …"

"John, I'm a witch. I'm very different from your sister but, like her, I'm a supernatural. I hope you can accept that about me. I don't want to keep any secrets from you. Not now … now that I … we …" Tracy had run out of words, having said all this in a rush, before she could change her mind. Now she waited for his reaction with baited breath. Her heart felt as though steel bands were wrapped around it, slowly squeezing and crushing the life right out of her.

John got it right away. He had no idea what her being a witch meant but he got that she had just opened herself up to him and it was really important that he reassure her. He didn't hesitate at all but swept her into his arms and began kissing her. He crushed her up against himself and then slowly brought his hands up to each side of her face. After kissing her so thoroughly she couldn't possibly doubt either his ardor or his passion, he broke away but continued holding her face with his hands. Staring into her eyes he said, "Tracy, I hope that answers your question … about my accepting who you are and what you are … but, if you need more convincing?" He slid his arms back down along her sides and held her close.

Tracy was overwhelmed, both with relief and with a lot of other feelings as well. John's kiss made her body feel on fire and her heart was pounding in her chest. His immediate reaction, so quick and so absolute, filled her with happiness. Then, as she realized he actually was waiting for her to answer his question, she giggled. "Umm … I guess I don't *need* more convincing. But, I sure would *enjoy* some more of that, John!"

Now John laughed and then brought his lips back down to hers. He didn't need to be told twice and he began kissing her with more fervor than ever before. Her arms went around him and she kissed him back, clearly abandoning all and everything, giving herself to him as completely and totally as she knew how. Finally, at the sound of another couple heading their way, they separated. Wow! John knew the rules about no public displays of affection or PDA's but it had been he who'd remembered the rules, not Tracy. Pointing to the river, he said, "Look how beautiful the view is from here, Tracy".

Tracy heard the sound of his voice but it took her another moment to focus. Then, realizing he was making conversation more for the benefit of the couple who were getting closer and closer, she said, "Yes, it's a glorious day to be out walking, John. Especially now that the summer is gone and the fall weather is here." They were both wearing coats, and with the breeze off the river, the outside temperature indeed felt cool. Inside, she was still on fire and held onto one of John's hands with an iron grip. Holding hands was okay and allowed by the rules.

They walked off the main path and waited until the other couple had passed. Then, Tracy smiled to herself and looked at John. "Missy told me I should give you a demonstration. So you'd believe me. You know … about being a witch and everything."

John was still enjoying the moment they'd shared and had almost forgotten about her being a witch. "Sure, go ahead. Show me things if you want.

385

But, if you say you're a witch, I believe you. After the way my crazy sister teased me when I was skeptical about her being a cat, I've learned my lesson. You won't turn me into a toad or anything, though ... will you?"

Tracy laughed at that and began to relax. John was really okay about this. Or, at least so far. She held up her hand, palm upward and drawing on all the energy around her, she concentrated and -- voila! A small ball of light appeared just above her hand and about three feet in front of them. She was still holding onto his hand with her other hand. While maintaining control of the light she'd created, she glanced at John. He seemed suitably impressed so she changed the ball of light into a ball of fire, keeping it still suspended in front of them.

John realized she was doing something normal people really couldn't do. He still had no idea what a witch was but, clearly, Tracy had some special powers if she could create light and fire like that. She had referred to herself and his sister as both being supernaturals. "That's pretty amazing, Tracy. Of course, you know that but I can't simply stand here and not say something. Ahh ... don't you need to say magic words and ... umm ... what about being inside a circle? I think I read somewhere that witches need to make circles, or something."

Tracy pushed the ball of fire upwards and after rising a few feet, it suddenly went out. "I see that I have a lot of explaining to do, John. Please ignore whatever you've read. Actually, though, we sometimes do use circles. When I'm with my coven -- which, by the way, I trust you'll not tell anyone about -- you won't right? Tell anyone about witches or covens or any of this?"

"Your secrets are safe with me, Tracy. Just as Missy's secrets are for her to tell, I'll never betray you or any of your secrets. Never! Trust me." He squeezed her hand to further reassure her.

"Well, we do make and use circles. It helps us reinforce one another. But, controlling energy the way I do doesn't require any circle or any magic words. I do it with my mind. I can draw on the energy that's all around, harness that energy and use it by exercising my will. Missy told me it's very similar when she Shifts -- she has this place she goes to in her mind and she also then needs to exercise her will."

John said, "I've seen the shimmer of light and felt the burst of energy when she does that. Even though she's behind a blanket that she always has someone holding in front of her, those are very noticeable. She hasn't really explained *how* she does it. And ... then she's a mountain lion. Tell me again why you think she's a witch."

"Oh, it's because she can regenerate, healing herself the way she does. Maybe you don't know too much about that part ... but, you do know how she healed Mike's sister Michelle, right? That's the other thing -- she not only can heal herself but she can heal others. And, you've felt her send out those energy pulses, right?"

"Yeah, she can definitely make you stop and take notice when she does that. So, that's something witches can do?" John realized he now wanted to learn everything there was to know about witches.

Tracy said, "Some witches can do that, but it's rare. Especially if they're using power or energy from within. I can't really do that. What I do is harness energy from around me. But, I'm told I have a lot of power compared to many witches. My Mom is also a witch but she's not nearly as powerful as I am. And, I'm still gaining power as I get older. Missy too. Who knows how much power we might develop? Witches seem to finally stop gaining power once they reach the age of about twenty five or so. That's when we're all fully developed."

"So, it's using energy. What about spells? Am I really safe? I won't wake up and start hopping around ... you know ... ribbit, ribbit, ribbit!" John laughed.

Tracy laughed at how he'd made each ribbit really sound like a frog was croaking nearby. "Well, I don't use spells. So, you're safe from me at least. I probably should warn you about what my real power is, though."

John was still chuckling and thinking how much fun it was, bantering with her back and forth. She really was a special person and way beyond compare to any of the girls he'd ever known. That she seemed to be tuning into him was thrilling. She had some more powers? Terrific, by all means. Bring it on! "Tracy, you had me at 'I'm a witch' and so you don't have to keep giving me any warnings." He looked around and they were quite alone. He wanted to take her into his arms and kiss her some more.

Tracy also looked around but she now released his hand and took a step away. "John, this will take me a few moments ... I'm going to change the weather out there." She then concentrated and as she quietly stood there, gazing out at the river, the air all around them changed. Although it was gradual at first, all of a sudden it was a lot darker. There were storm clouds overhead.

John realized Tracy really was doing this, making the weather change. He could definitely feel the complete change in atmosphere and she seemed to be off in some zone, oblivious to her surroundings. She lifted both arms upward and then, without moving at all for several seconds, she did something. He couldn't say just what she'd done but he immediately sensed that she indeed had done something. Then, in the very next moment, there was a loud crack and a bolt of lightning criss crossed out over the river, very visible as it arced downward into the water. This was followed by a loud boom of thunder.

Tracy turned and looked into his eyes. "There. That's my little demonstration, John. And, that's also pretty much it. I don't think I can do much else. I don't bend spoons or make objects float in midair or do any healing or send energy pulses out like Missy does. But, I do have a way with light, fire and lightning." She walked back over to him and slipped her hand back into his.

After processing what she'd just shown him, John looked into her eyes. "That was definitely impressive, Tracy. You're really something. Wow! I really don't know what else to say. You can control the weather …"

Tracy interrupted him right away. "Not exactly. I can harness energy. I don't make rain go away and have sunshine follow me around wherever I go." She moved closer and pressed herself up against him, suddenly wanting to be held. "I'm going to try something new, if you'll let me. Missy thinks this might work."

John wrapped his arms around her and hugged her close. "Sure, Tracy! Anything. Go ahead." He held her quietly and waited. After more than a minute had passed, he asked, "Will this new thing be anything we can share, Tracy?"

Tracy sighed deeply to herself and looked up at him, pushing herself back. "Thank you, John. That was really wonderful. You don't feel drained or anything? I mean, Missy was right. I have been drawing more energy from you than I've ever experienced before, even when in a circle with several other witches lending me power. I guess I can't really describe it any better than that. But, while you may not be a witch, you sure seem able to …" Suddenly she stopped and began blushing. The more she tried to think of ways to explain things to him, the more embarrassed and flustered she became.

John thought about her question for a moment. Did he feel drained? Was she somehow drawing energy from him? Then he began laughing. "Hey … it's not like we just had sex or anything … is it? I mean … I'd know if that had happened. I think. Wouldn't I?"

Now it was Tracy's turn to laugh. "I'm not going to attempt any further explanations, John. Maybe ask you sister about this. It was her idea. And, no. We did not just have sex. I was only … I mean, it's way too soon for …" Again, she stopped and began blushing.

John laughed and hugged her close. "I'll settle for a kiss, then. For now." He bent down and claimed his kiss and found her very pleased to be giving that to him. Very pleased, indeed.

"So, you were able to get all charged up again?" asked Missy. She was in Tracy's room, as both roommates were out and they could talk. Tracy had emailed her already, explaining how wonderful John had been and how she was falling for him, head over heels. She'd invited her to drop by when she got the chance and Missy was enjoying their conversation.

"You were absolutely right, Missy," said Tracy. "John made me feel like I was plugged into the source of all energy. *His* energy was exactly what I needed. But, you knew that already. You and Mike … well. I guess I can't even imagine how you and Mike might be."

Missy said, "Don't worry about it, Tracy. One day at a time. John seems happy enough with that, right? I mean … he's not putting any pressure on you or anything, is he? He seems to be just as excited about having a connection with you as you seem to be about all this. It's you he wants, Tracy. You as the person in his life. He's been with other girls. I think he'll always leave it for you to decide how things will go."

"Well, you were right about his accepting my being a witch. I'm sure you're right about him. We're going to be together for Thanksgiving, you know. He's coming to Texas with me to spend a few days there with my family. Then I'll be coming to Salem, staying with your family until returning back here. He wants me to be his date at that wedding for Alice and Mark. You've told me so much about them already. I'm really excited now. Six more weeks. It will be here before we know it!"

Cadet King finally managed to meet with Missy, finding her alone where they'd not be overheard by anyone else. They were outside and he'd been trying to find an opportunity for a couple of weeks, but that had not been easy to do. "Cadet McCrea, can I speak with you for a moment?"

Missy had scented him, of course, and knew he was there waiting for her. She had noticed him several times in recent days and was not quite sure just what to expect. He and Cadet Quigby had avoided her up until now. She was not worried but her curiosity was piqued and, noticing they were indeed well out of earshot from anyone else, she figured she'd hear what he had to say. She said, "Yes, sir!" and snapped to attention.

King said, "At ease, Cadet McCrea. Please, I just want to talk. Nothing formal or anything. Okay?"

"Okay, sir," said Missy. She waited to see where this was going.

"I want to apologize but can I ask that this conversation be just between the two of us? I'm not really able to say any of this except in private. But, I really am sorry for the way I treated you during Beast Training. I was wrong."

Missy was actually surprised, at first. "Well, I'm pleased to know that, sir. And, if you want this conversation kept secret, don't worry. I can keep things secret. I think you know that."

King said, "Yes, and that's another part of what I wanted to tell you. I want to thank you for the way you handled those friends of mine that night. You could really have made trouble for me and you didn't. At first, that really surprised me and I kept waiting for the shit to hit the fan. When it didn't, I realized you really were more interested in just helping your squad and winning top shot and that you were willing to overlook what I'd done. You really are amazing, Missy. I'm sorry, I really am. I hope you can maybe forgive me. We can't be friends or anything ... I'm not looking for that. But, I do owe you this. You have my apology and my assurance you won't have any trouble from me ever again."

Missy could see that he was being sincere. Maybe the good reputation she'd made for herself over the past few weeks had also influenced him. Women did indeed have a place at West Point. "Okay, Cadet King. Sir. I forgive you and accept your apology. I appreciate there are some people who really don't like women in the Army. And, maybe there are some women who don't belong. But, I'm not looking for any special treatment."

"Oh, I know, I know. At first, I just really thought you were a freak." King smiled at her and shook his head. "Actually, you *are* a freak, Missy. You're not like other girls. Shit, look at what you did to my friends. Four big football players and you ... well, I think you'd agree there aren't many people who could have done what you did. Male or female. And, you're not just top shot in your plebe class any more. From what I've heard, there's never been anyone who can shoot as well as you do. Everyone in Combat Weapons keeps bragging about you."

Missy laughed and began to relax. "Okay, I'll give you that. I am *not* a normal girl. Maybe I am a freak -- I'm not going to argue with you about that. But, I am dedicated to being the best Army officer that this academy can help me become. If you and I can share that common goal, who knows? Maybe someday we'll have to serve together in the same unit and hopefully then you won't be all that uncomfortable about that."

King smiled, "Good enough. I do want to warn you about Cadet Quigby, though. He and I were close until all that went down out there with you and your squad. With you getting top shot, he's taking that personal. You made him look bad as well as me. I deserve to look bad, after sending those guys in to mess with you. That was wrong and if you'd handled things differently, I might have been kicked out. So, I don't care about looking bad -- that was my wakeup call. And, it wasn't that big a deal, my looking bad. I'm okay now. I've been avoiding him ever since and have just been going forward here. But, I know he's holding a grudge, Missy. Watch out for him. He really hates you and he has a few other friends that still listen to him. Good luck!"

"Thanks, Cadet King." Missy realized she really was grateful to him. "I'll be extra careful. I already try very hard to follow all the rules. Now, I'll try even harder, knowing there are maybe those who might be looking to make trouble for me. I've heard a lot of sad stories about things that have happened to girls here at the academy and I don't want to someday be one of those sad stories."

Chapter Twenty-Eight
Oct 2018

Missy walked into the Visitor Center and then found the room where Robert Ulrey was waiting for her. She was wearing her dress grey uniform and could see he was impressed. "You know, Robert, lately I've been seeing you more often than I see my boyfriend. I'm not sure how I feel about that. I haven't seen Mike since Labor Day weekend but here you are." She laughed and he joined in and laughed with her.

"Hey, don't blame me. You asked for this meeting today, right?" Robert had exchanged several emails with her and they really needed to discuss a few things. Such as, her telling Marchitto she was a witch and what Les and Marsha had been able to hear from the surveillance tapes.

Missy had just returned from a busy week out in the field, where they'd been doing mountaineering, living in tents, rappelling down cliffs, crossing rivers on ropes and all sorts of small unit tasks and challenges. It had been a mix of tactics and survival. She'd thrived, loving every minute of it. Her squad had not been quite as enthusiastic but for Missy, the more extreme the better.

She'd done a little showing off out there, which everyone was still talking about. Rappelling down the cliff, facing forward and down rather than backward and up, holding onto the rope with only one hand while pretending the stick in her other hand was a rifle? Demonstrating how she could have been on the attack, racing down the cliff while shooting at the enemy while descending? Okay, that maybe had been a little extreme. Of course, with her reputation for marksmanship, no one doubted her claim. Her credibility had been well established.

Then, for the river crossing, did she really have to make everyone look bad by using only one of the ropes and going hand over hand, quickly reaching the other side in less than half the time for anyone else? That had been more than two hundred feet across and she'd been wearing an eighty pound backpack plus her rifle. Hand over hand? But, it wasn't really a competition and Missy had explained she was only doing things she knew she was fully capable of doing. She hadn't broken any rules and wasn't really trying to make anyone else look bad. This had been one of the last times they'd be out in the field and able to perform this type of training. Yes, they'd have some exercises during the winter but those would be different and it wouldn't be until the springtime before they'd be back out there for anything like this.

There had been the usual amount of marching, of course, and the usual amount of ribald marching songs. Yes, women now went to West Point. Sure, a lot had been toned down. But, guys were guys and the marching songs invariably ended up with some raunchy lyrics being yelled out at the top of their lungs as they all marched in cadence. One of their favorites, popular with servicemen for a hundred years or so, was about LuLu and the men she'd been with. It had a lot of variations, none of which were politically correct. Just when the lyrics would suggest something explicit, they'd skip to the beginning of the chorus.

> Bang, bang, Lulu; Lulu, bang, bang.
> Who's gonna bang bang Lulu, now that Lulu's gone away?
>
> LuLu had a boyfriend, his name was Diamond Dick,
> She never saw his diamond, but often saw his ...
>
> Bang, bang, Lulu; Lulu, bang, bang.
> Who's gonna bang bang Lulu, now that Lulu's gone away?
>
> Lulu had a rooster, she also had a duck.
> She put them on a table, to see if they would ...
>
> Bang, bang, Lulu; Lulu, bang, bang.

Upon her return to the barracks, there had been soccer practice and weapons training for competitions coming up, both for this weekend. She'd barely found any time to schedule Robert coming down to visit her. Having so little time was why she hadn't asked Mike to come down since Labor Day. But, she knew she had to deal with what she'd stirred up, now that Sal had gotten on to her. Even if she hadn't been concerned about saving those girls from being sent to Brunei, she believed it would have been necessary to come to terms with Sal … once he'd learned how she'd made that visit to Frank a year ago, that had become inevitable.

She explained all of this to Robert but he still was shaking his head. He looked at her and said, "But, did you have to say you were a witch? And, challenge him the way you did?"

Missy said, "Hey, who's he gonna tell? I mean, for him or Sal to go around complaining about witches would only make them appear pretty vulnerable, right? I know they can't afford that. So, tell me what you've learned. What have Ben and Sal been doing?"

Robert said, "Marchitto visited both Billy and Donny. He interviewed them each at their own places which was convenient for us, since we were able to listen in. Your surveillance system sure came in handy for that." He saw Missy nodding her head at him, so he continued. "Marchitto talked to Billy first, which was good, since Billy then was able to give Donny both a head's up and some direction on what to say. Bottom line, they didn't admit to grabbing you or killing Tony and they definitely didn't admit to naming Sal. But, when Marchitto asked if they'd ever met you, they were very vocal. They told him how you had to be some sort of a witch, without Marchitto even having to ask about that."

"I had kind of hoped for something like that. After all the times they've been calling me that

399

redheaded 'witch bitch' ... glad to know some good has come from that." Missy smiled.

"Yeah, that part really played right into your game quite nicely. They claimed you showed up at their hotel, knocked them out with some sort of a spell and then tortured them. You had Tony's folder with his instructions for kidnapping you and you had already taken care of Tony. They didn't admit to giving you anything and then they kept quiet about it when they returned to New York. They told Marchitto they didn't dare suggest to anyone in Sal's organization that they believed in witches. No, they hoped they'd seen the last of you."

Missy said, "Excellent! Did Billy mention how I cut off his little finger?"

Robert laughed. "Oh, yes. You were an evil witch, torturing them for hours but they never gave you anything. As proof of that, you've never acted against Sal before now, right? They claim you got all your info from Tony and Frank, not them."

"So, has Sal done anything about all this yet?" asked Missy.

"We don't have much inside information but we have learned Marchitto has apparently consulted with a couple of people who supposedly are experts on witches and witchcraft. This has all been on the QT and very hush-hush. Nothing that would suggest Sal himself was involved. But, Marchitto obviously has done some research and I'm sure Sal has been given a full report."

Robert smiled. "Perhaps your strategy isn't so bad, really. Like you say, Sal isn't going to run around talking about this. And, if you can somehow convince him to leave you alone? We'll see."

"Yes, but I haven't yet figured out how I'll do that. But, in case I need to visit him, that's why I've asked for all the details about his estate. Did you bring the aerial photos I asked for? You could zoom in from that government satellite spy camera for me, no problem?"

Robert said, "Yes. And, here are the details about all his utilities and about his elaborate security system. Even if you can knock out his electrical power, most of his security system will be back on line in just a minute or so. He has some huge generators out in one of his garages. What exactly are you planning to do, Missy?"

Missy smiled. "Now Robert, you know I'm only going to ask for forgiveness afterwards rather than ask for any permission now, right? You folks at "P" Branch really don't want to *interfere* or anything." She really emphasized the word *interfere* and they both laughed.

Ben Marchitto was once again meeting with Sal to discuss witches and witchcraft. These meetings were happening more frequently, now that he'd provided Sal with his various reports and there were fewer days remaining until the end of the month. Hard to believe how much work he'd been required to do, all because of some girl still in her teens. He'd been very careful. No one else knew anything about this. He knew better than that. Even without Sal constantly reminding him.

"So, what can she do, Ben?" asked Sal. "You don't think she can stick pins in some doll and actually give me hemorrhoids or anything, right? Shit. I can't believe some of the crap you mention in your reports about witches. My real problem is where there's smoke, there's fire, right? Even though ninety-nine percent of this has to all be bullshit … some of it might not be bullshit. And, you're telling me you believe her. She's a witch. She pushed your chair. So what?"

Ben said, "So, I also was able to verify just about everything she said. You already knew about her visiting Frank and what she did to Ramon. And, that guy Tony Gonzalez died in a car accident that maybe wasn't an accident. Then, those two guys she told me about that were killed by some large cat? There aren't supposed to be any cougars in Massachusetts but that's what killed those guys. A cougar. Very strange."

"Yeah, yeah, I get all that. And, she seemed to know all sorts of things about my organization. Not only about Billy and Donny … and, I'm still not sure I'm buying everything those guys told you … but, she even knew about your girlfriend Minnie? That Russian broad you've got stashed over in the Bronx? Billy and Donny don't know about her, which is why I'm not ready to just blame them for all of this." Sal studied Ben and then asked, "Or, does this witch read minds? Were you maybe thinking about that Russian broad when this witch Missy walked in? No, wait … you told me how

402

attractive this girl is ... so, maybe your brain immediately began to make some fantasy associations, right? You wanted to fuck this cadet in her uniform and so you then thought about your mistress? Jeez ... I don't know what to think."

Ben knew Sal was just venting. "No, Sal, that's not what happened at all. And, she certainly didn't learn about those girls going to Brunei from reading my mind. I didn't even know very much about them. I still don't. What are you going to do with them, anyway?"

"Well, I'm not ready to send them home and set up any fucking trust fund. I'm just not in any big hurry to ship them to Brunei yet. Tell me more what this witch might do. You said she might pay me a visit? She actually said that?"

"I don't know if I have her exact words but, basically, it was to tell you not to make her come out here ... if you didn't do the trust fund and everything by the end of the month, she'll be paying you a visit." Ben thought for a moment and added, "She didn't say what she'd do if she came out here, exactly, but ... she said that's what might happen. She'll pay you a visit."

"Okay, so tell me about my security. She can't get in here, right? So, what can she do?" Sal didn't like not being in control of any situation and this witchcraft nonsense was really pissing him off.

Ben said, "Well, there's the double fence all around, each fence twenty feet high with barbed wire and electricity. If she can somehow get over the first one, the dogs are always patrolling the twelve foot area in between them. If she can get past the dogs and climb the second fence, we would at least have been alerted by then. And, we have one of our guys at every possible entrance."

"What about crashing through the front gate? Or, maybe she puts some spell on our guard out there? Then, he lets her in?" Sal knew all this but wanted to hear it again. What might he be missing?

Ben explained, "The guard is pretty safe inside the gatehouse and, even if he wanted to let her in, he'd have to have our security chief okay it. That's how it works. He can't open the main gates unless our security chief first flips his switch on the console in the control room. Where all the video cameras are showing him everything."

"Okay. I guess we'll just have to wait and see. I don't like it but I also don't like the idea that anyone else might ever hear about any of this. From what you've put together in your report, she could have tried shaking us down a long time ago. Instead, she's at West Point of all places. Unbelievable!" Sal began looking at the huge file on Missy that Ben had provided. He'd already memorized it but was still finding it hard to believe all the things in that file. He began studying some of her photos all over again.

Missy's roommates Sharon and Kelsey were once again thanking Missy for saving their ass. Somehow, she'd managed getting their room ready for a last minute inspection that had caught everyone by surprise. Missy had insisted they step outside while she then had raced around their room, putting everything in order, and they'd survived the inspection with no one getting any demerits. Kelsey, in particular, was thrilled as she'd racked up many hours walking off all her earlier demerits and was really looking forward to the weekend coming up, without having to walk off any more.

"How do you manage getting all our stuff arranged so fast, Missy?" asked Kelsey. "And, how come we can't watch?"

Sharon laughed. "You know you can't watch her when she does her sparkly eyes magic, Kelsey. Don't mess with success!"

Missy looked at them both and smiled. "As long as you two don't actually *see* me doing anything that might be considered magic … why, then you can't ever be blamed for not *saying* anything about it. Not that what I'm doing is any violation of our Honor Code. But, I'm just looking out for you both. You know I always have your back and I trust you guys will cover for me."

They assured her that, of course, they'd always have her back -- no problem. Missy was counting on that … at least, she was counting on Sharon. Soccer season was finishing up and basketball season was just starting. Missy and Sharon had both made the basketball team and their first game was coming up on the second Sunday in November which was also Veteran's Day. There would be no classes the next day, since that Monday was the national holiday. Because the game was an away game, they would be staying Sunday night at a hotel in downtown New York City -- they didn't need to rush back to the academy and were being allowed a little bit of free time. And, since they were already roommates, Missy and Sharon were booked into the same hotel room. Very convenient.

Sharon played forward and Missy played guard. In addition to her ball handling ability, which was excellent, Missy had an amazing jump shot. She could jump several inches higher than other girls her height and this always surprised whoever was on the opposing team, who then would fail to block Missy's shot. She had developed her shooting skill in high school, of course, and was very accurate. Whenever a three point shot was needed, Missy could usually be counted on to make her jump shot go in. As this became more and more obvious during tryouts, Missy easily made the team. Then, during practices, the coach Irina Borovsky studied her even more closely and realized Missy indeed was a fabulous player.

Irina then talked to Missy's soccer coach, Kristen, and the more she heard about Missy, the more excited she became. Kristen explained how much Missy had helped with the soccer team and how, this season, they were finishing first place in their division and were going on into the playoffs. Missy's contributions, on and off the playing field, had been a big part of their success. While there was a bit of an overlap, with soccer playoffs and basketball starting up, they worked things out so

Missy was playing in all the games and only missing some practices.

Missy had decided on her plan. If Sal had still not set up the Roseanne Trust Fund and released all those girls by then, she'd be paying him a visit late that Sunday night, after that first basketball game. She would need Sharon to cover for her, since she'd be away from her hotel room for a few hours. Her Granddad McCrea always used to tell her to plan her work and then work her plan. She knew she definitely had her work cut out for her. But, she indeed now had her plan.

Chapter Twenty-Nine
Nov 2018

Missy studied Sal's double fence and was thankful for the wind, which was blowing her way and keeping her scent from reaching the dogs patrolling inside. She was high in the tree she had selected from the aerial photos and was confident she could indeed clear both fences. This required leaping from the branch she had crawled out on and sailing more than forty feet outward and dropping about thirty feet to the ground. Even with her little backpack on, which Mike had brought her and had double checked was securely in place after she had Changed, this was a leap she could easily make. She had been waiting for close to an hour, since once inside she planned on Changing again.

Mike had met her outside her hotel and so far, everything was working as planned. Sharon had been very understanding. Missy had explained this was some important sparkly eyes magic that she needed to do and she wasn't merely sneaking out to have sex with her boyfriend. Sharon had not wanted to know any more about it than that. If Missy said it was important and needed to be done, that was good enough for her.

Now she sent Mike a mental message. *I'm going in now.* She'd be sending him a few more messages tonight.

With one final look around, Missy gathered herself together, crouched down on the branch and then made the big leap pushing with her hind legs using all the power she could put into her jump. And, as she'd figured, it was enough. She cleared the barbed wire on top of the second fence with several inches to spare and landed silently on the ground below, inside. No alarms were being set off and she quickly loped towards the big house, set well back from the street. She was approaching from the side and about ninety degrees away from where the gatehouse was located.

There was plenty of cover for her approach as Sal's yard contained several trees and bushes. And, it was quite dark outside the perimeter of light from all the floodlights that were illuminating the area close to the house. She crept to a hedge just outside of the lighted area and Changed. Quickly donning the black sweatpants and sweatshirt from her backpack, along with black running shoes, she pulled her hair back into a ponytail and set the backpack aside for later.

She also had brought several tranquilizer darts, a blowgun and some duct tape. Thank you to "P" Branch for its unlimited resources and willingness to provide her some support. She occasionally had practiced with some blowguns back in high school and was quite certain she'd be accurate from anywhere within twenty feet. Thank you to self for all the extreme training she'd put herself through these past few years.

There were guards stationed at three entrances and two more were patrolling together, circling the house about every ten minutes. She'd been watching all this from up in the tree while she'd been waiting. This checked with the information Robert had provided. She waited until the two guys on patrol had passed by and then she followed after them, about a minute behind. As she approached the first stationary guard at the side entrance, she was able to stay out of sight and had no difficulty getting close enough for an accurate shot. He hardly felt the sting of the dart in his neck and then suddenly collapsed, without much noise. Missy wrapped his hands and feet with duct tape and added some tape across his mouth. Then, she moved on.

She made sure she stayed far enough behind the two guards on patrol so they were out of hearing range. She dispatched the second guard stationed in the rear and the third guard stationed out front, also taping them up as she'd done for the first guy, and then raced forward to be there when the patrol came up to where the first guy had been. Two quick darts caught them before they'd had a chance to notice anything amiss and she quickly had them taped up and set aside. She grabbed the .38 caliber revolver from one of the guards, a nice Smith and Wesson, and took his holster as well.

The .38 Special would only fire six rounds and wasn't as good as her M9 pistol; it didn't have much stopping power. But, it was simple. No rack to slide in order to chamber a round. Just point and shoot. She knew she would be accurate enough at close range, if she needed to actually shoot it.

Fifteen minutes had passed and five guards were down. She went inside the house.

Since it was close to midnight, she wasn't surprised to find no one downstairs on the first floor. She knew there was a control room in the basement where the security chief and one or two others were watching all the videos and monitoring Sal's security system. Too bad that system had relied so heavily on the double fence and the guys on patrol. She hadn't even needed to force any locks to get inside and she still hadn't set off any alarms. Sal really was old fashioned and hadn't taken advantage of modern technology very much. The file Robert had provided had clearly identified all the sensors and detectors that she needed to be concerned about and she'd easily avoided those and escaped detection so far.

She went upstairs where Sal had a second office, which was actually his study. From the briefing notes in Robert's file, she knew Sal preferred operating from that office. If he wasn't in bed with his wife, that's probably where he'd be. She noticed several scents as she made her way up the stairs, and one of them was Marchitto. She was able to hear voices and, sure enough, Marchitto was talking to someone. That someone had to be Sal.

Sal had two children but they were both away at boarding schools. Teenagers, one a Freshman -- his daughter -- and the other a Junior -- his son. From the sounds and scents Missy was getting, Sal's wife was in their bedroom which was located on the other end, away from his office. Missy could hear a TV playing in that bedroom.

She reached the top of the stairs and moved silently down the hallway, stopping outside Sal's office

411

door which was closed, probably so he and Marchitto would not be bothering his wife. She listened to their conversation for a minute which was all about some arrangement with one of the other New York families. Apparently, the split was not going the way Sal had agreed and Marchitto was explaining what Sal's options were for dealing with the situation. Missy smiled to herself. Life was complicated for poor Sal. So many decisions to make. She opened the door and walked in.

The two men were seated in easy chairs and had drinks on a table between them. The office was good sized -- about fifteen feet by thirty feet -- and there were bookcases all along one wall and a large flat screen TV centered on another wall. One wall had windows which looked out towards the front of the house and, as she'd anticipated, they could see the gatehouse down by the street. In the opposite direction, off to the side of the house, the large garage was also visible. This was the garage that housed the backup generators. This layout -- and the intel that Sal would most likely either be in this office or could easily be brought up here -- was part of what she'd based her plan on. When she walked in, both Sal and Ben stopped talking and looked over at her.

Missy raised the .38 revolver so it was clearly visible and said, "Ben, I'm sure you've told Sal all about me, including my marksmanship skills with a pistol, so I trust the two of you will sit right there and not make any sudden moves. From this close, I'm quite sure I could easily blow off someone's finger. Unlike when I removed a finger from one of your guys -- you've talked to Billy about me, right? -- I don't think this time anyone could sew it back on again later." She smiled at the reactions she was getting.

She looked closely at Salvatore; she had seen several photos of him, of course, but now she was finally seeing him in person. He was looking at her and she could see he also was making comparisons to various photos he'd seen before of her.

Sal said, "Obviously, you are this crazy person Missy McCrea that I've been hearing about. And, if you think you're going to get away with anything, you definitely must be crazy. I've got guys all around this place and ..."

"Well, I didn't bother with the guys in your control room. But, don't bother signaling them ... before they can get up here? You'll be missing more than a finger, Sal. Your guys outside? Resting comfortably. So, let's not bother with any more threats ... you know why I'm here, right? I'm quite sure Ben told you I'd be visiting if you didn't do as I'd asked. But, you haven't set up that trust fund yet, so here I am. The Roseanne Fund. For those girls you're holding. Do I need to go and release those girls myself, Sal? I can do that ... but, I want you to do more than just release them. You understand about that, right? I want them properly taken care of so you really need to establish that Roseanne Fund." Missy had walked up and was now only ten feet away. Their eyes were staying focused on the revolver she was slowly waving back and forth.

Sal said, "You're crazy all right. This is all bullshit and you're trying to shake down the wrong guy." He was still trying to pretend she was merely some deranged female whom he could easily handle. "You breaking into my home like this? You're going to really regret it, Miss West Point Cadet McCrea. You aren't going to shoot me. You'd never get away with that."

Missy put the gun in the holster she'd strapped on and said, "You're right. I'm not planning on shooting you. Ben told you I'm a witch, right?" She pushed out some energy -- just enough so both Sal and Ben could feel it. "You don't really want to mess with me, Sal. Let me give you just a little demonstration why not. I want you to call your guy out there on the gate. Tell him he needs to get outside and stand at least fifty feet away from that gatehouse. Can you do that, Sal?"

Sal and Ben looked at each other. Ben said, "She's going to blow up the gatehouse, Sal." Looking at her, Ben said, "Missy? You can't be serious ... what the hell do you think you're doing? You'd have to be crazy to ..."

Missy said in her most severe tone, "Call your guy right away, Sal. Use that phone right there. But, if you call anyone else? I'll change my mind about not shooting you and I'll blow your hand off. And, if you don't call him in the next thirty seconds? You'll have to explain to all his buddies how you let him become a crispy critter ... like those other guys I'm sure Ben told you about. Luis and Jose. Ben, you explained all this to Sal, right? About how when you mess with me you might die a horrible death ... you mentioned that part,

414

right?" Missy's eyes were now glowing because of all the power and energy that she'd brought into them.

Sal was very much impressed with Missy. He didn't dare make any attempt to do anything physical -- he'd read the file on her and he knew better than that. He figured there was no harm in having his guy stand outside the gatehouse and so he made the call. Missy then waved them both over to the windows and they came over to watch. They saw the guard open the door and walk out -- he then ran over to a spot about eighty feet away, on the other side of the driveway and just inside the fence.

Missy sent Mike a message. *Now, Mike. Have Tracy do it now.* She waited thirty seconds and then sent out a very noticeable pulse of energy. Just at that same instant, there was a loud crack and a bolt of lightning hit the gatehouse, followed by a second bolt. The gatehouse disintegrated and there was a small fire clearly visible. Thunder could be heard rumbling right afterwards, not far away.

Missy turned to Sal and said, "I know you realize that was lightning, right? You'll never prove that I did that, of course. But, in case my demonstration of witchy power isn't enough to convince you? Take a look over at your garage."

Having pre-planned targets was definitely a wonderful strategy. Missy had studied how this was often done for field artillery targets and she'd adapted the concept for her plan tonight. She was having Mike pass on her messages to Tracy who was with him outside, not far off, along with John and Tracy's Mom. Tracy had taken the one pass she was allowed and was using it for this three day weekend, since she hadn't used it earlier for Labor Day weekend. Her Mom had picked her up but John and Mike were with her now. They were all inside a circle that Tracy had set and Missy knew Tracy was drawing power from each of them.

As both men turned to look at the garage, Missy sent Mike her next message for Tracy. She timed another energy pulse just as Tracy's lightning cracked again, with several bolts coming down and doing some very obvious damage to the garage. Missy was quite certain this would be taking out the backup generators inside. And, Sal's two expensive luxury cars in there should likewise pretty much be scrap. Because Sal and Ben were experiencing her energy pulses at the same moment as these incredible lightning bolts, they couldn't possibly be doubting that she was doing all this. Now, even more thunder could be heard, booming loudly.

Missy had figured this little demonstration of what powers a witch might wield should probably be enough. But, she wanted to make certain Sal was a total believer -- any thoughts of retaliation needed to be completely wiped away; the safety of her family depended on that. So, she wasn't quite finished. "Sal, have I made my intentions clear enough, yet? Apparently, whatever Ben told you wasn't enough. I trust my little visit here tonight has convinced you? Let those girls go home and set up that Roseanne Trust Fund. I'm going to know if you don't fully carry everything out, exactly the way I want, so don't even think about crossing me. And, I've just now decided that I want an extra million dollars added to that fund ... in case I decide there are any other deserving young girls who need to be helped."

Both men were still speechless but they were staring at Missy and had clearly understood her. Finally, Sal said, "Okay, okay. You win. Fuck! A witch. Why do I have to deal with a fucking witch! This is unbelievable -- there is no way anyone would ever believe this, but you've convinced me. Fuck! Ben, take care of it." He turned and walked back to the chair he'd been sitting in earlier, but then he turned around again to stare at Missy. "How is shit like this even possible? Fuck!"

Missy smiled and said, "The extra million I want in that fund? That's because I had to make this trip out here to visit you, Sal. Don't make me come back again. And, don't ever try contacting me. Any future contact will all be one way, me to you. If you mess with me in any way? Or, with my family? Well, I'm not quite through yet. Here's a little more for you to remember me by." She sent Mike another message. *All and everything, Mike. Now!* She wanted Sal and Ben to see how much energy she was able to push at them and drawing on all she had, and all she was able to pull in using her connection to Mike, which now also gave her access to John and Tracy and Tracy's Mom, since all four were in that circle Tracy had set -- she pushed out the most energy she'd ever done before, all at once.

Sal and Ben were both knocked across the room, each ending up flat on their ass, while objects were sent flying in all directions. Missy's energy pulse was tremendous and the glass in the windows was all blown out. At the same time, the house was struck with lightning, again and again, and suddenly all the lights went out. The power was gone.

That was what Missy had asked Tracy for -- to continue hitting the house with lightning until she saw the lights go out. She had only an approximate location for just where the power lines were entering the house, since the utilities were all underground. She and Tracy had discussed this part of Operation Roseanne the most. Missy was going to be drawing on all the power she could pull at the same time that Tracy would be doing that, with bolts of lightning coming down again and again until finally the power was cut. Ah, yes, Missy loved it when her plan all came together!

Having all this energy and power they were tapped into and sharing? Awesome!

Since the generators had already been damaged by the lightning strikes on the garage, there was no power recovery -- everything went dark and stayed dark. All systems were out. Missy left the revolver and holster behind and quietly made her way out, going down the stairs and back out of the house. She could see just fine. The guards from the control room in the basement had all reacted to the lightning strikes by running outside and still had not even bothered going up stairs to check on Sal. Missy had no problem eluding each of them and returning to where she'd left her backpack. She stripped her clothes off and quickly packed everything back into the backpack, double checking to make certain she was leaving nothing behind. She also had wiped off the revolver and holster and had been careful not to leave her fingerprints anywhere else, so there would be no trace of her whatsoever.

Once she'd strapped the backpack into place, she Changed. This was the third Shift for her in only two hours but she had no problem doing that. She was still bursting with all the energy she'd been able to pull from the others and was actually feeling as though she were about to explode. Changing back into her cat form once again was now a huge relief, releasing some of that energy, and she immediately felt much more normal. Yes, being a cat was so much better! Whew!

She quickly raced over to the tree she'd selected during her planning of this operation and climbed up to a limb high enough for her to once again leap across the double fence. She gathered her strength and felt very good about this jump. Being able to pull energy from others was a new experience. She'd only been doing that from Mike before now, but this was much greater -- Tracy had described how it was but actually experiencing all this was really something else.

Missy landed easily on the ground, outside Sal's fences, and raced off into the surrounding area. She could scent everything and see everything and hear everything to a degree far beyond anything she'd ever done before and the exhilaration was amazing! That, even more than knowing how she'd caused so much damage to be rained down on Sal's property, was filling her with an incredible self awareness. She was a witch and a werecat and it was wonderful!

She had no trouble running all the way back to where Mike was waiting for her, along with Tracy and her Mom and her brother John. When she ran up to them and was obviously still amped up with power, they all began to cheer. She'd already sent Mike several messages that everything had gone as planned. She was indebted to each one of them for the way they'd helped her in all this. When she finally appeared, racing out of the shadows and jumping onto Mike, knocking him down, there indeed was a great deal of excitement being shared by the whole group.

Missy had executed her plan and they were all now very optimistic. Mission accomplished and message delivered. All that Sal would ever be able to find, or anyone else find for that matter, was evidence of some incredible lightning strikes which had somehow hit several locations all over his estate. His home, his garage, his gatehouse. Lightning. What terrible luck, right?

The guards Missy had taken out with tranquilizer darts would wake up the next day, only to learn they'd missed the whole thing. They each would be clueless as to what had happened to them. The guards from the control room were pretty much clueless as well. Sal and Ben would certainly not be saying anything about a witch or anything supernatural. No, that surely wasn't anything they'd ever want to discuss.

Missy did Change back, once Tracy and her Mom finally stopped making a big deal about how great it was for them to be seeing her in her cat form. Mike then drove her back to her hotel and, with only a quick kiss goodbye that somehow managed to convey all the love and admiration that he was feeling for her, he left her and drove away. She made her way up to her room and quietly went inside. Sharon woke up, gave her a questioning look, and when Missy gave her a reassuring smile and a thumbs up, she smiled back, rolled over and went right back to sleep.

Missy did not sleep. She was so filled with residual energy and emotion from all that had happened that she stayed wide awake for the rest of the night. Even so, she was fresh as a daisy the next day and joined her teammates at breakfast where they all were still congratulating one another on the big win at last night's basketball game. Missy's life at West Point could now get back to normal.

Missy was pretty happy about her big accomplishment. She was quite sure Sal would no longer be a problem for her. And, she was also pleased knowing she'd saved several young girls from ending up in Brunei, living in a harem as helpless sex slaves. Her "P" Branch buddies should be happy -- she hadn't even killed anyone this time. Sometimes -- being a wicked witch was wonderful!

A week later, Missy learned the Roseanne Trust Fund had indeed been established and was well endowed. There was also some info from Robert about all the young girls who were showing up back home, each with an unusual entitlement. There had never been any trust fund quite like this before. True, when all was sifted and sorted out, Sal was benefiting by a huge tax write-off, so it wasn't really costing him all that much. But, he clearly had gotten her message. He did not want her to make any return visits.

The media made a big deal out of all the mysterious lightning damage that Sal's estate had experienced. What an amazing amount of bad luck. Lightning hadn't just struck twice but had struck more than a dozen times ... all hitting Sal's property. This had never happened before. There hadn't even been much of a storm that night and most places nearby had only gotten some rain. It sure was strange how so much storm activity had all taken place out at Sal's home. Since it was well known that Sal was a mobster, heading one of the five families in New York, the editorials had gone on and on with speculation all about retributive justice and various other possible reasons why the heavens may have decided to dump so much of its venom all on Sal.

Missy was unable to thank Tracy enough; Tracy and her Mom had really come through for her. Tracy, of course, had thoroughly enjoyed the whole thing and having those three days with John had more than made up for any debt to Missy. Not only had she been able to use her witchy powers to the max, she'd been able to have John be there helping her, feeding her power. He was still not exactly sure what witches were all about but he was more enamored than ever with Tracy. And, Tracy's Mom was ecstatic about John being such a wonderful boyfriend for her daughter. Tracy really had never been so happy.

Of course, all her buddies at "P" Branch were pleased with how things were going. No, she didn't even need to ask for forgiveness this time. With Sal now so completely convinced to avoid anything at all associated with Missy, Missy's family, or anything else connected to Missy, they could back away from the close scrutiny they'd been giving Sal and his organization. Missy was safe and their non interference policy could continue. They soon ended the surveillance on Billy and Donny since that was no longer needed. Going forward, it didn't look like Missy would need much support. She seemed to have things pretty well in hand.

Epilogue
Nov 2018

The wedding for Mark and Alice was perfect. Even the weather had cooperated. They had never looked so happy and more than two hundred guests were there to see them make their vows. After the ceremony -- with the groom kissing the bride and then the two of them raising their joined hands high overhead -- they were greeted with a standing ovation. Everyone then regrouped over at the hall where the reception was being held and waited to welcome them there all over again. Everyone agreed there was a special excitement about this wedding.

Alice's Mom had done a fantastic job and it was obvious how devoted she was to making everything absolutely perfect for her daughter. Earlier, she had broken down completely when Alice had insisted on her being the one to give the bride away. Fortunately, there had still been a month after that for her to recover, prior to the actual event, and when she actually did appear with Alice by her side, there could not possibly have been anyone prouder or more radiant.

Alice's Maid of Honor was also quite radiant. Missy looked spectacular, wearing a dark red gown that matched her hair. She had her hair all done up in an elaborate hairdo, using extensions made from her own hair, along with some unique touches that Heather managed to include. Missy assured her sister that, in the unlikely event that the career in engineering which she was planning for herself didn't work out, she could safely fall back on being a hairdresser.

John, as best man, looked very handsome in his tux. His date Tracy was thrilled to be there and once the ceremony was over, she was constantly at John's side. Yes, she was experiencing an emotional overload. So much had happened during the past four months -- she still could hardly believe so much had been possible. John had flown with her to Texas and Thanksgiving with her family had been the best ever, for both of them. John explained he was now planning to attend law school and would be graduating from that when Tracy graduated from West Point. While no commitments were being made yet, Tracy was thrilled.

There was a brunch the day after the wedding, which the newlyweds stopped by for. They were flying to Hawaii for their honeymoon but wanted to say goodbye to all their closest friends. Once Alice and Mark were on their way, Missy and Mike then also left and went over to visit with Michelle and Aaron. They'd not had a chance to see that much of them, with all the wedding activity and due to Mike having been at Missy's for Thanksgiving.

Michelle said, "Hey, Missy? Is it too soon yet for making plans for another Mount Washington ski trip? During your Christmas break? I know it's hard to believe, but that's only a month away now and it's been almost a year since the last time we were all up there."

"Perfect! I'd love that and I know Mike will too."
Missy looked at Mike and sent him a mental message,
after which she began giggling and he broke out
laughing. She'd just promised their evenings for this trip
would definitely include some monkey sex up in their
room.

Mike could only hope -- this time -- she wouldn't
need to go off and perform any rescues ...

From the Author

Thank you for reading *Missy Goes to West Point*, my second book about Missy. I hope you enjoy reading about Missy and her friends as much as I enjoy writing about her. I've always loved stories about female characters with special powers along with stories about witches and werewolves. Future books in this series are planned, so keep checking on Amazon.

I hope you will consider leaving a review for *Missy Goes to West Point* on Amazon, letting others know what you think about this book and this series. Word-of-mouth is crucial for any author to succeed. Your kind words, even if only a line or two, will help others decide to read about Missy and inspire me to keep this series going for many more books. That would make all the difference and be hugely appreciated. Thanks in advance!

Made in the USA
Columbia, SC
15 October 2024

44433048R00233